THE FALL AND RISE OF GORDON COPPINGER

David Nobbs's first break as a comedy writer came on the iconic satire show *That Was The Week, That Was*, hosted by David Frost. Later he wrote for *The Frost Report* and *The Two Ronnies* and provided material for many top comedians including Les Dawson, Ken Dodd, Tommy Cooper, Frankie Howerd and Dick Emery. Apart from his nineteen novels, David is best known for his two hit TV series *A Bit of a Do* and *The Fall and Rise of Reginald Perrin*. His radio series *With Nobbs On* aired on Radio 4 in 2012.

Also by David Nobbs

DAVID NOBBS

The Fall and Rise of
Gordon Coppinger

HARPER

Harper
An imprint of HarperCollins*Publishers*
77–85 Fulham Palace Road,
Hammersmith, London W6 8JB

www.harpercollins.co.uk

This paperback edition 2013
1

First published in Great Britain by
HarperCollins*Publishers* 2012

A catalogue record for this book is
available from the British Library

ISBN: 978-0-00-748887-2

This novel is entirely a work of fiction. The names, characters and incidents portrayed in it are the work of the author's imagination. Any resemblance to actual persons, living or dead, events or localities is entirely coincidental.

Typeset in Meridien by Palimpsest Book Production Ltd, Falkirk, Stirlingshire

Printed and bound in Great Britain by Clays Ltd, St Ives plc

MIX
Paper from
responsible sources
FSC™ C007454

FSC™ is a non-profit international organisation established to promote the responsible management of the world's forests. Products carrying the FSC label are independently certified to assure consumers that they come from forests that are managed to meet the social, economic and ecological needs of present and future generations, and other controlled sources.

Find out more about HarperCollins and the environment at
www.harpercollins.co.uk/green

For Briget, Mark and Max

Acknowledgements

I must give huge thanks for the support and encouragement I continue to receive from many people at Harper, but particularly from Louisa Joyner, who has brought a fresh eye to my work, as well as great enthusiasm and invariably shrewd suggestions. I have also benefitted yet again from the brilliant editing of Mary Chamberlain.

I don't think I could continue, at an age when many people have long retired, without the great help of my wife the marvellous Susan, and of my agents, Ann Evans and Nemonie Craven Roderick.

Have no men helped me, I hear you cry. Oh yes. I am very grateful above all to Richard Hayter for his invaluable help with the financial details. Without his advice I would have found it hard to write this book.

So it had come to this

He woke with a sense of shock. He had no idea who he was.
Or where he was. Or who this woman was, sleeping so
peacefully beside him.

Oh God. Did he want to know who he was? Would it be
an unpleasant surprise?

Later, when he told his doctor, he would estimate that this
blankness, this disorientation, this absence of self, probably
lasted less than a minute, maybe not even thirty seconds. At
the time it seemed like an age.

What he also realized later – and this he didn't tell his
doctor, couldn't tell his doctor, couldn't tell another human
being ever – was that he had experienced, in that brief moment,
the first intimation of doubt. To most of us, plagued as we are
by doubt, this may seem incredible, but men like this man – I
feel it would be impolite, in a curious way, to give you his
name before he himself has remembered it – manage to live
without feeling any doubt at all, do things that would be impossible if they felt even a shred of doubt. Garibaldi, Hitler, Colonel
Gaddafi, could they have done what they did if they'd had
doubts? Not that I am putting our still unnamed hero in that
category.

He felt something that he had not felt in his life for a

very long time – real alarm. This was extremely disconcerting. He was always so completely in command of himself, prided himself on not needing an alarm clock because his body did what he told it to do; he was always in control, people thought him a control freak.

Well, that was something. That was a piece of knowledge about himself. He was a control freak. But today he was a control freak out of control. He was breaking into a sweat, he could feel the wetness of panic all over his skin.

Memory came back to him in small bits. Somebody calling him Gordon. He was Gordon somebody. This narrowed it down, but it really didn't help all that much. Then from nowhere, in the utter darkness of the bedroom, there flashed into his mind a vivid memory of Mr Forbes-Harrison, his maths teacher, calling out, in a grim yard behind a grim school on a grim, grey morning, 'You, Coppinger, where do you think you're going?' to which he had replied, to his own astonishment, as well as Mr Forbes-Harrison's, 'To the very top, sir.'

And with that 'sir' there came the thought that he hadn't called anybody 'sir' for a very long time. People called him 'sir' now. He wasn't just Gordon Coppinger. He was *Sir* Gordon Coppinger.

Now complete awareness flooded in, astonishing him. He was a great man and a rich one. He was a financier and an industrialist with a finger in many pies, 'not all of which are steak and kidney', as he used to say only too often, to prove that he still had a sense of humour, though many people thought it proved that he hadn't. He owned the twenty-six-storey Coppinger Tower in Canary Wharf. In his huge and luxurious yacht, the *Lady Christina*, based in Cannes, he gave holidays every summer to men of power and influence.

He was a patriot and a philanthropist. He had created the Sir Gordon Coppinger Charitable Foundation, which supported many good causes. He owned the Coppinger Collection, which housed many masterpieces. The football team that he owned played at the Coppinger Stadium. It was time to get up.

Or was it? Not quite yet, perhaps. He knew *who* he was now, but he still wasn't sure *where* he was. The darkness in the room was absolute, which suggested that he was at home, in the vast master bedroom, with its thick gold curtains and its thermal blinds. But suggestion wasn't enough. He needed to know.

The question of where he was had no great importance in itself, beyond the necessity of finding a light switch or risk walking in the blackness straight into a row of wire coat hangers in some hotel bedroom, as had happened to a friend of his. Make that an acquaintance of his. He didn't do friends. But until he knew where he was he couldn't be sure of the identity of the woman who was sleeping so quietly beside him.

If it was a woman. But that had all been a very long time ago, and, surely, if it was a man, after all this time, he would have remembered. No, it was a woman. Her gentle breathing was unmistakably female.

Just occasionally, the soft breathing became a faint, whistled, wistful snore, as if she was thinking, Surely my life should be happier than this? No man's snore could come with so many fancy adjectives attached to it. Male snores were loud, or beery, or catarrhal. Male snores were simple.

Were these slight snores Lady Coppinger's? He wasn't sure. Was he in the master bedroom of Rose Cottage, the cottage being ironic, and the rose reflecting Her Ladyship's greatest interest? Or was he in a hotel? Was this woman Francesca? Or Mandy? Please let him not be in Mandy's flat. He sniffed. No, he wasn't in Mandy's flat. There was a faintly unpleasant smell of stale humanity in the room, but Mandy's flat smelt of drains – distant drains, but unmistakable.

How could he ever have been so unwise as to go to bed with a woman called Mandy? Few names had more baggage

3

attached to them, few names screamed 'tabloid press' as much as Mandy. He had been lucky to get away with it this long. Mandy must go.

He was wide awake now, and shocked by the timidity of his thoughts. Her name was half the point of Mandy. The risk was everything. Was he going soft? He felt for his prick. Yes, he was, but that wasn't what he'd meant.

He tried to remember the events of the previous evening, but they stubbornly refused to come. Had he made love? He didn't think so. That suggested, but didn't prove, that he was with his wife. The fact that he couldn't remember also seemed to indicate, but again didn't prove, that he'd endured an ordinary Sunday evening at home.

Yes! They'd been watching the *Antiques Roadshow*. He'd said, 'Bloody morons, they've had it for thirty-five years and they haven't even noticed the maker's name'; she'd told him to shut up in a very unladylike tone; he'd said, 'I wish he'd break that fucking vase over Fiona Bruce's head'; she'd said, 'If you're going to be unpleasant leave me alone'; and then not half an hour later she'd ticked him off for not wanting to watch *Downton Abbey* with her. *Downton Abbey*! He'd explained that life was too short to bother with things that hadn't happened to people who'd never existed. She'd shouted, like a fishwife – was that fair on fishwives, if such people still existed? – that he was ruining her Sunday evening.

Yes, he was at home.

Lady Coppinger had watched *Downton Abbey*; he'd trawled the Net looking for references to himself, while slowly sipping a large glass of the sixteen-year-old Lagavulin and wondering from what revolting bottle Jack was seeking oblivion at that very moment, under some bridge or in some dark alley. Then he'd slipped quietly into bed beside Her Ladyship, planted the obligatory kiss on her cheek so softly that it could not possibly arouse her, switched the light off and gone straight into guiltless sleep, while she'd read a bit of some soppily romantic book by some much-loved authoress who in real life had been such a frightful snobbish bitch that she'd have been drummed out of Dudley with disdain.

He was at home with Christina. A cocktail of relief and disappointment swept over him, and suddenly he recalled the date and realized why he had felt that this was an important day. It was 31 October. Halloween. His wife's birthday.

Yes, he had married a witch.

No, he hadn't married a witch. That had been their little joke. It wasn't a joke now. She hadn't been a witch when he'd met her. She'd been as lovely and as full of promise as the dawn. She hadn't been a witch when he'd courted her, proposed to her, married her. She had been his innocence. He had turned her into a witch. He had fucked his own innocence.

He didn't like these thoughts, and he wasn't used to having thoughts that he didn't like. It was time to get up.

But he didn't. His body still didn't stir.

This was dreadful. Regret could play no part in his life. There wasn't time for regret. Besides, he had everything he wanted. How can a man have regrets if he has everything he wants? Because he didn't want to have everything he wanted? That was ridiculous. Because he didn't actually have everything he wanted? Because it was impossible to have everything you wanted, because what you wanted came attached to what you didn't want, as in fame and photographers?

Photographers! If he had known what was to come!

And yet – and again this only occurred to him afterwards – that morning he did have at least an inkling of what was to come. He had a presentiment. Perhaps, he would suggest to his doctor later, his blankness had been caused by his having, subconsciously, a presentiment that he was going to have a presentiment. His doctor, who was Scottish, would say that was a bit too fanciful for him. He would say that there must have been a physical cause, the position he had slept in, the supply of blood, maybe even some kind of very minor stroke. He would suggest tests. Sir Gordon would pretend to agree.

At last he began to move, easing himself slowly out of the king-sized bed. He padded carefully across the thick, luscious carpet in the utter blackness. He knew from long experience the exact position of the door. He placed his hand on the handle, turned it ever so slowly.

Lady Coppinger gave a low moan which seemed to Sir Gordon to be a rebuke of cosmic proportions, but she didn't wake.

He was relieved that his wife was still asleep, that he didn't have to face her yet.

So it had come to this.

The suspicions that would overwhelm him

He seated himself at the round rosewood (what else?) dining table in the exact centre of the gigantic dining room, whose panelling was as Elizabethan as it could be in a house built in 1932. The table seated twelve, and most mornings, as he breakfasted in solitary splendour, he derived pleasure from the sight of the eleven empty places.

He was smartly dressed in the clothes Lady Coppinger had laid out for him the previous evening. He had no colour sense. She did. You couldn't breed roses without having a colour sense.

Farringdon emerged from the kitchens and slid gravely towards Sir Gordon like a stately home on legs. He carried a glass of freshly squeezed orange juice and a pile of newspapers. Sir Gordon, who was still feeling quite deeply disturbed by his lapse of memory, tried to look the essence of calm, and gave a small, studied smile.

'Good morning, Farringdon,' he said, and he thought he detected a slight nervous quiver in his voice. Farringdon didn't appear to notice it, but then Farringdon would not have appeared to notice it if his employer had come in to breakfast naked. In the early days Sir Gordon had been slightly unnerved by Farringdon's eyes. There never seemed to be any expression in them. It looked, in certain lights, from certain angles, as if he had two glass eyes. Sir Gordon was used to this now. He found it restful.

'Good morning, sir. Sir has slept well?' said Farringdon gravely.

'Sir has slept very well, thank you, Farringdon.'

'That is good news, sir.'

The politenesses over, Farringdon got straight down to business, listing for Sir Gordon, in the unchanging daily ritual, all the pages of the newspapers that mentioned him: '*Telegraph* page seven, *Times* business page two, *Sun* page two—'

'Opposite the totty!'

'Indeed, sir.'

'*Mirror* page twenty-seven—'

'Page twenty-seven! That's a bit far back.'

'Indeed, sir, but perhaps the fact that it is a page lead will assuage the disappointment.'

Sir Gordon wasn't given to idle speculation, but even he did wonder sometimes if Farringdon had once discovered a night-school course on the Language of Butlers.

Farringdon went on to list articles in the newspapers that the team judged to be of relevance to Sir Gordon, mainly from the business sections. Important though their impact on his day's decisions might be, he would only turn to those after he had finished reading about himself.

Sir Gordon took it entirely for granted that several of his employees had been up since three in the morning, driving the early editions of the papers down to Surrey, where other early risers had hunted through them for stories relevant to himself; while yet more, in London, were at their computers finding and collating references to him on Twitter, YouTube, Facebook and, only slightly less important, news bulletins. He thought that his researchers trawled through every page of every paper. He hadn't heard of Google Alert.

He began the process of opening the newspapers at the pages that Farringdon had listed, and which he had not needed to write down. Sir Gordon was proud of his memory. His eyes swept contemptuously past several headlines that told of the sad state of our world in the autumn of 2011. Air-disaster fears soar as laser louts blind pilots. Thieves desecrate memorials to our war heroes every two days. Nineteen glasses of wine by the age of twelve. The behaviour of the lower orders from whom he had so thoroughly escaped was of no interest to him.

He found the first reference to himself in the business section's editorial comment:

Rumour has it that the City is bracing itself for a disappointing set of results from SFN Holdings. While this is not particularly signifi-cant in itself, SFN being a fairly small player in the global game, any bad news from the Coppinger empire is bound to be . . .

Farringdon arrived with a pot of tea, a jug of water, and a bowl of Coco Pops. Sir Gordon had a proudly sweet tooth.

'Thank you, Farringdon. English Builders' Tea, the best drink in the world.'

Farringdon raised his eyebrows in agreement. Agreement would have figured largely in his job description, had there been one.

'You can keep your champagne.'

Again Farringdon, who had no champagne to keep, raised his eyebrows in agreement, and moved off, in his slightly bent, tactful way. He was three inches taller than Sir Gordon, and found it sensible not to emphasize the fact.

. . . destabilizing at this sensitive time. Also, SFN is believed to be close to Sir Gordon Coppinger's heart, if such an organ can be located, as it is in his native and beloved Dudley.

'If such an organ can be located!' Cheeky bugger. Rather flattering, though. Except . . . wasn't he loved, despite his wealth, despite his ruthlessness, because he was British, not

Russian or Chinese? A British oligarch. A walking assertion that Britons can still become rich. A patriot. And famously possessed of charm. When he wanted it. When he needed it. Which was most of the time. Which could become irksome.

But could it be – no, it wasn't possible – that the press were beginning to attack him, to test the waters? And why print these comments anyway, if not to destabilize? They must know that SFN Holdings made a loss every year, though he hoped that they didn't know that making a loss every year was the whole point of SFN Holdings.

By the time Farringdon returned with the crispy bacon and scrambled eggs, Sir Gordon had already located another story about himself. Well, this one was about Lady Coppinger, variously described in the press as fragrant, elegant, enigmatic – what a gift she was to the world of adjectives, and to imagery taken from roses, as in the headline to this particular story.

A PIECE OF CAKE FOR THORNY CHRISTINA

It's a long road from selling Battenburg cake to breeding the champion climbing rose at the Baden-Baden October Flower Festival, but even that honour couldn't make Sir Gordon Coppinger's elegant wife Christina smile for long.

My German friend Gisela informed me yesterday that Christina didn't win many hearts as she accepted the prestigious Der Meisteroktoberbergsteinerrosigpreis for her George Clooney Perpetua, named after her favourite film star.

She popped in to the famous and elegant German spa town by private . . .

'Thank, you, Farringdon.'

. . . jet, made a brief speech without using a single word of German, and popped out as fast as her long but no longer quite so slim legs could carry her.

Gisela informs me that Christina did not endear herself to her hosts by wearing her Remembrance poppy throughout.

Can it be that the former confectioner's assistant and beauty queen – she was voted Miss Lemon Drizzle in 1980, Miss Danish Pastry (West Midlands) in 1982 and Miss West Bromwich in 1983 – was anxious to show her husband that she shares his fanatical xenophobia, or was there perhaps a more personal reason for the brevity of her visit?

Did she feel that she needed to get back to find out what Sir Gordon was up to?

Sir Gordon smiled. She would *hate* that. She would be furious at the slur cast on her famous legs. She would *loathe* the references to her days as a beauty queen. How the world would mock. Didn't she have the sense to see that the whole point of their lives was that they had gone up, up, up and so it was great publicity that they had once been down, down, down? Even Miss Lemon Drizzle can dream of leaving the world of cake far behind and breeding world-class roses. Christina could have been a heroine for our times, a walking representative, in her high heels, on her long but no longer quite so slim legs, of the social mobility so loved by prime ministers who had been to Eton.

And, to his great surprise, he felt a distant flicker of sexuality at the reference to those legs. He even felt stimulated by the thought that they were no longer quite so slim. Few men are turned on by perfection. You couldn't believe what was in the papers but it might be rather exciting to check on the accuracy of the observation. Good God. Was it possible – was it? – that this year his birthday dinner with her would not be an ordeal?

But . . . this apparently trivial diary entry also worried Sir Gordon just a little as he ate his exquisite, always exquisite, bacon and scrambled eggs. He didn't like that phrase, 'what Sir Gordon was up to'.

11

What he had been up to was Francesca Saltmarsh. He had taken the rare opportunity, while Christina was abroad, of staying the night. They had made love three and a half times. That half haunted him. Was he beginning to grow old?

Could the press possibly have known about Francesca? No. It was just a shot in the dark. No! If the worst they could come up with was a snide suggestion in a little diary piece, he had nothing to worry about. He was invulnerable, as his fellow 'Sir,' Jimmy Savile, had been, because the great British public would not allow him to be attacked. They loved him so much, just as much as he in his turn hated them.

No, his concerns were exaggerated. A second cup of good old British tea, and the world would be fine again.

But as he turned to the third article about himself, his world felt not quite so fine.

Climthorpe United's challenge for promotion to the Premiership faltered when they were held to a goalless draw by lowly Barnsley at the Coppinger Stadium in yesterday's late kick-off.

The Gordoners missed a hatful of chances, the best of which fell to taciturn Bulgarian striker Raduslav Bogoff. The fans in the Abattoir Stand have started to boo him every time he touches the ball, and the same message comes from the increasing number of placards being paraded around the ground. Their message wouldn't be shortlisted for the Man Booker Prize, but it gets its point across clearly and simply: "Bogoff, Bogoff."

Manager Vernon Thickness continues to defend the moody target man from the Black Sea resort of Varna. "He gives us different options, which the punters can't always appreciate," he explained in his post-match press conference. "He's creating the chances, and the goals will come."

Does Thickness really believe this, or is he no more than a mouthpiece for owner Sir Gordon Coppinger's ideas? And why does Sir Gordon persist with the surly Slav, when it is his express intention eventually to turn Climthorpe into the only all-British side in the Championship, and, whatever his motives may be, we have to applaud that intention.

Sir Gordon has stated that the clumsy seasider gives the team a dimension of subtlety which brings out the best in his British teammates. "I am British through and through and have got rid of no fewer than eight foreign players since I bought the club," Sir Gordon explained recently, "but I haven't yet found a British striker who gives me exactly what Raduslav offers."

The eponymous owner was not present in the Sir Gordon Coppinger Stand yesterday to see his Eastern European protégé miss yet more chances. Nor was Bogoff's lovely wife, the svelte Svetoslava.

Could it be that her presence in Britain, and her absence from the match, has something to do with Sir Gordon's continued faith in her hapless hubby?

Sir Gordon loved to read about other great men, and he knew that all truly great men had to be vigilant in their examination of themselves for traces of incipient paranoia. He was honest enough to wonder if there was a touch of the disease in his suspicion that there might be a connection between this story and the diary piece about Christina. Had the press decided to go on the offensive against him, albeit slowly and carefully, putting their toes into the ocean with little hints? Well, they were hopelessly on the wrong tack with Svetoslava. Apart from everything else, he didn't know when he had seen a less svelte Slav.

But even this very gentle rumour and tittle-tattle made him feel uneasy, and he wasn't used to feeling uneasy. He'd have liked a third cup of good old British tea, but it was out of the question. Great men can't be seen clambering out of their Rolls-Royces for a quick pee at the side of the Kingston By-Pass, or taking a bottle with them just in case. To be seen by Kirkstall performing awkward manoeuvres into a bottle on the back seat, it was unthinkable. The urination of great

13

men – and indeed of great women – must be hidden from the world.

Through the huge picture windows of the dining room he could now see that an unlovely dawn was creeping shyly in over the lush Surrey countryside. Dawns didn't break, they arrived mysteriously. As a boy he had sometimes stood by the window in the dark in that little house in Dudley, stop-watch in hand, waiting to record the exact second when it began to get light, in order to enter it into 'Coppinger's Almanac', his life's work. He had always failed, and the failure had made him furious. He never failed now, and he was rarely furious. Fury used up energy that needed to be stored for more important use.

He was pleased that it was such an unappetizing grey morning. What was the point of being driven to work by a chauffeur in a luxurious Rolls-Royce if the hoi polloi in their ghastly clothes were standing at their bus stops in warm sunshine? He hoped it would chuck it down this evening, so that all the trick-or-treaters would get soaked.

He turned, reluctantly, to the financial pages.

Insecurity grows. House prices fall. CBI wants tax breaks to help young unemployed.

What? Tax breaks? Help for the young unemployed? He almost choked on his last sip of tea.

China: Don't count on us to help you.

Bastards. Who was ever naive enough to think they would? He'd boycotted Chinese restaurants for five years now. That had shown them.

In a sudden surge of temper he flung the papers to the floor.

He clambered slightly stiffly out of his chair. That wouldn't do. He was only fifty-six, and fifty-six was the new forty-three.

He picked the papers up, smoothed them down, and put them in a neat pile.

Thank goodness nobody had witnessed his brief rage. He never lost his temper. He was always cool and collected. Nobody ever saw him ruffled.

He would have been astonished if he'd known that this would be one of the reasons for the suspicions that would overwhelm him.

It was going to be one
of those days

It was a day like any other, and yet it was a day like none other. Everything was as it usually was, yet nothing was as it usually was.

Every moment of every day in the life of Sir Gordon Coppinger (fifty-six), control freak, of Rose Cottage, Borthwick End, near Borthwick Magna, in the county of Surrey, was calculated, planned, and conducted with calm authority. On this grey Halloween morning, however, a ghost of anxiety sat on his shoulder, drove with him into that strange place known as Canary Wharf – half smart city, half urban village – accompanied him as Kirkstall steered smoothly past trim tower blocks whose names on their summits proclaimed the point of the place: Barclays, HSBC, Credit Suisse, J.P. Morgan, Coppinger.

The anxiety walked with him up the steps and through the wide glass doors into the great foyer of the slim, sleek, Coppinger Tower, affectionately known, because of its ribbed structure, and the delicate frond-like curves at its top, as the Stick of Celery. The Coppinger Tower stood a little off the centre of Canary Wharf, but commanded a splendid view over a long bend of London's river. At its top gleamed that single, powerful word, in gold letters: 'Coppinger'.

On this grey Halloween morning he took with him, past all the huge rubber plants, only the appearance of calm authority. He was more shaken by the manner of his awakening than he would ever admit. It was as if for those moments of blankness he had been outside his body, and it was as if he still hadn't quite slipped fully back in, didn't quite fit neatly yet. And he was aware, too, that he was, almost subconsciously, nervous about the evening. He was dreading the birthday dinner with his wife. The hope that he might enjoy it this year had withered in the cruel light of dawn.

'Good morning, Alice, how was your weekend? Did you and Tom do anything interesting?'

Alice Penfold, neatly groomed, intelligent, modern, confident receptionist, had slender legs and shapely knees that banished instantly any depression caused by the traffic on the Kingston By-Pass. Sir Gordon wished that she didn't have a stud in the middle of her chin and a ring through the left nostril of her sweet flared nose, but they had the advantage of giving out a strong signal that this skyscraper was not a stuffy place. She blushed, as if she really believed that the great man was interested in her puny doings. That was the extraordinary effect Sir Gordon had on people. He asked about the wretched Tom at least once a week, but he had no interest in the man, who was a keen cyclist and birdwatcher, the twerp. He could just imagine Tom, with his heavy binoculars, his orange Lycra and his spots, stopping to pee behind some sodden hedge in Sussex. Strange. That was the second time that morning that he had thought about peeing at the side of the road.

'We went to Brighton for the day, Sir Gordon. It was lovely.'

Brighton! Lovely! Dear God. And yet . . . he recalled a trip he had made, all those years ago, all the way to Llandudno, with Cindy on the back of his motorbike, and he felt, for Alice, a pang of envy, soon stifled with a slight, involuntary shake of the head – imagine it, a movement of the body that was unplanned, what was going on?

'Good for you.'

What a stupid comment, but Alice seemed pleased.

As he walked towards the busy lifts, Sir Gordon saw the cheery bulk of Siobhan McEnery entering the building, and he slowed down to speak with her. She greeted him with a smile as wide as the Shannon. There was a warmth about Siobhan McEnery that reached even into Sir Gordon's heart, and he wondered briefly what it would be like to take her to his secret seduction suite on the twenty-second floor. But then he wondered about this with most women.

'Good morning, Sir Gordon.'

'Good morning, Siobhan. Everything sorted for Saturday?'

Siobhan McEnery's unofficial title was Head of Fun. Her official title was Head of Corporate Entertainment. Sir Gordon stretched this to include making all the preparations for his great biennial Bonfire Night bash.

'Everything sorted, Sir Gordon. Oh, Liam and I are so looking forward to it.'

'And how's wee Ryan?' Sir Gordon asked as they entered the lift. The database that was his mind saved the names of all his employees' offspring.

Siobhan flushed with pleasure at this evidence of her employer's interest in her family. She little knew that he couldn't have cared less about wee Ryan.

'The wee mite's not so good this morning, Sir Gordon, but nothing to worry about.'

'I hope not.'

Siobhan got out at the fourth floor. As the doors closed behind her Sir Gordon gave a little shake of the head at the thought of sex with her. He realized that the only other occupant of the lift, a courier, had seen that shake, and this shocked him slightly. It had been the visual equivalent of talking to oneself. He *was* beginning to grow old.

The glass lift, built on the outside of the Stick of Celery, took him swiftly, smoothly, silently up to the nineteenth floor.

He smiled at the courier as if the unkempt oaf was his equal. As the lift rose it opened up a view of wharves and water stretching to the towers of the City of London itself, but he had no eyes for that. He had eyes only to turn in upon himself. He was remembering that he had always peed a lot, as a child, when he'd been nervous. He didn't remember that he'd ever been nervous since he was a child. But he wanted to pee now. Odd how peeing was dominating his thoughts that morning.

He walked from the lift to his office past the massed ranks of his employees. He had asked for the floor to be designed that way. He liked to see them all hard at work making him richer in their awful open-plan working space. In the ante-office to his own, enclosed office sat his secretary, Helen Grimaldi, these days more grim than aldi. She gave him her smile which suggested that she still remembered that Tuesday, and flicked her eyes towards a young man seated on the white settee. Sir Gordon recalled that he had three meetings this morning. He thought of them as if he could see them written in his diary: '8.30 Martin Fortescue, 9.30 Fred Upson, 10.30 GI.'

Martin Fortescue was the twenty-one-year-old son of a man he didn't like who had asked him to see the boy as a favour. He'd arranged for him to come in at eight-thirty, to test his punctuality. He was disappointed to see that the long streak of piss (oh no, another urine reference) was there already. His little lecture on the importance of punctuality would remain unspoken yet again. What was wrong with people, all turning up on time in these hard days?

The boy rose from his seat in the outer office, rose . . . and rose . . . and rose. Much too tall. And the innocence, the keenness. Sir Gordon suddenly felt as if he was seventy-seven.

'See you in a moment.'

'No problem, sir.'

Sir Gordon's office was enormous, as were his rosewood (what else?) desk and his sleek swivelling chair. There were four hard chairs and four soft chairs for visitors. Whether he seated you on a hard chair or a soft chair had huge significance. Half the wall opposite the door consisted of a vast curved picture window. On the rest of the wall there were just five pictures: a portrait each of Lady Coppinger looking arrogant, his elderly father Clarrie looking wise, his banker brother Hugo showing all the warmth of a cheque book, his artist son Luke looking artistic, and his daughter Joanna looking as though she had never had a man and wouldn't know what to do with him if she ever did.

There was no picture of Jack.

He kept the boy waiting for eleven minutes, just long enough to make him feel anxious, which would show he was the wrong type, not hard enough – or irritated, which would show that he was a different kind of wrong type, bit above himself. But the lad, to do him credit, seemed utterly unfazed. That's what Winchester and Cambridge did for you, gave you confidence, damn and blast it. That's what you had to find for yourself if you'd been to a secondary modern in Dudley.

He indicated the hard chair that he had placed in isolation at the other side of the desk.

'Did they offer you a drink? Tea? Coffee?'

'Yes, thank you. No, I'm fine, sir. I'm all right.'

Excuse me, but that's what we're here to find out.

'Winchester, eh?'

'Yes, sir.'

'Like it?'

'I think it was great. I felt privileged.'

You are.

A barge hooted urgently on the sullen river. Sir Gordon never found time to stand at his great picture window and look at the boats. All he saw when he looked at the window were the window cleaners' bills.

'Good school motto, Winchester. "Manners maketh man."'
Most stupid bloody motto in the history of mottoes. Manners
concealeth man. 'We certainly set great store by manners
here.'

'I can see that, sir.'

You can see nothing.

'So why do you want to work in the City?'

'It would be stupid to pretend that I didn't like the idea
of making a lot of money, sir, but I honestly do think it would
be the right career path for me.'

'It doesn't worry you that you might be setting out on this
. . . "career path" . . . at a time when it may be turning into
a rather rocky road?'

'I hardly think working for you could ever be described as
being on a rocky road, sir.'

Too smooth for his own good. Could be quite clever, though,
could fancy making a name for himself. Keep him well away
from Gordon Investments.

'I'm going to offer you a job, Martin, but . . . you're going
to have to prove yourself.'

'I would expect nothing else, sir.'

'Good. Good. If you accept it, you'll have to move to Stoke.'

That'll teach you for being six foot five.

'Stoke?'

'On-Trent.'

'Oh yes, sir, I know of it. The Potteries.'

'Exactly. Arnold Bennett country.'

'I'm sorry, sir. I'm not with you.'

'Arnold Bennett was a famous man from that region.'

'Oh, really. What did he . . . what was he famous for, sir,
exactly?'

'He invented a very well-known omelette.'

'Good heavens.'

'Full of smoked fish.'

'Good Lord.'

'I know.'

Sir Gordon swivelled idly from side to side in his large executive chair, as if he was weighing up what to say next, though he knew perfectly well what he was going to say next.

'I daresay you dream of getting rich overnight, but I want to test your mettle in manufacturing, Martin.'

'Manufacturing, sir?'

'Yes. I have factories that actually make things. I'm not just a money man, you know.'

'Oh, I know, sir.'

The first lie. Oh well.

'Have you heard of Porter's Potteries Pies?'

'I can't say that I have, sir.'

Avoided a second lie. Well done. Not a bad lad, sadly.

'Well, I have a finger in many pies, and they happen to be one of them.'

Didn't even smile. No sense of humour? That could be a problem, working for Porter's Potteries Pies.

'Porter's – they're the Wedgwood of the pie.'

'Ah.'

'Cut your teeth on them, and the world could be your oyster.'

'Thank you, sir. Do you . . . um . . .' A roguish look spread over Martin Fortescue's face. 'Do you ever put oysters in your pies? I know people used to.'

'Arnold Bennett, probably. No, we never have. Maybe you could explore the possibility.'

'Thank you, sir. I certainly will.'

Sir Gordon sent Martin on his way and immediately telephoned his father. Martin's father, not his own. No point in telephoning his own father. Not compos mentis. No longer wise. Very sad. Terrible, actually.

'Julian?' He was relishing this moment. He only wished he could see Julian Fortescue's self-satisfied face when he told him he was sending his precious son to a pie factory in the Potteries. 'I've seen your son, Julian, and I'm offering him a job. In my pie factory. In Stoke.'

'Stoke?'

'On-Trent.'

'I know where Stoke is, Gordon. Oh, Gordon, pies, that's marvellous, that'll take the smile off his face. And Stoke. All the way to Stoke. We were wondering how the hell we could ever persuade him to leave home. I can't thank you enough for this, Gordon.'

It was going to be one of those days.

'I really have shocked myself'

His second meeting was with Fred Upson, MD of SFN Holdings.

Fred was one of those people who irritated you by their passivity, and then irritated you even more by their passive acceptance of your right to irritate them. He was one of life's natural victims, and Sir Gordon, like most other people, couldn't resist a little bit of ritual humiliation.

He had to be careful, however, very careful. Fred knew where the body was buried, the body in this case being SFN Holdings. He would be committing professional suicide if he alienated Fred. Fred might perhaps suspect that he was being humiliated at these Monday meetings, but he must never be allowed to know it for certain. The relationship was on a knife-edge, but then the edges of knives were Sir Gordon's favourite territory.

He also had to pay Fred extremely well.

He moved the hard chair to an obscure corner of the room, and brought forward one of the soft chairs.

His meetings with Fred were always scheduled for nine-thirty, just early enough to make it impractical for him to get to Euston from Dudley that morning, and so forcing him to spend a night in the London that he loathed so much.

Fred was on time, of course, exactly on time, on the dot, as always. How irritating was that?

Sir Gordon indicated the soft chair.

'Make yourself comfortable.'

'Thanks.'

'Tea? Coffee?'

'Had coffee at the hotel, thank you. Vile. Put me off the stuff for weeks.'

'Something stronger, then?'

'Oh no. No, no. No thanks. Bit early for me.'

Fred had a drink problem. Offering him something stronger was just perfect – right on the edge of the knife.

'So, hotel not good?'

'Disgusting.'

'I thought we'd got you a new one, F.U.'

The edge of that knife again. Fred could hardly complain, they were his initials, but he must have resented it. He didn't show it at all, though, which of course made Sir Gordon want to say it all the more.

'You did, Sir Gordon. I've now tried the Ibis, the Travelodge, the Travel Inn, the Kwality Inn, the Premier Inn, the Outside Inn, the Innside Out, the Orvis . . .

'I think that's a shirt.'

'Oh, sorry. Anyway, it's one that begins with an O, and ends in tears. They're all awful.'

'Well, if you refuse to go beyond Euston Road, what can you expect?'

'Speaking about the hotel, I gave Helen a list of my expenses. They have rather piled up. If they could be . . . er . . . processed . . .' Fred Upson didn't quite have the courage to use the verb 'paid'. '. . . I'd be very grateful. Not that I . . . but . . . you know.'

'Absolutely. Helen will be processing them even now, if I know Helen.' Sir Gordon was almost tempted, just to see Fred Upson's face, to add, 'And I do know Helen. In the biblical sense.' But he resisted it. Mustn't give employees ammunition.

'Right. The most important matter is dealt with.' Sir Gordon smiled at Fred Upson, to show that this was, and at the same time wasn't, a joke. Fred Upson's expenses were a legend in the Stick of Celery. 'Everyone in my employ is the best at something,' Sir Gordon had once said. 'And in Fred Upson's case it's expenses.'

'So! To business! How are things at good old SFN?'

'You know how they are, Sir Gordon. They never change.'

'True.'

'I read that article about our results being disappointing. Strange that SFN should be mentioned at all, but rather re-assuring.'

'I wondered if they meant you were going to declare a profit.'

'Oh my God, no.'

'Actually, Fred . . .'

The phone rang. It was part of the ritual.

'Sorry about this.'

That was part of the ritual too. Sir Gordon wasn't at all sorry. In fact, he had instructed Helen to send through as many phone calls as possible during Fred Upson's visits. It was his little joke, for his own amusement only. Power can be boring, and absolute power can be absolutely boring. Fred might suspect that she was doing this, but he couldn't know it.

Helen didn't always do Sir Gordon's bidding. In fact, she was becoming less and less compliant. He couldn't sack her, unfortunately, or she would rearrange the vowels and issue a complaint. One unwise Tuesday he'd had sex with her for seven minutes and he'd regretted it for eleven years. But she did what he asked with regard to Fred Upson. She too found pleasure in annoying him. Mother Teresa herself would have found the temptation hard to resist.

26

'Coppinger,' he announced briskly into the phone.

'Me too.'

'Oh, hello Hugo.' He mouthed, 'My brother. Won't be long,' to Fred. 'How are you, Hugo?'

Hugo went straight to the point. Phones weren't made for small talk.

'Can you do lunch? The Intrepid Snail, one o'clock. A.A. Gill slated it, so it can't be bad.'

'Well, yes, but . . . any reason? Not that it matters.'

'No reason, except . . . well, two things, only one of which I would dream of mentioning on the phone.'

'Do you think your phone may be being hacked?'

'They wouldn't dare. No, I think *your* phone may be being hacked.'

'So what's the reason you *can* mention?'

'Jack. We must do something about him.'

'Ah. The Intrepid Snail, one o'clock, right.' He put the phone down and smiled insincerely at Fred Upson.

'Sorry about that, F.U. Where were we?'

'Your tone changed and became serious and you said, "Actually, Fred . . ."'

'Ah, yes. Yes. Actually, Fred . . .'

The phone rang again.

'Oh good heavens, so sorry about this.' He picked up the phone. 'Coppinger.'

'It's me, Dad.'

'Luke!' He mouthed, 'My son. Won't be long,' to Fred.

Fred gave him an 'I understand. It doesn't matter. He's family. I'm not. I'm just an employee' look which irritated Sir Gordon so much that he felt tempted to have a really long chat, except that no good could come out of a long chat with Luke. These thoughts had the suitable accompaniment of at least three vehicles rushing through the windy streets around Canary Wharf with sirens blaring.

'Is it a bad time?'

'Absolutely not.'

'That's a miracle.'

'So, how can I help?'

'I don't know if you can.'

Sir Gordon looked across to Fred Upson, sitting there so patiently, seemingly content to be ritually humiliated, and suddenly all irritation left him. He felt a stab of sympathy for the man. This wasn't good, he wasn't at home with sympathy the way he was with irritation, but he found himself wondering about Fred's home life, was he married, could he be married, what sort of woman could possibly . . . and then he realized that he hadn't heard a word of what his son was saying. This was awful. Get a grip, Gordon.

'So what would you advise, Dad?'

'Luke, I have a big problem here . . .' He shook his head several times, trying to tell Fred that the problem was nothing to do with him, or that the problem was a fiction. '. . . and I'm afraid I . . . I didn't fully catch what you said.'

'Well, how much did you catch?'

'Luke, it might be better just to tell the whole story again.'

'Are you all right, Dad? This isn't like you.'

'I know. I don't seem to be terribly like me today.'

'What?'

'Never mind. Get on with it.'

Sir Gordon felt that he was in danger of raising his voice, of losing his rag, and he never did that in the office. Well, never anywhere, but particularly not in the office.

'OK,' continued Luke. 'Look, you know my painting of the Garden of Eden?'

'Not specifically.'

'Well, I showed it to you last time you visited us, and you asked if it was Le Manoir aux Quat'Saisons.'

'Oh, that one. Yes, vaguely. Sorry.'

'Well, you may not like it, but Carmarthen Art Gallery think it's pretty wonderful. Or was.'

'What? "Was"?'

'It's been vandalized.'

'What?'

'Horrid words daubed all over it.'

Another siren. You'd have thought the world must be ending somewhere, but it was just another routine London day.

'What horrid words?'

'Well . . . sorry, Dad . . . "Fuck off".'

'"Fuck off"?' Sir Gordon smiled apologetically at Fred.

'Yes. And . . . "*Ffycia bant*".'

'"*Ffycia bant*"?'

'Yes. That's Welsh.'

'Welsh for what?'

'Welsh for "Fuck off".'

'I see. So somebody's told you to fuck off in two languages.' Good for them. Almost worth learning another language just for that. 'I think that's carrying nationalistic sensitivity a bit far.' He smiled apologetically at Fred once again. 'Not very friendly to you.'

'Not just to me, Dad.'

'What?'

'There's something else. That's why I'm ringing you. It says something else.'

'What?'

'"Like father, like son".'

'In two languages?'

'In two languages. Somebody out there doesn't like us, Dad.'

'It seems like it. Oh dear. What do you want me to do, Luke?'

'I don't think you can do anything. But the press know. I thought I ought to warn you.'

'OK, right. Thanks.'

He couldn't just ring off. He had to say something,

show – that surprise word again, that stranger from the unused pages of the dictionary of his mind – sympathy.

'And Luke?'

'Yes, Dad?'

'I may not understand your pictures. I may not like them. Probably I'm wrong, since they fetch such amazing prices, but . . . I'm sorry. Really. That's an awful thing to happen to an artist.'

'Well, thanks, Dad, I . . . thanks.'

Thank God we're on the phone, thought Sir Gordon. If we'd been together we might have hugged.

'Sorry about that, F.U.,' he told Fred after he had rung off, 'but it was important. My son's picture of the Garden of Eden has been vandalized.'

Fred shifted uneasily in his easy chair. He wasn't interested in Luke's troubles, but he clearly felt that he had to ask something.

'Was it blasphemous?'

'I didn't understand it well enough to be able to say. I suppose it could be some religious nutter. Plenty of them about. But part of the message read, "Like father, like son". I assumed that was us.'

'Could have been God the Father and Jesus the Son. They're pretty well known too.'

Sir Gordon looked at Fred Upson in astonishment.

'Sorry,' said Fred.

'No. No. I rather . . . fair point. Rather good, Fred. I . . .' I almost liked you there, for a moment. Couldn't say that.

'So what was it you were going to say to me when the phone went?'

'Obviously we still need to declare big losses, Fred.'

A smile played with the edges of Sir Gordon's mouth as he recalled the day he appointed Fred. 'So you are asking me to be MD of a loss leader?' 'Yes.' 'So you consider me the ideal man to run a firm that is a loss leader?' 'Yes.' 'I see.'

The smile died.

'But in the present climate, Fred,' said Sir Gordon, suddenly very solemn, 'we may not be able to afford to continue to actually *make* big losses. The office is costing too much to run. Declare more losses, make fewer. I want a report on potential savings on my desk one month from today. One month from today, F.U. Things could be going to get serious. We're going to have to up our game.'

Their eyes met again, and each held his gaze.

'You've shocked me,' said Fred Upson.

'I've shocked myself,' said Sir Gordon. 'I really have shocked myself.'

Can we be absolutely certain that they can't lip-read?

That anxiety, throbbing in his gut like the engines of a slow-moving ship, sharpened slightly. '10.30 GI.'

He pulled forward three easy chairs for the managers of GI.

Within minutes Keith Gostelow, Dan Perkins, and Adam Eaglestone were stretching their legs in their chairs. The heartland of Sir Gordon's empire was not a bastion of equal rights for women.

If a member of the public was introduced to Keith Gostelow, Dan Perkins, and Adam Eaglestone as the triumvirate who ran a major investment company, that member of the public would not be impressed. But no members of the public did meet them. That was not the nature of Gordon Investments.

'Any problems, gentlemen?'

Keith Gostelow and Adam Eaglestone exchanged a very swift, uneasy glance, a glance which excluded Dan Perkins. Sir Gordon's sharp eyes missed none of this, and he didn't like the glance. It suggested that there were problems – or, at least, that there was *a* problem.

'Keith?'

It was an acknowledgement from Sir Gordon that he had seen and understood the glance.

'Um . . .' began Keith Gostelow – floppy, anarchic hair; bad complexion. 'Maybe it's just me, but . . . and I'm not saying it's a serious matter, don't get me wrong, but . . . um . . . I have noticed . . . I mean, not widely, and not equally over the whole country, and perhaps more in long-term investments, but also in . . . in the long term . . . in short-term investments . . . a bit . . . but as I say, not widely, but enough to make me take notice . . . investment is . . . in some areas . . . in some fields . . . um . . . not great.'

'Poor?'

'Exactly.' Keith smiled, then the smile dissolved into slight panic. 'Well, I mean, no, not exactly poor, no.'

'But not great?'

'Exactly.'

'Adam? Your take on this?'

Adam Eaglestone – balding, short, shiny suit – was more fluent.

'Uptake is sluggish. I would say that this is entirely unsurprising in view of economic sentiment at this moment in time. However, I would offer this cautious addendum. Should the economic situation weaken still further – and I see no reason to be optimistic about this – I do think that a problem might arise, and should be guarded against, if it can be done without weakening confidence, because to weaken confidence might be to precipitate the crisis whose possibility was the cause of confidence weakening in the first place.'

'Thank you, Adam. Dan?'

'We're in the shit.'

Sir Gordon paused. The words of Dan Perkins – all muscle, face like granite – seemed to echo round the vast office. The clouds drifting slowly past the great picture window were just slightly coloured as if the sun was attempting to break through, giving them an unattractive muddy complexion which reminded Sir Gordon of the unpleasant waste matter in which, in Dan Perkins's pithy opinion, they were.

'So,' said Sir Gordon. He let the word hang there. It hung well, so he repeated it. 'So . . . if Dan's view is right, and if what you two were saying reflects that view – and I am of course absolutely shocked to hear this, but I respect you or I wouldn't have appointed you . . .' The sentence wasn't going well. Every man finds himself occasionally in the middle of a sentence which isn't going well. The average man struggles to its muddled end. A great man abandons it. Sir Gordon abandoned it and returned to the word which, since it had served him well twice already, might be expected to be effective again. 'So . . .' he said, and once more he let the word hang there.

'Do you think we should reduce the return by, say, for instance . . . um . . .' began Keith Gostelow.

Suddenly two men appeared at the window, one of them massive, with a broken nose, the other short, wiry and grimfaced. Sir Gordon's heart almost stopped. Ice coursed through his veins. He couldn't breathe. The tall man raised his gun. So this was it. Pie Producer Patriot Gunned Down in Canary Wharf Horror. He'd known that he had enemies, of course, but . . .

Then he realized that the gun was a mop. He raised his arm in greeting. The large window cleaner waved back, and then the two were obscured by a torrent of water.

'. . . or I mean maybe we should . . . um . . . I don't know . . . well, I mean, I really don't mean that I don't know . . .'

'Quiet,' said Sir Gordon. 'Careless talk costs lives.'

'Sorry?'

'That was a poster my dad kept. From the war.' He lowered his voice. 'Better not say too much in front of the window cleaners.'

Another look passed between Keith Gostelow and Adam Eaglestone. Again, it bypassed Dan Perkins. Sir Gordon hoped

34

that none of his three investment executives had noticed his brief panic. If rumours that his nerve was going got about . . . and was it going? Oh God. Was it? Was that what the waking-up incident had been about? As a result of all this, he found himself speaking in a sharp manner that shone light on his momentary weakness.

'You think I'm paranoid, Adam, Keith?'

'Um . . .' said Keith.

'Of course not,' said Adam. 'And I'm as security conscious as anyone, but . . . do you really think a window cleaner could hear what we're saying through double glazing?'

'It wouldn't matter if he heard what you and Keith were saying, anyway,' said Dan. 'I've never heard two people say so much about so little.'

'Dan, please,' said Sir Gordon. 'Let's not get personal. Let's not lose our nerve.'

His eyes met Dan's. He held the look. Dan broke away first.

'I'm security conscious, yes,' said Sir Gordon. 'Very much so. Maybe exaggeratedly so. No, of course I don't think they can hear what we say through what is actually triple glazing. And of course I'm not paranoid. However . . .' He paused. 'You three are the only other people in the world who know the truth about Gordon Investments. There are people who would pay highly for that truth. Keeping it secret is vital to our survival. Vital. They may be bona fide window cleaners. They may not. But, even if they are, can we be absolutely certain that they can't lip-read?'

We never said a word about Jack

There were only two people in the world, one man and one woman, whom Sir Gordon Coppinger regarded as his equals. He had felt it about the man from the moment he first read about him. Garibaldi was his hero, his mentor, his example. He had felt it about the woman from the moment she laid her sword upon his shoulder. But there was also one person in the world whom he regarded as his superior. His brother Hugo – his *elder* brother Hugo. How important is that word 'elder'. How irreversible is the luck of birth.

Sir Gordon belonged in Canary Wharf, that upstart city outside the City. Hugo belonged in *the* City. Huge swathes of British history seemed to accompany him as he walked arrogantly towards the Intrepid Snail. Even the fact that he had been knighted seemed to Sir Gordon, in Hugo's presence, to be a handicap. He was a man who had needed to be knighted. Hugo walked with the air of a man who has already been knighted by existence itself.

The Intrepid Snail was situated on the ground floor of what had once been a bank. The walls were dark and their panelling was centuries older than that in the dining room of Rose Cottage. In its sombre recesses there had been placed sculptures of snails in varying degrees of intrepidity. The restaurant itself, however, perhaps in a forlorn attempt to persuade the masses to enter with equal intrepidity, consisted of rows of scrubbed pine tables, and looked like an upmarket works canteen.

At one o'clock on this mild, windy Halloween day the masses had not been persuaded to enter. There were only two customers, middle-aged men in dark suits seated at a window table. They were leaning forward so that their heads almost touched and talking in such low whispers that they must either be indulging in deadly and important gossip or declaring a late flowering of homosexual love. The former seemed the more likely.

'More gastropod than gastropub,' commented Hugo Coppinger as his eyes took in the room in one brief glance. His well-cut suit bore not a trace of its cost. Its elegance was perfectly restrained. You would have sworn, if you hadn't known him, that there was a woman in his life who had chosen his shirt and his silk tie.

'It should be all right,' he said with doubt in his voice. 'It was slated by Giles Coren.'

'I thought it was A.A. Gill.'

'Him as well. It was slated by everyone. What do these food writers know?'

The contempt which he poured into the words 'food writers' was pure Hugo, thought Sir Gordon. He didn't know anyone who did contempt better than his banker brother. In the contempt stakes even Sir Gordon was an also-ran. And all this from a man born to humble stock in Dudley.

A waiter approached with the air of a man who has been disturbed in the middle of a nap.

'Have you booked?' he enquired in a contorted accent that neither of them could identify.

'I'm afraid not,' said Hugo, 'but perhaps you can squeeze us in.'

Either the waiter had no sense of humour or he was deaf

or he didn't speak English or he had heard that remark five hundred times before. He led them, as they had known he would, towards the window table next to the whispering duo. Sir Gordon strode as erectly as he possibly could, striving for the extra inch that would place him on a level with his brother. Hugo let his shoulders sag just slightly, in order to hide that fateful inch. The ruse worked perfectly. Both men looked exactly five foot eight and a half inches tall.

'Please!' said Hugo. 'We don't want to sit near these people. We have matters of the utmost secrecy to discuss, and so, no doubt, do they. This is the City of London in crisis, man.'

'You not want sit in window. Lovely view.'

'It's a disgusting view. I don't want to see it. I want to go right over there, far from what our mother, mistakenly but nevertheless accurately, always called the maddening crowd.'

Hugo plonked himself down at a table as far as possible from the other couple. The waiter, offended by having the table chosen by the customer, stomped off.

On each table there was a single artificial red rose, standing in a glass vase shaped like a snail.

The waiter emerged from the kitchens with food for the other table and the look of a man who was rushed off his feet. It must have been several minutes before he approached the two brothers. He handed them menus, and gave the wine list to Hugo, which irritated Sir Gordon.

'Unusually quiet, is it?' he asked.

'No, sir. Always like this, Monday. Tuesday too. Wednesday, Thursday, a little more busy. Friday, you never know. Friday is unpredict.'

'You do like chatting to people, don't you?' commented Hugo with just a trace of waspishness as the waiter ambled off. 'The famous charm, overcoming even the reticence of a waiter who hates customers.'

'I use it,' admitted Sir Gordon. 'I work it.' He paused. 'I think I despise it, actually.'

He took the wine list off Hugo.

'My turn, I think.'

'*I* invited *you.*'

'Irrelevant. We take turns.'

'Fine. I accept graciously.'

Sir Gordon had wondered if the menu would feature nothing but snails, but he needn't have worried. It didn't appeal particularly to these two men who could eat out anywhere at any time and were used to the best, but at least it wasn't over-reliant on the eponymous molluscs, although the chef's signature dish was snail bouillabaisse.

'Snail bouillabaisse. What the hell is that all about?' said Hugo. 'I'll tell you one thing. This French restaurant is not French. No Frenchman would insult their marvellous bouillabaisse in that way.'

Barely ten minutes passed before the waiter strolled back to take their orders. All the time Sir Gordon was wondering if Hugo really had suggested lunch because he had something important to say. He hoped not. He sensed that, if he did have anything to say, it would not be pleasant.

'Have what you fancy, Hugo,' he said unnecessarily.

'I won't have a starter,' said his brother. 'I'm eating tonight.'

He didn't enlarge on this information. He was a very secretive man.

'Me too. Dinner with my wife.'

'Ah! The domestic bliss that has escaped me. Or have *I* escaped *it*?'

Sir Gordon ordered a bottle of Margaux that was almost as old as the waiter and cost £210.

'Wait!' commanded Hugo as the waiter started to move off. He lowered his voice, even though every word was clearly audible to the waiter. 'Do you really want to spend that much?' He lowered his voice even more, but was still audible. 'The food isn't going to be worth it. And you don't need to impress me.'

39

'I hope you aren't hinting that I can't afford it?' said Sir Gordon.

'Of course not, Gordon. It's just . . . not necessary.'

'It is to me. I like fine wine.'

'Well, all right, then. Good. I'll enjoy it. Thank you.'

The waiter returned surprisingly quickly, opened the bottle with exaggerated reverence, and poured a small amount into Hugo's glass with ill-concealed hostility. Hugo handed the glass to Sir Gordon without comment. Sir Gordon rolled the wine round the glass, sniffed it, and nodded. He couldn't help feeling, in Hugo's presence, that he didn't quite know what he was nodding at, that he wouldn't even know if it was corked.

When the waiter had gone they clinked glasses in their usual manner.

'To "Our Escape from Dudley",' said Hugo.

'"Our Escape from Dudley",' echoed Sir Gordon.

'I haven't said this before,' said Hugo, 'but, you know, it's a bit of a miracle, you and I, from a secondary modern in Dudley, both so eminent in our different fields. I should think ninety per cent of the people I deal with in my work went to public school, and half of them to Eton. We owe a lot to our parents.'

'Well, of course. I hope I always acknowledge that.'

'Stop looking for evil subtexts in what I'm saying, Gordon.'

'Sorry. Bad habit.'

'No, but there they were, two good people, intelligent people, but . . . not special. Here we are – let's not beat about the bush – thoroughly special.'

'I suppose so.'

'Dad was clever. Mum wasn't clever exactly, but she had common sense in spades, and she had spunk. The last thing I want to do is be rude to Dad but he did lack spunk. But the combination of brains and spunk, in you and me, it just gelled. It's not perfect, I could definitely do with a bit more spunk and you could probably do with a bit more brains, but it isn't bad. Is it?'

'I never said it was.'

'You're looking for subtexts again.'

The wine was delicious and as they sipped and chatted Sir Gordon almost forgot his concern over whether there was a secret agenda for the meeting. He couldn't recall quite such a relaxed conversation with his brother as the reminiscences of old Dudley flowed. But all good things come to an end, and eventually their food arrived.

They ate for a few minutes in silent disbelief. Eventually Hugo plucked up the courage to speak.

'How's your veal?'

'It tastes like face flannel that has been marinated in Montenegrin traffic warden's phlegm.'

'So A.A. Gill was right.'

They both left half their food, and the waiter took their plates away with no comment and no surprise. They scorned the pleasure of looking at the dessert menu, and shuddered at the thought of coffee.

'We'll just enjoy the rest of the wine.'

'Very good, gentlemen.'

'Yes, it is,' said Sir Gordon. 'Pity nothing else was.'

His brother raised his eyebrows in surprise. The waiter made no comment and showed no reaction.

Hugo leant forward and dread entered Sir Gordon's heart.

'I suggested lunch for a reason, Gordon. I keep my ear to the ground. I'm picking up . . . rumours. Only rumours. And please don't believe that I believe them. There's usually no smoke without a fire, but no cliché is true all the time. Rumours about Gordon Investments. Rumours that . . . all is not well.'

'When you say "all is not well" do you mean . . . we're running into financial trouble?'

'Not exactly. Gordon, you can talk to me. We're family.

41

I'm here for you. We haven't always been close, not as close as we should, we haven't always got on as well as we should, but . . . damn it, man, I'm not good at being affectionate . . .' He paused, then lowered his voice still further, though now they were the only two people in the room. The other customers had left and the waiter was probably having forty winks after his exertions. 'People are suggesting – hinting – that the set-up of Gordon Investments is not altogether straight.'

'Not honest?'

'Yes. So people are saying.'

'And what do you think?'

'Gordon, I've studied the figures, and . . . I wouldn't go so far as to say that they don't add up. The returns you're giving people are . . . possible but perhaps not probable. Either you and your team are *very* good . . . *very very* good, or . . . well, I don't need to spell it out, I don't actually think I could spell it out. So really, I'm asking you, Gordon, I suppose, for reassurance.'

Suddenly Sir Gordon knew how desperately lonely he was. His mother was dead. His father was lost in the mists of senility. Circumstance prevented his getting any filial feeling from his son. His daughter was cowed by life. And his wife – oh, how he dreaded this evening – his wife would be merciless if the truth emerged. It was a moment of revelation that dwarfed everything else that had happened on this difficult day. It even seemed to explain to him the nature and cause of his disturbing awakening that morning . . . was it really only eight and a half hours ago? It had been psychic, a portent. Suddenly he longed to be close to his dear elder brother whom he had never really appreciated. Suddenly he longed to confess. Suddenly he realized just how heavy his burden had become, that burden that he had never even acknowledged to himself, that burden that had grown and grown while he had slept his guiltless sleeps.

Hugo, help me. Hugo, I've been the most frightful fool. Hugo, you do love me, don't you?

There were so many sentences that he found impossible to utter.

'Hugo, I'm telling you, I'm telling you honestly . . .'

The waiter, skilled at interruption like so many of his kind, came over with their bill, showing a surprising turn of speed.

Sir Gordon entered his card details.

'If I add a tip, does it get to you?' he asked.

'Oh yes, sir.'

'Good. Good. The question was purely hypothetical, of course.'

'I'm sorry, sir?'

'You will be. I'm not giving you a tip. You don't deserve it.'

'We closing in two minutes, sir.'

'Excellent news. The outside world is so much more appealing.'

Sir Gordon noticed that Hugo had noticed that he had abandoned his habitual charm. He really must abandon it more. The gratification you could feel from being rude was brief, briefer even than the gratification of sex, but it was enjoyable both in anticipation and reflection. And he did particularly dislike waiters. He would smile at the memory of his remark as he ascended towards his office that afternoon. Besides, what was the point of being powerful if you were always polite? Where was the fun? No, he had used his charm too much.

Sir Gordon abandoned these thoughts reluctantly, and turned back to his interrupted speech.

'Hugo, I'm telling you honestly, yes, I know the figures are difficult to believe, but I have very skilled men working for me, I have a marvellous organization honed over the years, I'd be a fool if I claimed that we can continue in this climate to give investors the returns they've become used to,

43

but there's not a shred of irregularity in what we do, and not even a particle of doubt in my mind that with my reputation, my record, my popularity, we will easily do enough business to keep our heads well above water and with no need of any form of illegality whatsoever.'

'Well, I'm very pleased to hear that,' said Hugo.

'I wish my mother was alive so I could say those words directly to her in your presence. Then you'd believe me.'

'I do believe you, Gordon.'

'I wish my father was compos mentis so we could go together and—'

'Gordon, I believe you.'

'Rumour doesn't help in difficult times. Can you scotch those rumours, Hugo?'

The waiter reappeared, jangling keys in one of the least subtle hints in history.

'We'll have to go. Gordon, I'm not a public figure like you but I have immense influence behind the scenes. I will do all I can to kill this creeping, insidious doubt. I just had to hear your denial of wrongdoing from your own lips. We had to share it as brothers. I've heard it. I believe it. End of story. Thank you for the wine, if not the lunch.'

They passed through the door without meeting the waiter's eyes. They heard the lock click angrily behind them.

And in the street – there in the City of London – the Coppinger brothers did something neither of them would have believed, when they got up that morning, that they would ever do.

They hugged.

Hugo walked away. He didn't look back. He never looked back.

And Sir Gordon thought, Good Lord. We never said a word about Jack.

The evening ended, as it had begun, in silence

We've all seen them, those married couples in pubs and restaurants, sitting there in silence, not a word to say to each other. It's easy to mock, feel a touch of contempt even, forget that maybe they no longer need to talk, know what the other is thinking without any necessity for words. It's easy to forget that they know so much about each other that it's almost impossible for them to think of any questions to ask each other. 'What sort of music do you like?' would be a devastating admission of lack of interest after twenty-nine years.

And Sir Gordon and Lady Coppinger had been married now for twenty-nine years. It felt like forty-nine. Their silence was not companionable, not shared. Their silence was prickly, and loud with all the things that were not being said. Their silence was deafening.

They were sitting at opposite ends of the oval table in the private room on the first floor of the Hoop and Two Colonels. It was a gastropub in these days when pubs in the country can no longer survive without being gastropubs. Sir Gordon liked it because it served largely good, plain, solid English food. Lady Coppinger disliked it for the same reason. If she ate there too often her legs would become even less slim than once they had been. There was nothing unusual about the place except its name. It was the only pub in the world called the Hoop and Two Colonels. Neither Sir Gordon nor Lady Coppinger was remotely interested in why it was so named. There was no money in knowing.

It cost Sir Gordon quite a sum to book the private room just for the two of them. The restaurant was full of atmosphere, crazy with beams, crammed with dressers laden with old plates. The private room was spare and pale and almost corporate. But it was difficult for them to eat in public. You never knew who'd be watching, finger on the button, ready to Tweet. 'Saw Sir Gordon and Lady Coppinger at dinner. Hardly spoke. Devoted? I don't think so.' Or to phone. 'You know who those are? Just popping out, sweetest, to phone the papers. Might be a photo opportunity, might bung me a few quid, might be able to get that trellising fixed.' People! Bastards!

The private room could seat twenty, so by sitting at the ends they formed a little parody of the aristocracy at home. This evening that just irritated Sir Gordon. This evening he actually wanted to talk. But he couldn't. He felt as if he was visiting a sick relative in hospital. Time dragged. Opening gambits died on his lips. After the ritual insincere 'Happy birthday, darling', the raising of his gin glass and her champagne flute – he hated flutes, he hated champagne – and her insincere 'Thank you, Gordon', she couldn't even bring herself to say 'darling' there was an aching silence while they waited to order.

If one is telling of a meeting in which nothing was said, what can one do but relate what was not said? Prominent in this category, from Sir Gordon, was 'What sort of a day have you had?', closely followed by 'Anybody phoned?', 'Any further disasters reported from the care home?', 'Has Luke forgotten it's your birthday again?', 'Was Joanna's card as uninspired as ever?', and, coming up strongly on the outside, 'Bought any more shoes today?'

From his wife there was no such profligacy. One silence

strangled all others in their infancy. 'Have you seen Mandy today?'

They gave their orders. Lady Coppinger's 'I'll have the coquilles St Jacques and the pork stroganoff' was a simple statement of defiance against the patriotism on which her husband traded. Sir Gordon's 'I'll have the hare terrine and the Lancashire hotpot' was spoken with the slight uneasiness that comes with the knowledge that every word one utters in public may be dissected for hidden meaning. The chef might phone the business section of a paper, whose gossip columnist might write, 'May we expect news of an investment in the north-west from the Sir Gordon Coppinger Group? Certainly on Monday evening at his wife's birthday dinner Sir Gordon chose not only Lancashire hotpot, but also hare terrine with Cumberland sauce. Straws in the wind? Maybe. But the north-west is one of the few parts of Britain in which Sir Gordon has no business interests.' And the hare terrine. Woe betide him if he ever came out against hunting. The waiter might remember that hare terrine and accuse him of hypocrisy on Facebook. Bastards, waiters.

Sadly, people do not always realize how difficult and stressful the lives of the famous are.

Once again, too, Sir Gordon had to order a bottle of wine that cost in excess of £200. If he didn't, his wife might wonder about the state of his finances. She might also discover – oh, perish the thought – that he had spent more on a bottle for his brother Hugo than he had on her.

Once the waiter had gone, Sir Gordon began to wish that he could end the silence, that they could talk, laugh, joke as once they had done. Christina was much more comfortable with the silence than he was. The silence put him at a disadvantage. And he was struck again by that sense of utter loneliness. This was awful. This was weak. He might be many things, but he was never weak. He must speak.

But to speak would be weak. He mustn't speak.

But he couldn't bear the silence any longer. He spoke.

His question was hardly worth all the agony that had preceded it.

'Do anything for lunch?'

The question shrivelled in her gaze.

'Of course not.'

'Why "Of course not"?'

'Gordon, I can't eat twice in one day.'

She'd read the article about her appearance in Baden-Baden! She'd seen the comment about her legs!

The wine arrived and saved him further humiliation for a moment. He spent more than a minute swirling it round his mighty glass and sniffing it.

When the waiter had gone, the silence was absolute. She crossed her no longer quite so slim legs and the rasping of tights on tights was deafening. It was awful to feel no desire in these circumstances. He was a man of prodigious virility. Surely he could summon up at least a smidgen of desire?

The need to speak conquered him again. Inevitably, the subject was roses. Roses were her life. She had won no fewer than thirty-seven prizes for her roses, in various parts of the world, and her two slim volumes, *Rose Breeding For Beginners* and *The Bush Pruner's Companion*, had winged their way to all her friends and most of her enemies.

Occasionally, when he caught her at work on her roses, he saw a trace of the enthusiastic, uncomplicated woman she had once seemed to be. Her face lost its wariness, its hauteur. It was still a beautiful face but it had slowly grown harder, thinner, more angular. He sometimes wondered if she had actually forgotten, over the years, that she had once been Miss Lemon Drizzle 1980.

He recalled her telling him, when they were courting, how thrilled she had been with the corner of his allotment her father had given her, how excited she had been when she first made carrot cake with her own carrots, how she had loved her very first rose bush. He had seen her slowly turn this new interest from a hobby to a business, from fun to finance, from colour to competition, from pleasure to prizes, from roses to rosettes. He had seen her stride through the Chelsea Flower Show like the goddess she now seemed to believe she was, as if she had bred not only roses but her own self as a lady of breeding. And he knew now that much of the responsibility for her transformation had been his. It was little wonder that his remark came out all wrong.

'Thought up any new roses today?'

Even to him it sounded sarcastic. It was a huge mistake.

'I do not think up roses. I breed them.'

She relapsed into silence, and the fact that he deserved it didn't make it any easier to bear.

'I do wish you had something to say, Christina,' he said. 'It is your birthday, after all.'

He noticed a flicker of astonishment in her dark brown eyes, and a brief glimmer of triumph. He had shown his weakness. She had reduced him to pleading, and to making a ridiculous non sequitur about her birthday.

The return of the waiter was quite a shock to Sir Gordon. The silence in the room had been so absolute that it would not have surprised him to have discovered that the rest of the pub had disappeared, that they were suspended in space.

'Which of you's the terrine?' the waiter asked.

This ineptitude cheered Sir Gordon considerably. It was what he expected from the public. It was what he expected from waiters.

'I am,' he said. 'Must be difficult to remember when there are so many of us.'

'Yes, sir.'

When the waiter had gone, Sir Gordon found himself wondering if there was a name for a person who hated waiters. A waiterophobe?

He also wondered how it was that he was starting to

wonder about things. It wasn't like him. There was no percentage in wondering.

He took a large mouthful of hare terrine, liberally spread with Cumberland sauce. At that moment, with cruel timing, Christina spoke.

'So, let's talk,' she said. 'What have you done today?'

Oh Lord. She had bowled a googly. He chewed his terrine at unnecessary length and pondered all the things he couldn't tell her. He couldn't tell her about meeting Fred Upson. She hated the man. His obsession with his expenses drove her into apoplexy. He couldn't mention Luke's paintings. In his eyes the fact that the boy had been shortlisted for the Turner Prize was a stain upon the whole family. He could tell her nothing about GI. To talk about his lunch with Hugo would be most unwise. And as for his afternoon . . . well!

The swallowing of the terrine could be delayed no longer.

'I gave a job to the Fortescue boy. Terribly public school. Bathed in naivety and enthusiasm. I've sent him to Porter's Potteries Pies.'

'Excellent.' She almost smiled. 'I hate that Fortescue man.'

He thought, but did not say, 'You didn't need to tell me that. It'd be easier just to tell me when you don't hate somebody.'

'And?'

'What do you mean – "And"?'

'And what else have you done? I hardly think that took all morning.'

He took another mouthful of the delicious terrine, and again chewed for as long as he dared.

'Oh, you know,' he said at last. 'Meetings and things.'

'You've become very secretive lately, Gordon. Particularly in the last seventeen years. So, nothing to report. The little lady wouldn't understand all those dreadful economics.'

'Well, since the world's economists don't seem to, you probably wouldn't.'

'Lunch?'

50

'What?'

'Did you have lunch?'

'No.'

'No lunch? Gordon! What's happening to you? You'll waste away.'

'Well, I mean, I had a quick sandwich. In the office.'

'Fetched for you by the grim Grimaldi?'

'Yes, as it happens.'

'What sort of sandwich was it?'

Suddenly there was too much talking – far too much.

'What is this – the Spanish Inquisition?'

'I'm interested. You always say you hate sandwiches, and now I learn you had them today and naturally I'm fascinated to know what kind of sandwich was so delicious that you overcame your habitual repugnance.'

'Tuna and cucumber.'

'Tuna and cucumber! Gordon, that is so Pret A Manger. That is so Network Rail. That is so Welcome Break. You cannot expect me to believe it.'

'I don't see why you shouldn't believe it.'

'Because Hugo told me you lunched with him.'

'Oh, was that today? Oh God, yes. Yes, it was. The tuna sandwich must have been Friday.'

Oh God. If my millions of admirers could see me squirming like this.

Christina smiled. It struck him how her smile had also changed over the years, hardened into a reaction not to the world but to her own thoughts about the world. It had become as spiky as some of her roses. Yet it still had a faint, disturbing echo of what it had once been.

'Why are you smiling?'

'I was thinking, what if your millions of admirers could see you squirming like this?'

'Have you finished?'

They hadn't heard the waiter come in.

51

'I see not a speck of food left on our plates. I think we may safely deduce that we have finished,' said Sir Gordon, clothing his sarcasm in a smooth smile.

'Thank you, sir.'

The waiter slid noiselessly out on shoes that must have been oiled with WD40, or perhaps with 'S'ssh! The Ultimate in Squeak Removal', made in Sir Gordon's factory on the outskirts of Droitwich and destined, he hoped and believed, to consign WD40 to the pages of history. Or was he being over-ambitious again, as he had been with Germophile? Germophile! He didn't even want to think about that episode.

In his effort not to think about Germophile, something Christina had said suddenly struck him.

'You've spoken to Hugo then?'

'I wondered how long it would take for that fact to sink in. Yes. He phoned, asked if he could bring anything for Saturday. I told him there was no need to bring anything except himself. I told him he was gift enough. The poor sap lapped it up.'

'Hugo isn't a poor sap, darling.' He regretted that 'darling'. 'Poor saps don't have houses in Eaton Square, Cap Ferrat, Venice, Rhode Island, and Bermuda.'

'He's a poor sap emotionally.'

'He's a banker.'

The opportunity for rhyming slang cannot have escaped either of them, but they said nothing.

'Who's the hotpot?' interrupted the waiter like a gunshot.

It had to be an act.

When the waiter had gone, Sir Gordon took a mouthful and discovered that the hotpot was a very hot hotpot indeed. He gasped, tried moving the meat around in his mouth so as not to burn any bit of skin too much. Few wives could have wasted such a moment.

'And your afternoon?'

While he dealt with his explosive mouthful, Sir Gordon

thought desperately about his desperate afternoon. What could he tell her? Jack wasn't mentioned in the house, which was hardly surprising in view of the gift that he had left her all those years ago, the gift that she had once, briefly, welcomed. (I could explain this now, but I choose to string you along. These are not generous times.)

Besides, how could he admit to his wife that he had felt unable, after his lunch with Hugo, to face the Coppinger Tower? He could never confess such weakness to her. And how could he admit that his heart seemed to have opened up, and that he'd felt an overwhelming *need* to see his younger brother, who had not quite enough of the family brains, not quite enough of the family spunk, not quite enough of the combination of brains and spunk that had been given to Sir Gordon and to Hugo by the brutality of chance. How could he admit to Lady Coppinger that he had hunted for Jack with the intention of trying to help him, even though Jack had rejected all help for ever?

And hadn't found him, not in Soho, not under the arches of Charing Cross, not in Waterloo, not under any of the bridges of London. And how the wind had blown.

'I just went back to the office actually. Caught up on some paperwork. Didn't see anybody.'

'Except the grim Grimaldi, presumably.'

Did she know?

'Except the grim Grimaldi, yes. She brought me her grim coffee, and a grim rock cake from the grim canteen.'

He felt a slight twinge of shame at his disloyalty in calling the canteen grim. The canteen and the adjoining restaurant on the eighth floor were fine. The only reason he didn't use them was because his presence inhibited everyone else from saying anything meaningful to each other. The strength of his ears was legendary.

Talk faded, fluttered feebly, died. Sir Gordon grieved, searched for answering grief in his wife's dark eyes, and found none.

'Have you finished?'

'Once again the total absence of any even minute morsels of food remaining on any of our plates or in any of the dishes would suggest that we are seriously deluded if we believe that we haven't finished.'

'Yes, sir. Very good, sir.'

If only he had managed to see Jack.

Could Jack have died?

How would they find out if Jack had died?

He became aware that Christina had been speaking.

'Sorry, I missed that. I was thinking,' he said.

'Gordon! How brave. Taking up a new activity at your age.'

He was so tired of her sarcasm – though not, curiously, of his own.

'So, have I missed anything interesting?'

'God, no. I just asked what you were doing tomorrow. I know my questions aren't very imaginative but I am trying because you said you wanted me to talk. '

'So you're trying new things as well. The obedient wife. Very nice.'

For a moment he thought he'd got away with it. He really didn't want to talk about tomorrow. Two events dominated tomorrow's agenda, and he didn't want to talk to her about either of them. But then she repeated the question.

'So what *are* you doing tomorrow?'

Tomorrow . . . lunching with the Earl of Flaxborough, who lives, not surprisingly, at Flaxborough Hall, which is, also not surprisingly, just outside Flaxborough, and in which 'a proposition of some interest will be put to you', according to the Curator of the Coppinger Collection, Peregrine Thoresby. What a feast of sarcasm about his glamorous life and his neglect of her that would inspire if he told her. And in the evening . . . well . . .!

'Tomorrow? Nothing much. Can't remember.'

'Oh, come on, Gordon. You always remember. You don't even need a diary.'

'No, honestly, tomorrow, routine bits and bobs, that's all. Tuesday's never very stimulating. Oh, and I won't be back for dinner. I have a meeting.'

'With Mandy?'

'Who's the tiramisu?'

He was grateful for the interruption; he had never been so grateful to a waiter, but he didn't show it.

'Has it not dawned on you yet that *I* choose the British dishes, because I am British and proud of it, and my wife deliberately, in order to annoy me, chooses the most foreign dishes she can find on the menu?'

'So you are the Eton Mess, sir?'

'Oh, well deduced, Mr Einstein.'

Oh God, now those dark eyes were gleaming. In his eagerness to show the waiter how much he hated him he had revealed to Christina how deeply she had got under his skin. What a disaster, what an Eton mess.

'You're avoiding my question. Are you seeing the marvellous Mandy tomorrow night?'

'I wasn't avoiding your question. The waiter interrupted, with the genius of his ilk. I didn't get a chance to reply.'

'You're avoiding it now. Are you seeing Mandy?'

'What is this obsession with Mandy?'

'That's what I ask myself. Are you seeing her tomorrow night?'

Why was he so reluctant to lie? Was he losing his nerve? Did he think she would be able to tell that he was lying?

'No, I am not seeing Mandy tomorrow night. I'm seeing two Croatian businessmen. Croatia's an up-and-coming country. I need to get in there.'

After that, they ate their delicious desserts in silence.

Suddenly the door burst open and a woman in her early thirties, wearing a witch's hat and a very short dress, lurched into the room, saw them, and shrieked with laughter.

'Oops, sorry, I thought it was the Ladies,' she said.

'No,' said Sir Gordon unnecessarily.

'Oh gawd, I'm bursting,' said the drunk young woman.

'Too much information,' said Sir Gordon.

'Do you know where the Ladies is?' the drunk young woman asked Christina.

'I have no idea,' said Christina frostily.

'Blimey, you're on your pud and you haven't been yet. You must have a strong bladder. I've got a very weak bladder. I go all the time. Pee, pee, pee, that's me.'

Oh, Christina, your face. Your fury. Your scorn. The lower orders, how common, how vulgar. Your denial of your birth, your childhood, your mum and dad, your moments of glory as Miss Lemon Drizzle. Oh, Christina.

He conveniently forgot, in his scorn of her scorn, that he also despised the lower orders. But, curiously, this evening he did not despise this intruder. Oh, silly drunk young woman in your witch's hat, he thought, I will help you find the Ladies.

And he did. Without difficulty. With charm.

And that disturbed him. Maybe he had only done it to irritate Christina, and he often went through rituals that he despised and hid his scorn in charm, but he found that he did not despise this young woman who might have very good reasons to get drunk. He found the incident rather endearing. He thought the young woman was fun.

That was worrying.

He returned, looked at his wife's icy face.

'It's odd. Today has been strangely dominated by urine. At breakfast I thought of the horror of needing to pee on the Kingston By-Pass. In the office, I imagined our receptionist's boyfriend peeing in a sodden Sussex hedge. In the lift I realized I needed to pee and then I found myself describing young Martin Fortescue as a long streak of piss – though only to myself admittedly – and then in the afternoon I found myself in agony, while I was searching for Jack, and I did something I've never done, I took an enormous risk, not a paparazzo in sight, but still a risk, I peed under Blackfriars Bridge. And now this poor girl with her weak bladder, what a day.'

Of course he said none of that. The evening ended, as it had begun, in silence.

A great deal nearer than the Solway Firth

Sir Gordon felt slightly uneasy on his visit to Flaxborough Hall. This was the real deal. Rose Cottage truly was only a cottage after all.

He felt uneasy from the moment Kirkstall nosed the Rolls-Royce up the long drive towards the beautiful Jacobean frontage, through parkland laid out by Perspicacity Smith centuries ago.

There were signs, it was true, of slight but disturbing decay. Some of the bushes needed pruning. Branches that had been ripped off trees by the recent gales still lay on the ground. The mellow red-brick walls were in need of pointing. A gutter here and there hung loosely. Drainpipes were rusty.

The eighteenth Earl of Flaxborough stood at the top of the steps to welcome them, almost as if Sir Gordon and Peregrine Thoresby were royalty. Here too there were signs of slight but disturbing decay. He looked frail. He seemed to have become slightly too small for his clothes. He was beginning to droop, as if his long legs could no longer bear the weight of his even longer body. He had stretched his thin hair bravely over his scalp, to little avail.

'I am so delighted to welcome you to Flaxborough,' he said, in a melodious voice steeped in history.

There was a slight stiffness to his walk as he led them through the great hall into a large drawing room. The chairs in which they sat felt as if dust sheets had only just been removed from them. A chill hung over the house. Damp clung to the walls like a nervous child. It would have been tactless to look at the plaster too closely.

'The bells aren't working,' said the Earl apologetically. 'Excuse me while I round up some sherry.'

Perhaps the Earl's stiffness was just a result of the damp, but when he had gone Peregrine commented, 'He walks as if he has the burden of history in his bones.' Peregrine had a great mass of curly black hair which made him look much younger than his forty-eight years. His voice was almost as posh as the Earl's, but thinner and more strident. 'Did you notice that little habit he has of glancing behind him? Is it fanciful to imagine that he is seeing seventeen Earls of Flaxborough marching behind him, watching what sort of a fist he is making of managing his inheritance?'

Taking an interest in other people had never been high in Sir Gordon's priorities, but he found himself examining the Earl more closely as he returned with a tray, a bottle, and three Georgian sherry glasses. Sir Gordon was sensitive enough to feel a little embarrassed at being treated by this aristocrat as if he was manna from heaven, but then there came that voice again – 'I have a sherry that I think will amuse you' – and the authority returned, Sir Gordon was in his thrall.

'I thought we'd have luncheon first,' said the Earl, after they had been amused by the sherry, 'and then examine the picture.' He pronounced it 'pickcha'.

Peregrine had refused to tell Sir Gordon what the purpose of their visit was. 'I'm sorry, I know how infuriating it is,' he had said, 'but I want your reaction to be instinctive and immediate.' Now it was clear that the Earl wanted him to buy a pickcha for the collection. Peregrine had explained that the estate was in deep trouble and needed to sell its assets. It was situated in an unfashionable part of the country – Bedfordshire – and was in the shadow of Woburn. The eighteenth Earl did not have a talent for showmanship. The house was seventy-ninth in the heritage top hundred. No elephants or giraffes wandered its grounds to delight the masses. No pop stars drowned the screeching of the peacocks.

Lord Flaxborough led them along a damp corridor towards the cavernous dining room. His wife arrived to join them as if she had been hiding in a secret passage. They lunched at a large table with the Earl at one end and Lady Flaxborough at the other, and of course it occurred to Sir Gordon that this was the real version of the parody he had performed with Christina in the private room of the Hoop and Two Colonels only yesterday – could it really have been only yesterday?

Lady Flaxborough was pale and slim and had a face like an overworked angel. She was painfully polite, asking Sir Gordon endless questions about his collection, his charitable foundation, even Climthorpe United. 'It must be such fun to own a whole football team,' she said, in a tone that almost but not quite concealed the subtext of 'What kind of an idiot are you?'

Sir Gordon, determined to begin to turn over a new leaf and talk to people about themselves, was forced to spend the whole luncheon behaving as if he was rehearsing the final run-through of a television programme about his life. Poor Peregrine was silenced too, bypassed utterly.

The luncheon was served rather slowly. In fact, it was thirty-five years late. It consisted of brown Windsor soup, roast lamb in caper sauce, and sponge pudding, and was served by a butler who looked like a gnarled oak and made Farringdon seem a complete imposter.

'I think you may be rather mystified by the red wine,' said the Earl, and they were, although Sir Gordon had to be careful not to end up too mystified; he needed to be fresh for the evening.

And then the meal was over and the moment came.

'If you'll excuse me,' said Lady Flaxborough. 'I will be so grateful to you, Sir Gordon, if you agree to help us dismantle our heritage, but I cannot bear to witness it.'

'I understand,' said Sir Gordon in a hoarse voice.

He didn't know whether protocol demanded that he attempt to kiss Lady Flaxborough on her white cheeks, but in the end he only shook her hand.

The three men climbed the main staircase, in the face of a northerly gale blowing from the bedrooms, and entered the long gallery, which was indeed long, but slightly less long than most of the other long galleries in the stately homes of England. Nobody ever said, 'When you go to Flaxborough, you must see the quite long gallery.'

They had the quite long gallery to themselves. The house was closed for the winter. The air was icy. Two small radiators were pointlessly hot.

The Earl led them to a rather small painting, a watercolour entitled *Storm Approaching the Solway Firth*. It was a Turner, dating from 1836. In the presence of its owner, who'd had more than fifty years to admire it, and of Peregrine, who was steeped in the language of art appreciation, Sir Gordon felt incapable of any adequate response. He was out of his comfort zone. Luckily, Peregrine spoke for him.

'Marvellous,' he said. 'A minor masterpiece, perhaps, yet a masterpiece. The colours more muted than in some Turners, but we know it's autumn and we don't know how we know and that is very clever. We know the storm is coming, we feel the unease, we may suspect that this will be the first storm of winter, yet the picture is almost still, but the stillness is fragile, the stillness is doomed, the boat looks so peaceful, the water is just gently ruffled, yet we know that the boat will soon be tossed and helpless. Magnificent. Will you buy it, Sir Gordon?'

61

'The provenance is utterly secure, I suppose?' said Sir Gordon, making it only just a question.

'Oh, absolutely,' said the Earl. He couldn't look Sir Gordon in the face. 'Let me put you fully in the picture, Sir Gordon. I have three pictures that have been earmarked for sale, with huge regret. All masterpieces but what else is one to sell if one needs to raise money? This, a Tintoretto, and a Monet. Our great institutions in this time of cuts cannot afford to buy everything, so the pictures will have to go to auction unless . . . unless a saviour can be found.'

A warm feeling crept over Sir Gordon. Saviour. He was a saviour. In moments like this he almost persuaded himself – perhaps occasionally did persuade himself – that this was why he had done it all, this had always been his purpose, to make money in order to use it more wisely than any government, in order to give something back to the nation he loved and, more important, the nation that loved him. He no longer felt uneasy in this house. He even felt a sense of triumph, and he longed to say, 'I'll buy all three.' Why not? That would show just how successful he had been, and just how generous he was.

But that would have been vulgar, and, however weak his position, there was still something about the Earl that forbad vulgarity in his house. Besides, there came with Sir Gordon's warm feeling a colder undercurrent, a trickle of sensitivity that marred his pleasure as he witnessed the unease of a man short of old money practically begging to be saved by new money.

Maybe Peregrine Thoresby could read his mind, and had sensed the danger. Certainly he leapt in pretty quickly.

'Clearly, even if we wanted to, the collection couldn't consider buying all three,' he said. 'There are limits even to our resources, and the publicity it would engender would create an excitement that we just would not be able to accommodate in the context of our other work and the rest of our collection and the inevitably finite resources of our building itself. So, Sir Gordon, I felt – and this is what I would strongly advise – that we should purchase the Turner. If all three go to auction, none of them is likely to remain in Britain. There simply isn't the money here to rival what there is in other places. Well, if the nation loses the Tintoretto and the Monet, they weren't ours in the first place. But to lose a Turner – even a relatively small work from someone so British, so quintessentially British, even, dare I say it, quintessentially English – would be a tragedy.'

Sir Gordon knew that the Earl and Peregrine would be capable of talking about the picture for at least an hour without being so vulgar as to actually mention money, so, however much he might regret it, however much it would suggest that his reactions and his motives were less spiritual than everyone else's, he would have to be the first one to raise the subject.

'So, what sort of sum are we talking about here?' he asked.

'I've taken the liberty of talking to the Earl about this, Sir Gordon,' said Peregrine, 'and we've arrived at a round figure, a very round figure, which we think is fair, in no way excessive, and which acknowledges that this is a relatively small work, and a watercolour, and his watercolours do not historically fetch as much as his oils.'

'I would be prepared to sell this picture to you,' said the Earl in his modulated tone, 'for twenty million pounds.'

'Fine,' said Sir Gordon. 'Consider the deal done.'

They shook hands. Sir Gordon was again bathed in the warm glow of the saviour. The Earl was relieved. Peregrine Thoresby was as excited as a child.

Sir Gordon felt happy as Kirkstall drove them speedily back to the Coppinger Tower. He was now the proud owner of *Storm Approaching the Solway Firth*. He was blissfully unaware that this was just the first of many storms that would approach, and that all the others would come a great deal nearer than the Solway Firth.

Those insidious doubts

The entry in his diary read, '*6.30. Dorchester. DDT (Kranjčar and Modrić)*'. Using the names of real people gave him a tiny frisson of risk. It was unlikely that Her Grimaldiship would recognize Kranjčar and Modrić as Tottenham Hotspur players, but it was just possible, and that element of insecurity added salt to the stew of deception.

'Well, Helen,' he said as he reached her desk. 'I'm off to see the Croatians.'

'Give my love to the Dorchester.'

'I will.'

Did other people have conversations as fatuous as that? he wondered. (Wondering again! What was going on with all this wondering? he wondered. And that was wondering *again*.)

'May I ask what DDT stands for?'

'Of course, Helen. You have every right to know.'

Their eyes met. A stab of desire caught him off guard. He was always vulnerable at the start of one of his naughty evenings.

Did she sense his sexuality? He thought she did. He thought he could see it in her eyes. He'd have to be careful. He ought to leave. A quickie with Helen was definitely not in the plan.

'It's the Dubrovnik Development Trust.'

'And what's that all about?'

'Developing Dubrovnik.'

'I'm sorry I asked.'

He lowered his voice.

'This is very hush-hush, Helen, but I can trust you.'

Her square face softened. She really did believe he was going to the Dorchester to meet two Croatian businessmen. What an opportunity.

'We're planning to build a shopping mall inside the walled city. I'm helping to fund it – for a substantial return, of course.'

'Inside the walled city. You can't. It'd ruin it. Where inside the walled city?'

'Near the harbour, at the end of that big long tiled main street.'

'But that's the best bit. You can't do this. I love Dubrovnik.'

He knew that.

'It's ravishing.'

And once I ravished you. No!

'Why? Why, Sir Gordon?'

'To keep the cruise ships away. They have up to five huge ships a day, pouring people in – in their ghastly shorts with their hideous white veined legs and their paunches and their tattoos, filling the bars and the shops and the restaurants, making life for the natives utterly intolerable. They have to make it ugly to survive.'

God, it was just believable.

He gave her a quick kiss on the cheek and noticed that she had the faint beginnings of a moustache. That really turned him on. He hurried away from the danger.

As he strode through the open-plan office, a few people were still at their desks. It was five to six.

'Well done,' he called out. 'Your diligence has not gone unnoticed.'

Kirkstall drove him to the Dorchester, dropped him off and went to park. As soon as his chauffeur was safely out of the way, Sir Gordon went outside and hailed a taxi. In the taxi he thought about the evening ahead. He was never at his best in taxis. Rich though he was, and even though he had just offered to buy a painting for £20 million, he hated the way the meter clicked up, up, up. He tried to ignore it, but found his eyes drawn back to it. 'That's one pound, twenty just for waiting at these lights,' he would say. Christina had once pointed out that he resented spending on taxis but paid a fortune to gardeners. 'They don't have meters on their foreheads,' he had said.

So now, in the taxi, it was natural that his thoughts should veer towards the negative.

Barely thirty-six hours had passed since that disturbing awakening, when he'd decided that he must end it with Mandy. But then he'd thought of that as a sign that he was going soft.

Should he end it? Were people becoming alerted to his sexploits, as the tabloids would no doubt call them? Insidious doubts began to assail him. Was he still invulnerable? Would his sexual appetite destroy him? Shouldn't he concentrate on his great work, his collection, his charitable foundation, his football team? Men with missions should be single-minded. What would his staff in those great organizations and his workers in his factories and all the people in the Coppinger Tower think if they knew that their esteemed leader stared at the meters of taxis in horror? What would they think if their charismatic hero was splattered across the tabloids as a sex addict?

Oh God, was he a sex addict? He hoped not. It didn't sound good when he read about other people who were sex addicts. They had to have treatment, for goodness' sake. How intolerably embarrassing that would be.

If only, with his appetite, his virility, his needs, his strength, he could resume sexual relations with Christina. It really was rather extraordinary that he couldn't.

He would have to grasp that nettle.

No, he must give Mandy up. She had served her purpose.

As he climbed the stairs to the second floor of her block of flats in Hackney – there was no lift – he noticed again that there was no smell of drains. The smell occurred only inside the flat, yet it was so faint that it seemed to be drifting in from outside. A conundrum! A conundrum that might perhaps have been easily solved if only Germophile had . . . but he must stop thinking about Germophile.

There she was, beaming plumply, sexy and generous, far too aroused for him to even contemplate disappointing her. He would let her down gently later. He owed her that much.

There was a smell of something else, dominating even the distant drains. It was the faintly sweet, temptingly disgusting aroma of cooking lamb. She had made one of her shepherd's pies.

They kissed hungrily, hurried to the bedroom, tottered on to the bed, clawed at each other's clothes – they couldn't get them off fast enough. He raised her rate of interest, he made his deposit, it was urgent, it was a meeting of needs, it was a contract, it was the execution of an agreement, it was over.

It had always struck him as pathetic that she tried to lay an attractive table in her cramped kitchen-diner. There was a single, rather tatty rose in a cheap vase. There was a flickering candle which would deposit wax over the Formica that wasn't even retro. She had placed the mats for the veg without a vestige of spatial awareness. The salt and pepper pots were dumped inelegantly in just the wrong place. It was a disaster, but she had tried. It made a vivid contrast to luncheon at Flaxborough Hall, where elegance hung in the air like a memory.

She would have to go.

He couldn't tell her just now, or, if he did, he would have to leave before the meal. He wasn't that cruel, to leave her with two portions of shepherd's pie to eat through her tears. Besides, the portions had not been generous at luncheon, and a man is always hungry when he has just agreed to pay £20 million for a picture.

But would she shed tears? Did she care a jot for him?

She poured him a glass of wine. In the first few months he had always taken a bottle, hugely expensive, wasted on her. She had said that she was perfectly able to buy good wine, she was his girlfriend, not a paid mistress. He knew that sometimes she paid as much as £9.50 for the wine they drank.

He took a sip and actually enjoyed the roughness that her palate could not detect. Sometimes the wines that he bought were so smooth that all the tension had been bred out of them. Yes, he could enjoy this. And as the top of the shepherd's pie began to crisp up the smell grew far more appealing, and he realized that he was very hungry indeed, even hungry enough to eat lamb for the second time that day.

'I hope this is going to be all right,' she said. 'It's only shepherd's pie.'

'It'll be just lovely. I've told, you, Mandy, I don't particularly like sophisticated food.' He realized that this hadn't sounded like the essence of tact, but she didn't seem to notice. 'Good old British simplicity, that's me. Besides, how can I criticize? I've never cooked anything in my life.'

Her large pale blue eyes grew even larger in astonishment.

'What, never? Not even boiled an egg?'

'Never. Not even boiled an egg. I have things done for me, Mandy. I have everything done for me. I haven't cut my toenails myself for a quarter of a century.'

'I can't imagine your life.'

She wouldn't be able to imagine the Earl of Flaxborough's either.

'I can't imagine yours.'

She served the shepherd's pie with cabbage and carrots.

He ate hungrily.

'Sex makes me hungry,' he said.

She blushed just a little. Her body was so uninhibited, but she went all coy when she talked about sex. She changed the subject hurriedly.

68

'I'm trying out a new girl this week. She's better with hair than with people.'

He didn't want to talk. He was actually relishing the food. The cabbage and the carrots were a little undercooked to his taste, but the pie itself was succulent, nicely seasoned, simple but unadorned, a success.

Sometimes when she talked about her salon he thought of other things, but today he actually found himself listening and wondering about this other world, so far removed from his, and even further removed from the Earl of Flaxborough's. How many worlds there were.

'That's the thing with hairdressing. You get people who're good with hair and useless with people and you get people who're good with people and useless with hair.'

He smiled. They shared a problem – the inadequacy of underlings.

'If you get somebody who's good with hair *and* people it's like gold, and then they emigrate to Dubai, and they never come back. There must be millions of hairdressers in Dubai. I don't know how you do it, finding people for eleven manufacturing companies plus your financial empire and your property portfolio and all your ancillary activities.'

He had once used the phrase 'my property portfolio and my ancillary activities' to her, to explain the cancellation of that month's visit, and she was one of those dangerous people who remember every single thing that is said to them.

'This is very nice, Mandy.'

He really meant it and she knew that he meant it and she blushed slightly again and he felt the first tingle of returning desire. Maybe . . . maybe he wouldn't tell her till after their second helping.

'Would you like a second helping?'

Her timing was immaculate, and completely innocent.

'Thank you. I would. Very much.'

Over his second helping he found himself making a request. He, making a request to her!

'Tell me more about the new girl. The one who's not good with people.'

'Why?'

'I like hearing you talk.'

Forget Hackney. It was Blush City, Arizona.

'She talks too much. I think they've told her in training that's what you do. Hairdressers can be overtrained.'

'Like footballers.'

'I was sorry you lost on Saturday. I always look for the scores.'

'Yes. Unfortunate. Go on. In what way does she talk too much?'

'Asks questions. I mean, the sort of women I get, they nod off or read magazines. They don't want her saying, "Are you doing anything exciting this weekend?" Because most of them aren't, and if they were they wouldn't tell her, would they?'

She chatted away and he didn't have to say much in reply and actually to his surprise he found it not unbearably boring to hear about this other world. There was apple crumble; he praised it and asked her if she'd made it herself and she said it was from Waitrose. They finished the bottle and he assured her three times that it was nice and she said, 'I won't wash up,' which was the nearest she would ever get to 'How about another fuck?'

This was one of his best evenings with her and he was amazed to find how much more he was enjoying it than his visit to Flaxborough Hall. He felt a twinge of pity for the eighteenth Earl, who would never hear anything about Hair Hunters of Hackney. The meal had been much better than usual, really quite edible, and she had worked hard over it, and it would have seemed heartless to have said, after that, 'Mandy, this can't go on, you know.' So he didn't.

This time he relished her unfashionable fleshiness, her large untrendy breasts, her full cheeks, her generous lips, the pleasure in her pale blue eyes. She once, in a rare moment of post-coital candour, had told him that his power turned her on, that it was exciting not to have been entered by her friend, the traffic warden, but by a man who had eleven manufacturing outlets in England alone. (Not to mention his property portfolio and his ancillary activities, though she hadn't mentioned those on that occasion.)

This second coming was so gentle, so relaxed, so slow, so synchronized, so lovely. You really could almost have believed that there was real emotion in it. You could almost have believed that he felt real affection for her. You could almost have believed – oh, he hoped not – that she felt some kind of love for him.

He didn't want to go home. He really did not want to go home. But he would, he almost always did, and when he didn't he almost always regretted it.

As he took his shower, washing all traces of sexuality off him (not that Christina would come near enough to him to notice, but this was one risk that wasn't worth taking), he felt really quite sad that he was destroying all the evidence. It seemed . . . tactless. Ungracious. And using her hot water too.

This was the moment when, if he was to tell her at all, he would have to tell her.

She mouthed her farewell kiss at him, careful not to undo the good work performed by the shower.

As he walked down the stairs he found himself wondering how a hairdresser could have such awful hair. But he actually found that quite endearing, and, as he stepped into the taxi that would take him to the Dorchester – in order for him to look as if he was coming out of the meeting he hadn't been to, so that Kirkstall could drive him to darkest Surrey and suspect nothing, although actually he suspected that Kirkstall suspected everything – he was really extremely glad that he hadn't given way to those insidious doubts.

Perhaps we have intruded enough

The dusk is pulled across the London sky like a merciful shroud drawn over a dead body. The short day is over. The long night is beginning. Nights are very long on the London streets, in winter.

For one of the men on the streets this Saturday evening, however, the night is perhaps not going to seem as long as usual. He has found a marvellous position, not exactly the best seat in the house, but the best space on the pavement. He has found a little corner, below pavement level, where warm air is being pushed out from the extractor fan of a posh London restaurant. He does not know the name of the restaurant. He does not know the name of any restaurant. He has not been in a restaurant for more than twenty-five years.

Before he settles down for the night he takes a swig from his bottle. The rawness of the alcohol warms him. He runs on alcohol. He starts each day with alcohol. It is the only thing that can cure his hangover. Maybe tonight, though, he will sleep right through, and need no alcohol. He certainly hopes that he will sleep until the restaurant's kitchen closes.

He puts the bottle down beside him, where it will be handy if he needs it during the night. He wraps his old stained rags around him and lowers himself carefully on to the ground. He will be relatively cosy, tonight, in his own sunken grotto.

Just as sleep is about to envelop him, there are two loud bangs from somewhere nearby. He is irritated rather than alarmed. He knows

72

what they are. They are not the signal to start a revolution. They are not the first shots in a gangland battle. They are fireworks. Tonight is Guy Fawkes Night. He knows this because he knows that November the fifth is Bonfire Night, and he knows that it is November the fifth because he always knows the date. There are often pages of newspapers bouncing in the wind along London's dirty streets, and although he may look half drunk and extremely filthy, he still has a good brain, and he has very little to feed it, so he grabs what scraps he can.

Now sleep will not come. He thinks back to all those Bonfire Nights in Dudley, watching the municipal fireworks display with his brothers, gasping with shared astonishment, which was about the only thing they shared. They weren't allowed to have fireworks themselves. There were a lot of things they weren't allowed to have. They weren't allowed to go to the swimming pool in case they contracted polio. He enjoyed the Saturday-morning film shows but his two brothers had grown out of such things, if indeed they had ever been into them. His elder brother almost certainly hadn't. He had no sense of fun. There hadn't been any point in playing games with him. He had no talent for games.

The middle brother, now, he had been different. He had been rather good at games, at make-believe, but he had never had the time. He had never had the time for anything, really, except for making money. He used to go to the baker's, buy cakes, take them home, and cut them into pieces – rather small pieces to be honest – and sell them by the slice. He preferred that to any game, which was a pity.

Does the man in the privileged position beside the warm-air outlet welcome these reminiscences, or are they an irritation which prevents him from sinking into the unconsciousness he craves, if indeed he does crave it? How does he feel about his lifestyle? Is he happy? Is he sad? Is he resigned? Is he bitter?

What goes on inside his head is actually the only privacy he has left in his life. Perhaps we have intruded enough.

Staring at himself with astonishment

This was the bit that he liked best – the moment before anybody arrived. He stood in the middle of the enormous drawing room, rich in plump settees and elegant standard lamps, two of them in the art deco style – who said he was a philistine? On the walls hung a Cézanne, two Pissarros and a Stanley Spencer – again, who said he was a philistine? Log fires crackled gently at both ends of the great room. They were known as the west fire and the east fire. Some people described this as affectation, but Lady Coppinger said that it was necessary in order to give definite and simple instructions to the servants.

He walked slowly through the ground floor of his 'cottage', and every prospect pleased him.

The rosewood (what else?) dining table, the long rustic table in the far kitchen and the trestle tables erected for the occasion in the conservatories were all beautifully laid with plates of rare beef, pink lamb, pork with liberal crackling, smoked duck, venison sausages, five moist whole salmon that had once been wild, six stuffed trout that hadn't been too pleased either – the old jokes were the best in Sir Gordon Coppinger's book. It was all so quintessentially British, to use

74

Peregrine Thoresby's favourite word. Not a salami or a snail in sight. Good old Siobhan.

In the vast entrance hall with its anachronistic Doric pillars, the two lovely Pembroke tables were bedecked with all the rich promise of alcoholic excess. On the table to the left were bottles of champagne and long antique flutes. On the table to the right bottles of red wine stood opened and breathing and were surrounded by glasses of a size to cheer the most sombre of hearts. All the wine was British. It pained Sir Gordon not to be able to serve great French wine, but his reputation as a patriot was paramount.

The serving staff stood at their posts, young enough, smart enough, alert enough and attractive enough to pass muster even to this stern critic. Good old Siobhan.

Oh, it was wonderful. The food elegant and untouched, the bottles full, the glasses gleaming, the carpets spotless, and Lady Coppinger safely in her dressing room deciding which shade of lipstick to favour and which necklace to wear.

He climbed the stairs with the energy of a young man, and made a final security check round the eight bedrooms, the three dressing rooms and the eight bathrooms, six of which were en suite. Everything was as it should be. He'd known that it would be but he was glad of the excuse to look round and admire his cottage without seeming smug about it.

He switched off the lights on the landing that would have seemed long enough and wide enough to be called a gallery if he hadn't been to Flaxborough Hall so recently, and peered out of one of the windows into the impenetrable dark. The rain hadn't amounted to much, the bonfire would burn well. In a couple of hours this dark sky would be alive with bright colours and sensational patterns.

He could just see, through the gently swaying trees, the lights in Top Field, where a marquee had been set up to serve beer and wine and pork pies and sausages (not venison) to the good people of Borthwick End, Borthwick Magna and

Borthwick Juxta Poynton. How generous I am, he thought, to allow them to marvel at the sensational waste of money which is at the heart of this evening at this critical economic moment in our island's story.

Yes, this was the bit he liked best. Soon they would be here, headlights frightening the owls in the trees that lined the drive, tyres churning up the grass in the Front Meadow and the Back Meadow, exclamations of astonishment as if they'd never seen tables laid with food before, the wild salmon and the unhappy trout skeletonized before his eyes, and the chatter, the roar of the trite remarks of 250 people, what *did* they find to talk about? The showy coats piled on the beds in the guest bedrooms, the crumbs and wine stains on the carpet, the soiled bowls in the many lavatories, it would be downhill from now on.

He braced himself against the invasion. He consulted the database in his head. He must be prepared.

People invited included his elder brother Hugo; his doctor Hamish Ferguson and Mrs Ferguson; his centre forward Raduslav Bogoff and his not so svelte wife Svetoslava Bogoff; his creative left-side midfielder Danny Templeton and Mrs Templeton; his goalkeeper Carl Willis and Mrs Willis; Keith Gostelow, Dan Perkins, and Adam Eaglestone from GI (Keith Gostelow and Adam Eaglestone accompanied by their better halves, Dan Perkins accompanied by his worse half); his daughter Joanna, accompanied by nobody; Siobhan and Liam McEnery; Field Marshal Sir Colin Grimsby-Watershed (retired) and Lady Grimsby-Watershed (retired); Admiral Lord Feltham of Banbury (retired) and Lady Feltham; Gloria Whatmough, Head of Charitable Giving, and her friend June Wellington; Peregrine Thoresby, Curator of the Coppinger Collection and his partner David Emsley; and, last but least, his son Luke and his latest girlfriend, Emma Slate.

People not invited included his younger brother Jack; his

deceased mother Margaret; Fred Upson; Martin Fortescue; Helen Grimaldi; Kirkstall; Alice Penfold with her stud and ring; Fiona Bruce; A.A. Gill; Giles Coren; the Mayor of Dudley; Mandy of Hair Hunters of Hackney; Francesca Saltmarsh of the Perseus Gallery with the sweetest little bedroom upstairs; and Jenny Boothroyd, Sandy Lane, Isla Swanley, Kerry Oldstead, Gill Goldthorpe, and Ellie Streeter, all of whom he had taken to his secret seduction suite on the twenty-second floor during the last six months.

The phone rang, loud and shocking in this last moment of silence.

A few moments later, Farringdon called out to him.

'A Mr Liam McEnery on the telephone for you, sir.'

'Thank you, Farringdon.'

He approached the phone as if it was an unexploded bomb.

'Coppinger.'

'I'm so sorry to bother you when you must be so busy, Sir Gordon.'

Yes, so get on with it.

'I'm afraid we aren't going to be able to come, sir.'

No Siobhan! What do I do if things go wrong? How selfish is this, to let me down at this late hour?

'It's the wee mite, sir.'

Oh, bloody Ryan. Might have guessed it. Children! Bastards!

'I'm afraid he's not well, sir.'

'Oh dear. Nothing serious, I hope, Liam.'

'I'm afraid it may be, sir. We've had to rush him to Great Ormond Street Children's Hospital.'

'Oh, I'm so sorry.'

This really is very inconvenient, though. Why are kids always so inconvenient? And who will orchestrate the evening now?

'Please give Siobhan my very best wishes, and tell her not to worry at all about the party, I'm sure her planning is absolutely foolproof.'

77

'Thank you, sir. She'll appreciate that.'

First arrivals. Suddenly Lady Coppinger sailed out from the harbour of her bedroom, exuding welcome, dripping with real pearls and false charms.

'Hello! Oh, you look gorgeous.'

'Well, so do you.'

'And that new rose you bred last year. Divine. What was it called again?'

'The Crimson Rambler.'

'Marvellous.'

'Thank you.'

They were off. It had begun. Siobhan was forgotten.

Who the hell are this couple? Quick, access the database of the brain, search. Ah, yes. Stanley Welton, the big cheese at Stilton (ha, ha) and Mrs Welton. 'How are Olivia and Toby?' 'Oh, how clever of you to remember.' We're off, we're at the races, who needs Siobhan? I can do this.

Chat, chat, chat. Sip, sip, sip.

The chosen footballers of Climthorpe United were among the first to arrive, awkward in their suits, none more awkward than Raduslav Bogoff. They had a Derby match against Charlton next day, and to invite so many of them tonight had been to indulge that love of risk that is an essential ingredient of the make-up of all great men.

'Good luck against Charlton tomorrow, Raduslav,' said Sir Gordon, 'and don't rush it in front of goal.'

'Oh no, Sir Gordon. Tomorrow I am cool. Tomorrow I am ice.'

'Excellent. And Raduslav? Don't drink too much tonight.'

'Oh no, I not, sir. I am Bulgarian. I no have this culture of booze.'

'Great stuff. Good man.'

The manager, Vernon Thickness, and his absurdly blonde wife Claudia walked in on either side of the little gaggle of footballers as if they were two sheepdogs directing them towards the pen.

'Hello, Vernon. Hello, Claudia. Going to stuff Charlton tomorrow, are we, Vernon?' asked Sir Gordon.

'Absolutely. Close down their wingers and they've no Plan B.' Vernon Thickness narrowed his eyes, which was difficult as they were narrow already. 'And don't worry about them drinking too much tonight. I'll be watching like a hawk.' He did his hawk impression. 'Anyone who drinks too much tonight is out. O U T. Out.'

Your spelling's improved, thought Sir Gordon. Let's hope your tactical awareness has too. But he didn't say this. There were some things even Sir Gordon didn't say.

They were pouring in now, and there was such a business of handing over coats and getting drinks that he had the unpleasant feeling of being surplus to requirements in his own entrance hall. He decided that it was better to return to the drawing room, which was filling up already.

Lady Coppinger approached him, gave him a sweet kiss on the cheek and said, 'Darling, you look gorgeous tonight.' She turned to the people who were drifting in the wake of her perfume. 'I'm so proud of my man.'

Sir Gordon almost showed his shock before he realized that this was a public performance, overdone in order to hurt him. And, briefly, it did hurt him. A shaft of pain went through him as he recalled the times when such things might have been said and meant.

The drink flowing. The noise rising. The locals in Top Field getting frisky already. The chauffeurs in the Back Meadow and the Front Meadow running their engines to keep warm. Cost of fuel immaterial, they don't have to pay. Global warming, global schwarming.

'More bubbly?' 'Please.' 'Crisis? What crisis?' Who cares about the Greeks anyway? They can whistle for those marbles.' 'No wonder they want them, they've completely lost theirs.' 'Very good! Quite right! Bastards!' 'Nobody pays tax in the whole of Southern Europe, they'll go to the wall and take us with them. Bastards.'

There was a sheikh in the room. He hadn't invited a sheikh. Hadn't got anything in particular against sheikhs, take them or leave them really, that was his attitude to sheikhs, but what was he doing here? Have to ask Siobhan. Oh, damn, couldn't. Better ask the fellow himself. How do you address them? Excuse me, Your Sheikhship, and I hope this doesn't sound rude, but who exactly invited you?

He started to part the crowds, feeling slightly like Moses, to get to the sheikh, but then he saw his dad, standing by the door looking utterly and totally lost. What was he doing here? Who'd invited him? He made his way over to Christina, who was holding court.

'Sorry to break in, sweetest –' God, that was difficult to say – 'but did you invite Dad?'

'Yes, all the happy family together, Gordon, on this very public occasion.'

'Bit risky, isn't it?'

'He'll be fine.'

Women! That was women all over. Make a gesture, create havoc. Better say nothing, though.

He hurried over towards his dad, feeling, though he was too anxious to realize it, a genuine shaft of emotion for the first time in the evening.

His father's cheeks were shrunken and his eyes were hiding in panic at the backs of their sockets.

'Dad!'

Say 'Dad' at regular intervals, and he just might put off that moment he dreaded, the moment when he had to face for the first time the fact that his father didn't know who he was.

'How are you, Dad?'

'I've lived too long.'

Quite right.

'No! Never!'

'Where am I?'

'You're at my house.'

'But it's huge.'

'I'm very rich, Dad.'

'Are you? Good Lord. I never was. Was I?'

'No, Dad, you weren't, but you did all right.'

'Did I? Oh, good. Where's Margaret?'

Margaret's dead, Dad. No point. Wouldn't remember, why hurt him?

'Probably checking her make-up.'

'That'll be it. Who's that boy over there who's in love with his hair and isn't in love with that woman who looks as if she doesn't wash?'

Good God. So few corners of the brain left active, and still such perception.

'That's your grandson, Dad. Luke.'

'Ah! Thought I recognized him. You must introduce me some time.'

He found a seat for his dad and looked round for someone to go and talk to him. His eyes lit upon a nun. A nun! What was she doing here? He hadn't invited a nun. What did Siobhan think she was doing inviting a sheikh and a nun? He must talk to Siobhan. Oh, blast. He couldn't. Perhaps he could ring the hospital. No. Insensitive. A picture flashed across his mind, anxious parents at a bedside. A wee mite struggling to breathe. Oxygen.

He managed to reach the nun. No time to ask her why she was here.

'Excuse me. I don't know you, but obviously as a nun you have compassion.'

Strangely attractive. He'd never had a nun. No! Gordon, get a grip.

'My dad . . . that's him in that chair . . . he's eighty-six

81

. . . he's got dementia . . . he's frightened . . . will you talk to him, calm him down? . . . Please.'

'Of course. Don't worry.'

'Thanks.'

'No problem.'

He was disappointed to find that even nuns said 'No problem'.

He tried to make his way over to Luke, but his path was blocked by Hugo, immaculate to excess and as supercilious as a cat.

'Posh do, Gordon.'

'Well, you know.'

'Yes. Keeping up appearances.'

'What do you mean by that?'

'Stop looking for hidden meanings. Anyway, I can see I'll have to pull my socks up next year.'

'Don't be ridiculous, Hugo. You top me every time. Last year was fantastic.'

'It was good, wasn't it? Still, this looks lovely. Where's Christina?'

'Oh, here, there, everywhere. Being charming.'

'Not *being* charming, Gordon. She *is* charming.'

'You don't live with her.'

Hugo gave the very faintest twitch.

'True. Very true.'

Sir Gordon edged closer to Luke. A quick look showed his father chatting happily with the nun. Maybe Siobhan had known what she was doing inviting her.

At last he was with Luke. They shook hands. The formality seemed odd, but a kiss was out of the question.

'Dad, this is Emma Slate.'

The worst yet.

'Delighted to meet you, Emma.'

'Really? Luke said you'd hate me.'

'Well, give me a chance. I haven't had time yet.'

Uneasy laughter. Good.

'I may as well tell, you, Sir Gordon –' there was a look of defiance on her face, plus an element of fear that if she wasn't careful she might look attractive to men she despised – 'that I came here under duress.'

'Not the quickest way. I recommend coming through Esher and Epsom. Any more vandalism, Luke?'

'Not yet.'

'Oh, don't be such a pessimist, Luke, why should there be any more?'

'I just have a feeling, Dad.'

'Luke gets these feelings, Sir Gordon.'

'Oh, does he? I wouldn't know, Emma. I don't know him as well as you.'

'Dad!'

'Well, I don't.'

'Whose fault is that?'

'Oh look, Luke, not today.'

'OK. Right. No, I think I must have – or *we* must have because you were mentioned as well – offended the Welsh in some way.'

'Well, that isn't difficult. So, Emma, are there a Mr and Mrs Slate?'

'No, I was produced by artificial insemination.'

'Emma!'

'I'm sorry, Luke, but I just hate telling people. It's such a conversation stopper. No, there isn't a Mr Slate or a Mrs Slate. Both my parents are dead, Sir Gordon. They drowned in Tenerife.'

Emma was right. It was a conversation stopper.

Now, as the buzz grew louder, the crowd thicker, he noticed, out of the corner of his eye, two people, the sight of whom demanded instant attention – his daughter Joanna, and a Greek Orthodox priest. It was no contest. He approached the priest with determination in his step.

'Excuse me . . . I don't know you . . . I'm . . . I'm Sir Gordon. Your host.'

'Lovely party.'

'Thank you. I . . . um . . . I have no wish to be in any way offensive, and I . . . I have no idea of how one is supposed to address a Greek Orthodox priest.'

'A Greek Orthodox *archbishop*.'

'Oh my goodness. Then perhaps I ought to call you "Your Beatitude".'

'That will do splendidly.'

'Good. I have to ask you, Your Beatitude, who invited you?'

'You did.'

'Me?'

'Well, not personally, but the invitation was from you.'

'You received an invitation?'

'I received an invitation and both as a Greek citizen and as a senior representative of Our Lord here on earth I find your attitude to me somewhat offensive.'

'I have to say that I am not thrilled by your attitude, Your Beatitude.'

'I will show you the invitation but I do so under protest.'

'There's really no need. I accept your word.'

'I insist.'

'Very well.'

The invitation looked exactly like the design that Siobhan and he had devised, and the words too were as they had agreed. If it was a forgery, it was a good one. He would need to phone Siobhan.

But could he? The image returned, Ryan's breathing now faint, Liam holding Siobhan's hand, a doctor and two nurses staring at the graph of the wee mite's heart; it was terrible, compassion flooded into Sir Gordon, and he had no defence against it, having hardly felt any for as long as he could remember.

He took his mind off it by wondering what it would be like to have sex with a nun, in her cell, right next to the Mother Superior's. It didn't work very well.

And then he realized that he had the perfect antidote to compassion right there standing in front of the east fire. His daughter Joanna.

It was the sagging of the shoulders that did it, he decided. The whole body might look better if she stood up straight. Even the clothes, which looked as if they'd been bought in a charity shop the day it closed down, might look better if she stood up straight. And the hair. He'd a good mind to send her a voucher for six free visits to Hair Hunters of Hackney.

Oh, Joanna, the day you were born . . . our hopes.

'So, darling, how are you?'

'Oh, you know, Dad. So-so.'

Never ill. Never well.

'Well, it's the time of year.'

Gordon, you can do better than that.

'Yes, I hate this time of year.'

You hate every time of year. Too hot. Too cold. Too wet. Too dry. Too average.

'Looking forward to Christmas?'

Oh, come on, Gordon, sparkle. It's Guy Fawkes Night.

'Not really, Dad. I don't much like Christmas actually.'

Not even positive enough to hate it.

'And it all starts ridiculously early these days.'

I entirely agree, in fact I'd go further, it's ludicrous, it's greedy, it's self-destructive, but can't we try to be positive tonight? It is a party. Abandon Christmas. Change the subject.

'How's the job?'

'Oh, you know.'

'Well, you could have worked for me.'

'Oh, Dad, don't. You know I don't want favours. You know I want to make my own way in the world.'

But you haven't.

'I know what you're thinking. You're thinking I haven't made much of a way, but it's my way.'

And you can't sing like Frank Sinatra either.

Suddenly, the banging of a gong broke through the rising chatter. More bangs, cries of 'Shh', and silence fell in the great triple-glazed, triple-gabled house specially designed for a soap magnate who needed two swimming pools and so amusingly called his mansion a cottage, ha, ha.

'Ladies and gentlemen,' intoned Farringdon. 'Your host, Sir Gordon Coppinger, wishes to say a few words. If you would make your way, as many of you as can squeeze in, to the drawing room.'

Sir Gordon hurried through to get to the front while he still could. Farringdon passed the microphone over to him. He tried not to look at the throng. He didn't want to see the sheikh, the nun or the archbishop. They sounded like a bad joke, but in fact their presence alarmed him. He didn't want to see his frightened dad, his listless daughter, his inept son, his insincere wife. He wanted to forget his unhappy life. What?? Unhappy?? No!!

He'd paused too long. He must begin. But to have had these thoughts at this very moment . . . how could he cope?

Of course he could cope. He was a great man, wasn't he? Wasn't he?

He coped.

'Ladies and gentlemen . . .' he began. 'Ladies and gentlemen . . . I'm not going to make a speech. Too many people make too many speeches. I'm going to say just a few words. As you may know, my brother Hugo and I host a Guy Fawkes party in alternate years, and this year it's my turn, so . . . welcome. Welcome, each and every one of you. Guy Fawkes Night. We celebrate a failure. How very British. Well, I don't much like failure. In fact, I think I can say that I'm a stranger to it. So, my simple message is this. Don't talk Britain down. Don't even contemplate failure. Cut the word "crisis" from your vocabulary.

Let's start tonight. Let's make this night a huge success. Ladies and gentlemen, you will find tables laden with food in the dining room, in both the conservatories, and in the far kitchen. Don't rush, there's plenty for everybody. Enjoy.'

The minute he had finished speaking he felt as if his words had been utterly hollow. He stood there in his crowded home, and felt utterly alone.

People began to queue for food. Many rushed. Others didn't rush because they were genuinely too polite. Some didn't rush because they didn't want to be seen to rush. A few didn't rush because they were cool. Luke didn't rush because he had to be seen to be cool. Christina didn't rush because she was the hostess. Joanna didn't rush because she didn't much like food. His dad didn't rush because the nun had abandoned him and he was utterly confused.

Sir Gordon walked up the side staircase, unseen, upstaged by hunger. His purpose was to telephone Siobhan from the phone in the master bedroom. He had to know whether she had invited the sheikh, the archbishop and the nun. If she hadn't, why were they there? Was there a plot to kill him? On Guy Fawkes Night? He wasn't a wimp, but he was frightened. Of course he was frightened. Very few people want to die.

And yet . . . didn't he court danger? Didn't he need it to spice up his unvarying diet of success? Yes, but danger was one thing, death another. He wasn't ready to die.

Danger. He longed for a sudden little bit of it. Perhaps he was a danger addict, not a sex addict. Perhaps he was a danger addict *and* a sex addict.

And here was the perfect way of having danger and sex.

He would make love to the nun in the bed he shared with his wife in the middle of his Bonfire Night party.

Gordon, this is madness. You are not a rapist. You are not an evil man. How will you persuade a nun into your bed?

With your famous charm.

But, Gordon, you are beginning to wonder about your charm.

87

It was a mad moment. It was over. The desire for sex and danger left him, the tide receded and he was a whale stranded on a beach.

He picked up the phone. Siobhan's mobile was switched off. It would be, you weren't allowed to have them switched on in the wards.

He hesitated. Even he, so used to having his own way, thought twice about ringing a children's hospital at a quarter to nine on Guy Fawkes Night.

He must find out.

He dialled.

'Hello. My name is Sir Gordon Coppinger.'

'*The* Sir Gordon Coppinger?'

'That's right. I want to speak to a lady called Siobhan McEnery. Her baby son Ryan is seriously ill in the hospital.'

'Is it important, Sir Gordon?'

'It's important or I wouldn't be ringing at this time but no, it isn't a matter of life and death and I will understand if she can't speak to me or doesn't feel able to.'

'I'll do my best, Sir Gordon.'

'Thank you. I really appreciate that.'

He waited, waited, waited. His heart was racing.

'Hello.'

Siobhan. He almost fainted.

'Siobhan, it's Sir Gordon here. I have to know. How's Ryan? How's the wee mite?'

'Oh, Sir Gordon, thank you so much for asking. He's very ill but he's holding his own.'

'Oh, thank you, Siobhan. Thank you. I'm so relieved. Get back to him, Siobhan.'

'Thank you, sir.'

He put the phone down and walked slowly away. He caught sight of himself in a long mirror. He stared with astonishment at the sight of himself staring at himself with astonishment.

Not such a useless lump
of a nun after all

He walked slowly down the stairs, out of silence into bedlam.

Almost without knowing that he was doing it, he took a plate and piled it with food. Almost without knowing how he had got there, he found himself back in the immense drawing room.

'Dad! Over here.'

Almost without making a decision he obeyed Luke and made his way over to the corner of the room, where there was a spare seat. Nobody, it seemed, had been that eager to sit with Luke and Emma, who had created a little artistic enclave by sitting with Peregrine Thoresby and his partner David Emsley.

'I *love* your Pissarros,' said Peregrine Thoresby, who was at his most effete and wouldn't be everybody's cup of mint tea in this gathering.

Sir Gordon finished his mouthful of smoked duck before replying. He needed the time. He was having trouble getting back into the social whirl after his experience upstairs.

'Well, I put on my walls only what I like,' he said at length.

'And that includes nothing by Luke?' asked David Emsley, who was big and solid and had played in the scrum for Rosslyn Park before coming out of the closet.

'Difficult one. I really don't want to be offensive,' said Sir Gordon. 'I only put on my walls paintings that I both admire and believe will enhance my house. If you think that makes me philistine, I am. I can admire Francis Bacon. I don't want him in my house. The same goes for Hieronymus Bosch and, I'm afraid, Luke Coppinger. It isn't a question of merit. It's a question of . . . domesticity. In choosing a picture I use some of the same criteria as I use in choosing a settee. Does it enhance the room? Fact of life, I'm afraid. You disapprove, Emma. I see it in your face.'

'Emma disapproves of everything,' said Luke proudly.

'I do not,' said Emma. 'How ridiculous. I disapprove of this party, yes. I'm sorry, but I do. Such waste, when billions are dying of starvation, and when it's just been announced that company directors voted themselves average increases of forty-nine per cent last year, and here you are wasting money on fireworks of all things, which are no use to anybody and frighten all the animals, and please don't point out that I myself have been eating your food and drinking your drink because it's all been laid out and will only be thrown away if I don't.'

There was silence. Luke seemed abashed. Even Emma seemed abashed. Sir Gordon felt very tired, too weak to face a challenge.

'You deny that you disapprove of everything, Emma,' said Peregrine Thoresby. 'So tell us. What do you approve of?'

'I approve of disapproval,' said Emma, 'because the world deserves it. I approve of alcohol, because it makes me feel good. I approve of cricket, because it's going to get Luke out of my hair for hours every weekend in summer if we're still together. I approve of bees, because they're clever and lovely and I like honey. I approve of rabbits, obviously.' Her most recent painting was a massive canvas of rabbit droppings. She looked at Peregrine and David. 'Oh, and I approve of homosexuality.'

'Thank goodness for that, eh, David?' said Peregrine.

'She's just saying it to be polite,' said David, and at the word 'polite' Emma snorted.

'Sir Gordon, you're a bit of an enigma, you know,' said Peregrine.

'Oh, I do hope so,' said Sir Gordon, but he said it without his usual conviction. He felt uneasy in this conversation.

'You can be so forward-looking with the collection at times, but you're regarded as a rather reactionary soul. We've never discussed this and I think we get on well, I hope we get on well. What's your attitude to gays?'

Sir Gordon wanted to tell them of his happy relationship with Dennis Hargreaves in Dudley all those years ago, but he couldn't think of a way of putting it that wouldn't sound a bit like boasting in this context, as if he was telling them that he wasn't narrow, he wasn't prudish, he too was a man of the world, a man of broad tastes. So he didn't. Instead he repeated something he had said at a seriously stuffy dinner party in Leatherhead.

'I have no objection to male homosexuality,' he said. 'I get on very well with homosexuals actually, but I loathe lesbianism.'

Throughout the house the conversation was buzzing merrily, people were beginning to go for desserts, soon it would be fireworks time, but in this corner there was a stunned silence. Luke broke it at last.

'That's ridiculous, Dad.'

'I don't want to be rude,' lied Emma, 'but it's ludicrous. How can you possibly justify it?'

'Two male homosexuals are two rivals out of the way,' said Sir Gordon. 'Two lesbians mean two lost opportunities. Simple self-interest.'

There was another, only slightly less stunned silence.

'Every decision in the world is made out of self-interest.'

'Oh bollocks,' said Emma, and she stormed off, to the extent to which it was possible to storm off in such a crowded room.

'Oh, Dad,' said Luke, and he set off after her.

'They're young,' said David Emsley. 'The truth still hurts them.'

The truth. Was it the truth? Sir Gordon wasn't sure any more. It didn't explain his phone call to Siobhan.

And then, shortly before ten o'clock, the guests trooped out into a night that wasn't quite wet and wasn't quite dry, that wasn't quite cold and wasn't quite mild, and they stood in their overcoats and their massed ranks right at the bottom of the garden.

Behind them, the house shone with light, a fantasy of gables and even a small turret, built in brick, rambling, almost mirroring a medieval house that had grown over the centuries, though this had grown in two days on the drawing board of a fast and not too punctilious architect.

Just beyond the fence, at the top of Top Field, the mountainous bonfire burst into life. The flames lit up the faces of the locals, beyond the bonfire.

Now the fireworks began. The Surrey sky was alive with double and triple rockets, meteors, comets, whistling tails, crackling willows, canopies of glittering starburst, noise and glitter and bursting greens and blues and reds. His guests ooohed. The locals aaahed. The guests aaahed. The locals ooohed. All was noise and light.

Dogs whimpered and hid. Cats hissed. Bewildered finches woke and fled. Nervous horses neighed and pranced and fell. Rabbits hared to their burrows. Sticklebacks in the streams felt the vibrations. Sir Gordon caught sight of the Greek Orthodox archbishop looking endearingly boyish and excited, and wondered again whether there was a plot to kill him or kidnap him tonight, under cover of all this excitement.

But most of the time his eyes were gazing into the sky, marvelling at the barrage of rockets, the titanium salutes, the wildly whistling missiles that burst into confusions of colours. Nobody noticed a frail old man slip through a gate with an agility beyond his years, but then he was nineteen again, he was in the Eighth Army, he was inspired by Monty, he was inspired by Rommel, who was that rarity, an enemy worth fighting. Nobody noticed him ride out the hail of bullets, dodge the wickedly whistling shells, and speed – well, totter, but it seemed like speed to him – towards the conflagration.

'There are men in there,' he cried, but his voice was frail, and nobody heard his cry. 'There are men dying in there.' But the noise was loud, and nobody heard his voice. But then he tripped, and the fall caught somebody's eye, and voices were raised, Sir Gordon and others heard the cries, Sir Gordon saw his father, slender and tottering in the glare of the flames, getting to his feet again, shouting desperately but oh so feebly, stumbling towards the flames, but oh so slowly, men were catching him, Sir Gordon was running but he was too late, too late, his father fell again, arms reached out for him, a log spat viciously, sparks flew, his father's straggly hair was on fire, his father screamed, then he saw his father pulled away out of the reach of the fire, there was a bag over his head, somebody was pressing the bag down so that the fire couldn't breathe, but his father couldn't breathe, Sir Gordon couldn't breathe, a great pain shot through him, he was having a heart attack, he was dying, he was lying and dying beside his dead father.

But Sir Gordon didn't die and neither, amazingly, did his father. They made them tough in Dudley, and besides, don't forget, Clarrie was nineteen again.

The bonfire burned on, the fireworks continued to explode, many people hadn't even noticed the kerfuffle beside the fire. Somebody found Dr Ferguson, who examined the old man with great tenderness. There beside the fire he was in the warmest place around. Dr Ferguson suggested that they let him recover a little from his shock before they moved him. And then, during the spectacular climax to the magnificent display, when almost all eyes were on the heavens, they moved Sir Gordon's frail, shocked father carefully, and carried him with infinite care back to the protection of the warm, wonderful house. Dr Ferguson said that to move him to hospital, a twenty-mile trip in an ambulance, to transport him to a bed when there was a bed here safe from MRSA, would be senseless. He himself would stay beside him, tend him, treat him, dress the burn on his scalp, comfort him.

'Well,' said Sir Gordon Coppinger to his spouse of twenty-nine years, 'do you think inviting him was sensible now?'

'It might have been a good, brave way for him to go,' said Lady Coppinger, the former Miss Danish Pastry (West Midlands).

Sir Gordon sighed. It was a sigh steeped in realism. She would always have the last word.

Some people knew what had happened and sent their condolences, but far more of the revellers had no idea that anything untoward had happened, such had been the splendour of the display.

There was mulled wine to round the evening off, and then, gradually, the guests began to leave.

'Next year will have to be pretty special,' said Hugo Coppinger to his brother.

'To next year,' said Admiral Lord Feltham of Banbury (retired). 'If we're invited, of course.'

'Time for us to retire, my dear,' said Field Marshal Sir Colin Grimsby-Watershed (retired) to Lady Grimsby-Watershed (retired).

'Did you enjoy the fireworks?' said Sir Gordon Coppinger to his daughter Joanna.

'I don't much like fireworks actually,' said Joanna Coppinger to her father.

'Well,' said Sir Gordon Coppinger to Emma Slate, whose *Rabbit Droppings Near Hornchurch* was said by one critic to have lent a completely new and translucent complexion to the meaning of art. 'There have been many panicking cats and dogs, ponds and marshes full of frightened frogs and terrified toads, well over a hundred expensive cars pumping carbon monoxide into the air, lights blazing in every room of a house of hugely unnecessary proportions, vast amounts of fine foods likely to be thrown away, most of which were produced by rearing and keeping animals in very dubious conditions indeed, and one dreadfully startled old man. Have you enjoyed it?'

'Oh, Sir Gordon, I have. I have,' wailed Emma Slate. 'Does that make me a bad person?'

'No,' said Sir Gordon Coppinger. 'It makes you human.'

Their eyes met. She wasn't his type at all. His father had been right. She wasn't very clean. And there had to be something a bit insalubrious in the mind of a woman who could create a picture of rabbit droppings. But sexual attraction didn't run along smooth lines. There weren't any rules. And he did wonder if there was just a chance that he could steal her off Luke. That would be fun.

'You're pissed,' said Sir Gordon Coppinger to Vernon Thickness. 'If we don't win tomorrow you're on your bike, sunshine.'

'We will hammer Charlton Unthletic tororrow. We will larecate them utterly. One–nil. I promise you that,' said Vernon Thickness to Sir Gordon Coppinger.

'A message for you, sir,' said Farringdon to Sir Gordon Coppinger. 'A lady rang and left a message. A Siobhan McEnery. I believe her husband had rung earlier.'

Sir Gordon's heart almost stopped yet again.

'Yes, Farringdon, yes. And?'

'She said there was no need to get you personally.'

'Yes, yes, but what was the bloody message?'

'I apologize for my slothful delivery, sir.'

'Shut up, and tell me.'

'Yes, sir. Sincere apologies.'

'Tell me!'

'Yes, sir. She thinks you're the most wonderful man in the world.'

'I don't care about that. How's the child?'

'The doctors are confident that the wee mite will pull through, sir.'

'Oh, Farringdon. That's wonderful.'

'Yes, indeed, sir.'

'That's terrific.'

'A most apt adjective, sir.'

'Better than fucking the arse off the most beautiful woman in the universe.'

'My sentiments entirely, sir.'

Sir Gordon suddenly realized that he was going to cry. He didn't know why he should cry at this news, it was absurd, but there it was, and he didn't want Farringdon to see him cry. Farringdon had many virtues, but being easy to cry in front of was not one of them.

He turned away hastily, tears streaming down his face. Suddenly he saw the sheikh and the Greek Orthodox archbishop approaching in the distance, deep in conversation. Whatever they were after, he didn't want them to see him cry either. He turned on his heel, saw a door, couldn't remember what it led to – well, it was a house of many doors – opened the door, slipped into whatever was on the other side of it, and hid. He found himself in a cupboard. There were cleaning materials on the floor (if only those had included Germophile!) and coats on hooks.

He could hear the two men approaching.

'I think I left my cope in here,' said one of them.

That stopped Sir Gordon's tears.

'Oh well, it's pretty chilly out there. You won't be able to cope without your cope,' said the other, the sheikh.

They both giggled. Sir Gordon couldn't see anything funny in it.

'When did you recognize me?' asked the archbishop.

'Just as the light from that fantastic finale was dying away, actually. I caught your face and I thought, "That's not a Greek Orthodox archbishop. That's Tim Walpole."'

'I don't think I'd ever have recognized you if you hadn't told me. Pretty good disguise.'

'Pretty cheesy. Both of us.'

'Yeah, well, it's a pretty good old Fleet Street tradition, corny disguises.'

One of them opened the door at last. Sir Gordon cowered. He began to be terrified that the dust would make him sneeze. He was furious, furious that members of the British press should infiltrate his house in disguise, furious that he found himself in the humiliating position of hiding from them in his own house, furious that he could do nothing about it because he would be an object of ridicule if the press found him hiding from them at his own party in his own house, furious that, when they were behaving in such a farcical manner, his would be seen as the most farcical situation of all should he be discovered.

'Ah. Got it. Got yours?'

'You know, I don't think this is my cupboard.'

Sir Gordon sensed them moving away through the door, but then they stopped.

'Did you pick up anything?' asked the sheikh.

'I'd hardly tell you if I did, but no, not a thing. Certainly no sex, and as far as I could see, getting on very well with his wife. Wasted evening, but fun. He was very funny talking to me, though. He actually said, "I am not thrilled by your attitude, Your Beatitude".'

'No! Rich. And great fireworks. Best I've ever seen. Couldn't take my eyes off them.'

'Me neither.'

At last one of them began to close the door, very slowly, still deep in thought and conversation.

'Who was the nun, do you know?'

'Well, I'm wondering if it could be Diane Travis, that useless lump on the *Mail*.'

The door was fully closed at last. Sir Gordon wondered

how soon he dared leave the cupboard. He tried to feel again the joy he had experienced on learning that Ryan, whom he had never met, was likely to pull through. But feelings aren't like that. Not a vestige of it remained.

This was absurd. He had to leave the cupboard. It was ridiculous to be frightened of leaving a cupboard in his own home. Garibaldi had captured Sicily with an army of 1,000 men, more than 300 of whom were lawyers. Garibaldi wouldn't have been frightened of stepping out of a cupboard in his own home. He would never forgive the press for putting him in this position. Interviews? Stuff them from now on.

There was no alternative but to go for it. He opened the door of the cupboard, disentangled himself from several coats, and crept out.

There was nobody in sight. There probably hadn't been for at least ten minutes. The party was over. The guests had all gone. His staff were busy clearing up. He sat and drank a large glass of Lagavulin and then went to bed, where he slept badly and had disturbing dreams about nuns.

In the morning his father was fine apart from a blistered scalp and even less hair than before. He remembered not a thing about it. Joanna had also stayed the night. Sir Gordon asked her how she had slept and she said, 'Oh, you know, so-so.'

Farringdon had brought him all the papers at breakfast. He'd turned to the *Mail* first.

COPPINGER FATHER ALMOST A GUY AT BONFIRE PARTY
It was the vanity of the bonfires at a huge thrash given by Sir Gordon Coppinger at his palatial country home last night, and it almost caused the death of his 86-year-old father . . .

Not such a useless lump of a nun after all.

'Shame'

He found it ironic that he was having lunch on Remembrance Day with a man who was suffering from Alzheimer's.

Remembrance Day. It had barely touched him in previous years. He had even thought that perhaps it was morbid to continue to grieve for things that had happened so long ago.

This year they had been driving over to his father's care home to take him out for an early lunch; they had been passing through the village of Borthwick Juxta Poynton when everything had stopped for the two minutes of silence, and he, who for years had carefully avoided being somewhere where he would need to observe the silence, had been shamed into stopping too. He'd caught sight of a couple of teenagers, one of them a pretty girl, standing in silent respect. Pretty girls could lead Sir Gordon towards all sorts of thoughts, some of them best not mentioned. This girl led him towards a feeling of remorse – vague, not quite grasped, not fully understood. He was still feeling out of sorts with himself as he escorted his father and his wife into the Dog and Duck.

'I've never been to this pub before,' said his father.

Sir Gordon didn't think there was any point in telling him that he had been there only four weeks ago.

'How nice to see you, Mr Clarence,' said the head waiter

to Sir Gordon's dad. 'I've got you your usual table in the alcove. You will be looked after today by Julio.'

'Blithering idiot,' said his dad to Sir Gordon. 'Thinks I've been here before. I hate waiters.'

Perhaps being a waiterophobe could be inherited, thought Sir Gordon, and then he thought, Waiterophobe! What an ugly word. Greek too. Don't want anything to do with the Greeks. They created democracy, now they're destroying it. They're not living in the real world. They're dragging us all down with them. No, Dad's phrase is simpler. I'm a waiter hater, that's what I am.

The dining room of the Dog and Duck was quite a simple space, the tables laid with spare elegance, the white walls decorated only by pictures of Old Borthwick. The table in the alcove gave them privacy. Sir Gordon could sit with his back to the throng. This meant that he wouldn't be troubled by punters, and today for the first time he thought of another advantage. If he was assassinated he wouldn't see it coming.

Joanna arrived five minutes late and flustered because of it. Why did the girl find everything so difficult? She squeezed into her seat, scraping her chair along the floorboards as she did so.

'Aren't you going to introduce me to this young lady?' asked her grandfather.

'This is Joanna, your granddaughter, Dad.'

'Hello! I wonder why they've been keeping you from me. Or have they been keeping me from you?'

Joanna blushed. She found dealing with her grandfather distressing.

'Where's Margaret?' her grandfather asked.

'She's visiting her sister, who isn't well,' said Sir Gordon.

'Oh. Shame.'

Their smiling waiter, Julio, bustled up to them.

'Good afternoon, ladies and gentlemen. Good to see you again. Better in than out, eh? Nice and warm. And you looking so well this Remembrance Day, Mr Clarence. And the ladies, so lovely. And the poppy so suiting your dress, Lady Coppinger. What would you like to drink, lovely ladies?'

Sir Gordon ordered the most expensive bottle of wine on the list.

'Very good, sir. A beautiful choice.'

'What's the soup of the day, Julio?' asked Lady Coppinger.

'I will find out for you, madam.'

'You do that,' said Sir Gordon. 'Perhaps instead of poncing around telling us how wonderful we are –' and calling Joanna lovely, which is ridiculous – 'you could find out a bit about the food before you come to serve us. Just a suggestion.' Even as he was saying this he wished that he wasn't. But he needed to find peace, and he had yet to learn how to find peace in himself except by declaring war on someone else, which wasn't really awfully encouraging, at fifty-six.

Joanna went bright red. Julio looked thunderstruck. So did Christina.

'That's the way to deal with them,' said Clarrie as Julio stomped off. 'Put them in their place.'

'I would suggest, Gordon, that you abandon charm at your peril. Without your public popularity you'd be nothing,' said Christina.

'My success does not depend on my being admired by waiters, Christina,' said Sir Gordon. 'If it did, I'd be happy to lose everything. Everything.'

Joanna looked from one to the other, twitched, and said nothing. If you said something, Joanna, I might act on it, thought Sir Gordon. If you ticked me off, I'd find a way out of my self-imposed predicament. I can hardly let Christina see me bowing to her judgement. I am now committed to being rude to the waiter throughout the meal.

Julio returned with the news that the soup was Stilton and broccoli.

'Oh dear,' said Joanna before she could stop herself, and

she found – how resourceful she was in this one respect – yet another shade of blush.

They ordered their meals. Joanna asked for a small portion. Her grandfather plumped for the lamb.

'You don't like lamb, Dad. You say it smells of animal and it gets in between your teeth.'

'Don't be silly, Gordon. I love lamb. I always have. Lamb's my favourite.'

The wine arrived. Sir Gordon rolled it round and round in the glass, sniffed it several times, and said, 'It'll do.'

Joanna refused a glass. 'Oh, not at lunchtime,' she said.

'Just a small drop for my father,' Sir Gordon told Julio. 'They don't like him having too much.'

The waiter poured the old man three-quarters of a large glass, and looked at Sir Gordon defiantly. Sir Gordon was already tired of this, and wished the meal could start all over again.

'I read that article in the *Mail*,' said Joanna.

Sir Gordon gave her a deft kick under the table.

'Ow! You kicked me,' she said. 'That hurt.'

'Sorry,' said Sir Gordon. 'It wasn't meant to hurt. I don't know my own strength.' He whispered the words, 'Dad doesn't remember anything about it.'

'What don't I remember anything about?' asked the old man.

'Dad! You're supposed to have bad hearing,' said Sir Gordon.

'What don't I remember anything about?'

'That day when Auntie Millie fell down a manhole in Malmesbury.'

'I don't remember that.'

'That's what I said.'

'I'm not surprised, though. She always was pretentious.'

'What's pretentious about falling down a manhole?' asked Christina.

'Malmesbury,' explained Clarrie. 'The alliteration.'

Sir Gordon couldn't believe what good form his father was on, or how upset Joanna looked. She was the nearest he had ever seen to being angry.

'I wasn't going to quote what the article said,' she persisted now. 'Credit me with a bit of sense.'

Shocked by her boldness, she found yet another shade of blush.

'I just thought it was very sort of snide, Dad. Sort of suggesting you hadn't sort of looked after him.'

'Looked after who?' asked Clarrie.

'No one you know,' said Sir Gordon, and to Joanna he said, 'Quite right. I thought that too.'

He knew that he hadn't come out at all well from the article. The journalist disguised as a nun had juxtaposed the fact that his father was in a care home with the fact that they had eight guest bedrooms in Rose Cottage. She hadn't made the connection. She hadn't needed to. He had felt again, on reading it, that he was no longer utterly untouchable. He would have to tread carefully, and under those undreamt-of circumstances it might be unwise to continue to be rude to waiters.

He would have to have a talk with Siobhan in the morning. He would have to find out if she'd invited those three journalists. He hoped fervently that she hadn't. She was one of the few people in the world whom he really liked. Suddenly he felt appalled that he hadn't enquired after Ryan for a whole week.

Their starters arrived, two brought by Julio, two by a gauche assistant who would never make a waitress.

They ate in a silence that pained Sir Gordon. Christina was determined not to be cheerful. His father no longer understood the art of conversation. Joanna never shone. It was all going to be up to him. He looked at the etching of Borthwick Magna High Street in the nineteenth century, and had a sudden wish that he had been born into a different era. Which was ridiculous, because he would never have risen above his humble station if he had. He sought inspiration from the horses, the pretty dresses, the bonnets, the raised hats of the gentlemen. No inspiration came, yet he must speak.

'Unlucky loss for the lads on Sunday,' he said.

'What lads were those, Dad?' asked Joanna.

'*The* lads,' said Sir Gordon scornfully. Did she understand nothing? 'My lads. My team. Climthorpe United. We lost two–one away to Charlton. Bogoff missed an open goal in the last minute. Unlucky!'

'Sam Bartram was the best goalkeeper I ever saw in my life,' said his father.

'Sam who?'

'Bartram. Kept for Charlton. Marvellous. You can't have forgotten him.'

'Dad, he was before my time.'

'I'm so old that nothing was before my time. A save he made against Derby County was the best save I have ever seen. Where's Margaret?'

'She's visiting her sister, who's not well.'

'Oh. Shame.'

Their main courses arrived, and Julio poured more wine.

'Congratulations,' said Sir Gordon. 'You've hardly spilt any.'

He just couldn't help it. Maybe he was addicted to insulting waiters as well as to sex and power.

'This is lamb,' complained his father. 'I don't like lamb. It smells of animal and it gets in between my teeth.'

'You can have my beef,' said Joanna. 'I don't mind which I have.'

'That's very kind, young lady. You're a star. You must come again.'

'She's your granddaughter Joanna, Dad.'

'Ah. Forgot. Sorry.'

Sir Gordon had sympathy with him over this. If Joanna sat on a cushion, she'd leave almost no impression.

104

Christina ate with all the delicacy of the refined. Every mouthful denied her origins. Clarrie ate fast and greedily, as if he'd forgotten that quite soon he would have finished and all his pleasure would be over because he wouldn't remember it. Joanna pushed her food around and took tiny mouthfuls so that nobody would notice that she wasn't eating very much. It was a sad, sad scene and Sir Gordon thought how awful it would be if all those brave men who had given their lives so that others might be free could see what his family had done with their freedom. He found it hard to bear this thought. Something had to happen.

Something did. And it came from Joanna, of all people.

Sir Gordon said to her, 'Don't you like your food, Joanna? You aren't eating much.'

She turned on him like a cornered rat.

'You don't like anything I do, do you? You don't like what I am, do you? Perhaps you're forgetting, Dad, that what I am is your fault. You have made me what I am.'

There was a stunned silence. Only Joanna's grandfather didn't look stunned. He said, 'Funny woman. Who is she?'

Joanna's blush was her greatest yet. She looked appalled at what she had said.

Christina was on the edge of her seat, relishing her husband's discomfiture.

And Sir Gordon? He couldn't believe what he had heard. It's hard to be utterly appalled and absolutely delighted at the same time. It takes it out of you. It makes it difficult to respond.

He strove to find in himself the arrogance to say that her accusation was balderdash. But he couldn't. He knew in his heart that there was much truth in it, and this appalled him, how could it not? But he also felt a sense of elation. His daughter had shown spunk. She had shown that there might just possibly still be hope for her in life.

He wanted to say, 'What nonsense,' or 'You ungrateful

wretch, after all we've done for you,' or 'How mean is that, after all we've spent on you?'

He couldn't.

He wanted to cry, 'Bravo!'

How ridiculous was that?

It was as if time stood still. He had read of such moments and now he was in one. Later, when he reflected on it, he couldn't estimate how long the silence lasted.

Joanna stood up. He felt that she was going to rush out of the room and burst into tears in the Ladies.

'Sit down, Joanna – please.'

He was astounded by the desperate pleading note in his voice. So was Christina. So was Joanna, who sat down slowly. Only his father, shovelling food in and missing his mouth quite a lot, remained impervious to the tension of the moment.

'Well now,' said Sir Gordon at last. 'Well now, if that is true, my darling, maybe it's time I did something about it.'

Christina looked at him in real amazement. Joanna, overcome by embarrassment, blushed yet again.

'Where's Margaret?' asked Clarrie.

'She's visiting her sister, who's not well.'

'Oh. Shame.'

His night's work is done

It is ten past four in the morning. A faint rain is falling. A man walks briskly along a narrow, slowly decaying street on the edge of Manchester city centre. There is anger in his heart, a black spot in his soul, aggression in his trousers, a large stone in his pocket, a sharp knife in his left hand and a tin of black paint in his right hand.

He stops outside a small gallery, too smart for the street that it's in, but the rent is cheap.

He puts the knife and the paint down.

On the door of the gallery there is an electronic entry box with numbers from 0 to 9 and a sign saying 'Press hash and speak'. The young man does not press hash or speak, since there is nobody there. Now comes the moment of truth. He has been given the four numbers which will open the door without activating the gallery's alarm. He has memorized them. But has he been told the truth, and has he memorized them correctly?

The gallery is between street lamps, and the light is dim. He peers at the entry box. He can just about make out the numbers. He holds his breath. His heart is racing as he presses the buttons.

The door opens. He breathes out heavily in his relief. He enters, closes the door, moves to the back of the room.

He daren't put the light on, and he can barely see the picture, but he has practised in the dark and believes that he will be able to paint the angry words legibly enough.

He takes a brush from his pocket, opens the tin, dips the brush into it and begins to scrawl the two angry words across the painting. 'Fuck off'. He gets pleasure from this, but later he will reflect that he does not get quite as much pleasure from it as he did in Carmarthen. All life's pleasures pall with repetition.

Now he does a more difficult bit. He paints two more words, in a foreign language. This time the language is not Welsh.

Next, he paints a more difficult bit still. Four words, but they have to be quite small. And he has to paint them in English and in German also. Not easy in the dark, and he cannot see if he has made them legible.

He puts the lid back on his tin of paint, gets some crumpled newspaper from his trouser pocket, packs the paper round the paint-brush and stuffs it back into his trousers.

He gets the knife out of the pocket of his bomber jacket and savagely makes three angry cuts in the painting.

He puts the knife back in his pocket, picks up the tin of paint, walks to the door, and peers out. The street is still deserted. Manchester sleeps.

He puts the tin of paint on the pavement, closes the door, holds it firmly closed with his left hand, and presses the same four numbers. The door locks.

He looks round. Still there is nobody about.

He puts on a pair of gloves, takes the stone from his pocket, walks into the middle of the street, takes aim and hurls it at the window of the gallery. It strikes the middle of the window, which shatters beautifully. He is a cricketer, after all.

Every bone in his body urges him to run, but he can't. Not yet.

He goes over to the shattered window and kicks at the glass with his strong black boots. Two swift kicks with each foot and the gap in the window is large enough for a man to step through.

He has gambled on his belief that even if anybody did hear the noise of breaking glass they would be so used to it, or perhaps so

108

frightened by it, in a British city centre in the middle of the night in the twenty-first century, that they would just turn over and go back to sleep. It seems that he is right. Anyway, his luck holds. He walks away, and within seconds he has disappeared down an alley. His night's work is done.

A serious mistake

Sir Gordon Coppinger – financier, industrialist, property magnate, patron of the arts, supporter of many charities, patriot, football lover, yachtsman, waiter hater, and sex addict – awoke feeling very disturbed and very small. Once again, it was hard for him to believe that he really was Sir Gordon Coppinger, financier, industrialist, property magnate, patron of the arts, supporter of many charities, patriot, football lover, yachtsman, waiter hater, and sex addict.

He hadn't slept well. He had dreamt. Oh God, how he had dreamt. He'd been at Ypres. The denizens of the Coppinger Tower were being instructed to hold the line. The Third Battalion the Hedge Fund Managers were giving way to his left, the Royal Welsh Financial Advisers on his right were in retreat, and he was afraid, afraid, afraid. At his side Helen Grimaldi was hurling bombs at the enemy with her bare hands. In front of him a shell hit Alice Penfold – face, nose, ring, stud, lips were shattered and gone – and he was afraid, afraid, afraid. He had woken streaming with vile sweat that stank of the lamb he had eaten for lunch.

He swiftly realized what had caused this dream. Remembrance Day had not ended well. He had settled down to watch the *Antiques Roadshow*, intending to annoy Lady

Coppinger with contemptuous comments on the people who had so undeservedly inherited beautiful artefacts that they were incapable of appreciating, only to find that it was a special Remembrance Day edition, full of the memorabilia of people who had laid down their lives so that he could live. He had found himself being moved by their heroism, moved to tears which he had tried desperately to hide from his wife, moved by emotions and doubts which he had tried desperately to hide from himself.

He wasn't used to bad dreams. He wasn't used to being moved by emotions and doubts. What was going on?

Furiously he scrubbed himself clean in the shower – scrub, scrub, scrub – washed the sweat out of his tangled hair – wash, wash, wash. He caressed his manhood with affection, and already, by the time he stepped out of the shower, he felt a great deal better. Over breakfast alone at the great round table he thought of his hero Garibaldi and tried to gain inspiration from him. By the toast and marmalade he had almost regained what he would have called his sangfroid if he allowed himself to use French words. By the time he stepped into the Rolls-Royce, he thought that he was himself again.

He thanked Kirkstall for his driving, stepped out of his car, and strode firmly through the sunshine into his tower. He tried to look as if he was Garibaldi leading his Redshirts into Naples. But then he saw Alice Penfold, and he was reminded of his dream.

Oh God, that vision, her death. Oh God, those doubts. But how wonderful that she was still alive, her face untouched, the perfect pale skin, the lively blue eyes, so innocent behind her reception desk, not dreaming that she had been dreamt about.

That innocence was a challenge. So were the stud on her chin and the ring in her sweet flared nose. How could she have done such things to herself? Yet the fact that she had

111

done so intrigued him. Yes, he had enjoyed – still was enjoying – many conquests, but life would be unbearable, for a sex addict, without the prospect of fresh fields to conquer, and Alice struck Sir Gordon as one of the freshest fields he had ever come across.

'How's Tom?'

'He's good.'

Damn.

'Terrific.'

'We saw a lesser spotted woodpecker at the weekend.'

He felt such a sharp stab of pity for Alice's puny existence that he was almost tempted to invite her up to his suite on the twenty-second floor there and then. This did shock him.

Suddenly he knew beyond all doubt that he must change many things in his life. This evening he was seeing Francesca Saltmarsh. He must tell her it was over. He must stop messing about. He was a great man. He must start behaving like one.

He took the lift to the fifth floor, home of the offices of his charitable foundation. Gloria Whatmough, Head of Charitable Giving, was in her mid-fifties, like him, and, unlike him, she was rather big. She wasn't fat, but everything about her – mouth, nose, breasts, knees, stomach, hands, feet, voice, handshake, handbag, earrings – was large. That might not have mattered too much if she hadn't been so obviously in love with him. He felt that if he ever dropped his guard she would devour him.

Gloria rose from her desk like a waterspout, steamed towards him, crushed his hand as if it was a beetle, and said, 'I've put us in the Elgar Room,' in the penetrating voice of a person from the upper echelons of society who has never had one moment's doubt that everything she said would be fascinating to everyone within half a mile. Yet, amazingly, she went down well with the charities. Her assurance over-whelmed them and comforted them. Her posh tones made people feel they could trust her.

All the many conference rooms in the Stick of Celery were named after famous Brits. The Elgar Room had a green carpet, white walls and a walnut table and chairs. On the walls were pictures of Elgar: Elgar at his desk looking as if he was composing; Elgar walking in the Malvern Hills and looking composed; Elgar leaning on his bicycle to gaze at the sturdy beauty of Hereford Cathedral.

Sir Gordon sat at the head of the table. Gloria Whatmough plonked herself down at his side, and put her right hand on his left knee so briefly that a moment later he found himself wondering if it had just been another bad dream.

'It's so wonderful of you to have saved the Turner,' she said.

'How do you know that?'

'Good news travels fast.'

'Bad news travels faster. How many are we seeing today?'

'Just two. Both interesting, I think.'

The first appointment was with a vicar, the Revd Daniel Barnstaple.

Paunchy, likes his food. Untidy, greasy hair. Dreadful pullover. No woman in his life. Listen!!!

But it was no use. Today he couldn't concentrate. He heard snippets – '. . . lost my faith' – but he kept thinking of Francesca and how he would break it off. '. . . words I have to intone seem more hollow by the day.' And Joanna, his thoughts turned to her. '. . . But what else can I do? You can have jobs before being a vicar but you can't get jobs after being a vicar.' He must do something about Joanna. He had promised. '. . . overwhelming scientific evidence about how the world began.' Yes, he knew what he would do. It was a brainwave. '. . . Trapped. I feel trapped.' Yes, he would have a trip with Joanna, he would call it off with Francesca, he had saved a Turner for the nation, he felt a whole lot better. '. . . There are large numbers like me, you'd be surprised. I can bring you depressed vicars and vegetating

113

vergers.' Gloria was staring at him. Did she know he wasn't listening properly? Concentrate, Gordon. '. . . backsliding bishops and disillusioned deans.'

He had got the vicar's message, but what did the vicar want him to do? He hoped he hadn't missed that. He glanced up at Elgar. The great man looked as if he was saying, 'I've got your number.'

'So what exactly do you want me to do?' he asked.

It was all right. The vicar hadn't got round to that.

'Set up a charity for vicar support,' said the Revd Daniel Barnstaple. 'All denominations welcome.'

After further discussion, Sir Gordon promised to think about it, and this seemed to be as much as the vicar had dared to expect.

'So what do you think about that?' Sir Gordon asked Gloria, when the vicar had gone.

'Oh. Oh, Sir Gordon,' simpered Gloria Whatmough, blushing at the honour of being consulted. Little did she know he had only asked her because he couldn't be bothered to think about it himself. 'I think we need to go into it further. Religion and politics, you know. Dangerous subjects.'

Sir Gordon agreed all too readily, and then felt ashamed of himself. Garibaldi wouldn't have agreed so readily. Oh dear, he must stop thinking about Garibaldi. He tried to think again about Joanna, but Francesca Saltmarsh pushed her way in.

The second visitor was a beautiful fiery Welsh lady called Megan Lloyd-Phillips. Her trousered legs were as long as a Welsh Sunday and her bright eyes were as dark as slate. Sir Gordon's heart almost stopped at the sight of her, and he forgot Francesca Saltmarsh for at least fifty seconds. He tried frantically to hide his attraction for Megan Lloyd-Phillips from Gloria Whatmough. A jealous, disaffected Head of Charitable Giving was the last thing he needed.

Tricky situation, said the eyes of Sir Edward Elgar.

'I'm Megan Lloyd-Phillips.' She made the words sound like poetry. 'Education is my concern. Dumbing down is my abomination. The need to win votes from the hoi polloi renders democratically elected governments impotent against dumbing down. The bright must not be stifled by the dumb. The dumb can be inspired by the bright.'

She looked straight at Sir Gordon and his heart stopped.

'Language is my passion.'

His prick surged. He was in serious danger of blushing! Desperately he thought about Garibaldi. Desperately he thought about biscuits. Be nice to have a biscuit named after *him*. Can I tempt you to another Coppinger? No, didn't sound right, sadly. Oh God, Gordon, listen.

She was talking about the Internet, and about texting.

'. . . not serious perhaps, but corrupting. I want to reverse the closure of libraries. I want to be able to say that all the arts are important, as an essential not a luxury, but that literature is the most important of all because words are the tools by which we communicate. I am concerned for the future of books, and therefore eventually for the future of language, and therefore, ultimately, for the future of thought itself.'

'Wow!' said Sir Gordon. The moment he had said it, he wished that he could take it back. An amazingly beautiful woman had spoken beautifully about the importance of language, and he had said, 'Wow!' This moment would haunt him.

'That's all absolutely fantastic,' he said, 'but where do I come in?'

'I want you to head a literacy campaign.'

He laughed.

'I can hardly read.'

'Exactly! That's why you'd be *so* right. So many people when they talk about books talk so poncily that other people feel inferior to them. But you, you could do it, and nobody would feel inferior to you.'

'Thank you very much.'

'Oh, I meant it as a compliment. I hope it didn't sound . . . I'm sorry.'

'No, no, it's all right.'

He wanted to say, 'I'll do it,' but he managed to resist it. It would never do for him to decide before he had consulted Gloria.

As Megan Lloyd-Phillips walked out of the room, her elegantly swaying bottom eloquent with invitation, Sir Gordon felt rather sad. Things were changing. They had to change. He would never accept the invitation of that glorious backside.

'Well?' boomed Gloria.

He must be very careful what he said. He just hoped that she hadn't noticed the attraction.

'I'm tickled pink by the idea of heading a literacy campaign.'

'She wouldn't be easy to work with.'

So she had noticed.

'I think I could handle her, Gloria.'

'Well, it's up to you.'

'No, no, I want you to agree. I made you Head of Charitable Giving because I valued your judgement.'

'Oh. Oh good Lord. Well, yes, I think it is rather a sweet idea. You and literacy. It's so . . .'

'Inappropriate?'

'Yes. Well, no. No. Oh no. No.'

She stood up.

He stood up.

'An interesting little session, I feel,' she said.

'Very.'

Just a pity I didn't meet Megan Lloyd-Phillips twenty years ago. No!

Gloria pushed her face towards him, ready for a kiss on each cheek. He was tempted to shake her hand but remembered her crunching handshake just in time, and dutifully kissed her. She made a little noise at each kiss.

The lift rose silently to the nineteenth floor, depositing people at the seventh floor (home of the London offices of four of his factories including the one making S'ssh! – he recalled a planning meeting at which they had debated for two hours how many 's's it should have in its name), at the eighth floor (restaurant – God, he was hungry), and at the eleventh floor (Coppinger Collection administrative offices – controversy there: the collection people wanted their offices to be on site and not in the tower, which made sense and he would have to give way one day, damn it).

Now he was on his own in the lift as it slid up the outside of the building. He noticed that the buildings were all now under cloud, but through a narrow gap in the clouds a strip of sunlight was sparkling across the river like a diamond bracelet. Even he felt moved by this dramatic beauty. And then the sun was gone, the day was grey, the river was sullen, and the sparkle had gone from him as well. As he walked through the great open-plan office, through the throng of earnest workers, he suddenly felt, as he had never felt before, All these people depend on me.

He stopped at Her Grimaldiship's desk, and ordered lunch – a pork pie in the end – with an indecision that Garibaldi would have despised.

'Oh, your son rang,' said Helen.

'Oh dear.'

'Twice.'

'Oh dear.'

'He said it was urgent.'

'Oh dear.'

He had been given custody of a great masterpiece. He had been asked to head a literacy campaign. He could do real good. He could go down in history as a great man. Or he could fool around with hairdresser Mandy, gallery owner Francesca, travel guide Sandy and all the others. History, and recent history in particular, was littered with the fallen reputations of great men who had believed, in their hubris, that they could get away with folly. How could he not have been above all that? How could he have allowed himself to be so foolish, not just with all those women, but with Gordon Investments, SFN Holdings, his unintentional foray into the murky waters of Pump and Dump over the Germophile affair, and all the other lesser matters – dodgy audits, price-fixing cartels, treating sales of fixed assets as profits – that could destroy him if they were made public. Oh, if only he could start again, and do it right.

He needed to set his life straight, and rapidly. It would be painful, but great men had to be prepared to endure pain.

He would start tonight.

Tonight he was seeing Francesca.

He had tried to break it off with Mandy, and had failed. It would be easier with Francesca. She was worldly. She was strong. She could get men with a flick of her fingers. She would not be destroyed.

But oh, oh, oh, he didn't want to break it off. He ached for Francesca's slim, taut, gymnastic body.

You're sick, Gordon, he told himself.

Tonight he would break it off with Francesca.

He must ring Luke before Luke rang again.

No. He needed to speak to Siobhan. That was more important. He dialled her extension. She told him she could be with him in ten minutes.

Ten minutes. Plenty of time to talk to Luke. He dialled, but found his fingers dialling not Luke, but Joanna's firm.

'Paleface and Snitch. How can I help you?'

'Oh hello. Could I speak to Joanna Coppinger, please?'

'May I ask what it's in connection with?'

'It's a personal matter.'

'I'm afraid our employees are not permitted personal calls.'

'Well, could you just tell her that her father rang, then? Sir Gordon Coppinger.'

118

'She may have gone for an early lunch. I'll just check. Hold on, please, Sir Gordon.'

'Thank you.'

'Putting you through, Sir Gordon.'

'Thank you.'

'Dad!'

Surprise. And alarm.

'Hello, Joanna.'

Hesitancy. Uncertainty. Would Garibaldi have been hesitant and uncertain with his daughter? Come on, Gordon.

'What's wrong, Dad?'

'Nothing's wrong, darling. Nothing at all. Why do you assume something's wrong?'

'Because you're phoning me.'

'Darling, you're my daughter, it's natural that I should phone you. What are you planning to have for lunch?'

'Oh, I don't know. This and that. Why?'

'No reason, just they wondered if you might have gone to lunch.'

'It must be urgent, Dad, for them to have put you through. We aren't allowed personal calls. They're very strict about it.'

'I think my name still counts for a bit, Joanna.'

Why had he added that pessimistic word 'still'? He felt a bit shocked.

'I suppose so.'

She sounded reluctant to admit it. He felt a spasm of irritation. It was so unfair of her to be stifled by his success. But he mustn't be irritated. This was a new start. Policy really, but perhaps touched with something more genuine. He found himself hoping that she would agree to what he was going to say.

'I wondered . . .' It was enormous, this, in context. Even Garibaldi would have hesitated. Forget Garibaldi, Gordon! 'I wondered if you'd . . . um . . . if you could come out with me tomorrow.'

'Come out with you? You want me to come out with you?'

You always were quick on the uptake. No. No sarcasm, even in thought.

'I want to take you somewhere.'

'Good Lord. Where?'

'It's a surprise.'

'Oooh.'

'Not a surprise sort of surprise. Just . . . I don't want to talk about it on the phone. People listen.'

'I'm intrigued, Dad.'

'Good. That's good. It's nothing unpleasant, Joanna. Nothing to dread.'

'I know. I am a bit of a one for dreading, aren't I?'

Good. Good that she could say that.

'It's just . . . I've things to look at and things to deal with and you're the only member of the family who can really help.'

He heard her gasp. He could imagine her surprise, embarrassment, pleasure. He found it rather nice that he could give her pleasure. Should have tried it earlier. Garibaldi probably . . . no.

'Thanks, Dad.'

She was moved. So easily moved. It really wasn't much. Not when the alternatives were Christina, Luke, Hugo, Jack, or his father.

'Do you think you *can* get the day off?'

'I'll jolly well try.'

That's the spirit.

'Your name might clinch it for me.'

It bloody well ought to.

'I mean, I never do take time off.'

'Well, there you are then.'

'I'll ring you back, Dad.'

'Great.'

Sir Gordon put the phone down gently. It had been a very

120

ordinary conversation, but in the context of his relations with his daughter over twenty-six years it had been very extraordinary indeed. And he hoped, hoped with an intensity which astonished him, that she would be able to come.

Luke. No, there wasn't time now before Siobhan arrived. Although she was Irish, Siobhan was always punctual.

He began to grow anxious. Anxious about Ryan. His heart was racing. His throat was dry. This was ridiculous. He had never gone to bed with Siobhan. He wasn't remotely attracted to her. He had never been to her home. He had never even seen Ryan. Why was he so concerned about the boy? Because of the vivid image that he had, the wee mite struggling for life, the beat of his tiny heart showing on a screen, the anxious parents at the bedside, gripped by love of an intensity that he had never experienced.

'Good afternoon, Siobhan. Thank you for coming. Sit down.'

'Thank you, sir.'

She filled the easy chair provided. She was a big girl. She filled the room, too, with her personality. She radiated warmth.

'How's the wee mite?'

His voice quivered with anxiety. She gave him a surprised look.

'He's out of danger, sir.'

'Oh, I'm so pleased, Siobhan.'

The relief. He could not believe the relief that flooded through him.

'So what . . . um . . . what was wrong with him exactly?'

'They called it a childhood virus. In other words . . .'

'. . . they didn't know. Siobhan?'

He saw her become slightly wary at his change of tone. Oh, he hoped she hadn't done anything wrong.

'Siobhan? Did you invite three journalists to my Guy Fawkes party?'

'I certainly did not, sir. I would never do such a thing.'

'I know. I didn't think you could, but I had to hear you say you hadn't. They had invitations. Perfect forgeries.'

'Who would do such a thing?'

'Well, it has to be one of my guests. That's what shocks me. Nobody else could have seen an invitation, so nobody else could have forged them. Thank you, Siobhan. And I'm so pleased about the wee mite.'

He could delay ringing Luke no longer. What was it about the boy that depressed him so, apart from the obvious fact which almost nobody knew?

'You rang, Luke?'

'Yes. It's happened again, Dad.'

'You mean . . .?'

'Exactly. In Manchester. Little gallery. The Degas Gallery. Somebody bashed the window in last night and just walked through and buggered up my *David and Goliath Seen as Two Sunflowers*. Same message. In two languages again.'

'Welsh, in Manchester?'

'No. German this time. It looks as though the Welsh thing was just to put us off the scent. And the same message at the bottom. "Like father, like son". In German as well. Somebody out there hates us both, Dad.'

'Fred Upson, my MD at SFN Holdings . . .'

'The one you like me to phone and interrupt when you're seeing him?'

'That's the fellow. And you did interrupt me when you phoned me the first time and I told him about it – it was only polite after he'd been interrupted – and he said he thought father and son might refer to God and Christ.'

'Could be, I suppose, but although David and Goliath are biblical figures this isn't exactly a religious painting. I think it means us. Anyway, the police have been, thick as two planks, didn't even get the Van Gogh reference. And of course the local press turned up, so, second time, bound to get in the papers. I know you think all publicity is good publicity, but I don't.'

'Did I say that? I do come out with some bollocks, don't I? I certainly don't believe that now. In fact, I'd be grateful if you could keep it all out of the press as much as possible, Luke.'

'OK, Dad. Will do. It's hardly all my fault, though, is it? And it's my paintings so it's far worse for me than for you, right?'

'Right. Absolutely right. Sorry. How's Emma? Still with you?

'Dad!'

'Sorry.'

'She's fine. Great girl.'

I'll never be able to steal her off you now. All that sort of thing is over.

'Yes. Yes, she is. Thanks for letting me know, Luke. And Luke?'

'Yes, Dad?'

'I'm being selfish. Of course it's worse for you.'

'Thanks, Dad.'

He said goodbye and put the phone down. He walked to the wide picture window, looked out, away from the river towards the West India Dock, and said out loud – as if to Canary Wharf and the Thames and the West India Dock and HSBC and J.P. Morgan and the world – 'I wish I liked him.'

The phone rang. He walked towards it. It gave a little hesitation and then picked up its tone again. Joanna!

'Hello, Dad. It's me. Dad, I can come.'

'Oh, that's great, Joanna. That's great. I'll pick you up at nine.'

He put the phone down, and realized to his astonishment that he meant it. It was great. It really was.

It was amazing. He was fifty-six, he had a grown-up son and a grown-up daughter, and for the first time in his life – he truly believed it was the first time – he really felt like a father.

It was a great feeling. It was a good moment.

It didn't last long. His chief accountant, chief of his many accountants, phoned.

'May we talk?' he asked.

'Of course, Wally.'

'Somewhere neutral, Sir Gordon. Not in your office or mine.'

'Oh my God. You don't want people to know we're meeting. You've got something serious to say.'

Sometimes Sir Gordon wished that he wasn't quite so quick on the uptake.

'I suggest the Wordsworth Room on the fourth floor,' he said.

And so it was among a host of golden daffodils – subtlety doesn't have a huge part to play in decorating a tower block – that Sir Gordon Coppinger had a rather sobering conversation with his chief accountant, Wally 'Proboscis' Frobisher. The nickname referred to his large nose, about which he was very sensitive, although he hid his sensitivity by constantly mentioning it. 'I'm the only large-nosed non-Jewish accountant in London,' he would say. Some people said that his nose had lengthened over the years from sheer curiosity. Sir Gordon needed to handle him carefully after the Germophile business.

'Nice holiday?' Sir Gordon asked.

'Fine,' said Wally. 'Came back to disturbing news, though.'

'Oh?'

'I'll get straight to the point. Have you promised to buy a Turner for twenty million?'

'How do you know that?'

'Bad news travels fast.'

'*Bad* news?'

'I think so.'

124

'Surely it's great publicity?'

'There is that.'

'What then?'

'It's a large sum.' Wally Frobisher gulped nervously, and he was not a nervous man. Nor was he a boring accountant, incidentally. It is a myth that all accountants are boring. Wally had been a stand-up comedian in his spare time. Now he was more interested in re-enacting the Wars of the Roses in a wood near Stevenage. But what he was going to say to Sir Gordon Coppinger would test the mettle of a very brave man. 'You do not have a bottomless pit of money.'

Sir Gordon was silent for a few moments. He looked stunned.

'What?'

'You do not have—'

'I heard you the first time. Surely, Wally . . . surely I . . . I thought . . . I mean . . .'

'You have vast amounts of money on paper, Sir Gordon, but you also have vast outgoings, and things in certain areas are not as good in these difficult times as they have been.'

'God, I hate daffodils.'

'What?'

'I looked at the wall for comfort and all I saw was daffodils. I don't like them.'

'I'm a crocus man myself.'

'What areas, Wally?'

'Well, property, for example. Prices dropping in some places. Property empty in other places.'

'We can sell and get heaps of money.'

'True, but not quickly, and it might not be much use unless we could do it fairly quickly, there are so many considerations. Besides, if we put too much on the market too quickly it may deliver a destabilizing message.'

'Anything else?'

'Manufacturing. Some factories are doing all right, some

125

aren't, but profit margins are narrowing over the whole spectrum.'

'Sell some off?'

'You might sell one. Sell more and again it could destabilize. The trouble with your situation is that if you try to realize too many of your assets people will realize that you need to realize them. You're in real danger of becoming a hostage to your reputation.'

'Anything else?'

'Investment. Just how secure is Gordon Investments, Sir Gordon?'

Sir Gordon could hear the faint warning noises of a reversing lorry far below. At this tense moment it seemed a symbol of his situation. He glanced up at Wordsworth and thought, Fuck you. What have you got to look so smug about? What do you know of pressure? Anyone can piss off to a study and write down words that rhyme.

'I'm very popular, Wally,' he said. 'People trust me. Investment is good. News of this sale would boost that investment. Wally, are you saying I can't afford this picture?'

'No. And may I say that I so respect your calm reaction, the absence of any hostility or anger towards this unwelcome messenger? No, I'm not saying you can't afford it. All I'm saying is, you have vast outgoings, you have huge staff costs, this building leaks money, you have a preposterously large yacht, you buy pictures, you buy sculptures, you sponsor arts events, you support charities, you run a rather unsuccessful football club – ah, now you do look angry with me – and it's my judgement that you should curb these activities a little. Even you are not entirely immune to the basic laws of economics. There is money, but not as much as there was, and it isn't – and perhaps never really was – a bottomless pit.'

'You recommend that I back out of buying the Turner?'

'I do. You haven't sent the cheque, have you?'

126

'Of course not. I never pay straight away. Right. I'll back out then.'

'Just like that?'

'Just like that.'

'On my say-so?'

'On your say-so.'

'Thank you.'

'It's just another form of conceit really, Wally. I appointed you because I thought you were brilliant, and I'm very proud of my judgement of people.'

It was a sober Sir Gordon who took the lift up to the nineteenth floor, and he knew that after this shock it would not be easy for him to call it off with Francesca Saltmarsh. He was consoling himself with the thought of her body already. Displacement activities didn't come much better than sex with her.

He decided not to phone the eighteenth Earl of Flaxborough from his office, for fear that Helen would eavesdrop. He wouldn't ring him from the Rolls-Royce either; he trusted Kirkstall but he was too proud to speak of it in front of him. No, he would phone from the taxi which would take him to Francesca's bijou house from the Athenaeum, where Kirkstall would drop him for his supposed meeting with a non-existent Russian who wanted him to take a share in the Hermitage in St Petersburg.

But you know how it is, it's no good making important phone calls from moving vehicles, and Sir Gordon was sorry for the Earl and reluctant to phone him, so he decided to put it off until the morning, when he would feel stronger.

And that turned out to be a serious mistake.

'A perfect memento'

There she was, smiling slenderly, tall and supple, far too aroused for him to even contemplate disappointing her. Besides, he needed her. He had been more shaken by his conversation with his accountant than he would admit.

She moved in a sophisticated, arty world, posh rather than bohemian. She had, he didn't doubt it, other lovers. Better-looking lovers. Younger lovers. But they did not pour into her the power of their millions, the throbbing vitality of their factories, the surging danger of their vast loans and debts. Also, she was a snob, and he doubted if any other of her lovers had been knighted.

He would let her down gently.

His entry into her was glorious. They coiled like snakes. They writhed like gymnasts. It was astonishing. It was brief. It was over. He was freed from his dreadful need, and he felt that she was at peace too.

It was tempting to lie there, to sleep, to dream, but he was hungry, and she was a very good cook.

They ate in her exquisite little dark green dining room. She put some music on. Tchaikovsky. Always Tchaikovsky. Once he had asked her why it was always Tchaikovsky. She had said, 'He's my favourite composer, and you are my favourite lover.' There was no arguing with that. He poured into her elegant Orrefors wine glasses the 1976 Saint-Joseph that he had brought. It had velvet depths and mellow shallows. It tasted of long summers and cool autumns and rich, healthy earth, with teasing faint traces of apple and blackberry.

Francesca served him a daube. As she lifted the lid, South Kensington suddenly smelt of Provence. The room was filled with the scent of herbs and garlic and wine and rich, rich beef. How he relished it. How his gastronomic hypocrisy excited him. Because his popularity with his public was so tied up with his patriotism, he could allow himself to enjoy the splendours of foreign food only in conditions of the strictest secrecy.

'Not sold any Coppingers yet?' he enquired, between delicious mouthfuls.

'No, but I will.'

Francesca had two of Luke's pictures hanging in her little gallery, on the ground floor.

He told her about the two outbreaks of vandalism against Luke's work. She said that she was confident of her security system. Here in London you had to be. London was not like Carmarthen and Manchester.

'Do you really believe Luke's pictures are good?' he asked.

'I never said that,' she replied. 'I said that they will sell. I actually think there's something rather unpleasant about his work. As you know, I've met him, and I have to say I didn't like him very much.'

Was there a potential link here? That phrase, 'Like father, like son'. Could he weave that into the conversation? Maybe we are alike. Maybe there's something rather unpleasant about me too. Francesca, maybe you'd be better off without me. I . . . um . . . I think we should stop seeing each other.

Bit tortuous. Not convincing.

And why spoil a glorious Provençale daube?

'He and Emma Slate are an item, aren't they?'

'Yes.'

She had finished her main course. She ate fast, urgently, energetically. He was savouring every slow, rich, gently garlicky mouthful.

'There's an article about her in this.'

She picked up an arty magazine he'd never heard of, opened it, and began to read. It was difficult to concentrate as the Tchaikovsky moved excitingly towards a climax on this evening of climaxes. She almost had to shout to be heard. He'd have preferred to read the article himself – he didn't like being read to – but she loved reading to him, and it was never any use protesting about this to her, or indeed about anything else.

'One of the most extraordinary of our modern artists is 26-year-old Emma Slate, whose life's ambition is to show the British people what beauty can be found in ugliness, writes Tamsin Darbyshire.

'I caught up with her at her bijou flat in an up-and-coming corner of Stoke Newington. She was dressed in jeans that were full of holes and a T-shirt which bore stains that might have been hollandaise or might have been something worse.

'Emma sprang to fame with pictures like Mould on a White Loaf in Sussex *and* Young Financial Adviser's Bin After Destruction by Urban Fox. *Among the pictures in her latest exhibition at the Nosworthy Gallery is a very large canvas called* Rabbit Droppings Near Hornchurch. *I asked her if she was serious about painting rabbit droppings or if she was just trying to stimulate publicity by being controversial.*

'"Oh, that's what everybody says about artists who try to do something different," she exploded. "Look, most art makes me sick, it's so bourgeois. I've been round galleries, seen the things people buy, endless paintings of Venice, canals, Little Venice, little canals, squares with plane trees in Southern France, dappled sodding sunlight, Scotland, sunsets, sunrises, steps to red doors, steps to blue doors, sunshine and shadows, bourgeois shit.

'"I find beauty in the unexpected. Take my rabbit droppings picture. These are the glistening remains of food, the bits even the rabbit can find no goodness from, but the earth can, it still nourishes the earth, the goodness remains, the goodness continues, it's the cycle of life, it's the cycle of existence, and the world says, 'Show me a pretty cottage.' It's shit."

'"But so is your painting, literally," I pointed out.

'"Exactly," she said. "Congratulations. You've seen the point."

'"Why Near Hornchurch?" I asked.

'"Because that's where I painted it," she replied, as if it was obvious and I was stupid. "There was actually a glorious sunset that evening, so that was a huge stroke of luck."

'"But you didn't paint the sunset," I pointed out.

'"No," she replied, "but you see, what isn't in the picture, what you don't see, is as important to me as what you do see. There's just a hint, if you look carefully – and I hope people will – that the reds in the sky are reflected in the second dropping from the left, hinting that I could have painted something much more conventional, much easier."

'I asked her if she didn't think most people would find this argument ridiculous.

'"I don't paint for 'most people'," she retorted, "but if people do find it ridiculous, that's great. I think our world is ridiculous."

'Rabbit Droppings Near Hornchurch *is priced at a cool £20,000. I have to admit that I didn't dare ask Emma Slate if that was ridiculous.'*

'What does Luke see in her?' asked Francesca. 'She's not exactly pretty, is she?'

'No, but . . .'

Sir Gordon paused.

'"But"?'

'Nothing.'

'You fancy her! You've thought about taking her off Luke, pinching her from your own son. My God.'

A perfect cue. I did think of it. I'm a monster. You'd be better off without me. I think we should end it now, Francesca.

Tell her now.

'Chocolate roulade?'

I will, he decided. I'll tell her straight after the chocolate roulade. Well, her chocolate roulade *is* superb. And I do have a very sweet tooth.

But by the time he had enjoyed two helpings of the chocolate roulade, he felt that gathering urge again. An urge, not a need – no longer swift, savage, and selfish, but gentle and considerate. It would be altogether more seemly to tell her after he had made love to her with tender courtesy and generous unselfishness, so that her last memory of him would be his worship of her beauty, rather than his stuffing his mouth with two helpings of chocolate roulade. Altogether more seemly.

And that was how it was. Intense was the joy he drew from her long, lithe limbs. Intense, he was sure, was the joy she was getting from the joy she knew he was getting.

'Francesca, you are the most beautiful woman I have ever seen.'

'You say that to all the girls.'

No. Only to some of them.

It was time to leave. He got out of bed. They stood, together, at the side of the bed, in her perfumed bedroom, in front of a splendid eighteenth-century mirror that had been left to her by a rich aunt.

He decided to tell her now.

He couldn't. He couldn't tell her while they were both still naked. It would be . . . absurd . . . inappropriate . . . discourteous.

But did he actually have to tell her . . . ever? Couldn't he continue to get away with it? Wasn't he invulnerable? Wasn't he a great man? Wouldn't he be able to rise above any scandal?

No. He knew now that it was not like that. If it had ever been, it was no longer.

If he didn't seize this moment, he wouldn't tell her tonight. When they were both dressed, habit would take over, he would be unable to resist the opportunity of seeing her naked again. He would persuade himself to take one last chance.

To do it now would be dramatic, momentous, worthy of a man who dared compare himself to Garibaldi. To do it now, when he stood facing her in all her loveliness, would be a heroic renunciation. She would see it as such. She would take it as a compliment to her beauty, to her sense of style, that he had done it like this and not in a commonplace manner at the door.

'Francesca?'

Her mouth dropped open. She went white.

'Oh my God,' she said. 'I do not like that tone, Gordon.'

'I'm going to have to stop seeing you. I'm so sorry. I really am. I—'

'I see. Just like that. One helping of daube, two helpings of chocolate roulade, two fucks. Thank you very much. Huge fun. Bye-bye.'

'Yes. Dreadful. I have to be a good boy from now on, Francesca. It's just the way it is. I regret it deeply.'

'*You* regret it?'

He thought she was going to hit him.

'Francesca!' he said. 'Don't spoil everything right at the end.'

She smiled.

'Of course I won't spoil everything right at the end,' she said. 'I've too much style for that.'

'Precisely. You have so much style.'

'We've both given each other great pleasure, and we should neither of us ever forget that.'

'That's wonderful, Francesca. That's so wonderful.'

'Just a second,' she said. 'Stay there just a second.'

133

She left the room. He stood obediently, mesmerized by the drama of the moment. She returned with a camera.

'I want to remember you just as you are tonight,' she said. 'That way I will feel that I have you with me always.'

She took a quick photograph. Just one.

'A memento,' she said. 'A perfect memento.'

That didn't make Sir Gordon
happy at all

He picked her up at her flat in Shepperton at four minutes past nine. He tried not to feel upset at being four minutes late. He mustn't be obsessive.

Shepperton. A name drenched in glamour. What films they had made, in years gone by, at Shepperton Studios.

But there wasn't much glamour left in the studios now, and there was no glamour in the rest of the place. No glamour in Joanna's little attic flat in a grey terrace. No glamour in Joanna herself. She had tried to look smart for this mysterious outing, bless her, she had tried, and she did look quite smart, but she also looked like a forty-three-year-old employee on her way to work, not a twenty-six-year-old on her day off.

He kissed her on her pallid cheek. Even this degree of contact embarrassed her.

She had trouble getting her seat belt into the slot. He had to help her. She blushed.

'Sorry, Dad,' she said. 'I think I must be a bit nervous. This is all so . . . unexpected.'

He was pleased that she had acknowledged that she was nervous.

'I'm a bit nervous too,' he admitted, as he nosed the

Rolls-Royce into the last of the morning rush-hour traffic on the main road. 'Apart from anything else, I'm not used to driving any more. I gave Kirkstall the day off. I wanted it to be just the two of us.'

He could see that she was trying not to look pleased. Why did people try not to look pleased?

Soon they were on the M25, travelling in the clockwise direction. The traffic was heavy, but moving freely. Sir Gordon moved particularly freely. Speed limits were not meant for the likes of him.

Joanna was gripping the sides of her seat.

'Relax,' he said. 'I may be a bit rusty, but I'm a very good driver.'

'I'm sure you are, Dad, but I'm not a very good passenger, I'm afraid.'

He relented, almost sticking to the speed limit as they drove on past the turn-off for Heathrow.

He knew that she was longing to ask him where they were going. It wasn't just to tease her that he wasn't telling her. He was curiously reluctant to talk about it, to admit it.

They turned off on to the M40, northwards. The traffic was less heavy now; he put his foot down just a bit, and then a bit more. She seemed more confident now, and at last, she found the courage to ask the question.

'So, Dad, where are we going?'

'You'll see soon enough. Well, actually, not all that soon. It's a long trip. Just enjoy it.'

Big birds were drifting in the thermals over the rich beech woods of the Chiltern Hills. Neither of them knew that they were red kites.

'I am,' she said, so long after his remark that the words had become detached from it.

'Sorry,' he said. 'You are what?'

'Enjoying it.'

'Good.'

'It's pretty countryside.'

They drove in silence for a while. Sir Gordon was thinking how shocked Joanna would be if she knew what he'd been up to last night. He was trying not to think about last night, it made him feel very uneasy, he even felt – yes – a sense of shame.

He was trying not to think about this morning too. His purchase of the Turner for the nation had been in all the papers. He could never back out of buying it now. It shook him considerably that this should worry him. And that was not the only story about him in the newspapers that Farringdon had brought him with his orange juice. It wasn't good any more to be daubed across all the newspapers practically every day.

'I wonder what all these big birds are,' said Joanna.

At the mention of birds, Sir Gordon saw Alice's pretty face, staring at the big birds with Tom in his bicycle clips – did people wear bicycle clips any more? How little he knew. And that thought shocked him. It shocked him even more that he would never see Alice naked, never again see Francesca naked, oh God, how had he got himself into this corner?

They passed the turning for Oxford. He wondered if she was disappointed that they weren't going there. It occurred to him for the first time that after all the build-up she would be extremely disappointed by their destination. He should have told her. Too late now. Be odd to tell her now.

He began to wish that he wasn't going.

He thought again about those other headlines in this morning's papers, undoing at a stroke the goodwill engendered by his purchase of the Turner.

Coppinger Son in Second Painting Shock
Vandals Attack Coppinger Painting
"F*** Off, Coppingers."
Does Someone Hate Sir Gordon?

Some of the leader writers even wove articles connecting the Turner with Luke's work, comparing Turner and Luke, and not to Luke's advantage. It wasn't good for investors to see all this. It wasn't good for Megan Lloyd-Phillips to see it.

He would never see Megan Lloyd-Phillips naked.

He was plunging into depression. This was dreadful. He wasn't used to this at all.

Don't just sit there like a lump, Joanna. Say something.

'Lot of Eddie Stobart lorries about.'

Hardly Oscar Wilde, but, bless her, she was trying. He suddenly felt a surge of affection for her.

'I'm so glad you could come,' he said.

She blushed, of course, but he knew that she was pleased.

On, on, on they went. He turned off the M40 on to the M42. They passed Birmingham on their left.

'Not much further now,' he said.

'I'm enjoying being driven, actually,' she said.

She had said more positive things this morning than he could remember her saying in twenty-six years.

He cut off along the A446, passed the Belfry Golf Club on the right, joined the A38, bypassed Lichfield. Joanna pointed out the three spires of the cathedral in the distance. He hadn't known that Lichfield had a cathedral.

He turned on to the A513 at Alrewas, passed a little café in a lay-by with a large Union Jack blowing in the breeze, and turned left into a much narrower road. Now that he had come all this way, he had to force himself not to turn round and just go home. How ridiculous was that?

He turned in to the car park of the National Memorial Arboretum.

'This is a memorial planted in honour of all the British military personnel who died serving their country in battle,' he said.

'I've not heard of it,' she admitted.

'Nor me, sadly, till I watched the *Antiques Roadshow*. Let's have a bit of lunch first.'

They entered the visitor centre. A guide proudly explained that the arboretum covered 150 acres of reclaimed gravel donated by Redland Aggregate (now Lafarge), and that 50,000 trees had been planted. Sir Gordon wanted to tell him, I've done my bit for charity myself. How pathetic was that? He resisted the urge, of course. Joanna would have blushed herself to death.

They lunched in the light, airy, immaculate café. Sir Gordon had beef lasagne; Joanna plumped for breaded plaice, which she ate with more enthusiasm than she usually managed to find for food. He was hungry too after the long drive. His lasagne was surprisingly good. He didn't know why he should be surprised by this.

A note on the table said, '*Cake of the Day, Victoria Sponge, baked by Tony*'. A chef walked past behind the serving counter.

'I wonder if that's Tony,' Sir Gordon said.

Joanna looked at him in utter astonishment.

He wanted to say, I can be human, you know.

He asked her if she was disappointed by their secret destination.

'Not disappointed, no,' she said. 'Not thrilled either. Just sort of . . . interested, I suppose.'

'Day off with your dad, could have been more exciting?'

'Well, yes.'

They walked out into the arboretum, and made their way along a path towards the main memorial, which stood gleaming white on top of a small hill built like an old English burial mound. The curved concrete of the memorial gleamed impressively in the winter sunshine.

They walked in silence, slowly, sombrely, among avenues of trees. The trees were still young: the arboretum had only been open since 2001. But the trees, unlike the people they commemorated, would live to their full maturity.

They climbed up wide steps to the monument. A school party was coming down, moved to respectable behaviour by the experience. On the monument were carved the names of all the people who had died in the service of our armed forces since the Second World War. Almost 16,000 names. There was a slight gap in the monument on their right, with a carved soldier pointing to it. On the wall, by the gap, were inscribed the words, *'Through this space a shaft of sunlight falls at the eleventh hour of the eleventh day of the eleventh month.'* Sir Gordon felt moved almost to tears. He fought them off. He didn't want Joanna to see them. Why?

To his amazement she put her hand in his and squeezed it. Only a few hours ago he had been sad that she had been unable to show that she was pleased. Now here he was, hiding his tears from her.

They were two of a kind.

No. They were so very different. Only in one aspect were they united – in the fact that they found it so hard to be united.

There was a view to the south over gravel pits and woods. They could hear the distant roar of vehicles on the main roads, people passing by without a thought for dead military personnel, people therefore by definition, and most unfairly, cast as less compassionate than they were.

Was it compassion that Sir Gordon felt? Well, perhaps a bit, but compassion is about other people and Sir Gordon was still very much tied up in his own feelings. He was facing the vastness of all this loss; the wastage of all this largely male humanity; the death of the best, the most brave, the most needed; and what he felt was that most self-centred of sorrows, shame. Shame at how he had lived the life these men had died for. A cliché, yet when it was filled out with the millions he had earned, the tax he had avoided, the scams he had created, the people he had cheated, the women he had toyed with, the son he hardly spoke to, the daughter whom he had almost destroyed with the burden of his egocentric expectations, the wife he had ceased to love, the brother he had lost so little sleep over, well, it was a cliché no longer – it was a sharp, individual suffering unique to himself.

They walked the afternoon away among the monuments and trees. Sir Gordon realized that the family had never gone for walks. He couldn't recall one single stroll, in all the years.

They were moved, together, in silence, by the Stone of Reconciliation – surrounded by trees planted jointly by people who had fought on opposite sides and later become friends – and by a single gaudy fairground horse, commemorating members of the Showmen's Guild, fairground folk who had died in conflict for their country.

In a far corner, beside the River Tame, there was a memorial that Sir Gordon could scarcely bear to look at. It was called 'Shot at Dawn', and was in remembrance of 306 British servicemen court-martialled and shot in the First World War for military offences, branded as cowards, posthumously pardoned by the government in 2005. Each soldier was remembered individually by a single wooden post. Six trees represented the members of the firing squad. There had been six of them so that none of them would know for certain that he had actually been the one to kill a fellow countryman.

'That's where I would have been,' muttered Sir Gordon in a very low voice. He didn't know whether Joanna heard.

They walked slowly back to the visitor centre, past deeply moving monuments, some impressive, some heart-rendingly modest. There were many things Sir Gordon could have said, wanted to say, didn't need to say, and so didn't say.

All he said was, 'Shall we try Tony's sponge?'

They ate their Victoria sponge in silence.

'Well done, Tony,' said Sir Gordon.

Joanna smiled. Her smile was lovely. Why did she smile so seldom?

The light was beginning to fade. The sunset was cold and

cruel. The darkness of night was falling on the great darkness of history. The last stragglers were making their way to the car park, with memories perhaps of very individual loss. The world was a cold place.

The car was a cold car, but cars, unlike worlds, can be easily heated.

It was a long, dark drive back, through a land of snaking headlights, of narrow escapes, of poisonous emissions.

'We were told that one day most people would be able to work from home,' said Sir Gordon.

'You never have,' pointed out Joanna.

Nobody could work in the same house as Lady Coppinger. Sir Gordon thought this, but did not say it. He had many faults as a husband, but he had never run down his wife to his children.

'I was referring to ordinary people,' he said.

'The houses built for ordinary people are too small to have offices,' said Joanna, 'so that bright idea never had a chance.'

'Good point.'

He hoped that he had managed to keep the surprise out of his voice.

The M42 was very slow, but that meant that the rush hour would be well and truly over by the time they reached the M25. On motorways you hunt for the smallest consolations.

Shortly after they had come off the M25 to begin their descent into Shepperton – the journey had taken so long that he felt as if it had been a flight – Sir Gordon pulled in to a roadside pub cum restaurant, part of a chain (next day he couldn't even remember its name). He had always avoided chains, but luxury would have been obscene today.

He ordered a gin and tonic, Joanna said she could manage a small sherry, and he ordered a bottle of house red.

'For me this is living a little,' he said. 'I've never ordered the house wine before, anywhere.'

'Do we need a bottle?' she asked. 'I won't drink a lot.'

'No, but I will. I need to today.'

'But you're driving, and you aren't used to driving.'

'I'm used to drinking, though, and I have a hard head, I'm sturdily built, I'm having a large meal, I'll be under the limit, and if I'm not they won't charge me anyway when they find out who I am.'

They ordered stuffed mushrooms followed by rump steaks with all the trimmings. Sir Gordon asked for his rare and said, 'You like it well done, don't you?' He hoped this didn't sound like a criticism, but Joanna said, 'I know. I'm very conservative. I'll tell you what. I'll have it medium.' 'There's no obligation,' he said, and she said, 'No, I know, but you're right. I'm not adventurous enough. I'll tell you what. I'll have it medium rare. I just don't want any blood. Not today. I've seen enough about blood being spilt today.'

The waiter sighed impatiently.

'Don't you dare sigh,' said Sir Gordon. 'You're lucky to work here from whatever godforsaken hole you've escaped from. Joanna is my daughter, I am her father, and this little conversation is of huge importance in the unfolding drama of our relationship, so do as you're told and now piss off.'

The waiter glared and muttered, 'I know who you are.'

'What did you say?' said Sir Gordon.

'I know who you are. I've friends who are waiters. Half the waiters in London know how rude you are.'

'Fetch me the manager this instant,' said Sir Gordon.

'No,' said Joanna.

'What?'

'No, Dad. No. Please. Today's been . . . well, I just don't want to spoil it. Forget it, please, waiter. And you know you were rather rude.'

'Yes, I . . . I'm sorry, sir, madam. Thank you, madam,' said the waiter, and he beetled off hurriedly.

'Thank you,' said Sir Gordon to Joanna, when the waiter had gone.

'Surprised? Didn't think I could be so forceful?'

'Absolutely.'

'Well . . . to say that I've enjoyed today would be a bit obscene, it's been harrowing, but . . . well . . . neither of us has said anything, we haven't needed to, and maybe I shouldn't, maybe it'll spoil it, but I have to. I've enjoyed being with you.'

Their drinks arrived and they clinked glasses.

'And I think I know why you asked me to come with you, Dad,' she said.

'Oh?'

'Yes. I think you wanted to show me how all those lives had been cut short so cruelly, and how lucky I am to be alive, and how awful it is that I'm what you regard as wasting my life. You're telling me to be braver.'

'You flatter me, Joanna.'

'What?'

'I wasn't thinking of you at all. I was thinking of myself. I knew it would be a difficult day for me. I've ignored these things, Joanna, but I can't ignore them any more. I feel so . . . so small.'

She looked at him in amazement.

'I feel . . . I could never have been so brave.'

'You don't know, Dad. You can't know. Those boys, I don't imagine many of them thought they could be so brave. I think you could have been.'

'I couldn't. I know.'

'You can't know.'

Their stuffed mushrooms arrived. They were obscenely large. The economy of the food industry puzzled Sir Gordon. The less you spent, the more you got. No greasy spoon ever served nouvelle cuisine.

'I've done lots of things I feel very ashamed of, Joanna. And I knew today would make me feel very very bad. So . . . I asked you to come with me not because I cared about you. I cared about me. I asked you because I needed you.'

144

'I . . .'

'What?'

'No.'

'Oh, come on, Joanna.'

'It'll sound so pathetic.'

'What? Tell me. You can tell me.'

'I think that's one of the nicest things anyone's ever said to me.'

They were hungrier than they thought. Joanna was suspicious of the medium-rare steak at first, but ate the lot. In fact, they both finished every mouthful, including their onion rings. Sir Gordon had never seen Joanna eat so much, and it made him very happy.

He drove her back to her flat, and kissed her goodnight at the gate, and hugged her, and that made him happy too.

But it would not have been seemly if a day spent visiting the National Memorial Arboretum ended in happiness.

As he was driving along the M25 at ninety-eight miles per hour in an anticlockwise direction, he was chased and then stopped by a police car.

The policeman asked him for his name and address.

'Sir Gordon Coppinger, Rose Cottage, Borthwick End. I . . . um . . . I have the Coppinger Tower in Canary Wharf. I run the Sir Gordon Coppinger Charitable Foundation. And the Coppinger Collection. And I own Climthorpe United. You may have heard of me.'

'I'm very pleased to meet you, sir,' said the policeman.

'Thank you. I'm also a friend of your chief constable, and several senior police officers with salt in their blood regularly take summer holidays in the Mediterranean on my luxury yacht.'

'I'm very happy for them, sir,' said the policeman. 'Now would you step outside the car and blow into this bag?'

That didn't make Sir Gordon happy at all.

It began to rain

He was even less happy the next morning. He'd been charged with drink-driving, he'd got home at twenty-seven minutes past three, his Rolls-Royce was in a police compound, and there was yet another major Coppinger story in the newspapers. In several papers there was a striking photograph of him full-frontal in the nude, with a complete rear view in the splendid eighteenth-century mirror that had been left to Francesca by a rich aunt. And there, behind him, was a reflection of Francesca in all her glory, standing by a corner of her unmade bed, in the act of taking that very photo.

News of his arrest for speeding and drink-driving would follow as night follows day.

Well, he was a big man – although, even at this dire moment in his fortunes, part of his distress at the photograph was that it showed so clearly that Francesca was two inches taller than him. But he was a strong man, he had brought this storm upon himself, there was nothing for him to do but to ride it out bravely. Yesterday he had doubted his physical courage. Today he would need all his moral courage.

'I should tell you, perhaps, sir, that Her Ladyship is cognizant of the incident,' said Farringdon gravely.

'How so, Farringdon?'

146

'The telephone rang all day yesterday, sir.'

'Oh my God, did it? Poor Christina.'

'Yes indeed, sir. We attempted to contact you. Astonishingly, sir, it seems that neither you nor Miss Joanna consulted your mobile telephones all day.'

'I suppose we didn't. It was a strange day, Farringdon. Intense. We were in a kind of cocoon, I suppose. So . . . um . . . did Her Ladyship say anything . . . well, of course she must have, what I mean is, did anything she said reveal anything about her reaction? Although that's a silly question, she can't have been pleased.'

'Delighted would not be the description of her reaction that I would instantly choose, sir, but she did say one rather surprising thing, with a little smile that, if I may be so bold, seemed to me to contain an element of malice, such as I have from time to time seen, if I may be permitted a touch of political incorrectness, on the female face.'

'Yes, but do get on with it, Farringdon. What did she say?'

'She said, "Mandy won't be pleased."'

'Thank you, Farringdon.'

He couldn't possibly get to work on time. It was more than his life was worth to leave this morning without facing his wife.

He consulted the diary in his mind and found, for the first time, that it failed him. He would have to ring Helen Grimaldi to check on his appointments, and rearrange them.

He asked Farringdon to take the newspapers with the offending photograph to Christina with her breakfast. She almost always had breakfast in bed. She was most definitely not a morning person.

It was appropriate that it should be the *Daily Mirror* that used the huge headline:

Mirror, Mirror on the Wall
Sir Gordon's Love Reveals It All

147

He couldn't believe, in retrospect, that he had been so naive as not to realize that Francesca had been trapping him with that photograph. It struck at the very essence of his image. He was very disappointed in her, and yet he was honest enough to acknowledge that she had every right to be bitter. He had used her. But surely it was a privilege, even for a time, even for so beautiful a woman, to be allowed to enjoy his favours? Surely she should show some gratitude for that?

No. He didn't even convince himself on that one. And he had to acknowledge that in her statements to the press she had not been savage; within the confines of her betrayal of him she had not been vicious.

Time, that shrewd tease, passed slowly. Outside, astonishingly, there was a dawn like any other. Surrey's beauty remained untouched. There had been no earthquakes. At last Farringdon reported that Christina was awake. He had delivered the papers to her. Sir Gordon telephoned Helen, who had not yet arrived, and left a message for her to ring him if engagements needed to be changed. Christina would have seen all the papers now. She would have finished her tiny breakfast.

He walked slowly to the bedroom. He wished that he had never been born.

She was sitting up, propped on several expensive pillows. She had pushed her breakfast tray away. She had eaten only the yolk of her egg and half a slice of toast.

'Good morning, Christina,' he said.

'Is it?'

'No. Oh, my darling, I'm so very sorry.'

'Easy to say.'

'Not very, no.'

'And a bit late.'

'I know. I agree.'

'How could you?'

All too easily.

'I ask myself that.'

'How do you reply?'

'I tell myself I've been a fool. A complete fool.'

'I don't disagree.'

'I wouldn't expect you to.'

A tactless sun emerged from behind the clouds and bathed the bed in a warm glow.

'Darling?'

'I sort of wish you wouldn't use that word, Gordon.'

'OK.'

'It's meaningless in context.'

'OK.'

'If I was your darling—'

'You've made your point, Christina. Christina?'

'What?'

'You've said it's too late to say I'm sorry, and I agree. Is it really too late to . . . try again?'

'What do you think?'

'Obviously I don't think it is or I wouldn't be asking you.'

'Have you also broken it off with Mandy or was that all over already?'

The sun went in again. The morning seemed much darker than it had been before its appearance. The sun was really not being any help at all.

'No. I haven't told her and I haven't broken it off, but I will, of course.'

'She won't be pleased.'

'No.'

'Gordon, is that it? Francesca and Mandy. Or are there others?'

He hesitated. It was like a bridge player wondering whether to play the king. Once they'd hesitated, you knew they'd got it. She knew now that there were others. There wasn't any point in denying it. In any case, he hoped he wouldn't have denied it. A clean break. A new start.

'There are others.'

'How many? I can give you a pencil and paper if you need it.'

'Don't. There are . . . were . . .'

He began counting on his fingers.

'Oh dear. Both hands!'

'Only just. Six. Six others. Oh God, Christina, I'm sorry.'

'You'll be getting advice from Tiger Woods.'

'Don't. Christina, I'm not going to ask you to forgive me, I don't see why you should, and the past is far less important than the future. I'd understand it, I really would, if you decided to walk away from me. There are two very different reasons why I would like it if you didn't. One of them's more important than the other, but they're both important. No, to be honest they're probably equally important.'

He sat down on the bed, as close to her as he dared.

'One of the reasons is money. If you leave, of course I'll give you a settlement. Enough to live on, including shoes.'

'Gordon!'

'Sorry. Enough to live on, not mean, but probably not as generous as you would hope for and expect.'

'Really? And why is that?'

The sun came out again, shining straight on to his face, blinding him.

'I don't know if you suspect anything, most people don't, but – what a time this is for confessions – things aren't too brilliant. Oh God, this sun. I'll have to move.'

He moved round to the other side of the bed, where he sat with the sun shining on the back of his head.

'Not brilliant? I thought we were incredibly wealthy.'

'We are, but . . . money isn't real. Money is just promises. Forget that and you're in trouble and I've almost forgotten it. We aren't in big danger, not while people have confidence in us, but I have . . . probably . . . overstretched myself a bit. And there are a few things . . . well, two really . . . well, three actually . . . where I may not have been wise. They might be . . . not awfully amenable to close examination.'

'Illegal.'

'No! Just . . . stretching things. Don't look frightened. We're all right. It's just . . . the confidence factor. I need people to remain confident about me. I need to keep out of the press . . . I know, all my fault. But you leaving . . . now . . . well, it might tip things over the edge. No reason why you should care. I've let you down. I'll understand if you go. But it could destroy me, destroy everything. And . . . you would get much less money from me than you would otherwise. Much less. Sorry, but it's a time for being frank.'

'And the other reason?'

'The other reason is that I want to rekindle our love.'

The sun went in again at that very moment, the bastard.

'You were thinking that one of the two reasons was more important than the other, and then you decided that they were both equally important. Before you decided that, was this one the more important reason or the less important one?'

'The more important. Then I just thought, to be brutally honest, because of how I've conducted my business, the money really is just as important, sadly. Being realistic. Being brutal.'

'Do you seriously think we really could possibly feel again for each other what we once felt?'

'I don't know. I hope so. Put it this way, and perhaps two negatives do make a kind of positive. I don't know that we can't.'

Christina gave a faint smile and bit the nail of her right thumb. This was a habit of hers that she seemed to have grown out of. Sir Gordon was rather encouraged by it. He knew that it wasn't contrived.

'I'll give it some thought,' she said.

'Good,' he said. 'That's great. In fact, under the circumstances I think it's extremely generous.'

'So do I,' said Lady Coppinger.

It would be good to report that the sun came out again at this moment. But it didn't. In fact it began to rain.

A great deal of pain

Things got worse. Sir Gordon talked to the press, admitting his affair and bitterly regretting it, but giving the impression that it was an isolated lapse. When will they ever learn, the rich and the famous?

It didn't cross his mind, softened as it was by all the years of people yielding to his every whim, that any of the other girls would trouble him. But they did. The papers were phoned by Jenny Boothroyd, Sandy Lane, Isla Swanley, Kerry Oldstead, Gill Goldthorpe, and Ellie Streeter, all telling of affairs with him. As always when a celebrity of any note was found to have had lots of extramarital affairs, articles and advice about sex addiction poured out.

'You'd think it was the worst offence in the world, Farringdon,' commented Sir Gordon at breakfast one morning. It was only Farringdon to whom he felt able to talk about it.

'Yes, indeed, sir.'

'I never forced myself upon anyone.'

'I would have been astounded if you had told me that you had, sir.'

'Impotence is far more serious, Farringdon.'

'I believe that it would be most unpleasant, sir.'

'Imagine if Adam had been impotent. We wouldn't be here now talking about it.'

'A most disturbing conjecture, sir.'

Farringdon walked slowly towards the door to the near kitchen. Then he turned.

'I wonder if that would be a good thing or a bad thing, sir,' he said.

Of all Sir Gordon's conquests, only Mandy from Hair Hunters of Hackney didn't contact the press. He sent her an email to tell her his reasons for what he had done, and to say how sorry he was to have to end their affair, and to promise her a proper letter.

He wrote that letter. He thanked her for the support and pleasure that she had brought into his life. He knew now that he was taking a huge risk in writing, but he still trusted her. He felt that unless there was someone he could trust, he would sink into depression. He told her that he was going to try to make a go of things with his wife. He wished her well with her salon, and hoped the new girl would turn out to be as good with people as she was with hair, and wouldn't ever go to Dubai.

Every morning he braved a huddle of photographers at the gates to Rose Cottage, at the end of his mile-long drive past Top Field, Middle Field and Bottom Field. Every morning he was shouted questions by journalists as he arrived at the Stick of Celery. Every morning he had to try to ignore the looks of all his staff, and especially of Alice Penfold. Every morning, as the lift took him high above the river, he wondered how all this was going down with the people of Britain.

He talked to the press and to the television cameras and told them that he was ashamed of what he had done. Every second of every interview was humiliating and distressing for him. He promised the nation that he would never stray again and would devote himself to mending his relationship with his beloved Christina. He even managed to play the patriotism card yet again. 'It's not easy, you know, for a man of virility and yet of susceptibility, of strength and yet of weakness, to resist the temptation presented by the lovely young ladies of these blessed isles.' Hugo had once commented that if his brother ever fell into the sewers he wouldn't come up smelling of shit, he'd come up boasting that British sewers were the best and cleanest in the world.

More articles appeared from the experts on sex addiction. Fierce debate took place about him on Twitter. He was public property. It was endless. It was horrid.

He took Joanna out to dinner and apologized for his treatment of her mother. She confessed that she had been seriously embarrassed when her mother had won a prize for an extremely striking pink hybrid tea rose which she had bred and had called Fragrant Joanna.

'I know she meant it as a tribute to me,' she said. 'I know I should be grateful. But I hated it. It's everything I'm not. Couldn't she see that? Or did she mean it? Was she being cruel? She can be cruel.'

'I think it was just blindness. She has tunnel vision where roses are concerned. And anyway, Joanna, people develop at different speeds, you know. I think you may be beginning to blossom. Now your cheeks are pink. Just like Fragrant Joanna.'

'People mocked me at work. They all used to sniff when I came into the office. "Oooh. It's fragrant Joanna."'

'People can be cruel.'

Now her cheeks grew even more like a blush rose. She told him that she had a boyfriend whom she had kept secret because she knew that her father would regard him as a nerd. He told her that he was no longer in a position to be contemptuous of nerds, and would like to meet him.

At the end of the evening, he said, 'I've really enjoyed being with you.'

Other aspects of his life went less well.

He hunted for Jack without success.

He dreamt of Megan Lloyd-Phillips making love to him on the pitch at the Millennium Stadium while Katherine Jenkins serenaded them with 'Land of My Fathers'. It was hours before he could even begin to recover from the sorrow of finding that it was a dream. He would have preferred a nightmare, so that he could have the pleasure of discovering that it hadn't happened.

He took Luke and Emma to watch Climthorpe United lose 1–0 to Leicester City at the Coppinger Stadium. Raduslav Bogoff missed a penalty in the eighty-third minute. The mainly masculine crowd, who had greeted Sir Gordon with ribald but affectionate songs at the start, were booing and shouting at him by the end. Luke glowered throughout. Emma kissed Sir Gordon and said, 'Never mind, we love you.' Luke glowered even more.

Sir Gordon gave Christina time and space, and on the surface they got on better than they had for years. Despite the growing frustration of his new sexless life, however, he found it impossible just yet to attempt to resume sexual relations with her, and she showed no sign of wanting to do so with him. He felt that they were living through a phoney peace, the outcome of which was still uncertain.

He received worrying financial figures from his bacon factory in Wiltshire, and very worrying figures from his electrical business in South Wales, where sales of washing machines and dishwashers had slumped. But there was encouraging news from Porter's Potteries Pies: Martin Fortescue was making a good impression, sales were steady, and they would soon be launching their new line of steak, kidney and oyster pies to a traditional old English recipe.

Mandy wrote back to say that she appreciated his letter and she wouldn't ever dream of hurting someone who had brought a lot of pleasure into her life and had never promised her anything. She was ashamed that some members of her sex had behaved like cows. The new girl had turned out to be a cow also, but luckily she'd got another job, she didn't care whether it was in Dubai or Swindon.

His three managers at Gordon Investments trudged up the bleak stone stairs from the thirteenth floor – they didn't want to be seen in a lift, that might spark a rumour – and this time there was no interruption from the window cleaners so they were able to speak frankly. Their views diverged slightly when they were asked by Sir Gordon, 'So, lads, the truth about our position, please.'

'Um . . . the truth . . . ah . . . well . . .' began Keith Gostelow, who had developed a small boil on his neck since their last meeting. 'That's . . . um . . . that's a tall order, because we're in . . . well, I don't say crisis, not at all, there is no . . . well, no crisis as such . . . not as such . . . because . . . well, look, there have been . . . you know . . . in the press . . . on the TV . . . well, haven't there, and it's unfortunate. But I mean, you know . . . different people, different thoughts, there are signs that some people . . . well, like Berlusconi was in Italy, I suppose, though not as much as Italy, I mean, let's face it, this isn't Italy . . . I mean, is it? It isn't. But . . . there we are . . . I still think we can be in business. If. If. I . . . um . . . I'm sure you know what I mean by that.'

'I concur with some of Keith's analysis,' said Adam Eaglestone, who was wearing new shoes which he had already scuffed. 'I do tend, though, towards a marginally more pessimistic scenario. While I think that at this moment in time, despite publicity much of which is unfavourable, despite the truth of some of what Keith says as regards an element of admiration certainly from a masculine perspective, in analysing the balance of the influence of the extensive coverage given to your *ex officio* activities on our incoming and outgoing flow scenario, I also think that if we can at this moment in time draw a line under this publicity, if we have assurances that

156

there are no more skeletons in the bedroom cupboard, we can survive.'

'I think we're fucked,' said Dan Perkins.

Sir Gordon was sufficiently alarmed by what his three managers said to seek another meeting with his brother Hugo. It was a decision that would cause him a great deal of pain.

He was gone

This time, unusually, Hugo opted for dinner. He chose a very new restaurant in Clerkenwell. It was called Oliver's Oven. Oliver, who was actually Romanian and not at all alliterative, but wanted to cash in on the Jamie jamboree, described his food as British Fusion – Heston Blumenthal meets Mrs Beeton – so it was patriotic enough for Sir Gordon to be seen in.

The walls were red and black, and the lighting was dim and red, which meant that large areas of the restaurant were black. Sir Gordon could hardly find his way through the dark busy room. The tables were close together and the place was crowded and noisy.

'I told you I wanted privacy,' shouted Sir Gordon once they had sat down.

'It's trendy,' shouted Hugo. 'Nobody's interested in anybody else. They're all up their own arses. It's perfect.'

They both ordered the house aperitif, a throat-scalding cough mixture beloved of Gypsies in the Transylvanian hills, and Hugo chose large glasses of Yorkshire Chablis to go with the lemongrass and nitrogen potted shrimps, and a bottle of Petrus, easily the most expensive on the wine list, to accompany the tamarind and mint tea infused toad-in-the-hole.

They had to lean forward till they were almost kissing each

other before they had a chance of understanding what the other was saying.

'That's Alan Peabody over there,' said Hugo.

'Who's Alan Peabody?'

'You really are a philistine. He's one of our greatest Shakespearean actors. He has nothing interesting to say as himself so this place is perfect for him. The girl he's with has no idea he's boring her stiff. This drink's perfect. Lots of coughs about. So, poor old Gordon, eh?'

'I've brought it all on myself, Hugo. I'm not complaining, and I can take it.'

'But you wanted to talk to me about something. I hope I can't guess what.'

'What do you hope it isn't?'

'Gordon Investments.'

'Ah. Well. I'm afraid it is.'

'Ah.'

'Yes. Quite. You know how you asked . . . is it straight?'

'Yes.'

'I told you it was.'

'Yes.'

'It isn't.'

'No.'

'You know?'

'Yes. It was my view that . . .'

Hugo was interrupted by the arrival of their lemongrass and nitrogen potted shrimps. They ate for a while in silent disbelief.

'You were saying, Hugo?'

'Yes. Yes, I was. If I made an assumption that . . . a certain type of . . . dishonesty . . . was endemic to the operation, which I did, using my mathematical skills, then I would have to say, Gordon, that you have been considerably cleverer than . . . a certain other person . . . varying your returns really rather brilliantly . . . but, even so, over the length of

159

time, your investors have been getting sums that cannot be accounted for honestly. My dear, dear brother, will you tell me straight? Is Gordon Investments one great big Ponzi scheme?'

'To be honest I've never quite grasped what a Ponzi scheme is, but if you mean that we pay all our returns out of the incoming investments, and never invest any of the investors' money at all, then yes, it is.'

'Oh dear. Oh dear, oh dear, oh dear.'

'I'm sorry, Hugo. What an embarrassment for you. You a giant in the banking world, and your brother the British Bernie Madoff.'

'Appalled though I am, Gordon, I have to confess to a sneaking admiration. I wouldn't have thought you could get away with a scheme of that magnitude in this country in this day and age.'

'Unlike Madoff, I haven't been too greedy. Unlike Madoff, I am well known and loved and trusted. Practically untouchable, Hugo.'

'That may be true of the past, Gordon. I fear it is true no longer.'

Sir Gordon didn't admit that he had a secret fear that Hugo might be right.

'Well, maybe all is not lost, Gordon.'

A waiter came and removed their plates. He didn't ask them if they had enjoyed their starters.

'Oh, Hugo, I'm so glad I've told you,' said Sir Gordon. They were both having to lean forward to make themselves heard through the roar of inanity, but Hugo was right. Nobody was listening. Security was total in this temple of egotism. 'I feel such relief. I wanted to tell you at that lunch at the Intrepid Snail. I'd had a bad day. My centre forward wasn't scoring goals, Luke had had a painting vandalized, you asked me about Gordon Investments, and I longed to say, "It all fits into my day, I'm afraid, Hugo. Bogoff, Fuck off, Madoff."'

Hugo looked mystified by this, as well he might.

'I couldn't believe it – three years ago, was it? – when the Madoff news broke,' said Sir Gordon. 'I thought, That bastard's stolen my thunder. Which is ridiculous, as I could never have boasted about it so there could never have been any thunder. But I thought, If it ever comes out, people will think I'm just a copycat, getting my little ideas from America.'

'Your ostrich burgers, gentlemen,' said the waiter.

'Thank you.'

'Doesn't it worry you, Gordon, that people will get hurt?' asked Hugo gently.

'People don't get hurt. Everyone gets paid. They don't know that the returns aren't real. Their money's real.'

'But if you don't get the investment money in, you can't pay the returns out.'

'But I always do get the investment money in. This ostrich burger has a funny taste. What is it?'

'Yes, but are you going to continue to get the investment money in sufficient – could it be ostrich, by any chance? – in sufficient amounts in the current – coconut? Is there some coconut in it? – in the current climate?

'Well, I've always thought so. I've always hoped so.'

'But your name is suddenly plastered all over the papers, Gordon, in unsavoury contexts.'

'Well, this is it. This is why I'm . . . Hugo, I didn't order an ostrich burger. I ordered toad-in-the-hole.'

'Good God. So did I. I was so involved in all this I didn't notice.'

'Nor me. Do you want to just carry on or do you want to change?'

'It's not exactly nice but would the toad-in-the-hole be any better?'

'I don't expect so. So shall we just . . .?'

'May as well.'

'Hugo, I have to say . . . there's a real risk that one day

– quite soon, possibly – there may not be the money to pay. You know what that means.'

'Arrest. A long prison sentence. Unless . . .?'

'Unless?'

The waiter hurried over.

'Gentlemen, you didn't ordering ostrich burgers.'

'Yes, we know,' said Hugo.

'But you eating them. You shouldn't eating them if you didn't ordering them.'

'You shouldn't have served them,' said Sir Gordon.

'I know, but I said, "Your ostrich burgers, gentlemen." You said nothings. Absolutely much nothings whatsoever.'

'We were busy with very serious matters. It didn't register.'

'But now Mr Peabody, he has no ostrich burger, nor his companion. Mr Peabody is famous actor, very good Macbeth, he much hate toad-in-the-gap, he say it horrible, what to do?'

'I am sometimes rude to waiters and I am trying hard to turn over a new leaf,' said Sir Gordon, 'but I am here to discuss matters of life and death, not of farce. The fault was yours. You must clear it up. I suggest you take these away, bring us our toad-in-the-gap as you call it, and order fresh ostrich burgers for Mr Peabody.'

The waiter glared at Sir Gordon, swept the plates up angrily, said, 'You said nothings. You should have said somethings,' and stalked off angrily.

The brothers sat in silence for a while. Hugo seemed exhausted and Sir Gordon didn't want to seem too eager to find out what Hugo had meant by 'unless'.

'Where were we?' asked Hugo at last.

'You talked about a long prison sentence, and you said, "unless . . .", raising my hopes. Unless what, Hugo?'

The waiter banged two plates on the table.

'Your toads-in-the-gap, gentlemen.'

'Please, please, please, waiter, just go away. Unless what, Hugo?'

162

'Unless I can help you.'

'Could you?'

'I don't know. I'm not a public figure like you, but I do have immense influence globally behind the scenes. This toad-in-the-gap's marginally better than the ostrich burger, actually. Gordon, it is not inconceivable that I might be able to raise enough money, off a few shores, in a few secret accounts, with the aid of a few rich friends and investors, to support GI sufficiently to set it on a legal basis from now on.'

'Could you really? I have one or two banker friends, you know. Friends who've . . . enjoyed a little holiday on my boat. Surely there are a few favours there to be called in?'

'Gordon, I'm sure your boat is lovely – it would be rather nice as your brother to be invited some time and have the chance to see if it is – but even a luxury holiday in the Med is small beer compared to the sums I imagine we'll be talking. Send me a list of names, though, that'd be useful. All this may take time, though, Gordon.'

'I'm starting to think that I might not have very much time.'

'I'll be as quick as I possibly can. Top priority, Gordon. Top priority.'

'Well, thank you. That's fantastic.'

'I . . . um . . . I'm in line for a pretty big bonus, Gordon, *entre nous*. If it was enough to make any difference I'd willingly give it to you, but it won't be.'

'How much do you expect?'

'About a million, give or take the odd hundred thousand. It would just be swallowed up.'

'Yes.'

'Why did you start?'

'Start what?'

'This scam. Why?'

'It was so easy. I always thought that one day I'd regularize it. Never seemed to need to, so never got round to it.'

'Oh, Gordon.'

'I know.'

'How are the books?'

'What?'

'GI's books. I presume you have books.'

'Oh yes. Immaculate. Full details of every transaction ever made. Utterly convincing. Thoroughly detailed. Everything adds up. Perfect.'

'Except that they're a complete fiction.'

'Except that they're a complete fiction.'

The strain of making themselves heard had told its tale. They both felt tired, and they sat in brotherly silence for a few minutes as they mopped up their main course.

The waiter cleared away their plates. He asked, brusquely, but not quite to the point of being rude, if they wanted to see the dessert menu.

'I don't,' said Sir Gordon. 'I've had one and a half main courses.'

'No. Nothing for me,' agreed Hugo. 'Important things to discuss. Can't risk any more farce.'

'Are there still important things to discuss?' asked Sir Gordon when the waiter had gone.

'Yes.'

'Oh.'

Sir Gordon leant forward. The babble in the restaurant was growing even louder as the drink spoke.

'Fire away, Hugo,' he said nervously.

'Just one question. One last question, Gordon. There's nothing else shady in your world, is there?'

Hugo's sharp, almost colourless eyes stared piercingly at his younger brother. Sir Gordon met the gaze, mirroring its intensity.

'Nothing, no.'

'There are no more revelations to come?'

He wanted to tell Hugo, tell him about SFN, tell him about Germophile.

He couldn't. He just couldn't.

He hadn't the courage.

He had used up his store of courage over the last forty years of taking risks, of not being afraid.

It was a sobering thought. He took a large sip of wine and wondered if he'd ever be able to get drunk again.

He must reply. Already the delay might be making Hugo suspicious.

'Absolutely not. It's usually the small things that get you found out. With one big enormous fraud, I can't afford anything else not to be above board.'

'Good. Good. Good thinking. Clever.'

'I wish our mother was still alive so we could—'

'You did that bit last time.'

'Well . . . what can I say, Hugo, except a huge thank-you?'

'What are families for, Gordon? What are families for?'

Sir Gordon phoned for his car.

'Give you a lift?'

Hugo said that he would walk.

'I love walking in London. It keeps me fit, and I always see something I can disapprove of.'

'Just one last thing,' said Sir Gordon. 'When we last met you said we needed to discuss it. We didn't. Jack.'

'Oh God, yes. No, we didn't. Jack. Well, what *can* we do, Gordon? We can't do anything unless we find him.'

'Maybe we ought to make a concerted effort to find him.'

'Yes. Yes. Good idea. Yes, we must. We will. Ring me.'

They walked to the door together, Sir Gordon lifting his shoulders and neck, Hugo letting his sag, five foot eight and a half each of them, those rich and loving brothers.

At the door they hugged.

London seemed strangely quiet after the restaurant. As so often, there was rain in the air.

Hugo strode off. Sir Gordon stepped into the back of his car.

'Evening, Kirkstall.'

There was no reply.

The car set off with a jerk. He'd never known that before from Kirkstall.

He looked at Kirkstall's neck.

It wasn't Kirkstall's neck. It was a thicker neck, a very solid neck. The backs of necks can be very illuminating, and very frightening. A cold spasm of fear and shock ran through Sir Gordon.

He reached for the door handle, almost got there before the click of the locks.

'Locked.'

'Let me out.'

'Don't be silly.'

Did he recognize the voice? He wasn't sure.

'Where are we going?'

'You find out.'

'Why are you doing this?'

'You find out.'

'Let me out.'

'Don't be silly.'

The driver drove fast, but not stupidly, not drawing attention to himself. Sir Gordon tried to see where they were going, but by the time he thought of this they were already in streets he didn't recognize. Back streets. Mean streets. Decaying streets. Not streets he'd know.

'You won't know anywhere. Bad streets. Not your sort of street.'

Sir Gordon found it unnerving to have his thoughts read like that. He reached, very slowly, very silently, for his mobile, which was in the right-hand pocket of his trousers. It was difficult to prise it out. He had to half sit up and try to manoeuvre it past tissues and keys.

'You use your mobile, I shoot. Not to kill. To maim. Nasty. Beside, you don't know where you are. Not at all. So no use. No use at all. So don't be silly.'

166

They continued in silence. Suddenly a new worry struck Sir Gordon.

'What have you done with Kirkstall?'

'Oh, you think of him now, Mr Big Shot.'

'I do. I care about him. If you've hurt him . . .'

'He not hurt, not bad. He not dead.'

'He'd better not be.'

'You think you know me. You don't. You never seen me nowhere. I am nothing to do with them. I am paid. Paid assassin.' He laughed. 'But I don't kill you. Only maim. Not paid enough assassin.' He laughed again.

Sir Gordon had been concerned for some time that his luck seemed to be running out on all fronts, but now he had a huge stroke of fortune, or so it seemed. The car passed a building that he knew. It was the smallest of all his factories, the very first one he had bought. It made kettles. There was no mention of his name on its frontage, just a large sign announcing '*Kwality Kettle Korporation*'. He had a soft spot for it and its corny name. It was the runt of his great litter.

The driver turned down the side of the factory and pulled up. Sir Gordon knew the name of this insalubrious road. It was Pirates Lane. Clearly, whoever was abducting him had no idea that he knew the area. Small-time guys. He grew more hopeful.

'Out you get. I go now, far away. I see nothing. And don't bother with registration number. It's your car.'

'And supposing I don't get out.'

The driver whipped round, pointed a pistol just to the left of Sir Gordon, and fired. The bullet just missed his ear and shattered the rear window.

'Next time I hit.'

Sir Gordon got out of the car as quickly as he could and leant against the side of a wall as if in fear and shock. He hoped he looked like a man about to faint. Within seconds the car was gone. There seemed to be nobody about. In a moment he had his phone out, he had dialled 999, he had told them who he was and where he was. Then he heard footsteps, iron boots ringing on tarmac. How many feet? Lots.

He knew the area. He had examined it fully for safety before buying the factory. He had been very thorough in those days, and he never forgot. The road was a cul-de-sac ending in a high railway wall, but on the left, halfway along the road, there was a narrow alley, which led through to a parallel road, up which he'd be able to escape.

It was very dark. There were only two street lights in Pirates Lane, and one of them was out. He walked briskly towards the alley. Just as he approached it three men came out of it, all wearing balaclavas. They caught him off guard. They were all round him before he could draw breath. They knocked him down. He struggled and managed to get to his feet, kicking and landing a very satisfactory blow on one of his assailants' private parts. The man screamed in pain. Sir Gordon was tough. He punched, he kicked, he fought fiercely. A right-hander got one of the men full on the nose. He fell backwards on to the other two, and they toppled over in a heap. These men weren't brilliant fighters. He could beat the three of them.

But then there were the men behind him. He had a quick peep. At first he could see nothing but darkness, then he saw three more men, also wearing balaclavas, dressed in black from head to foot, marching in the middle of the road towards him, their blackness not detaching itself from the blackness of the night until they had come very close to him. Only three. He had already held off three men, and for a second his spirits rose. But maths had been his least bad subject at school, and he still knew that three men in front of him and three men behind him added up to six men altogether.

And as he tensed himself against the three men he had knocked over who were now advancing upon him again, the three men in the street behind him jumped on him. Now all six were on him. He fought like a tiger, he landed blows that he had no right to land, he fancied he had endangered another man's Saturday night. But with six men in that grimy little street in East London he stood no chance. Knowing where he was hadn't been such a stroke of luck after all.

He was on the ground now; they were pummelling him with their boots, a dreadful blow struck him in the balls. He heard a train and wondered if it would be the last train he would ever hear. They were kicking his ribs, his knees, pulling his hair. It was the ribs that they went for most, bash, bash, bash, both sides, systematic. A couple of punches crashed into his face, and one of the men stepped on his arm, but it was the ribs, the ribs, the ribs, and he couldn't bear any more. Soon it would be over. Soon he would die. So what? Big deal. It couldn't come soon enough.

And then an urgent voice called out, 'Enough, you guys. Enough. Don't want to kill him.'

And they stopped. He lay on the ground and nobody was hitting him. He could hear them walking away. They had finished. He would live. Perhaps.

That voice. It rang a chord. A distant chord. Too distant. Who were these people? Investors who had lost cash over Germophile? What a moment to start worrying about people he had wronged.

He tried to move and couldn't get his body to work. A huge pain ran through him. He sensed that he had an internal injury. Something had ruptured. Something serious, a vital organ, had ruptured. He was dying.

He heard a car approaching. He was lying in the middle of the road and he couldn't move. He'd seen pheasants dying after being hit by cars. Once he'd run over a pheasant himself, and he'd gone back to run over it again to put it out of its misery. Christina hadn't been able to believe that he'd been so kind, and neither had he.

169

Perhaps the car would deliver that same service for him. He tensed his body, waiting for the impact, hoping, dreading.

But the car stopped. Now he heard sirens. Men were running. There were cries and shouts and shrieks. A dog barked, and then again more faintly. The sirens were fainter now too, and so were the cries of the men. Everything was fading. He was going, going, going. If he was dying he would wake up next morning and think, 'Bloody hell. I haven't woken up this morning. I must be dead.'

That was a strange thought. Maybe it was his last thought. A strange thought to end a rich life.

He was going, going, going.

He was gone.

He might yet be able to save his fortune

He awoke with a sense of shock. He had no idea where he was.

Everything was white – blindingly white. The glare of it all hurt his eyes. For a moment he thought he was lying on a bed of snow, that if he moved so much as one muscle he would slide, slide, slide to his death in a dark ravine which the sun never reached. Then he realized it was just a bed. It was a narrow bed, narrower than he had slept in for many years. And he was lying on his back, which he never did. And he was in the middle of the bed, which he never was. And he was alone in the bed, which was also very unusual. And wonderful. To be alone in bed, without Lady Coppinger or some woman from whom he would have to extricate himself, what luxury. Relief flooded over him, and he enjoyed a moment of the purest anticipation. Any second now he would give his legs and arms a glorious, slow, long stretch, and there would be no indignant female to cry 'Ow!' as his nails scratched her unintentionally.

He tried to stretch, and a thousand pains shot through his body. He had never felt such pain. He passed out.

He came back to consciousness very cautiously, dimly

remembering that he had been beaten up. Suddenly he recalled everything, from that awful moment of shock when he'd seen that the back of the neck of the driver of his car was not the back of Kirkstall's neck. He felt the same fear all over again. The memories of strange necks linger.

He tried, very carefully this time, to move first his legs and then his arms. At the faintest motion the pains began again. He felt most dreadfully sore. He had no confidence in his body, or in the integrity of any organ in it. He felt that he consisted of a thin bruised skin stretched over a sea of ruptures and leaking blood. Kidneys, liver, spleen, pancreas, prostate – in his fears these were all seriously damaged. In his fears death would creep over him from the inside.

His left arm was in a sling. His right leg was raised and in plaster. He began to sweat. Sweat poured off him. He felt slimy.

A bell pull was hanging down from the white ceiling, dangling over the white bed. He was wearing a white night-shirt.

He didn't know if he could find the courage to move his right arm sufficiently to reach the bell pull. He moved the arm half an inch, then a whole inch, flexing himself against further severe pain. There was pain, but it was bearable. It seemed that the right arm was intact. He moved it further, with slightly more confidence. He grasped the bell pull, gritted his teeth, and pulled. The action of pulling produced agony right through his body. He gasped.

It seemed to be ages before anybody came. He began to panic. He had been abandoned. He had realized by this time that he was in a private room in a hospital, and he had heard tales of how nurses resented private patients in private rooms, and in fact to his amazement he found himself wishing that he was in a long ward with beds on either side, and people in the beds, any people, any activity to help him take his mind off his pain.

172

He forced himself to remain calm, to conquer his fears. He imagined Garibaldi coming to visit, with Megan Lloyd-Phillips. 'This beautiful woman tells me you are a very brave man. I congratulate you,' said Garibaldi. 'I admire brave men.'

Then at last a nurse arrived. She smiled and said, 'Good morning, Sir Gordon.' And then she added what he thought was just about the most stupid question he had been asked in a lifetime of stupid questions. 'How are you feeling?'

He told her. She flinched.

'Are you right-handed?' she asked.

'Yes. Why?'

'Oh good. Only my little boy would love your autograph. He's autograph mad and we all support Climthorpe.'

'Excellent,' he said faintly, 'but how about a cup of tea first? My throat is parched.'

'I'll see what you're allowed,' she said.

She came back a few minutes later with a cup of revoltingly weak, milky tea. He tried to complain, exclaim, 'Call that a cup of tea?' but the words died in his throat; he was vulnerable, he was sweaty, he was weak, he'd had all his greatness knocked out of him.

'Thank you,' he said.

'No problem. Yes, we all love the United. That's me and my husband John and our son Ted. John's a plumber. Should you ever . . . when things get back to normal. I'll dig up one of his cards.'

Do shut up. Do . . . shut . . . up.

'Thank you.'

'Though none of us can understand why you play that Bogoff. He gets an occasional goal but his first touch is terrible.'

Mind your own business. This is not the time. You're a nurse. Fucking nurse me.

'Well, I'll leave you to it. Try to get some rest.'

What else do you think I'll do? Press-ups?

She came back almost immediately, with a bedpan.

'Forgot to give you one of these. Very important.'

His heart sank. He realized in a flash just how awkward every single action was going to be.

He closed his eyes so as not to be able to see his tea as he took a ghastly sip. When he opened them, a doctor was standing there, smiling encouragingly. Two women stood behind him, both smiling encouragingly. One of them was pretty. This made no impact on him. His heart was racing. He didn't want to hear what the doctor had to say. He wasn't ready to face a moment of truth.

'Well, well. Who's a lucky fellow?' beamed the doctor.

'If this is luck, I'd hate to be unlucky.'

'No, seriously, you are lucky. A broken arm, a broken leg, three broken ribs. That's all.'

'Good Lord. Only that. My lucky day.'

'I'm serious, Sir Gordon. They have given you one hell of a going-over, but we don't think you have any serious internal injuries. Bruising probably, not nice at all, but you will live.'

In Pirates Lane last night – had it been last night, how long had he been unconscious? – he had believed that he was going to die and he had been in such pain that he had welcomed it. Now, in hospital, he knew how deeply he didn't want to die. He would have said, if asked, that he was not afraid of death, never had been. The extent of the relief he felt at those three words from the doctor – 'you will live' – gave the lie to that. It flooded through his stale, bruised body. He was going to live.

'It sounds as though they knew what they were doing,' he said. 'Experts were they?'

The doctor gave a much smaller, somewhat evasive smile, and the two women behind him, presumably junior doctors, gave similar smiles. Sir Gordon was puzzled.

'I've no idea, sir. Not my area of competence,' said the doctor.

The doctor discussed his condition, estimated the time his

recovery would take, depressed him utterly, and reiterated how lucky he was. The two female doctors nodded in unison. Then all three smiled and left the room. For about ten seconds Sir Gordon felt huge relief. Then he felt crushingly lonely. He had to face the fact that he was in for a prolonged period of difficulty and inactivity. The prospect was appalling.

But he was a fighter. Look how he had fought against those six men, who sounded so expert, so skilled in how far to go in their violence. Perhaps they were Mafia men, or men from some other secret society, Triads perhaps, whose areas of activity he had somehow inconvenienced. Perhaps they were the hired assassins of rival businessmen. Whoever they were, he might regain a bit of lost stock with the great British public. They loved a fighter. They loved a plucky loser. Yes, as a plucky loser he would be able to restore his reputation, which was now so vital to his financial survival.

The nurse returned, smiling.

'You have a visitor,' she told him.

She sounded as if she was sure he'd be pleased, but he felt a sharp dread. He wasn't ready for visitors. He certainly wasn't ready for Lady Coppinger. Or Hugo. Or Luke.

To his relief it was none of these. It was Farringdon.

'Ah! Farringdon!'

Farringdon couldn't quite suppress the shock of pleasure that he got from the unmistakable warmth in Sir Gordon's voice.

'This is a most distressing conjoinment, sir.'

'Yes, indeed, Farringdon.'

'I understand that you have escaped serious internal injury, sir.'

'Yes, I've been lucky. Or perhaps my attackers knew what they were doing.'

'I doubt that, frankly, sir.'

'You know something about them? Who were they, Farringdon? Mafia men?'

'No, sir.'

'Some other secret society?'

'Not exactly, sir.'

'Desperate business rivals?'

'No, sir.'

'Investors who . . .'

He stopped. He couldn't even talk about the Germophile affair to Farringdon.

'What, then?'

'Waiters, sir.'

'Waiters?'

'Waiters, sir.'

'Men who wait at table?'

'Yes, sir.'

'I have been beaten up by six waiters?'

'Yes, sir.'

'Oh my God.'

'Yes, sir.'

'Do we know why?'

'Yes, sir.'

'Why?'

'It would seem, sir, that there are elements in the waiting fraternity who feel that they have been treated by you with less than complete professional respect.'

'I see.'

'A small group of them decided to . . . um . . . in their . . . in their words . . . I find it difficult even to say them to you in quotation, sir . . . "teach the arrogant bastard a lesson". I'm sorry, sir.'

'No, no, not at all. I asked you why. You had to tell me. Farringdon, do you . . .?'

Sir Gordon tried to move his body, even an inch would provide some measure of relief, but the pain was too great.

'Do you regard me as an "arrogant bastard"?'

Farringdon paused before replying.

'You have the natural pride of a man who has achieved what you have achieved, sir.'

'Thank you. Beautifully put. Will you put your arms under my back and help me change my position, Farringdon? I'm desperate.'

'No, sir.'

'What?'

'I would not dream of prejudicing your recovery by trespassing on the expertise of the medical staff, sir. I will ring for a nurse.'

Sir Gordon sighed. That would involve more smiling.

'I hope this business about the waiters hasn't reached the ears of the press, Farringdon,' he said.

'I regret to say that it has, sir.'

Cold fear crept into Sir Gordon's heart.

'It has?'

'Yes, sir.'

'How has the incident been reported, Farringdon?'

'In the main with headlines of such inappropriate levity, in the context of your injuries, that I fear that large sections of the media are beyond redemption, sir.'

'Give me examples.'

'I'd rather not, sir.'

'I order you to.'

'"*Are you the punch on the nose, sir?*" "*I didn't order a kick in the goolies.*" "*Making a meal of Sir Gordon.*" "*A service charge Sir Gordon will never forget.*" "*'Is Coppinger a lousy tipper?' asks Jake Throstle.*"'

'Oh my God. I'm an object of ridicule, Farringdon.'

'I find it hard to disagree with that assessment, sir.'

'And Her Ladyship, Farringdon. Have you spoken to her?'

'Yes, sir.'

'And?'

'She is very upset, sir. She told me she was appalled.'

'By what has happened to me or by what I have done to deserve this?'

'I have always found it politic not to include in the remit of my responsibilities any element of exploration into the inner workings of Her Ladyship's mental processes, sir.'

'Very wise of you, Farringdon. Farringdon?'

Farringdon's eyes looked more like glass than ever.

'Yes, sir?' he said cautiously.

'The way you talk. Now that we're here, now that I'm like this, who are you really, Farringdon?'

'I beg your pardon, sir?'

'Oh, Farringdon. You don't really talk like that, do you? Not at home. Not with your friends. You talk like that because you expect people like me to expect you to talk like that. You talk as you do because of what I was. Ouch.' Sir Gordon winced as pain flooded through him again. It really felt as if a main artery had been severed. 'Sorry. Bit of a heavy subject at a time like this, but it's our only chance.'

'I beg your pardon, sir?'

'Couldn't you say something like "What the fuck are you on about?" Couldn't you talk like a human being?'

'I don't know if I could, sir. Not after all this time.'

'Oh, come on. Try. We're close. We see each other every day, yet we behave like master and butler. We waste our lives together. We could be friends. We can here. Now. This is our chance. You weren't born a butler, Farringdon. The midwife didn't say, "It's a butler." Who are you?'

'I was born within the sight of bow legs, sir.'

'I beg your pardon. Oh God, now I'm saying it. What *do* you mean?'

'It was a joke, sir.'

'Oh. Sorry. A joke?'

'I wasn't born within the sound of Bow Bells, but I was born in a slum, where people are ugly and deformed.'

'Oh, I see. I get it. Very funny, Farringdon. Very droll.'

'Thank you, sir.'

'Don't call me "sir", not today. And I won't call you Farringdon. You must have a Christian name.'

'Yes, I do, s . . . sorry.'

'And it is?'

'Brian.'

'So, what was life like for young Brian?'

'Bleeding awful. Five kids in a tiny, dirty house. Rats everywhere. One bog. If we could have been said to have been in anything, as a family, it was fish. Dad had a wet fish shop in West Thurrock, Gran had been on the herrings down Lowestoft, they wanted me to go into fish, Mum said fish was in my blood, I said I hated fish. I did. I hated it. Bleeding eels. Terrible. I worked as a porter for a while, I was covered in sores, I had eczema something chronic. I literally scratched a living. You're tired. I've talked too much.'

Sir Gordon gave a faint smile.

'Yes, but . . . we'll finish the story later. How the fish man conquered his eczema and became a butler.'

'You taking the piss?'

'Not really. No, not at all . . . really. I wasn't born into my world either. What a farce our times together have been. Change all that, eh?'

They shared a smile, and this time the smile was welcome.

'You're right, though. I am tired. Pull the bell again, will you, and then go?'

'Righty-ho.'

Farringdon pulled the bell.

'Thanks, Brian.'

'No probs, Gordon.'

Again, the moment Farringdon had gone, Sir Gordon wished that he was still there. He was a prey to dark thoughts. How had it come to this? How had he, a national icon, cocooned in the nation's affections, turned into an object of ridicule? He couldn't afford to be an object of ridicule. Gordon

Investments would collapse, and with it his whole business world.

Still nobody came. Nobody would ever come. He would die, privately, in his private room.

He was now in mental turmoil, and the urge to try to lift himself up, in an attempt to relieve his physical discomfort, was irresistible. He was gripped by a kind of claustrophobia. He just *had* to change his position. And he did manage to move just a little, barely a couple of inches, and at a cost of sharp pain, pain worse than any discomfort, yet preferable to it, because in enduring pain one at least gains some satisfaction from the exercise of bravery, but in enduring discomfort there is no satisfaction at all.

And Sir Gordon found that the exercise of this physical courage, slight though it was, brought with it the capacity to discover some mental courage as well. His mind had always worked at its fastest in a crisis, and it worked fast now. Within minutes he was no longer despairing of the ridicule he was receiving in the media. Within minutes he was planning his fightback. Within minutes a door had opened – not, sadly, the door of his private room – and he had seen, beyond the door, a tremendous opportunity for publicity. He had never needed it more. He might yet be able to save his fortune.

'Siobhan,' said Sir Gordon, 'you're a genius.'

Siobhan McEnery, Head of Corporate Entertainment, and Gavin Welland, Head of PR, came round the next morning. It seemed Sir Gordon's name still carried sufficient clout for normal visiting times to be ignored.

The next morning. It felt like the next year. How the evening had dragged. Why did visiting time in hospital take away almost all capacity for conversation?

With Christina, of course, painful silences had long been the norm. Their everyday life for more than a decade had seemed like visiting time. But he had sensed, last night, that she was softening towards him. 'Oh dear,' she'd said, when she'd seen his condition. 'This rather puts the question of . . . resuming our conjugal relationship . . . on to the back burner, doesn't it?' He'd remembered how she had shocked a dinner party in Godalming, when a loss adjuster had asked where they'd been on their honeymoon, and she had replied, 'Down on each other, mostly.' The loss adjuster, a hard man as loss adjusters have to be, had splattered salmon-and-haddock fish-cake all over the table. And now, sounding utterly absurd in 2011, she talked of 'resuming our conjugal relationship'.

Joanna's arrival hadn't cheered things up enormously.

She'd been easier with him than she had ever been – Christina had raised her eyes in surprise tinged with envy when she'd told her dad how pleased she'd been that he took her to the arboretum – but she wasn't going to turn into Joan Rivers overnight, and Christina was even more surprised when Joanna said, 'Kev sends his best. He's looking forward to meeting you, Dad.'

Luke and Hugo had arrived together, having met, to mutual horror, in the foyer. The sight of either of them entering on his own would have been enough to depress Sir Gordon in his current state, but their entry together had been almost more than he could bear. Yet each of them had unwittingly caused one of the only two moments resembling pleasure that the evening provided.

Hugo had cleared his throat, looked even more solemn than usual, and said, 'This probably isn't the right time to mention it—' and Joanna had interrupted, 'Then perhaps you shouldn't.' She had blushed and apologized, but Sir Gordon had warmed to her even more. The look of utter astonishment on his brother's face had been a delight to see.

And then Luke had said that Emma had wanted to come but he knew it would be like Piccadilly Circus in the room so he'd dissuaded her, and Joanna had asked what she was painting at the moment, and Luke had said, 'It's a secret, she doesn't like to talk about her work too soon, but I can tell you it's going to be even larger in scale than *Rabbit Droppings Near Hornchurch*,' and Sir Gordon had said, 'What is it? Badger droppings?' and Luke's jaw had dropped, and he'd said, 'How on earth did you guess that?'

Oh God, with what fervour he had wanted them to go, and, when they had gone, with what yearning he had wanted them back again.

A nurse built like a shot-putter had lifted him with astonishing gentleness, and lowered him into a new position. Despite her care it had been agonizing. He had felt as a shot would feel when it was put if a shot had nerves. But the new position, what joy it had been – until that in its turn had slowly become uncomfortable, until he had wanted to scream.

If he'd been in a public ward, he would at least have moaned. With luck a nurse would have asked him what he wanted. Here he'd been alone, alone in the world in the middle of a massive hospital, abandoned, cast away. At any moment he could have pulled the bell, but he hadn't. As each slow second of each long minute of each interminable hour ticked by, a man used to having every service provided, every wish fulfilled, every task done for him, had forced himself to live that long night without complaint. Any man can endure a second, and what is a minute composed of but seconds? Any man ought therefore to be able to endure a minute. And what is an hour composed of but minutes? No problem. Tick, tick, tick. He could do it. Tock, tock, tock.

Why had he been so determined to hold out? He'd had plenty of time to consider that question. Because he had feared that he was incapable of courage? Because he didn't want to be the scourge of nurses as he had been of waiters? Because he'd felt guilty? Because he'd felt ashamed? Because he was too proud? Because he was stubborn? Because he was vain? Because his publicity machine would need a photo of him surrounded by smiling nurses as he left the hospital? He was lovely, a model patient, we'll miss him, he gave us all a lovely box of chocolates, he's going to confront the Prime Minister about our wages. There was nothing grand about him. It was like he was one of us.

But oh, the night had been long, and even a man can't think about himself for ever. Sir Gordon had known all along that sleep wouldn't come until he fell into deep slumber five minutes before it was time for them to get him up. He had tried the standby that had served him well in his rare moments of insomnia. Women. He had thought of riding his motorbike from Dudley to Llandudno with Cindy on the back, all those years ago, to have great sex on a great day on the Great Orme. Nothing. No excitement whatsoever. He had thought of Mandy, for whom every day was a bad hair day. Nothing. He had thought of Francesca, sleek and snobbish above her gallery. Nothing. Megan Lloyd-Phillips and her fiery Celtic beauty. Nothing. All the other women he had taken to bed when his diary said that he was at a business meeting. Nothing. The nurse, practising putting the shot on a deserted beach under a full moon in all her buxom nudity. Zilch. Only one woman, of all the women he had met, all the women he had won, all the women he had not managed to conquer – oh, there had been some, quite a few actually, who hadn't been interested in his power and his fame, some who had even been put off by the directness of his manner – only one who that night had given him the slightest feeling of sexuality. Alice Penfold with her ring and her stud. Strange. But even with Alice, lovely Alice, the stirring had been faint. These waiters had bruised his ego, his soul and his prick. Maybe, in the course of their violence, they had actually done him a favour. Maybe they had cured his sex addiction.

Well, morning had come, the sun was shining, he was propped up on three pillows, and now, at last, Siobhan McEnery had arrived, her warmth filling the room.

'Oh dear, oh dear. Just look at you,' she said.

'I don't want to.'

'I'm sorry. I shouldn't have said that. And you know, you don't actually look too bad. So, you wanted to see me. How can I help?'

It was happening again. It was so very odd. He had that image of Ryan again in hospital, a frail, pale, freckled, red-headed baby fighting for his life. And now *he* was fighting for *his* life, but he had to find out about Ryan first. This was ridiculous. He could barely bring himself to ask, so frightened was he of hearing the answer.

'How's the wee mite?'

'Starting not to be so wee. He's all right. He's grand. He's over it all now. He's fine.'

He reached out and patted her thigh, and it occurred to him, even as he did it, that it was the first time he had patted a woman's thigh without any element of sexuality.

'Oh, I'm so pleased,' he said.

'Thank you. It's wonderful the way you care.'

'Yes, it is. It's a source of great wonder to me.'

She gave him a strange look, but he didn't notice. In his relief over Ryan he was free to forget the little boy entirely.

'Have you sorted the mystery of the three journalists with the forged invitations?' she enquired.

'No,' he said. 'I looked through the guest list and I found twenty-seven people I didn't trust. Hopeless.'

'It really wasn't me.'

'Siobhan. Please! I know.'

Gavin Welland arrived, out of breath and looking a little stressed. Unkind people said that he always arrived a few minutes late, out of breath and looking a little stressed, in order to give the impression that he was busy and overworked. Sir Gordon didn't care. He did his job well. People who didn't do their job well didn't stay.

'So sorry I'm late,' said Gavin. 'Busy day. Flaps on all sides.'

'Not a problem. I'm not going anywhere,' said Sir Gordon. 'Now. These waiters. Fame is perceived, not real. Success feeds on success. I need the press on my side over these waiters. I need them badly.'

'You have a plan. I can tell,' said Siobhan.

'I do. I will turn this business to my advantage. With a little help from the two of you. Your flair. Your talent.'

'Thank you, sir. You're too kind,' said Siobhan.

'Not many people have said that. It must be the reason I like you so much. Pull up a chair. Can't leave a woman standing, and your sitting on the bed is not an option in my condition. I'm sure there's a chair for you too, Gavin.'

Siobhan pulled up a chair and sat down. She sat with her legs apart, as women only do when the thought of sex has not even occurred to them. Gavin found a stool with no back, and perched uncomfortably.

'So, how can we help, sir?'

'Siobhan, I want you to book the largest private room in London for a huge dinner party which I will throw.'

'And who is this party for, sir?'

'You know me, Siobhan. You know me, Gavin. You have experience of the way my mind works. You know the press. You both have a feel for publicity. Guess.'

'No pressure, then,' said Gavin.

Siobhan grinned.

'None at all. Seriously. No pressure. Just a bit of . . . well . . . fun. I'll be so excited if you get it.'

'You don't think that's pressure?' said Siobhan.

'Think.'

They thought. Siobhan got there first.

'Waiters,' she said.

'Yes!! Well done.'

She beamed.

'That is a good idea, sir. That's stunning.' She blushed. 'Oh, I shouldn't have said that, since I've just thought it.'

'Not at all.'

To really enjoy a woman's company, and to feel no sexual desire for her, and to know that you needn't feel embarrassed about not feeling any desire, because you know that she knows you don't and she doesn't feel any desire for you, and she knows that you know that, how wonderful that is, how rare it is.

'A dinner for twelve hundred, fifteen hundred waiters, as many as we can fit in,' said Sir Gordon. What do you think, Gavin?'

186

'Brilliant,' said Gavin. 'An apology to the profession, an act of very public remorse. Splendid. With you as one of the waiters.'

'Oh, great. No, that's good.'

'"I never realized what a difficult job it is," says tycoon.'

'Marvellous.'

'A great opportunity for patriotism. An all-British menu. All-British wines.'

'Well done, Gavin. This is starting to look good.'

'Superb,' said Siobhan.

'A lavish menu. No expense spared.'

'May I suggest not lavish, sir?' said Siobhan. 'Generous, but not tactlessly extravagant in hard times.'

'Fine. Point taken. Terrific.'

'Waitresses too?' asked Gavin.

'I don't need remorse over waitresses. I don't think I've ever been rude to them. And none of them beat me up.'

'Maybe,' said Siobhan, 'but an all-male event is dodgy publicity. Some waitresses, I think.'

'OK. I trust your judgement, Siobhan.'

'How do I choose the waiters?' she asked. 'Contact restaurants across the whole spectrum – Fat Duck to greasy spoon?'

'Absolutely. Leave it to them to choose who they can spare. Oh, this is wonderful. It ticks every box. And the world sees me being generous, as if I don't have a financial problem in the world.'

'Which you don't, surely?' said Gavin.

'No. Of course I don't.'

He exchanged a long look with his PR man.

'Brilliant. You must tell the press straight away, Gavin. And you will do this beautifully, Siobhan, it's right up your street.'

'Thank you, sir.'

'Any worries?'

'Absolutely none,' said Siobhan.

'One,' said Gavin.

'Oh? And that is?'

'Who will serve the waiters, sir?'

'Well, waiters.'

'But which waiters? Which waiters are going to be happy to serve meals at the biggest dinner party for waiters the world has ever seen?'

'You don't think they'll all be so moved by my tribute to their profession that they'll be proud to serve?'

'I think they'll be very upset that they've not been invited and have to serve other waiters, and very jealous, and so it will be very divisive.'

'Gavin's right, I'm afraid,' said Siobhan.

'Well, there must be a solution.'

'There is,' she said, 'but it's expensive.'

'Please, Siobhan, I'm not mean. I was never mean. Your solution?'

'You give another, smaller dinner party for the waiters who served at the party for waiters.'

'And who serves them?'

'Waiters who were present at the original party.'

'Tremendous idea,' said Gavin. 'So good that by the time I get back to base it'll be my idea.'

He smiled, to show that he was joking, but neither Sir Gordon nor Siobhan was utterly convinced that he was.

'Siobhan,' said Sir Gordon, 'you're a genius.'

Flat, flat, flat

It's a time for uncomfortable nights. It's agonizing to spend a whole night in a cubicle in a gentlemen's convenience, ready at any moment to raise one's legs above the level of the slit at the bottom of the door, in case the nightwatchman is so diligent that he peers underneath it.

The intruder felt a sense of excitement as he entered the toilet in the evening, just before the art gallery closed. This excitement has long gone. And he doesn't dare fall asleep in case he snores. He's not a regular snorer, but anyone can emit the occasional rasp, and the nightwatchman might have keen hearing.

He curses himself for not owning a watch with an illuminated dial. What kind of a criminal is he? Somehow, though, it has never occurred to him that all the lights would be off in the urinal, in a land where millions of bulbs glow unnecessarily all night.

Every so often the utter silence of the long night is broken by the automatic flushing of the row of urinals. He estimates that this is happening every half-hour. If he is right, it is half past two in the morning. But is he right?

The flushing of the urinals makes him want to pee. Well, the only advantage of his nocturnal location is that he hasn't far to go. But the noise of a stream of urine hitting water can sound deafening in the middle of the night, and he has to direct the flow to the side of the bowl in order to avoid this. And he daren't flush it.

Wryly, he reflects that these considerations are not the stuff of heroism.

He thinks that he has heard the nightwatchman's slow, steady tread three times as he tours the gallery. Now he hears it again. This is clearly a man who takes his duty seriously.

Should he make his move now? No, it's too early. The trick will be to do it after the nightwatchman's last tour of inspection.

The urinals flush three o'clock – he has to trust his calculations. They flush half past three. He feels the need to pee again. They flush four, half past four, five, half . . . Well, you get the idea.

He hears the footsteps again. They fade away. He thinks it must be about ten past six. This is the moment. It's now or never.

He unlocks the door of his cubicle very carefully, tiptoes across the floor of the lavatory in the pitch dark, arms outstretched in front of him. He opens the door very carefully. It gives the faintest squeak, which sounds terrifyingly loud in the silence.

The gallery is in almost total darkness, but the tall windows on the outside wall are not curtained, and a dim, sodium light trickles in from the sleeping town.

He tiptoes to his target, gets a small tin of paint and a brush from his jacket pocket, and opens the tin, which he had eased the day before so that it would open without difficulty.

His task this time is easier. All he has to do is paint two large letters all over the painting. Now for a few moments he is happy. The tedium of the night is forgotten. He paints angrily, rapidly, joyously, orgasmically.

He takes a sharp knife out of the inside pocket of his jacket, and makes three angry incisions on the painting. As he does so, he is shocked by the depth of his hatred.

All the time his heart is racing, and his ears are straining. But nobody comes, nobody hears, nobody sees.

He takes a calculated risk, returning to the gentlemen's toilet by a circuitous route so that he can have a peep at his watch in the stronger sodium light by the windows. He can just make out the time. It's twenty-seven minutes past six. His calculations have been correct.

He tiptoes back to the Gents, opens and closes the door carefully, and breathes a great sigh of relief, just as the urinals strike half past six.

He has, perhaps not surprisingly, taken against the cubicle in which he has spent thirteen and a half hours. He decides to spend the rest of the night in the adjoining one, just for a change.

His hatred has all gone. In retrospect it seems sad, stupid, pointless. His mission has been successful, but he feels flat, flat, flat.

Back into the real world

Sir Gordon was leaving the hospital that morning. He viewed this with very mixed feelings. He had been bored, bored, bored, but he knew that even in his short stay he had become institutionalized, his body had learnt to respond to the rhythms of the place.

Now he had to find the courage to resume his battle for survival. He wasn't ready for such a challenge. His ribs ached. He had a leg and an arm in plaster, his internal bruising was hanging on stubbornly, he was still an ill man.

He had been visited in hospital by Adam Eaglestone, who had shown him the latest figures for GI. Investments had dipped dangerously close to the level of returns when the press had been reporting his sexual shenanigans, with investment by men marginally up, but investment by women hugely down. They had recovered somewhat with Gavin's press release about his dinners for waiters; so now he just had to hang on until the publicity over the dinners reignited the affection the nation felt for him, the boy made good, the patriot, the lovable rogue with a heart of gold.

His telephone rang. He had been allowed to keep and use his mobile.

'Coppinger.'

'Good morning, Sir Gordon. Fred Upson here.'

'Fred! How are you?'

'I'm fine. But how are *you*?'

'Not so bad, but I'm still in hospital, F.U. I don't have access to any expenses forms.'

'Sir Gordon!'

'Sorry. Couldn't resist it. Laughs are few and far between in hospital.'

'I know I have a reputation, but I only ever claim for what's justified.'

'I know you do. I'm only teasing. How can I help you?'

'Have you heard this morning's news?'

It felt as if a clammy hand was grabbing Sir Gordon's neck.

'No. Nobody's brought me a paper yet. What's happened, F.U.?'

'Another of Luke's paintings has been vandalized. In the local gallery.'

'Oh no. What is going on? Somebody somewhere doesn't like me. Or him.'

'Or me.'

'What?'

'There's a different message this time.'

'What message, F.U.?'

'*F.U.*'

'*F.U.*?'

'*F.U.*'

'What do you mean, "*F.U.*", F.U.?'

'I mean that the message scrawled on the painting is just that. Two huge letters. "*F.U.*"'

'Oh dear. Nasty.'

'Painted with anger, apparently, and the usual deep cuts with a knife.'

'Oh dear. Not nice.'

'It looks as though I'm the real target.'

'Well, one of the targets.'

'Who's doing this, Sir Gordon?'

'I don't know. This is a very disturbing development.'

'You're telling me.'

'Somebody who knows the company well enough to know who you are and that I call you F.U.'

'Exactly.'

A porter entered the private room, with a wheelchair.

'They've come for me, Fred. To take me home. In a wheelchair. I'd better go. I'll have everything investigated, Fred. And we'll talk. Rely on me.'

'I do, Sir Gordon. I do. But . . .'

'I hope this is quick, Fred. They're waiting for me.'

'It's just . . . I've never much liked being called F.U. Do you think, after this, you could . . .?'

'Done, Fred. Point taken. Not funny any more.'

'It never was to me.'

'No. Of course not. I'm sorry, Fred. Fred, I mean that. Really sorry. It was childish.'

'Thanks. Give my sympathies to your son, will you?'

'What?'

For a moment Fred Upson's remark made no sense to Sir Gordon.

'Luke. The ruination of his paintings. Such a very personal attack. Must be disturbing.'

'Of course. Of course. Thank you, Fred.'

The porter wheeled Sir Gordon out of his private room into a world of activity, nurses sitting behind a desk strewn with documents, phones going, a doctor striding on long legs, a tiny nurse struggling in his slipstream, a woman with staring eyes and unkempt hair standing in the middle of a corridor looking lost and terrified.

He wanted to go back to his blindingly white, excruciatingly boring room.

They went down in the lift, Sir Gordon in his wheelchair, a nurse beside him carrying his little bag of possessions. On

194

the ground floor there was a shop and a café. He wanted to buy a book in the shop and sit in the café and read. Read anything. He wanted to escape.

The main doors of the hospital slid open at the approach of his wheelchair. A cold wind blew into his face. There was his Rolls-Royce, the rear window repaired already. There was Kirkstall, looking none the worse for his ordeal. But the car wasn't surrounded by smiling nurses holding up placards saying '*We love you, Sir Gordon*'. It was surrounded by cameramen. And camerawomen. Camerapeople. And reporters. A forest of flashlights. A bombardment of questions. He clambered stiffly out of his hospital wheelchair, and limped back into the real world.

An opportunity had been lost

The Christmas decorations were going up. It irritated him that they seemed to go up earlier and earlier every year. It irritated him that he couldn't lift a finger to help. It irritated him most of all that he wouldn't be able to go back to work until after the Christmas holiday at the earliest. He had no talent for idleness, not a shred of interest in any hobby that would take his mind off his frustration at being trapped in his home at this critical time in his fortunes. He limped and snarled round the house like an injured badger.

He told Christina, shying uncharacteristically from the indelicacy, that he was finding it difficult even to wipe his own bottom. He had always done it with his right hand, and now that was impossible. She offered to do it for him, and he was appalled.

'I couldn't have you doing that,' he said. 'You're a lady.'

'Oh, for fuck's sake,' she said. 'Nobody's going to see.'

But that wasn't the reason. He just couldn't bear the thought, the humiliation.

'There's nothing degrading about it, Gordon,' she said. 'Every bum needs wiping.'

I know. Even Garibaldi's.'

She looked at him in astonishment. He had never mentioned Garibaldi to her.

'Garibaldi?'

'He was a great leader. Even great leaders need their bums wiping.'

They got a nurse in to help him undress, wash, shave, wipe his bum, dress. He tried not to feel humiliated. He couldn't. He fancied the nurse. That was dreadful. How could you make advances to someone who has wiped your bum? How could you make advances to a nurse in your own home? He had sworn to be faithful. The nurse went away for the weekend and they got a relief nurse. To his enormous relief he didn't fancy the relief nurse.

Christina sulked because he wasn't allowing her to help. He told her he was sparing her the humiliation. That didn't wash. Nor, when the nurse wasn't there, did he.

'You're beginning to smell sometimes,' said Christina. 'I wish you'd let me do things to you.'

And that only led him to thinking again of the one thing he couldn't do to her, and of all the women he fancied whom he would never have, must never have.

The nights were awful, his flesh crawled under the plaster, he knew – perhaps that is too strong a word – he *sensed* that a massive crisis was brewing, he wanted to get on with it, he wanted to face it and begin to show his mettle, to erase these creeping doubts about whether he was brave enough to show his mettle.

And there was all of Christmas to endure first.

Things were difficult with Farringdon too.

'Ta very much, Brian,' he said when Farringdon brought him his juice at breakfast the first time that he managed to struggle down to breakfast.

'No probs, guv'nor,' said Farringdon in his cockney accent.

197

There was a moment's silence. Neither of them knew what to say next. Farringdon would usually walk straight off, but today they both felt something more was needed.

'What's the weather like, Brian?' asked Sir Gordon.

'Fucking parky, mate. Freeze the knobs off a brass bedstead.'

'Oh blimey. Glad I don't have to go out.'

They were trying to be their real selves, and it was sounding stilted and ghastly, like a cockney script written by a man who had never been further east than the Strand. They sounded less real, as their idea of what their real selves were, than they did as the characters they had allowed themselves to grow into.

'Brian?' he said when Farringdon brought him his toast.

'Yeah, Gordon?'

'May I ask you something?'

'Course.'

'I think I'm beginning to get better.'

'Great stuff, Gordon.'

'Do you know why I feel that?'

'Haven't a fu . . . sorry. Haven't a clue, mate.'

'You can swear in front of me, Brian. Expect at home you always swear all the time.'

'That's at home, innit? This is here. Doesn't seem right, not at breakfast. Not in this 'ouse. Not talking to you. Can't bleeding do it, know what I mean? You was saying you was feeling better, did I know why, and I don't, so, tell me, Gordon. Why?'

'I'm feeling better because I wake up feeling unbelievably randy, Brian. And I was thinking, you, Brian, man of the world, you must have felt randy sometimes when it wasn't the right moment.'

'All the time, Gordon. Don't tell me about it.'

'Well, what do you do about it?'

'I think about things that aren't sexy.'

'Sometimes I think everything's sexy. What isn't sexy?'

'Dunno. Not when you put me on the spot like this, sir.'

'Don't call me sir.'

'I find it difficult, sir, cos . . . well . . . that's what you are. Biscuits.'

'What?'

'I think of biscuits. Cos I don't find biscuits sexy, sir.'

'Not even Hobnobs?'

'Not even Hobnobs.'

'What else, Brian?'

'I dunno, sir. I'm . . . Sir, you're not going to like this, but . . . I can't do this.'

'You can't do what?'

'I can't butle when you call me Brian.'

'Butle?'

'Be a butler.'

'Ah. Slow there.'

'I'm not comfortable when I don't call you sir, sir. It don't seem right. It don't seem appropriate, know what I mean?'

'I actually know what you mean very well, Brian.'

'I mean, I suppose if we went out on the piss together you could call me Brian and that would be all right, but in here, with the silver condiments and that, and the fancy napkins and all, I don't know if I can do it if I'm Brian, sir. I'd much rather you called me Farringdon.'

'I see. Oh well.'

'You're disappointed.'

'Well . . . not really. No, I have to admit you're right. It doesn't sound right you calling me just Gordon . . . It sounds . . . naked. I might want to be just Gordon but I'm not.'

'Exactly, sir. Wellingborough, sir.'

'What?'

'Wellingborough.'

'Wellingborough?'

'My auntie lives there. In my opinion it is not a sexy place. Imagining I'm in Wellingborough does it for me, sir.'

'I don't think it would do it for me. I've never been there.

It's hard to imagine a place you've never been to. I might add a brothel or two and then I'd feel really sexy.'

'I'm sorry, sir.'

'No, no, Farringdon. You did your best.'

'Thank you, sir. And I will set my mind to thinking of other, perhaps more efficacious aids to celibacy.'

'Thank you very much, Farringdon.'

Farringdon was Farringdon again, and seemed to be relieved. Sir Gordon was Sir Gordon again, and although he too felt elements of relief, he also felt rather sad. He felt that an opportunity had been lost.

He would need a long,
hot bath

Christmas Day arrived at last at Rose Cottage. Sir Gordon awoke early, and with a feeling of slight dread.

In his youth, when he had seized every moment in which it was possible to earn money, he had once worked as a temporary Christmas postman. There had been a delivery on Christmas Day. Trains and buses had run on Christmas Day. On Christmas Eve, Hugo, Jack, and he had helped, with huge excitement, to put up pastel-coloured streamers across the walls of their little terraced house in Dudley. Now the decorations had been up in the streets for almost two months and in most houses for about three weeks, and many people seemed to have been on holiday for at least a week. He was tired of it all before it had even begun. We lived now in a world of vast excess, and he lived in more of a world of excess than almost everybody, and he hated it, but he was trapped, trapped, trapped.

Sir Gordon's memories of his childhood Christmases were not all good. He'd been driven frantic by those long afternoons and evenings when everyone was far too full of food, and a huge, slow-moving anticlimax had settled over the British Isles.

Christmas Day at Rose Cottage ran to a very different and very rigid routine. A late, full English breakfast, a walk into the village to be seen at church and to post handwritten letters of condolence through the front doors of villagers who had suffered any kind of misfortune in the past twelve months, a walk back from the village. Visitors were invited to arrive between half past two and three, at which time they listened to the Queen's Speech. Then they were served tea and a small slice of Christmas cake. At four o'clock the champagne would be opened with a flourish, they would toast absent friends, and then Sir Gordon would start handing out the presents which had been sitting under a tree so large it might almost have been a present from Norway. At half past five they would sit down to their Christmas dinner. Today there would be eight of them – Sir Gordon, Christina, Hugo, Luke, Emma, Clarrie, Joanna . . . and Kev. Yes, today they were going to meet Joanna's boyfriend at last.

As he lay there, feeling sexually aroused, Sir Gordon hit upon a subject for reflection that proved far more successful in dousing his desires than either biscuits or Wellingborough. He thought about the products of his factories, and how they had performed in the shops in the run-up to Christmas. There had been a welcome lull in press coverage of his doings, a reassuring stability in the affairs of Gordon Investments, where the feared rush of Christmas withdrawals had not happened. He had no firm figures for sales of his products, but it was already clear that there had been no seasonal bonanza. 'Patchy' had been the uninspiring adjective most favoured by his sales people.

Sales of some products like S'ssh! were unaffected by Christmas – very few people were such unromantic cheapskates as to wrap a household lubricant as a gift. Equally, the hoi polloi were not likely to be able to afford to give many Coppinger Electric Cars. Kettles were perhaps more possible as a gift, but it seemed as though his kettles had remained in the shops in great numbers, staring out at the high streets like rows of bored penguins. Also, there was every indication that his new alternative-energy toy range had failed to please. Very few children would, it seemed, be unwrapping little wind farms, or doll's houses with solar panels. So much for the caring middle classes, thought Sir Gordon. On the other hand, sales of his National Espresso coffee machines, fuelled by the simple slogan *'Coppinger* – The *name for Coffee'*, had been lively, and considering they were a new line this year, the Christmas puddings launched by Porter's Potteries Pies had done reasonably well. Elsewhere, in the worlds of carpets, electrical goods, jams, and settees, things had at best been flat. He particularly regretted having gone into settees. If you ever watched commercial television, you realized that Britain was a nation awash with unsold settees.

All in all, a happy result for a man seeking to dampen his sexual ardour, but not sufficiently consoling to a man who is beginning to wake up to the fact that he has overreached himself and that there may be a rocky road ahead.

At last he felt that it was late enough for him to get up. He switched his bedside light on, leant over, kissed Christina on the cheek, and said, 'Happy Christmas, darling.'

'Happy Christmas, Gordon.'

Promising. Not very promising – she hadn't said 'darling' – but her saying 'Gordon' had invested the words with at least a degree of warmth. With any luck she wasn't going to be awkward about their change of plan. He didn't think he could bear it if she was awkward today.

Part of the change of plan had been forced on him by his injuries. He could hardly have walked to the village and back. Actually, it was a good excuse as he had begun to realize how absurdly feudal that walk, and those letters of condolence, must seem to the village in the twenty-first century. He'd bought Rose Cottage, not inherited it, and, bizarrely, in Britain, in country circles, it was far more prestigious to inherit a house you couldn't afford to run than to buy one with your own money and live in luxury in it. Also, it had dawned on him that the last thing these good people wanted just before their Christmas dinner was to be reminded of their misfortunes. Seeing things from another person's point of view was still a novelty to him. Sometimes, as now, it disturbed him.

The rest of the change of plan was altogether more controversial. He wasn't going to church. He was being driven by Kirkstall, through the quiet Christmas morning streets, to his brother Hugo's house in Eaton Square, and from there, he and Hugo would go in search of their younger brother, Jack. They would be back, of course, in time for the Queen's Speech.

Sir Gordon didn't believe in God – he went to church because he thought it was what the people from the Big House should do in a village – and, to be fair to him, he was no longer so convinced of his own importance as to have thought, if he had believed in God, that the Almighty would have had time to arrange for him to find Jack just because it was Christmas Day. Nevertheless, he had an absolute conviction that he would find him, and he took three enticingly wrapped presents with him, after a splendid breakfast, with Lady Coppinger utterly charming, almost in parody of a Lady of the Manor, in full 'Would you be so kind as to pass me the marmalade?' mode.

Hugo drove; he didn't trust anybody else with *his* Rolls. The weather was mild and grey, not at all Christmassy, and parts of London felt as if they had been evacuated due to the approach of some huge natural disaster. They couldn't drive everywhere, of course. They kept having to park so that Hugo could explore narrow alleys, and dark arches, and windy parks, and all the places where bearded, smelly people lay in bundles of old rags, or sat staring blankly at the inhospitable scene, or held out their hands in the hope of seasonal charity. Sir Gordon had to sit in the car and wait, nursing his injured leg and having thoughts that were as dark as the alleys.

As they drove, Sir Gordon plucked up his courage – how strange that this confident man now needed to find strength in order to ask simple questions – and said, 'You said you might be able to provide finance to set up Gordon Investments on a sound basis, Hugo. May I ask how that's going?'

Hugo paused a while before replying, and Sir Gordon remembered that he always had, and how it had infuriated him as a boy. Weighing up his responses. How irritating was that?

'Slowly,' said Hugo slowly. 'Very slowly. These things take time. Several banks are involved. It's far from a good time for some banks. They need assurances, assurances which under the circumstances aren't easy to give. We're getting there, we really are getting there, Gordon. I won't let you down, I promise.'

The irritation melted away. For all their differences, they got on pretty well. Sir Gordon realized, perhaps for the first time, on that strange Christmas morning, that among all his complicated feelings for his brother there was love, despite that disturbing sense of inferiority which Hugo did nothing to dispel.

It was unfortunate that Hugo chose that very moment to confirm that it was now definite that he was going to get a bonus.

'Oh, well done. How much?'

'Two point three million.'

'Not bad.'

'Deserved, Gordon. That's what those cretins out there don't understand.'

'I'm not a cretin, Hugo, but I'm not an economist or a banker either. In what way is it deserved?'

'I have saved the bank far more than two point three million. Far more. I just dread it getting into the press. The cretins will have a field day if it does.'

'I'm not going to tell.'

'Of course not, but other people know and I have enemies.'

Hugo parked his Rolls for the seventh time that morning, at the edge of an arch behind Charing Cross Station. A bundle of brown rags stirred, rose like an Indian rope trick, grabbed a bottle of meths, belched, and said, 'Fuck off.'

Jack.

Hugo helped Sir Gordon out of the car, and handed him his crutches. He struggled slowly over towards Jack.

The boy with the slightly delicate features was unrecognizable. The young man with the beard that had always underlined the weakness of his face rather than hiding it had disappeared. Here was a man 120 years old, with long straggly yellowing hair. As he unravelled in front of their eyes he gave off a stench of piss, shit, sweat, and alcohol. This was their brother.

A very tall, extremely thin man, a pencil of a man, a skeleton of a man, stood and watched their meeting, watched with a look in his eyes that was deeply disturbing – knowing, intelligent, caustic, eyeing them as if they were the gates of hell. His smile was a rictus of despair. His presence, his nearness, his interest made Sir Gordon's blood run cold.

'Don't be nasty, Jack,' he said. 'It's Christmas.'

He wished he hadn't said that, even before Jack said, 'Not for me it fucking isn't.'

'I know. I know. Jack, we've brought you some presents.'

'I don't want your fucking presents.'

'We've brought you our fucking presents because we care about you,' said Hugo.

'Couldn't resist showing me your fucking Roller, eh? Bastards.'

'No,' said Sir Gordon. 'No! Please, Jack, not at all.'

'It's the only car I have,' said Hugo.

'My heart bleeds for you,' said Jack.

'Please give us a chance,' said Sir Gordon.

'Give you a chance? What chance did you give me?' shouted Jack.

'Every chance. We've tried to help. You wouldn't accept it,' shouted Sir Gordon.

'We've made overtures in good faith. You've rejected them all,' said Hugo.

Their words were snowballs which splattered against the wall of Jack's hatred and then disintegrated.

'Please accept our presents, Jack,' pleaded Hugo.

'Don't try to give me things,' said Jack. 'You think giving me things can make me forget what you took away from me, you fucking bastards.'

'We've tried before, Jack,' said Sir Gordon, 'and now we're trying again. It may not be much, but we've dragged ourselves from the warmth of our homes to come and see you.'

He felt the absurdity of his words even as he spoke them, so he wasn't surprised by Jack's reply.

'Well, try dragging yourselves back again, will you?'

'Anyway, I'm leaving the presents,' said Sir Gordon. 'There's a bottle of decent wine, and a scarf and gloves in case it gets cold this winter as they forecast.'

'Oh. Fantastic. That's changed my life,' shouted Jack.

Sir Gordon felt that he was about two foot high. How come it was a boxing match? How come Jack was winning every round? How could all this be?

'Now if you fucking asked me home . . .' said Jack.

'You know we can't do that, Jack,' said Hugo.

'Hugo!' said Sir Gordon.

'What?'

'Jack's right. That's the only thing that could make any difference now.' He turned to Jack. 'Come home with us. Come now.'

Hugo led Sir Gordon away from Jack, till they were almost out of earshot. Jack watched them like a wary urban fox.

'You can't do this. Think of Christina.'

'I know. Difficult.'

'Think of Joanna, bringing her boyfriend for the first time.'

'It might relax him. Seeing the problem that's Dad. Meeting the problem that's Jack. He'd be relegated to disappointment number three.'

'Oh, Gordon, it's not possible. Look at the state of him.'

'I know. You'd need the Roller fumigating.'

'It isn't that.'

'I know. But I have to do it, Hugo.'

Sir Gordon broke away and returned to Jack.

'Well?' said Jack. 'What have you decided?'

'I'm asking you back. With us. Now. I mean it.'

'It's too late.'

'It's only quarter past twelve.'

He regretted his stupid joke even before it fractured on Jack's scorn.

'Please, Jack. I really do mean it.'

'I believe you do,' said Jack much more quietly. 'I really believe you do, Gordon. But no. It really is too late.'

'Please.'

'Can't you understand English? It's too fucking late.'

Afterwards, Sir Gordon wondered if he should have pressed still more. But he took Jack's refusal with an element of gratitude and relief. He had tried. He had meant it, but . . . perhaps it was just as well. Christina. Dad. Joanna. Perhaps it was just as well.

'I'll be back,' he said.

'Take your fucking presents. They're an insult,' said Jack.

'OK.'

'But thank you.'

Sir Gordon looked at Jack and suddenly wanted to hug him. He moved forward.

'Don't hug me. I don't want you to. I stink. Get away from me.'

Jack looked terrified.

'Right. Right. But we'll be back, Jack.'

'We'll be back,' echoed Hugo.

They walked back to the car, Sir Gordon painfully slow on his crutches, Hugo not daring to offer help to his obstinate brother. They had to pass the tall, thin, yellow man. His grin was terrible, and constant, as if it had been knitted on to his face.

As they got into the Rolls, Sir Gordon let out a huge, long sigh. In his sigh there was relief, disgust, regret, hope. Too many emotions all at once.

He felt that, when he got home, he would need a long, hot bath.

There was no chance

It had not been the best of Christmases, but it had not been the worst either. But oh, he was tired. He had tried too hard, he had realized that he was trying too hard, he had tried too hard not to try too hard, it had all been exhausting.

Christina had tried too. She also had tried too hard, realized that she was trying too hard, had tried too hard not to try too hard, and she was exhausted too. He was very grateful to her. With the gratitude came desire.

It might not be easy, with a leg in plaster and an arm in plaster, but in a few minutes he was going to do something he hadn't done for over a year. He was going to make love to his wife.

Did they perhaps fear that this might be their last Christmas?

They sat by the west fire, staring at its dying embers as if they expected something dramatic to happen, separated yet united by their exhaustion, a million miles away from each other, yet closer than they had been for ages.

'Clarrie get to bed all right?' she asked.

'Yep. It was extraordinary. He had a moment of complete clarity.'

'Clarrie's clarity.'

'Yes.' He gave a half-laugh. 'I was tucking him up, as if he was a child, which he is, and he said, "They weren't bad, those Christmases in Chorley Avenue, were they?"'

'Good Lord.'

'I know.'

Good Lord. Shorthand for 'Good Lord, after his not even knowing who you were earlier, that's barely credible.'

I know. Shorthand for 'The tricks the brain plays really are quite extraordinary, but wasn't it awful, that moment?'

They were talking in a married couple's shorthand, there in the last warmth of the embers. They hadn't done that for a long while either.

Yes, it had happened, the moment he'd dreaded, and it had happened so suddenly and so directly that he had been stunned. He had approached his father with a present, he had been on the point of saying, 'For you, Dad,' and his father had said, 'I don't know who you are, but you're very kind.'

Sir Gordon repeated the scene to himself now, beside the west fire. Was Christina repeating it to herself too?

'Dad, I'm your son. Gordon.'

'Ah, yes. Yes, of course. Of course. Yes. I got muddled, Gordon. I thought that was my son over there.'

'That is, Dad. That's Hugo.'

'Ah. Yes. Hugo.' And then, astonishingly, 'Where's Jack?'

Lying in a bundle of rags by the Embankment.

'He couldn't come, Dad. He's on duty.'

'Ah. Shame. Well, better open this, I suppose.'

The awful thing about the presents was that there had been so few for Kev. The piles had mounted, and there had been almost nothing for him. He hadn't looked embarrassed, though. He'd sat there, quietly, speaking when spoken to, smiling when something was amusing, and just occasionally when it wasn't. Not a bad-looking lad, really, for a postman.

It was as if Christina had read his thoughts. That hadn't happened for a long time either.

'So, Gordon, our daughter is in love with a postman.'

'In love?'

'I think so. Don't you?'

'I don't know. I don't think recognizing love is one of my greatest talents.'

'No.'

Silence.

'Are you shocked?'

'I'm disappointed, Gordon. Aren't you?'

'Well, I suppose so, but . . . I mean, I suppose I'm disappointed that Joanna is so . . . what's the word?'

'Disappointing?'

'Well, yes, I suppose so. Well, no, I don't really. I just mean, I wish she found life easier. Christina, don't take this the wrong way, but thank you for hiding what you felt about Kev.'

'What do you mean?'

'I could see you thinking, We've come so far and our daughter's marrying a postman.'

'Marrying?'

'I expect so. I hope so. What else is there for her? And he's a very nice postman. The nicest postman I ever met.'

Silence.

'Actually, probably the only postman I ever met.'

They shared a little laugh. What a night it was becoming, there by the dying west fire, for things that hadn't happened for a long time.

'Do you know what she said?' he asked.

'How could I?'

'Yes. Stupid the things we say. She said, "Kev is gentle, and he's a man, and I think those things together make a gentleman."'

'Joanna said that?'

'Yep. She said, "He gives nice presents to customers who've been good to him when they move home."'

212

'Good Lord.'

'I know.'

Silence.

'Maybe he doesn't need to stay a postman. Maybe you can give him a job.'

That would be irresponsible. He'd be safer as a postman. The thought struck Sir Gordon like a container full of kettles.

Silence.

'Well, what am I going to tell Lady Carberry? What am I going to tell Mrs Fitch in the village?'

'Oh, Christina.'

Silence.

'Then there's Emma. "How are your children doing?" "Oh, terribly well, Lady Carberry. Joanna's marrying a postman, and Luke's shagging a girl somewhat to the left of Lenin who's currently working on a painting called *Badger Droppings in Wiltshire*." Gordon, is this what we left Dudley for?'

'OK, but we have a good life.'

So far.

Silence. Sir Gordon thought about how he had once considered trying to steal Emma off Luke. It seemed like years ago. It had been on Guy Fawkes Night. Fifty days ago. Today, looking at that square jaw, set in defensive mode against the insults she anticipated from the world in response to the insults she had heaped upon the world, he hadn't been able to believe what he had thought then.

Silence.

'Hugo was on good form.'

'Yes.'

Silence. Nothing more to say about Hugo, it seemed.

The fire was really dying now. The colour was draining from its cheeks.

'Time to go to bed.'

'Yes.'

213

She gave him her arm, and he limped to the lift. There had been much debate over installing a lift, all those years ago. He was glad now that they had.

They entered the master bedroom, that vast, pale pink, frilly, feminine room. She helped him undress. It was Christmas Day, and tonight there was no nurse.

He felt shy. He felt embarrassed about letting his own wife see his body. How absurd was that?

They washed at the two adjoining basins, side by side, she totally nude, he nude except for plaster. He cast a quick glance at those legs that had been described as no longer quite so slim. The sight of the fullness of the thighs excited him. He could feel himself getting erect. The erection embarrassed him.

He cleaned his teeth more thoroughly than he had done for months.

He struggled into bed.

She came towards the bed. He gazed at her. Her stomach was no longer quite so flat. And she was blushing.

She climbed into the bed beside him. She didn't look at him, but her hand stroked his good arm.

'Are you feeling a bit shy?' he asked.

'Slightly. Isn't that ridiculous?'

'Very. I am too. Oh, Christina.'

It was absurd. He was too shy to kiss her breasts, suck her nipples, run his hand between her legs. And, when he touched her, he could feel her stiffen. He was the only one who should stiffen. As he had.

The only thing he wasn't too shy to do was to clamber on top of her. It wasn't easy. He had to keep his right leg off her body. The touch of plaster was not known to be sexy.

To begin again, how hard it was. To return to those years of sexual pleasure was all the more difficult because of all those years. He hadn't dreamt that it would be like that. She opened her not quite so slim legs as if by rote. He attempted

214

to enter her. He realized that it wasn't going to work. Had Mandy and Francesca and all those other women come between them? Had it been impossible for her to forgive and forget? Was this an act of bravery on her part, rather than desire? Was it just too difficult with all the plaster? Would even Garibaldi have found it difficult with a leg and an arm in plaster? Garibaldi. Where had he sprung from?

Now that Garibaldi was in the bed with them there was no chance.

It's wasted already

One couldn't have said that the early days of 2012 were happy days exactly, not for the world, not for Britain, and not for Sir Gordon Coppinger. But they weren't the worst days that the world has known, or that Britain has known, and they weren't the worst days that Sir Gordon had known either, or was soon to know. They were best described, perhaps, as the Doldrums. Not much fun, but perhaps to be cherished none the less, in view of the storms that were to come.

He did face, however, one great problem. It was the problem many men have faced and many men will face. It was – there's no getting away from it, there's no way of avoiding it – the problem of sex.

With Christina there was an uneasy, slightly embarrassed peace, but embarrassment was so much more pleasant than hostility that he barely felt it to be embarrassing. They had come a long way together in these last weeks. They had managed to cobble together some kind of construction out of the rubble of their love. Their love was like a precious vase that has been broken, discarded, found in the back of a cupboard and carefully but not entirely successfully restored. It might look all right on a table, but if you put flowers and water in it you would find that it leaked. They were tender together. Sir Gordon knew that Christina was being more tender than he deserved, in view of his revelations. There was something about her again of the old Christina. But there was the problem of sex.

He pretended to himself that his broken leg was the cause of his impotence with her, but he knew in his heart that it was not so. He knew in his heart that he was inhibited in the present because the present just could not live up to the past. It was overwhelmed by the past. He thought of suggesting that they should go out to dinner and pretend that it was a first date, that they knew nothing about each other. But he knew it wouldn't work. It would be altogether too twee a procedure.

It was all so ridiculous. His desire for all the other women there had been in his life grew and grew. He had never been celibate for any length of time before. But he had promised Christina – and the nation through the press – and he would not break that promise.

He was a sex addict without sex.

The absence of Mandy hurt him physically. The thought of Francesca's body was so disturbing that he felt that he would continue to have difficulty walking even after the removal of the plaster from his leg. As for Alice Penfold, he had to pass her every morning. It was agony. His only consolation was that he knew that if she hadn't got her ring and her stud it would have been an even greater agony.

He longed to talk to another human being about all this, but to whom could he talk? Other men had friends. He'd been too busy to have friends. He could talk to Farringdon, but not intimately. The two of them had tried to be intimate and natural in each other's presence, to be their real selves with each other, and it hadn't worked. He needed a man he could unburden his soul to in a quiet corner of a crowded pub. He knew no such man.

217

The only person he could unburden himself to was his brother. They met at an upmarket Indian restaurant. Indian restaurants were fine for patriots, curry having been subsumed into British culture. The Cardamom Queen specialized in street food twenty-seven times more expensive than it would have been in any street. The tables were widely spaced and separated by oriental screens. The service was excessive.

'I had to choose somewhere so expensive that nobody left wing could afford it,' said Hugo. 'My photo was in the papers today.'

'I know. The bonus.'

'Some bastard leaked it. And they've all chosen the smuggest photos they could find. I won't give it back. I will not. I've earned it. It's my right.'

'It doesn't help either of us. Yet more press coverage for Coppingers. Yet more bad press coverage for Coppingers.'

'No. Too true. So what is it you want to discuss, Gordon?'

It's very hard to talk about the intimate details of one's sex life when a sip of water is poured into your glass every time you have taken a sip. And there was that other matter to be discussed, and that too must not be overheard. Sir Gordon decided to get that out of the way first. It was, after all, hugely more important.

'How . . . um . . .' Oh God, why did he feel so nervous about this? Because he had never begged before, he'd never had to beg before. 'How . . . um . . . are you getting on with the . . . you know . . . the . . .' Hugo gleamed and listened and didn't help him out and for a moment Sir Gordon almost hated him. '. . . the . . . well, the rescue package, I suppose I'd have to call it.'

'Gordon, the important thing is . . .' Hugo paused while his water glass was topped up. '. . . that when we do offer you a sum, it's sufficient. More than sufficient. If it isn't, it fails, you're down the drain, the money's lost, wasted. We're talking an enormous sum here. I wouldn't mention it in a restaurant. Look, I'm getting there. Believe me. Next week I'm going out to . . .' He paused while his wine glass was topped up. '. . . St Helier, and from there to Zurich. After that I'll know more. What I'm trying to do isn't easy, Gordon. These are difficult times, and this is a difficult sell. We're talking of rescuing you from a scam, Gordon, and nobody wants to get their fingers burnt. I'm afraid you just have to hang on and be patient. I'm doing all I can for my little brother.'

'I know you are. I'm sorry.'

'Was that it?'

'"It"?'

'Was that what you wanted to discuss?'

'Oh. No. It was . . . thank you.' He paused while the waiter opened their napkins for them. 'Thank you.'

The waiter moved off.

'I wish they didn't hover so much,' said Sir Gordon, 'but I can't afford to be rude to waiters this week with the big dinner coming up. I'm trapped.'

'Don't talk about it. Tell me quickly before one of them comes back.'

'It's . . . sex.'

'Ah!'

'That was an enigmatic "Ah!"'

'Was it?'

You secretive bastard.

Sir Gordon told Hugo about his problems with Christina. He told him that he was going to stick to his promise not to be unfaithful.

'I don't know about you,' he said, 'but . . .'

'But here come the starters.'

'Oh God.'

After the waiters had given them their chickpea fritters in the manner of Nagpur's market district Sir Gordon described to Hugo the depth of his frustration.

'What about . . .?' It was Hugo's turn to hesitate. These were men of the world, they were brothers, it should be easy. 'What about . . . mast . . .?' And then a waiter was there again, topping up. At last he was gone. '. . . urbation?'

Hugo looked very embarrassed. Sir Gordon felt that he had been relieved not to have had to say the whole word in one go. This evasiveness angered him and stimulated him.

'It doesn't work for me,' he said. 'I tried this morning, but I was playing hard to get.'

Hugo smiled faintly. It was his I'm-afraid-top-bankers-don't-find-that-sort-of-coarseness-terribly-funny smile. There had always been something irritatingly prudish about Hugo.

'I don't know about you,' Sir Gordon said, 'but I've had wonderful sex.' He paused, as if remembering. 'I adore women. I suppose I've been lucky.' He had no idea about Hugo's sex life. He'd tried to draw him out with his 'I don't know about you', but it hadn't worked, and he realized that he wasn't going to be told anything. How could he plough on without encouragement, without reaction, without any kind of information? But he did plough on. 'Sexual fantasy just doesn't work for me. I've had too much of the real thing.' He wasn't meaning to boast, but he was aware that it sounded like boasting. Did Hugo have problems? Was he just alienating his brother? He'd meant to ask his elder brother for help, it wasn't turning out like that, it was going wrong, it would be better to stop. 'I just don't know how to cope, Hugo.'

'I'm not the man to ask about such things,' said Hugo.

What was he to read into that? He told Hugo about Farringdon's suggested method of concentrating hard on things that weren't sexy. Hugo had no better offer to make. He wished that he hadn't raised the subject with him.

As he tucked into his quail served on the bone in the style of the roadside stalls in the legal district of Jaipur, he realized that Farringdon was his best, indeed his only, bet.

'While we're here,' said Hugo, lowering his voice ominously

220

as if they were about to embark on a subject even more personal than sex, 'while we're here, you promised me, the last time we had dinner together – the night you were attacked – you promised me that there were no more skeletons in your cupboard.'

Sir Gordon's heart began to fibrillate. It was coming.

'I did, yes.' He could hear just a faint hoarseness in his voice. Hugo knew. So why deny it?

'I have heard talk about Germophile,' said Hugo.

Sir Gordon couldn't breathe. His throat was closing. His claustrophobia was enveloping him like fog.

'Germophile?' He feigned astonishment.

'People are wondering if it was a case of pump and dump.'

'I don't even know what that is, Hugo.'

'Oh, Gordon, don't pretend to be so naive. You bought into the development of a wonder cleansing agent called Germophile. Don't pretend you don't remember. There was talk that one application on a hard surface could kill bacteria for a month. There was talk of its wiping MRSA off the map.'

God, those hopes. The prospect of such glory. Anyone could have been carried away. He just didn't want to talk to Hugo about it. Not now. It was too painful.

'Of course I remember. It didn't work. There were side effects. It turned out not to be feasible.'

'In the meantime you had bought into a crap company near Great Yarmouth, you announced that you were going to explore the making of Germophile there, shares rocketed, it proved unfeasible, shares plummeted, people lost a lot. It's being suggested that you and your cronies sold out at the top and made millions, and hid the fact that it didn't work till you'd safely dumped your shares. People are saying . . .'

Sir Gordon felt an urgent need to interrupt. He looked round for a waiter, and Hugo hesitated.

'Need more wine,' said Sir Gordon.

The wine bottle was empty. Suddenly there wasn't a waiter

to be seen. It was the way of waiters all over the world; it was like police sirens, they kept you awake every night until it was your turn to be burgled.

At last he managed to attract a waiter's attention.

'People are saying', resumed Hugo when at last the wine had been brought, examined, recognized, opened, swirled, and poured, 'that you never intended to process Germophile.'

Sir Gordon exploded.

'Never intended? Never intended to be the one to save people from fatal hospital infections all over the globe? Are you mad? Are you out of your mind, Hugo?'

'All right,' said Hugo hurriedly. 'All right. I'm pleased to hear you say this. I'm pleased to see you so angry. I'm re-assured. I believe you. I'm sorry, Gordon, but I had to be sure. You're asking for a vast sum and my people are going through everything with a toothcomb.'

They finished the meal talking about easier subjects, about their mother, sadly and safely dead, and about their father Clarrie and their brother Jack, sadly and not safely alive. They both knew that they could have been doing more for Clarrie and Jack, so neither of them could feel embarrassed or triumphant on the subject in each other's company. Both knew it was a safe subject for conversation, just so long as the conversation didn't lead to their planning to do anything.

He realized that for discussion of the problem of sex, Farringdon was his only option. This made him feel very lonely. A wave of regret passed over him for all the thousands of conversations with Jack that he had never had, but should have had.

Next morning he asked Farringdon if he had any ideas of other unsexy subjects for him to concentrate on.

'You might find post offices a helpful resort in this connec-tion, sir,' suggested Farringdon. He was the consummate butler again. No vestige of Brian remained. Yet things had changed, in that Sir Gordon knew of the existence of the invisible Brian, in that they both knew that their exchanges were not entirely real, that they were performing a stately conversational dance together, and would have to for as long as they were master and butler. Not a happy thought. 'In my experience post offices are blessedly devoid of sexuality.'

'I have a problem with that,' said Sir Gordon. 'It's at least thirty-five years since I was in a post office.'

Little Chefs were another suggestion. Again, Sir Gordon had no real experience of them.

'My sheltered life is becoming a disadvantage,' he said.

Motorway service stations proved more useful. He could imagine those. He had failed to avoid them entirely in his travels.

'Tax demands,' continued Farringdon.

Sir Gordon felt that it would be insensitive to tell this hard-working and honourable man that the tax demands he received, though not pleasant, were so much less than they should have been that he actually found thinking about them quite stimulating.

Nevertheless, and not without difficulty, he did construct for himself a short list of aids to sexlessness. In fact, the very game of selecting things that were sexless became a distraction in itself, and thus turned into another aid to sexlessness. It developed into a bit of an obsession. He decided to make an alphabet of it – his ABC – his Alphabet of Boons to Celibacy. On the one hand, one might say that nothing could indicate more clearly how he had changed than that this most purposeful of men should spend so much time in such an apparently fatuous pursuit. However, one might also look at it as evidence of his continuing purposefulness that he could use such a seemingly time-wasting enterprise for practical ends.

It may seem indulgent to go into detail on this subject when so many events are about to crowd in upon Sir Gordon's life, but his highly subjective list is quite revealing about his character, and, besides, since such chaos is soon to fall upon his head, it's only compassionate to linger for just a little while on this period of comparative calm.

The first complete version of Sir Gordon's Alphabet of Boons to Celibacy was Asparagus (by making your pee smell it should render the penis vaguely unattractive, and as it comes up an asparagus bed looks disturbingly like rows of green penises emerging from the soil); Boils (particularly those on Keith Gostelow's neck); Clamping of cars; Dentists; Enemas (he could imagine that these might excite some people, but surely not the British?); Finland; Garage forecourts; Hobbies (all hobbies, notably trainspotting, stamp collecting and golf, seemed the epitome of sexlessness to Sir Gordon); Isthmuses (an ugly word, and the least prepossessing of all land formations in geography); Junket (his mother Margaret had believed junket was good for the treatment and the prevention of sore throats, so you had it whenever you had a sore throat and whenever you hadn't); Kettering (it sounded more like a process than a place. 'Are we going kettering tomorrow?'); Luke (there is a reason which will become clear very soon); Morris dancers (to handle phallic symbols in a dance and still not be sexy was quite an achievement); Nails (he had a phobia about having his toenails cut); Orpington; Parables (so smug and so pat); Quorn (the meat substitute); Roses (too many in his life due to Christina); Swindon; Tattoos; Undertakers; Volvos; Wellington boots; X-rays; Youth clubs (he had never found one he could bear to go to twice in the whole of that great lost opportunity, his youth); and Zoos (he hated to see people staring and pointing at animals).

And so he managed to survive from day to day. Joanna got engaged to Kev. Sir Gordon walked past Alice Penfold and thought about having his toenails cut by a stamp-collecting Morris dancer in Orpington. The plaster was removed from his leg and arm. That night, he and Christina had an awkward little hug. She stroked his prick. It stiffened, but not enough. She gave his sound arm an affectionate stroke, gave him a very quick kiss on the cheek, and turned her face away from him. He suspected that she might be crying.

He attended, and served as a waiter at, the greatest dinner for waiters the world has ever seen, in the Dorchester on Park Lane. The press coverage was immense. He learnt how very easy it is to be a waiter, and how very difficult it is to be a good waiter. The waiters and waitresses ate potted Morecambe Bay shrimps, roast Hereford beef with Yorkshire pudding and horseradish, sherry trifle and English cheeses. They drank English wine, Welsh cider and Scottish whisky.

Sir Gordon recognized the waiters who had served him in the Intrepid Snail, the Hoop and Two Colonels, the Dog and Duck and Oliver's Oven. He apologized to all four of them individually. They lapped up his charm and their dinner. Two days later, the same menu was served, in a smaller function at the same hotel, to all the waiters who had served at the first meal. The only person to wait at table at both functions was Sir Gordon, the hero of the hour, the good sport whose photograph appeared in every newspaper, the patriot who once again was good news and with whom therefore one's money must be safe. Money poured into Gordon Investments. His future might still be saved, with or without the help of Hugo, whose rescue mission was proceeding so slowly.

Two days after the second dinner, Joanna visited Rose Cottage to have a preliminary discussion about the wedding arrangements. She went on her own, because she felt that it might not be an easy meeting. She told them, with fear but also with determination, that she and Kev wanted a quiet wedding. 'And it's me as much as Kev, if not more so,' she insisted.

'You can't have a quiet wedding,' said Christina. 'You're my only daughter. It's bad enough . . .' She stopped hastily.

'You were going to say, "bad enough your marrying a postman",' said Joanna.

'I was,' admitted Christina. 'I'm so sorry, and I shouldn't have said it, but . . . there it is . . . it's how I feel.'

'That's not nice, Mum. I love him. He's lovely.'

Sir Gordon, sitting in the middle, watching them, felt like an umpire at Wimbledon.

'You're a snob, Mum.' Joanna didn't find this easy. She was shaking. She was very distressed. 'And you weren't much once yourself, were you? You were . . .'

It was Joanna's turn to stop.

'You were going to say, "Miss Lemon Drizzle",' said Christina.

'Your mother doesn't think any the worse of herself for having been Miss Lemon Drizzle 1970 . . .'

'1980,' barked Christina. 'How old do you think I am?'

'1980. She's proud of it. It was a great achievement at the time. And she doesn't think any the worse of Kev for being a postman.' He couldn't believe that he'd become a peacemaker. 'It's just that we've moved ourselves up in the world, we've made sacrifices to do so. I personally don't think you're coming down in the world by marrying Kev, but you would be by having a quiet wedding. You'll look beautiful . . .'

'I won't.'

'To me you will. Coming down the aisle . . .'

'Aisle? What aisle? I don't believe in God, Dad. All the scientific—'

'Yes, yes, yes, we needn't go into that, neither do I, but I do believe in Church.'

'What?'

'For weddings. I believe in wearing white . . .'

'I can't wear white. I've . . .'

She blushed.

'Joanna! That doesn't matter. That's so utterly irrelevant

226

in 2012. Congratulations, incidentally. I'm . . .' It was Sir Gordon's turn to stop hastily.

'You were going to say, "surprised". You were going to say you didn't know I had it in me.'

'Joanna! Well, no, well, yes, I was going to say . . . well, not surprised exactly, well, yes, surprised, I suppose, in a way, because . . . well, I mean, less lately but you've always been . . . I'm saying too much. I daresay you can't imagine me and your mum . . . doing it.'

Christina threw him a caustic look and he blushed.

'It's the greatest day of a mother's life,' said Christina. 'I wasn't saying I don't like Kev. As a matter of fact, I do. You couldn't not. I can't pretend he's my idea of a dream catch, but I like him, and if you are going to marry a postman, I'm glad it's him and not some other postman, and I really will look on the bright side and think of all those postmen you're not marrying, and I hope you'll be very happy and I think you will, but, don't spoil my day.'

'It's my day,' said Joanna. 'I want a quiet humanist wedding with no more than twenty guests. I couldn't take any more than that. I'm not . . . I'm not brave.'

'In your way you are,' said Sir Gordon.

'I'm sorry. I know this is awful news for you. Waste of this house. Waste of all your money. Waste of all your fame. Waste of everything you've achieved.'

'Oh, don't feel guilty about that,' said Sir Gordon. 'It's wasted already.'

She is even more astonished

It is seventeen minutes past three in the morning. At last in this mild winter there is a sharp night frost. Rhubarb growers are rubbing their hands with delight, and the man who is walking along the pleasantly prosperous and elegant little street in South Kensington would be rubbing his hands to keep them warm for the task that is soon to come if they weren't full. There is anger in his heart, a black spot in his soul, aggression in his trousers, a large stone in his pocket, a sharp knife in his left hand and a tin of black paint in his right hand.

He stops outside a small, smart, expensive gallery. He puts the knife and the paint down on the pavement by the door.

On the door of the gallery there is an electronic entry box with numbers from 0 to 9. He has sat from time to time in the small coffee shop over the road, lingering over a coffee and a slice of cake, and watching. At last he has seen what he is looking for, the lady who owns the gallery returning home. She has pressed four numbers on the entry box and entered the gallery. She has not switched off an alarm. Clearly when she goes out she does not set an alarm, if she has one. Maybe her insurance is such that she does not live in dread of a burglary. This does not surprise him. He has met her. She is one cool customer.

But does she have an alarm and does she set it at night? He

228

believes that she may not. He is gambling on what he knows of her character, her coolness, her confidence, her smugness about her little gallery which is not really so great.

He is gambling even more about the four numbers that he is going to press on the entry box. He knows that she is a big fan of Pyotr Ilyich Tchaikovsky and he believes that she may well have a sentimental and superstitious streak. He is guessing that she will have done the obvious thing and set the numbers at 1812, believing that nobody who would even consider breaking into her gallery could know her well enough to be aware that she is a fan of Tchaikovsky. Or would be well informed enough, being by definition a low type because a burglar, to have heard of the 1812 Overture. She is an intellectual snob; she listens to Radio Three and he is gambling also that she will not know that Classic FM uses this number for its phone. She wouldn't be seen dead using it if she did know.

Yes, he is doing rather a lot of gambling, but there is no real danger. If the numbers that he presses are wrong, he will simply walk on and go home. Nevertheless, as he presses the four numbers, he holds his breath, and his heart is racing.

The door opens. He breathes out heavily in his relief. He realizes just how eager he is to perform his act of vandalism. He hates the woman who owns the gallery and is probably even now fast asleep in her bijou flat upstairs.

He believes that this woman has gone to bed with his father. He is wrong, she hasn't – she has never met his father – but it is this belief that fuels his anger and his energy as he closes the door very quietly and moves to the back of the room.

He daren't put the light on, and he can barely see the picture, but he is an old hand at this now and he believes that he will be able to paint the angry words legibly enough.

He places the paint can on the floor, and takes a brush from his pocket. But the brush has started to slide down a hole in the lining of the pocket of his elderly jacket, and it is reluctant to come out. As he strives to free it he leans over slightly and overbalances. He saves himself from falling, but his foot kicks the paint can. The noise seems huge in the quiet of the night in this peaceful little street. He stands stock-still, listening. He can hear nothing. He doesn't believe that the noise was as loud as he had feared in his shock. His heart calms down, but his throat is dry, he longs for a glass of cool water.

He takes the lid off the tin and dips his brush into the paint. The room is flooded with light. The gallery owner stands there, tall, slim, stark naked, her stern face softened by sleep. She is more beautiful than any naked woman he has seen, and he has seen a few. He freezes in fear and astonishment.

She is even more astonished.

'I do not listen to your calls. Ever.'

He woke with a sense of shock. He had no idea who he was.

Oh, he knew his name. He knew that he was Sir Gordon Coppinger. But what did a name amount to? What sort of a man was he? In what did a man's personality and identity reside? In what did *his* personality and identity reside? What was his essence?

He didn't know any more.

Did he still want to be an entrepreneur, a financier, a businessman, a manufacturer with his finger in many pies?

He didn't know any more.

Did he still want to be extremely rich, to order bottles of wine that cost more than £200, to invite senior police officers and important people in radio, television, and newspapers on to his luxury yacht? Did he still want to work the system and exploit the system?

He didn't know any more.

Would he still wish, if he could get away with it, to be unfaithful to the woman lying so peacefully beside him, at every possible opportunity, whenever an attractive woman presented herself, which would almost certainly be often?

He didn't know any more.

Or did he wish to continue to work to repair his marriage, which had seemed a not entirely hopeless quest in recent days?

He didn't know any more.

He felt himself getting at least partially erect. Could he not turn now to Christina and take her swiftly and gloriously?

No, he couldn't.

It was time to get up, but he didn't want to. Just ten minutes more in bed, safe, cosy, half asleep, that would be very nice.

What was he thinking of? He had thought himself a great man. Other people thought him a great man. He must behave as a great man. Did Hannibal say, 'My feet are sore. I wonder if I've been marching a bit too far too fast'? Did Alexander the Great complain, 'I don't feel too good today. I wonder if I've got a bit of a cold coming on'? Did Julius Caesar exclaim, 'The Rubicon's wider than I thought'?

He leapt out of bed, showered, washed, and dressed, ate his breakfast swiftly. Kirkstall made good progress on the Kingston By-Pass. Soon the Rolls was gliding to the smoothest of halts outside the Coppinger Tower. Sir Gordon thanked Kirkstall, stepped out, and strode positively into the building. This was his dream, it was his signature on his message to the world, it was his palace. How could he be reluctant?

His heart stopped as he entered the foyer and saw her behind the reception desk. Alice Penfold, her cheeks still pink from the wind she had struggled against on her journey in by bicycle. His prick rose like a razor clam brought to the surface by its hole in the sand being filled with salt. Desperately, he began to plan a tour of isthmuses with his dentist. It didn't work very well. He didn't know enough isthmuses. A bit of research was needed there. Or maybe he ought to replace isthmuses with something else. How about . . . iodine? He hated the smell of iodine, and this morning the thought of it worked where isthmuses had failed.

On an impulse he rose right to the top of the building, to the twenty-sixth floor, past HR and PR and GI and his own office and Property and his secret seduction suite. More and more of the Thames became visible, a silver streak snaking towards the sea, turning back on itself in horror at the idea of being subsumed into the ocean; yes, it seemed to Sir Gordon that even London's river had an identity crisis.

He climbed the short flight of stairs that led on to the roof garden. He pressed the four numbers on the entry box that opened the door only for a few privileged people in the building. Access to the roof garden had to be worked for.

It was a glorious winter morning, crisp, sunny, cloudless. London was softened by the very faintest of mists. He strolled along the marble paths between the rose beds. There were examples of all her roses in the gardens of Rose Cottage, but this was Christina's greatest achievement, her life's work, the ultimate proof of her irresistible rise from the world of lemon drizzle cake. He had mocked, yes, at times he had mocked. He didn't mock today.

Her roses were stunted now. It was impossible to tell her Apricot Carpet from her Scarlett Johansson. They were nothing. But come May their glories would begin and they were so planned that the coordinated colours would blaze until November. It was all extremely clever. She had cross-bred some marvellous roses, of exquisite shades, some startlingly bright, like the flattering Gordon's Glory, some extremely subtle and seeming to change with every breath of wind. She was as successful with floribunda as she was with rugosa. She had won international prizes for climbers, ramblers, ground cover, bushes, and miniatures. Yes, from time to time a magazine would feature this rooftop garden. But to see it in situ, in its perfection, that privilege was given to a very, very few. That had of course been the whole point of it, but how he regretted it now. And with the regret came – yes – love. Not lust. Not desire. Love for

233

his wife, not for her body but for what she was, for what she said, for what she did, for her achievement in building this secret garden. It was his first experience of – he wouldn't have thought of the word, but there was no alternative for it – *spiritual* love.

And with that there came a huge wave of regret that he had not cherished her achievements sufficiently, not found time to take more than a polite interest, mocked them to others as much as he had praised them.

He walked over to the edge of the garden. Not right to the edge. He would never have admitted it, but he suffered slightly from vertigo.

He looked out over Canary Wharf, to the towers of Barclays, HSBC, Credit Suisse and J.P. Morgan. And here he was on top of Coppinger. It wasn't the tallest tower, he hoped that he hadn't been vulgar in his pursuit of wealth and power, but it was his and it was a great achievement.

He looked down at the West India Dock, lined now with bars and restaurants, with long open terraces in front of them all. This area would come to life for everyone in spring, just when the roof garden would come alive for the privileged few.

Once, this great river and her warren of docks had been alive with trade in commodities. Now one commodity dominated all others. Money. And money should never have become a commodity.

He shivered. Why did he shiver? Well, it was a cold morning, but there was no wind at all, the sun held at least a memory of warmth, and he was well wrapped up. No, he shivered because his doubts came floating up the river on that sneaky little wind.

He recalled the words of his accountant, Wally Frobisher. He did not have a bottomless pit. His balance sheets dealt in enormous sums, but they still had to balance. This had been a profound shock, more profound than he had realized at

234

first. Gradually, since his meeting with Wally, sums of money, even relatively small sums, had meant something, they had no longer just been meaningless figures beyond comprehension. Now the doubts of the night assailed him again. He had used so much of his money to such good ends. He had earned so much of his money through honest enterprises. Why, oh why, had he been tempted into the realms of fiction? His tax returns were fiction. The books of Gordon Investments were fiction. The whole of SFN Holdings was built on fiction. Why, why, why? It had all been so unnecessary.

He found himself walking back to the edge of the roof garden. His vertigo was calling him, and its call was irresistible.

There was a wall but it wasn't high. It would be so easy to throw himself over it. That would solve all his problems.

No.

No, no, no.

But he felt the pull.

Come on, Gordon. Show a bit of courage.

He climbed on to the low wall. His heart was hammering at his ribs, which were still slightly sore. His head was swimming. He must be brave. He forced himself to look down. Oh God, there was nothing between him and the pavement twenty-six storeys below. People were ants. A bus was a Dinky Toy. His head was swimming. He was going to faint. He was going to fall.

He closed his eyes, and jumped off.

It was only a jump of two foot six, and he landed without difficulty.

The hammering slowed. He staggered to a bench, sat down, tried to get his breath; he couldn't, he was choking, here in this space open to the wide sky he was suffering from claustrophobia. He couldn't be.

A wave of fear swept through his body like a tsunami as he realized just how close he had been to deciding to jump off the other way.

Gradually he began to breathe more normally, and now a cold sweat broke out all over his skin. Now he found some comfort in the fact that he had been brave enough, he with his fear of heights, to stand on that wall.

No, he still had a tremendous amount to live for. He was exaggerating his crisis. There were areas of concern, yes, but he was still rich, he was still popular, he would be a little more cautious and he would triumph.

He was almost convinced.

He walked down the bare stone stairs to the nineteenth floor. He didn't fancy the confinement of the lift. He was not yet sufficiently recovered from his self-imposed ordeal.

He strode past the desks of his employees, hard at their work. He tried hard to look just a bit like Garibaldi.

He smiled at Helen Grimaldi and thought of iodine.

'A lady called Francesca rang,' said Helen. There was the faintest tinge of jealousy in her voice, and this after seven minutes eleven years ago.

He was glad, when she mentioned Francesca's name, that he had been thinking about iodine.

'She wants you to ring her back. She sounded . . . shaken.'

He wanted to rush into his office, but he made himself walk with measured tread, take his coat off, settle himself in his chair, have a quick look through the papers on his desk. He wasn't going to give Her Grimaldiship the satisfaction of knowing that he was anxious.

'Hello, Francesca. It's Gordon.'

'I'm sorry to ring you in your office, Gordon, but the strangest thing has happened.'

'Oh?'

'The gallery was broken into last night.'

'Oh, I'm sorry.'

'Yes. I heard him and I rushed down. Didn't stop to put anything on. Stark naked.'

Iodine. Iodine.

236

'He was just about to paint on the bigger of Luke's two pictures.'

'Oh no. What is all this about?'

'Gordon, it was Luke.'

'What do you mean?'

'Luke's been vandalizing his own paintings, Gordon.'

'What?'

'He was standing there, brush in hand, looking wild and angry.'

'Oh my God. He must be having a breakdown.'

'Gordon, I rang the police. I mean, I felt I had to. You know, insurance and everything. I had to call the police straight away.'

'Of course. Of course you had to. No problem, Francesca. I'm sorry you had to endure this. What an arsehole that boy is. Where is he anyway?'

'Well, the police took him away. For questioning.'

'Right. I'll find out where he is and see him. Oh God.'

'Gordon, I miss you.'

More iodine, applied by a trainspotting undertaker wearing wellington boots in Finland.

'Careful, Francesca, my secretary listens to my calls.'

'Oops. Anyway, I'm sorry to have to bring bad news.'

'No, no. *I'm* sorry you've had to experience this.'

He put the phone down, put his coat back on, and left his office.

Helen Grimaldi's square face was like a rock. The sun was catching her burgeoning moustache.

'For your information, Mr Coppinger,' she said, 'I do not listen to your calls. Ever.'

And felt an answering squeeze

'Is there any chance of pleading diminished responsibility?' asked Mr E.A. Land, of Weinstock, Weinstock, Land, and Weinstock. He was a fussy little man with shiny trousers. He looked a bit like a rodent, and didn't seem at all out of place in a cramped police cell with just the faintest residual smell of urine from a less couth criminal. There was a small, barred window, and no furniture except for a bare table and four hard chairs.

'I'm not pleading sodding diminished responsibility,' shouted Luke. 'My responsibility has never been less diminished. This is part of what all this is about. Responsibility. You've never taken responsibility for me, Dad. Too tied up in making all that sodding money.'

'That of course is entirely true,' said Sir Gordon, 'but shall we try not to shout?' He turned towards Mr E.A. Land. Mr E.A. Land was the sort of man Sir Gordon loved to tease. He longed to say, 'I think your judgement is somewhat awry, Mr Land, perhaps as a result of being an island.' When Mr Land looked perplexed, he would explain, 'A small piece of Land entirely surrounded by Weinstocks.' No, it was utterly inappropriate, it wasn't the time. Luke was in big trouble and in any case it probably wasn't funny.

'I'm pleading guilty,' said Luke.

'What to?' asked Sir Gordon. 'You haven't been charged yet, have you? What can he be charged with, Mr Land? Is it an offence in law to vandalize your own paintings?'

'When the paintings are in a gallery I would have thought that the ownership invested in the creator of the work of art under any normal contractual arrangement would entirely prohibit his breaking and entering and causing fundamental damage to said work of art,' said Mr E.A. Land.

'I only actually had to break and enter once,' said Luke proudly. 'I've done rather well, I think. Though of course I did cause fundamental damage every time.' He turned to Mr Land. 'I've got you here for a rather unusual purpose, Mr Land. I want you to plead not only guilty for me, but very guilty.'

'There is no such plea in English law, Mr Coppinger.'

Sir Gordon tried not to flinch at the mention of Luke's surname.

'I know. I know,' said Luke. 'What I mean is, I'm proud of what I've done. I want you to point out to the jury—'

'If it's a jury case. It may not be.'

'Well, the jury if it is, the judge if that's who it is – emphasize my irresponsibility, the damage, the way I mocked Welsh nationalism, the distress caused to Fred Upson, the damage to the safety reputation of the gallery in Dudley, the cost of repair, the fear suffered by Francesca Saltmarsh, who is of a very nervous disposition. Lay it on. Ask for the maximum sentence.'

'I can't do that,' said Mr E.A. Land. 'It would destroy my reputation.'

'Sod your reputation,' said Luke. 'I'm serious. What I've done is important. If you can't do that for me, you can sod off.'

'I beg your pardon?'

'Consider yourself dispensed with, Mr Land.'

'I do,' said Mr E.A. Land. 'I consider myself utterly dispensed with. I consider myself sacked.' He stood up, drew himself to his full height, which was a bit of a mistake as he was only five foot three, stomped to the door, turned, and said, 'I leave with great pleasure.'

'The pleasure is mutual,' said Luke. 'What a happy moment in a grim world.'

When Mr E.A. Land had left, the two men were silent for quite a while.

At last Sir Gordon spoke.

'Why are you being even more unpleasant than usual, Luke?' he asked, and he added, rather wearily, 'And why have you done all this? And why the hell do you think you can be a martyr over it, for God's sake?'

'You've never behaved like a true father to me, have you?' said Luke. 'You've never liked me.'

Was this the moment to tell him that he wasn't his father? It was tempting, but no, it wasn't.

Perhaps he would never tell him.

'At times I have made genuine attempts to like you, Luke,' he said. 'You have to admit you haven't made it easy.'

For a moment Luke didn't reply. When he did, his voice was softer, and his face took on a boyish, vulnerable look, as if his anger lad left him, and left him without protection.

'I do admit that, Dad. Sorry.'

'Bit late.'

'Yes.'

'I will try to behave like a father to you over all this.'

'Bit late.'

'Yes.'

Suddenly, at this tense moment of all moments, in this bleak place of all places, Sir Gordon wanted, for the first time in his life, to be friends with Luke. Father and son, no, not possible, but was it too late to be friends?

'Supposing you tell me, quietly and rationally, why you

have done these very strange things, which on the face of it seem completely mad?'

'Partly to hurt you, Dad. To get at you. To embarrass you. Awkward stories in the papers. Bad publicity.'

'Yes, well, it's worked.'

'Sorry.'

'No. No. I can understand. I can't have been easy to live with.'

'You've mocked me. You've despised me. I wanted to show you that I amounted to something.'

'Well, you've done that, though how one would describe what you've amounted to is questionable.'

'I'm sorry, but I hate what you stand for.'

'Perhaps I don't like it much either.'

'Oh, come on, Dad.'

'People change.'

'No.'

'You know best, with your vast experience of life, of course.'

'There you go again.'

'Sorry.' Sir Gordon rubbed his chin with his right hand, felt the comforting bristles, the reassuring though now suddenly unwelcome virility. He was beginning to feel his claustrophobia coming on – another secret. It was as if the walls of the cell were slowly closing in. He began to sweat.

'Are you all right?'

'Claustrophobia. I get claustrophobia.'

Was Luke astonished that he had a weakness or that he had admitted the weakness? Or both?

'I'll be all right.'

'We could ring.'

'No.'

He felt better already, now that he'd admitted it. And the admission, and the fact of the claustrophobia, had shifted the dynamic of the meeting, had shown that there might have been a chance of a proper relationship between father and son, even though they weren't father and son. This revelation made Sir Gordon feel very sad.

He couldn't believe the way the meeting was turning out. He couldn't believe that he no longer felt hostile to Luke.

'There's more to it all than that, though, isn't there?' he said quietly.

'What?' This had surprised Luke.

'I pay you the compliment of believing that there's some kind of philosophical element to this. I think you're very muddled, but I do believe you're a thinker, and not an altogether stupid one.'

'Well . . . that's pretty clever of you, Dad, actually.'

'At the eleventh hour we discover that we have underestimated each other,' said Sir Gordon.

Their eyes met. It was not an easy meeting, but it was the best meeting their eyes had ever had. Sir Gordon was still feeling claustrophobic, but he could tolerate it, the walls weren't sliding towards him any more, he could breathe if he made deep, slow breaths.

A police officer entered and said, 'Five minutes, Sir Gordon.'

Sir Gordon nodded, and the policeman left.

'Tell me about it,' Sir Gordon said. 'Tell me your motive.'

'I've been brought up to believe that cash is king,' said Luke. 'In our household that message has been drummed into me left, right, and centre. Cash, cash, cash. King, king, king. Animals live to eat. We claim to be better than animals, but if we live just to make money, are we any better? Our lives in our family have been entirely dominated by money.'

'True, Luke. So true. Go on.'

'I hate the way the values of the artistic world are corrupted by the values of the materialistic world.'

'But we can't separate them unless you give your pictures away. You're a businessman as well as an artist, unless you give your pictures away.'

242

'Well, I don't mind that, we have to live, we can't charge four hundred pounds an hour like Mr E.A. sodding Land. But pictures bought as investments, pictures fetching totally unrealistic prices, Van Gogh never selling a picture and now they're worth millions, it makes me cry. My pictures, which you don't rate . . .'

'Luke, I don't rate all sorts of artists, even famous ones. I don't rate Gauguin. I'm hard to please.'

'. . . My pictures, which you don't rate . . . Really? Don't you? I don't rate him either. Why have we never talked about these things?'

'I think you may be more to blame than me on that.'

'Oh God.'

'And I share your view about Van Gogh. It's almost too tragic to think about.'

'Anyway, my pictures, which you don't rate, are starting to fetch ridiculous prices. I don't want that. I want to stop it. Hence, my revolt. Hence, my wanting to go to prison.'

'Oh, Luke, prison would be horrid. You don't want that.'

'I don't lack courage.'

'I don't doubt it, but this isn't worth being a martyr over.'

'Well, anyway, there you are, Dad. That's it. That's my story.'

Sir Gordon drummed his fingers on to the scratched and no doubt germ-infested table. He didn't know what to say.

'You may find your pictures even more valuable because of what you've done,' he said at last. 'Even the ones that are damaged. They have history. They have provenance. They could be like unperforated stamps.'

'Oh God, do you think so?'

'Look on the bright side. If that happens you'll still have made your protest and you'll have more money, so that'd be a result. But Luke?'

Luke caught his change of tone and suddenly became cautious.

'Yes?'

'Don't take this the wrong way, don't fly off the handle, but that isn't why you've done it, is it? For publicity? To up your prices?'

'No!'

'Because it wouldn't be a bad plan.'

'No! I'm not like that. And you're going to say you wish I was. I'm sorry, Dad. You and I have absolutely opposite attitudes to money. Hard to think we're father and son.'

Oh, it was so tempting to tell him the truth. So many lies in his life. So tempting to become free of them all. But, if it's wrong to lie, that doesn't always make it right to admit the lie. He must live with it. He mustn't let sleeping lies dog him.

That wave, that tsunami, came hurtling back through him. Earlier that day he had been on the verge of killing himself. How awful that would have been, when there was unfinished business to be done. Unfinished business with Luke, with Joanna, with Christina, with Hugo, with Jack, with Keith Gostelow, Dan Perkins, Adam Eaglestone, and thousands of other employees. He wasn't the only pebble on the beach. People despise clichés, but sometimes a cliché is a revelation.

'I'm not sorry for what I've done, Dad,' said Luke very quietly. 'I can't be.'

I see your point. What you've done is ridiculous, but I do understand. I even admire it to a certain extent.

He couldn't say any of that. Luke wouldn't believe him.

Sir Gordon's arm reached out over the table, and he shook Luke's hand. He squeezed it encouragingly, and felt an answering squeeze.

244

What hope is there?

It was just one article, in the colour supplement of one newspaper. Millions of people would never read it. But it was a Sunday newspaper, and Sunday was the day when newspapers still held quite a grip on the British public, and this was a very popular newspaper, and it was the cover story, with a rather striking photograph of the three of them, not taken together of course, but united digitally (a hint of the disaster to come, though of course he couldn't know that).

There it was, for a million or more people to read, and talk about to other people:

The Coppinger Who Didn't Make It. A Shocking Family Secret Revealed

The newspapers had made hay with Luke's vandalism. It hadn't been good publicity, there was no way he could pretend that it had, and it had dented the feelgood factor created by the dinners for waiters. But it hadn't been a complete disaster. It had evoked a certain amount of sympathy for Sir Gordon as a wronged parent, as the father of a wayward child, as a victim of Modern Art, which was always a villain in the British public's eyes. He had expressed his support for Luke.

That had gone down well. No, it had been far from a complete disaster. The downside had been that there seemed to be constant publicity about him, one way or another, leading to a perception that things were unstable in the world of the Coppingers. Too right they were, but that must be hidden. And the controversy over Hugo's bonus, the sight of his brother smiling smugly in all the newspapers, didn't help.

And now there was this. He passed the supplement to Christina without a word, and buttered another slice of toast.

She was a slow reader. She seemed to be digesting it a word at a time. There was no way he could tell, from her expression, what she was feeling, but he noticed that her face, in concentration, when she was trying neither to please nor to repel, was still beautiful. The chin was perhaps a little more prominent, there was a faint hint of darkness under the eyes, there were a few lines above the lips, but she could still have passed for Miss Lemon Drizzle in a fading light.

As she read, it dawned on him just how much he was becoming a creation of public opinion. This made him angry. It didn't help that it was all his fault. Patriot, man of charity, supporter of the arts, he had created that image and people had forgiven him his wealth and his yacht in exchange for it. They had liked him.

Oh, if only he'd been honest. If only he could start again. He could be all this and honest too. Well, almost all of it. But now his whole future depended on Gordon Investments surviving, and that depended on his remaining popular until Hugo produced his rescue plan. But he was beginning to doubt that Hugo could produce his rescue plan. He was beginning to wonder if Hugo was as powerful a force in global banking as he made himself out to be.

This article was therefore a great nuisance. They should never have done it. They should have told the truth. But how could they have known what public property he was going to become?

Christina handed the paper back to him without a word. Farringdon entered, began clearing away their plates.

'You have breakfasted well, I trust, or as well as can be under the circumstances?'

Yes, thank you, Farringdon.'

'I doubt it's much consolation, but sentiment in the kitchens is very much on your side, sir, madam.'

'Thank you, Farringdon.'

When Farringdon had gone, Sir Gordon read the article again, more slowly this time, with greater concentration, hoping to remember every word.

They came from a modest family background in a small town in the West Midlands, and they scaled the peaks of the financial world in very different styles, but Sir Gordon and Hugo Coppinger had a secret. They had a younger brother, Jack. And Jack scaled no peaks.

While Sir Gordon cavorted with bankers and financiers on his luxury yacht the Lady Christina *in the Med and the Adriatic, and Hugo lived more austerely in his homes in Eaton Square, Cap Ferrat, Venice, Rhode Island, and Bermuda, brother Jack was living in squalor in the alleys and dark arches of London.*

Tipped off by a fellow vagrant . . .

Sir Gordon knew exactly who that had been. He could see him now, a tall skeleton with an eerie, humourless smile, staring at Hugo and him.

. . . I caught up with him (a silly phrase really! He didn't take much catching. He was entirely immobile) in a gloomy subway under the glamorous-sounding Fulham Palace Road in Hammersmith. He had a long, unsavoury beard, and was wrapped in filthy blankets and rags which bore testimony to his scanty diet over, in all probability, several years.

The subway stank of urine, faeces, rank alcohol, sweat, grease, dead rats, and something worse. That something worse was Jack.

Jack Coppinger, the youngest of the three brothers, did better at school than Sir Gordon, though not as well as Hugo. What went wrong, to send him to such depths?

"I didn't have the drive or the ambition," he told me, taking a swig from a bottle of industrial alcohol. He admits that he is never sober nowadays. "I was a dreamer. I don't think either of them ever had a dream. There wouldn't have been time. All they were interested in was money. They hardly ever had time to play with me.

"They chose very different routes to riches. Hugo chose the professional road. He was a swot. Nobody liked him, but he didn't care. He was the man exams were designed for. School, university, he excelled, and soon he disappeared into the banking world. Switzerland specializes in secret bank accounts. Our family produced a secret banker.

"Gordon left school at 15 and did nothing but earn money and save it to use to earn more money. Fair play to him, he worked hard, and, unlike Hugo, people liked him. They didn't see, as I did, that behind the smile there was only hunger.

"They are very different as people. Hugo is incapable of love. Gordon overflows with love, but it is all for himself. If he was a contortionist he would f*** himself twice a night.

"I was bright, but diffident. Shy. Hugo isn't shy. He just thinks talking to people is pointless. I didn't talk to people because I couldn't think of anything interesting to say. I had a crippling lack of confidence, and they helped to destroy me.

"I'm not going to say that they were truly cruel. They never beat me up. They just offered me no encouragement. I was a nuisance that they tolerated. If we played a game, they would seek a reason to break it off.

"They rose in the world, left Dudley behind them, and I rarely saw them, but their legacy lived on in me. I admit it, I felt jealous of their success, bitterly jealous, particularly Gordon's as he was

*so public and always so f****** pleased with himself.*

"I can't say the things that went wrong for me were their direct fault, but if they had been different it might none of it have happened. I started drinking to boost my confidence. I had to be pissed to enter a room where a party was being held.

"I lost two jobs because of my drinking, one as head baker in a confectioner's where Sir Gordon's wife Christina once worked when she won Miss Lemon Drizzle 1980, and the other in a firm making a rival to Durex which folded – the rival, not the sheaths. How people mocked. 'Can I have a packet of three?' People can be very nasty when they detect weakness. I once asked Christina out and she refused me very nicely. She was a great girl in those days. You can imagine how humiliated I felt when she went out with Gordon and married him. I wouldn't have been so upset if she'd been really nasty to me, but I think she pitied me.

"I was pissed when I met my wife, pissed when I got engaged to her, pissed when I married her and pissed when we conceived.

"She couldn't cope with being a mother. I don't want to name her as she still lives in Dudley and has made some sort of a life for herself, but she walked out on us when Luke was three weeks old.

"I couldn't cope. In fact, I had a bit of a nervous breakdown, I was in a loony bin for a while, you can't call them that now but not calling them that doesn't change anything.

"Gordon and Christina had been in America for a while where he made a lot of money – what else? – and they came back at just this time. She'd had a hard time giving birth to her daughter and she'd been told it was a risk to have another kid. They wanted another one and here was one and nobody knew she hadn't been pregnant because she'd been in America and so it all made perfect sense to take Luke and pretend he was theirs.

"Gordon can be very persuasive. The way he presented it, I couldn't cope, adoption's to a certain extent a lottery, here was a ready-made home where the boy would be loved and brought up well and I would be able to see him and nobody would know he was actually my son, and not Gordon's, so it all made perfect sense. Which it did, that's the awful thing. Gordon is so f****** lucky."

I asked Jack if Gordon had been true to his promises. A cold wind blew down the subway as he considered his reply. He shivered, despite all his layers of rags.

"Partly, I suppose. I think Luke was brought up well, nobody did know he wasn't Gordon's, and I was able to see him, at first. But they never loved him. I think Christina tried but couldn't cope with the fact that he wasn't hers. Gordon was too busy, he should never have had kids of his own or anybody else's. And my seeing Luke didn't work, because I couldn't act as if I was anything more than an uncle. Daddy's odd brother. Don't mind Uncle Jack, he drinks, and he's not quite right, but he's harmless, so be nice to him. F*** that."

He stopped, as if exhausted by his own rhetoric, and a single tear ran from his eye into the discoloured forest of his hair. He took another swig from his bottle, and burped. I had to duck to avoid the stench.

I asked Jack if he wanted me to reveal the secret about Luke. Was it fair on Luke?

"He's an artist, isn't he? Searching for truth, he once wrote. Well, I can help your search for truth, I thought. Can't see it can do him much harm now he's grown up, to be honest. Maybe against your principles to print the truth, but I'd love it. Can't bear the way they just possessed my boy when they talked to the papers and on television. Specially when he was nominated for that prize. Serve 'em right if it comes out. Up to you, of course."

Well, we have published it. We believe that people who live through the sword of the public eye, and that includes Luke Coppinger now, must be prepared to perish on that sword if the truth demands it.

I asked Jack how long he had lived on the streets.

"I dunno. Haven't kept a diary lately." He gave a smile that was so bitter it seemed to freeze on his lips. "Twelve years? Fifteen?"

"Have you had any contact with Gordon and Hugo during that time?"

"Oh yes. Look, don't think they are absolute monsters. Just flawed, selfish human beings. Obviously Gordon has done more than Hugo, he's in a position to offer me jobs, and he has done . . . twice in fifteen years. Obviously with strings attached, needing to clean myself up etc. But he did it with such a sense of doing the right thing, it was nauseous, it stuck in my gullet, and my gullet is not a good place to be stuck in these days."

I asked him when he last saw either of his brothers.

"Christmas morning. That did surprise me. They found me quite by chance. Brought me presents, nicely wrapped. Scarves and socks and booze. I mean to say – what f****** s*** sort of a c****** thing to do is that?"

Suddenly, to my surprise, Jack Coppinger's voice went at least an octave lower. I saw just a flicker of warmth which cut through the chill of the subway, a ray of humanity that almost stifled the stench.

"Gordon asked me to come home with him. Imagine it. On Christmas Day, me like this, in his home. It was the sort of ridiculous invitation that he would make, the sort that was perfectly safe because there was no risk of my accepting, but – do you know – I think, for the first time in our lives perhaps, I think he was sincere. Yes, I do. Hugo was horrified, but no, give Gordon credit, I think this time he really thought I might say yes, and he could deal with that."

I asked him if that meant there was hope that something better might come out of all this in the future.

He stroked his ghastly beard and thought hard. "No," he said at last. "It's too late. It's always too late. People should always realize that, and always do things earlier."

So what of the future, I asked.

"I have no future," he said. "I have no present either. And my past ended fifteen years ago."

A cold thought to end a cold interview in a cold place.

Sir Gordon folded the paper up neatly and placed it on the table. He looked across at his wife. He gave her a feeble little smile. She gave him a feeble little smile back.

'Not really all that unfair,' he said.

'I suppose not.'

'We'll have to go and see Luke.'

'I suppose so.'

'Do you know one thing that really upsets me about this? One thing that really worries me?'

'How could I?'

'No. Stupid way to put it. It's this. The editor of that paper has been on my yacht three times. If my bribes aren't working for me any more, what hope is there?'

I hope we haven't

They met in a private room in the staff quarters, not face to face through a grille with a row of prisoners and visitors, and with warders staring at them grimly. The governor had told Sir Gordon that he was granting him this privilege in view of the enormous importance of the news he had to relate to Luke.

Sir Gordon had expressed his surprise and concern that Luke had not been released straight away on bail. The governor had told him that, since violence was involved, Luke was to be assessed by a police psychiatrist.

Sir Gordon hadn't been proud of his response to this.

'But damn it, man,' he had said, 'he's *my s* . . . well, no, he isn't.'

The governor had spoken to him as if to an anxious mother.

'I'm sure he'll be granted bail very soon,' he had said.

Sir Gordon had felt humiliated. He, Sir Gordon Coppinger, humiliated.

A warder led Luke in. He didn't look dramatically different, perhaps slightly paler as if starved of sunlight, perhaps slightly thinner as if starved of food, but was that just in Sir Gordon's imagination? He also looked wary, cautious, on guard, ready to endure grievous verbal harm. Oh Lord. Sir Gordon hated to see that wariness.

He didn't know if Luke had seen the article; did they get the papers in prison, did they have time to sit around on a Sunday idling through the supplements?

'Hi, Dad.'

It looked as if he had not seen the article, and nobody had told him of it.

'Hi, Luke.'

Sir Gordon hated the word 'hi', though not quite as much as he hated the word 'hiya'. He had joked that this was how they were taught to speak English these days in hiya education. But in critical times small prejudices don't seem important, and he was finding, greatly to his disappointment, that things that had always annoyed him were beginning to annoy him less. It was sad to let go of prejudices, but sometimes you had to, and he garnered a very small morsel of pleasure in saying 'hi' to show brotherhood to Luke, since he couldn't show fatherhood.

'You don't look too bad.'

'I'm fine, Dad.'

'Are they treating you all right?'

'I'm OK.'

That wasn't quite an answer, but Sir Gordon let it go.

There was a moment's silence. He must jump in, grasp the nettle. But before he could formulate the difficult words, Luke spoke again.

'What do you think of Emma, Dad?'

'Emma? The person or the artist?'

'Either.'

How had he got trapped in this conversation? How could he break into his momentous confession? How could he not answer without being rude? Better answer and wait for the next gap.

'She's on her mettle all the time. On the defensive. As if she represents not just herself but the whole feminist movement and mankind's historic search for social justice. It's

254

therefore hard to judge her as an individual. If you and she can be happy together I'll be very pleased. You could do worse, and if that's a bit lukewarm I'm sorry. Lukewarm. Play on words. If she warms Luke, that's good.'

Luke looked at him in astonishment. He could change the subject now. Easy as pie. 'Luke, there's something else I need to tell you.' But he wanted to talk on. They were starved of talk, Luke and he. He was starved of talk altogether. Real talk. 'As to her work, I find it utterly ridiculous, but I find her defence of it, her explanation of it, strangely plausible. That's something I haven't come to terms with yet. But I don't think many people will want to put it on to their walls.'

'But that isn't the point, Dad.'

Sir Gordon could see dangerous rocks ahead. What is the point? One's art. But you have to live. Oh. Right. It's coming back to money, I might have guessed it. He had to swerve to avoid those rocks or there'd be another cruise ship disaster. He had to seize on all these mentions of 'Dad'. He'd never have a better opportunity. Courage, Gordon.

'You're saying "Dad" an awful lot today, Luke.'

'Do you know, Dad, I've never really been able to think of you as my dad. Not really truly. Lately . . . well, just these last few hours since I got caught really, I've . . . I don't know . . . I just suddenly . . . I feel a lot closer. I wish, you know, we'd had conversations about art and things.'

'Cling to that, Luke.'

'What?'

'Cling to that feeling.'

Luke began to look paler still.

Sir Gordon looked round the room as if in search of inspiration. There was none. It was a dull little interview room that might have been anywhere. Only the view of the high walls, the barbed wire and the floodlights outside the walls revealed that this was a room in a prison.

'We've been allowed to meet in here, Luke, in private,

because I have something very important to say to you. There's been an article in a Sunday newspaper, about . . . about your uncle Jack.'

'The pisshead.'

'Correct. The . . . as you put it . . . pisshead. Luke, I . . . oh Lord . . . look, Luke, I . . . am not actually your father.'

Luke's mouth opened, but no sound emerged.

'I hate to tell you now, when you're in here, but . . . if you found out, from someone who's read this article . . . Luke, I don't know what to say. I think it might be just as well if you read this now. You can get the whole truth as you read, and neither of us will have a chance to say anything we might later regret.'

He could see that Luke was devouring the article, rushing headlong to the part about him, then stopping dead, barely able to believe what he was reading. Outside, the brief winter afternoon was coming to an end, the lights outside the wall were on. Sir Gordon shivered.

'Uncle Jack's my dad.'

'I'm afraid so.'

'My mum! My mum isn't my . . . oh God. Christina isn't my mum.'

'I'm afraid not.'

'My mum's some inadequate woman in Dudley whose name we don't know.'

'I'm afraid so.'

'I've just lost both my parents.'

'I'm afraid so.'

'Fucking hell.'

Sir Gordon didn't feel he could say 'I'm afraid so' again.

'Why hasn't Mum . . . oh bloody hell. Why hasn't Christina come too?'

'I suggested she didn't. It's all my fault. It's because of what I am that we are what we are. I wanted to take responsibility. And I thought it might all be too emotional for her.

She wanted to come, but we talked and . . . um . . . we decided.'

'Why the hell did you never tell me? How the fuck could you lie to me like this?'

'I wish I had one simple answer, Luke. We thought we would never need to tell you. We thought you might not want to know. We didn't know how to tell you. We didn't want to tell you. We thought it might destabilize you while you were growing up. And then, well, you were grown up, your father was – well, you said it – a pisshead . . . your mother, none of us even know her name. We thought it was for the best, but for whose best, I now don't know.'

'You should have told me. You should have fucking told me.'

'I know.' He didn't know. He still didn't know. 'I know. Luke, I'm going to go. I'm going to go because it wouldn't surprise me, if I stayed, to find you saying awful angry things to me. Better to remember the conversation we had before I told you, when we talked to each other like two human beings. Everything has changed, so how about a new start?'

'I can't speak. I'm absolutely shattered. I don't know who I fucking am now.'

'That's the only thing that hasn't changed. You're still you.'

'How could you do this to me? How could you?'

'Talk to Emma. I suspect that beneath all that shit, there's real strength there. Do you want to keep the article?'

'No, I do not.'

Sir Gordon called the warder in.

'Thank you. We've finished,' he said.

Oh God, he added to himself, I hope we haven't.

Beyond Gravesend

The body of a man drifts down London's river on the ebb. It is evening. The water is dark, but the lights shine brightly.

The body moves in very slow circles on the flowing, swirling tide, but always its progress is towards the sea. It passes between St Thomas' Hospital and the Gothic excesses of the Houses of Parliament. Only in Pugin's tower for Big Ben is there true elegance, but the man wouldn't have noticed this even if he was still alive. He was never interested in this building. He never believed that anything good would come to him out of it.

The corpse drifts unseen past the London Eye, past Cleopatra's Needle and the South Bank, whose stern, spare concrete buildings give no hint that fun and riches can be derived from the arts. Even if this man were not so very dead, he would not recognize these buildings. He had never been in the National Theatre, the Royal Festival Hall or the Queen Elizabeth Hall. Some people might think that it is no great sorrow that he is dead. Others might say that for many years he had not been fully alive.

His body passes the sombre perfection of Somerset House and the stately elegance of the Temple. It does not notice a dark building with the glamorous name of Sea Containers House.

On the north bank, the great domed bulk of St Paul's Cathedral is almost hidden by modern developments, one or two of them cheap and hideous. Wren churches peep from between the office blocks like shy owls sizing up the dangers ever present in the dusk.

The body floats past the well-proportioned old building that once housed the City of London School. It swirls gently underneath Tower Bridge, which does not need to rise to let it pass. Now it is passing a city of wharves. Once trade was king here. Now the wharves are desirable apartments, with lines of restaurants on their ground floors. It is more than twenty-five years since the man whose body this is went into a restaurant.

Now as evening turns to night the last revellers are leaving the dockside pubs. The tide takes the body past the tower blocks of Canary Wharf. A few lights still burn brightly in some of the offices of the Coppinger Tower. Men and women are working late into the night to try to ensure that their careers are not going to be dead in the water also.

On, on, on floats the body, past Greenwich, where time is mean but architecture is generous. The estuary widens. The river passes under the great bridge at Dartford. The smells here are of salt and silt and sewage.

The swirling currents and the falling water maroon the body on the marshes beyond Gravesend. The night is cloudy now. The sky is dark. The only lights are the flashing messages for ships from lighthouses. Water birds are asleep in the reeds. A marauding owl screeches. The salt water laps the body.

What a suitable resting place this body has found for itself. A lonely liquid place, at the end of a lonely liquid life. On the marshes, beyond Gravesend.

Fred Upson went pale

Every phone call now was a potential banana skin. This one was more like an overloaded container ship carrying a cargo of bananas.

'It's Fred Upson, Sir Gordon.'

That on its own was enough to depress him.

'Hello, Fred.' No more of that F.U. business. That had been childish. 'How can I help you?'

'The . . . um . . . the tax people want to inspect the books.'

That wasn't good, but . . . shouldn't be a problem.

'That's not a problem, is it?'

'Not in itself, but . . . um . . . they want to inspect the warehouse.'

'Shit.'

Sir Gordon found that he had swivelled slowly round. He now had his back to his desk. There was no comfort in the grey sky.

'Why? Did they say?'

'Check that everything matches up, that the books are a true reflection etcetera.'

'Do you think they suspect anything?'

'Hard to say. Must do, I suppose, or why would they do it?'

'True. Good point. Oh hell.'

He couldn't bring himself to swivel back to face his desk.

'When are they coming?'

'Um . . . tomorrow, actually.'

'Shit.'

'Yes.'

'Have you been in touch with Mac?'

'Yes.'

'Good man. Is he still up for it?'

'Oh yes. He's actually quite excited.'

'Good Lord.'

'Sir Gordon?'

'Yes?'

'I'm actually quite excited too.'

'What??'

Sir Gordon stood up in his astonishment. Even though nobody could see him – not a window cleaner in sight – he felt foolish and sat down again.

'Can you imagine how boring this job has been for me, Sir Gordon?'

'Well . . . I suppose so, yes, yes, I suppose so. I hadn't looked at it that way.'

He hadn't looked at it any way. He hadn't spent a nano-second wondering how Fred Upson felt about his job.

'So Fred, Operation Big Mac it is.'

'Operation Big Mac it is.'

Archie Macdonald, known to all his friends as Big Mac, was the nearest to a friend that Sir Gordon had ever found in his whole life. The two of them had left school together at the age of fifteen to seek their fortunes. Archie, whose family were originally from Kirkcaldy, had always been more narrow in his outlook than Sir Gordon. He'd worked his way up from tea boy, via jobs in six different factories, to being managing director of his own import-export business. The Scots were known for having the vision to travel the world in the cause of work, but there is an exception to every rule, and Big Mac was the exception to this one. His work had never taken him more than six miles from the house in Dudley where he'd been born. His import-export business was strictly legitimate, but in the world of spread betting he was a legend in the West Midlands, and so Gordon (not yet Sir Gordon) had been emboldened to make his unusual suggestion. He would pay Big Mac an annual retainer in exchange for the use of his warehouse in a crisis. Now the crisis had happened, and Big Mac, who had obtained quite a lot of money for doing absolutely nothing at all over the years, was being true to his word.

Every sign in his warehouse, in every place where the name '*Macdonald*' appeared, would have to be replaced by a sign that said '*SFN Holdings*'. Every container, every tin, every box, every file in every cupboard, every piece of equipment, every safety instruction, every notice from duty rosters to appeals over lost cats, would have to be examined and replaced if need be. On every container of any kind and size, the notification of contents would have to be consistent with the paperwork at Head Office. And it would all have to be done in one night. And when the inspection was over, everything would have to be put back again, also in one night.

It was, in one sense, a huge risk. Most of the notices would simply be placed on top of the other, the genuine notices. Lift one, and the scam would be revealed. But it was Sir Gordon's contention that the risk was actually minimal. Why should a person do that, unless he (or she) suspected that one import-export firm actually imported nothing and exported nothing and had got away with that for almost twenty years and had hundreds of notices ready at the drop of a hat to replace all the notices in another import-export firm owned by a man who was happy to let them do this. It was his contention that a man (or woman)

262

with the imagination to invent such a bizarre proposition would not be working for HM Revenue & Customs or the police.

Besides, Fred Upson was a Rotarian and a Methodist. He played golf. He was on the committees of two charities. There was no reason to suspect a man like him. And Sir Gordon . . . well, he was Sir Gordon.

Fred worked with a very small staff in the Head Office. Only two of them knew the firm's dark secret. They would join Fred and Sir Gordon in spending the long hours of the January night in the tedious task of replacing all the signs and labels. One or two others might have suspected but realized that it was not in their interests to investigate. In blowing the whistle they simply would put themselves out of a job whose wages were a nice little bit above average. If they had known that the figures they worked on so diligently bore no relation to any reality, it could scarcely have made the job any more boring than it was already. Fred had told Sir Gordon that he was worried about members of staff wanting to visit the warehouse. Should he declare it out of bounds? That was the trouble with Fred. No imagination. Sir Gordon had told him to tell the staff that they were more than welcome to visit the warehouse whenever they wished to in their spare time. That had done the trick. Nobody had ever been near the place.

GI had a much larger staff, working on the actual deposits and withdrawals, and on the fictional investments made on these deposits, and on the fictional profits out of which the withdrawals came. Again, some may have suspected what was going on, or that something was going on, but most probably didn't look at things too carefully. Sir Gordon called Keith Gostelow, Dan Perkins, and Adam Eaglestone to a meeting, held not in his office or in theirs, but inconspicuously in the Byron Room on the eleventh floor.

He felt very uneasy, and he didn't meet their eyes as he

spoke. Instead, he gazed fixedly at a rather impressive portrait of the Ancient Mariner. It is perhaps a sad reflection on the level of cultural awareness to be found in British industry that not one person had ever appeared to notice that the wrong picture had been hung in the room. One must presume that knowledge of the works of Byron and Coleridge was scant in the Coppinger Tower.

Sheepishly, he explained the position at SFN Holdings. They were appalled, and didn't take much persuading to agree to go up to Dudley to help. Keith Gostelow would have to put off a meeting with a dietician whom his doctor thought might help him with his susceptibility to boils and pustules, and Dan Perkins would have to cancel a visit to the theatre with his wife, but none of this mattered. If the truth about SFN Holdings emerged, the whole empire would crumble. They were all in this together. Even Big Mac himself helped with the actual labour. As he put it, 'I think it's dead romantic, working at night. The world's asleep, but we're still at it. It makes me feel like I'm important.'

'You'd find romance in a shithouse, you,' commented Sir Gordon.

Sir Gordon could barely have tolerated travelling with his three GI executives, and he couldn't drive himself. His drink-driving charge, which his mind had buried beneath all his other worries, had suddenly surfaced and produced a year's driving ban and a fine of £1,000. His only consolation had been that in the context of his other scandals this news had been greeted with all the impact of a blancmange being thrown into a lake.

Kirkstall, however, seized the chance of driving to Dudley and back twice in two days as if it was an opportunity granted to few men.

Sir Gordon, Fred Upson and their various helpers assembled at the Macdonald warehouse, which was in a nicely obscure position right at the end of a large, dreary industrial estate.

There was no access from the back, which was on the edge of scrubby woodland. Nobody, therefore, except criminals would be likely to see them during the night hours. There would be no passers-by. There were no places to pass by to.

Fred Upson and one of his two assistants brought parcels of labels from the SFN office, and the long night's work began. Some of the work was heavy. Containers were piled five deep, and Sir Gordon decided that they would need to slide the top container off the one below it sufficiently to replace the Macdonald label with an SFN Holdings label, however unlikely it was that HM Revenue & Customs would actually go that far in their search. On the bottom three containers in each pile of five they would just have to believe that HM Revenue & Customs wouldn't want to examine the tops of them. They would need to use a crane to get to them.

Fred's assistant, with Big Mac, listed the contents of all the containers and emailed the details back to his other assistant in Head Office, who began the task of printing new labels that reflected accurately the contents of such of Big Mac's containers as they felt had even the remotest risk of being opened.

Sir Gordon went to the chippy just before it closed, and bought haddock, chips, and mushy peas for them all. It was the first time in thirty-five years that he'd been to such a place and he was a bit flummoxed when they asked if he wanted salt and vinegar on the chips. 'I'll take your advice,' he said. They advised him to have them, and so he did. He found it all a bit embarrassing.

They sat on hard chairs, surrounded by containers, in this great cold hangar of a building, devouring their fish and chips with salt and vinegar, and their mushy peas, eating with their fingers in silent contentment, feeling like a team working together. They actually felt a sense of achievement at the end of the meal. Nobody can eat mushy peas with their fingers without feeling a sense of achievement.

It got colder and colder as the night wore on. It was windy and some of the work involved climbing ladders outside. Bats flew close to them and strong men felt afraid. And there was always the fear, unlikely though this was at the back end of this semi-derelict industrial estate, that somebody might see them.

Nobody did.

The steadiness of their progress kept them working in harmony. In fact, there was only one small fallout all night. That occurred at about half past four in the morning, when the job was almost done. As Fred Upson and Sir Gordon were climbing stairs to offices on an upper floor that covered half the warehouse, Fred touched a banister that had a sign warning *Wet Paint* hanging from it. The banister was still tacky, and he left a perfect handprint.

'Why did you do that?' asked Sir Gordon.

'To see if it was wet,' said Fred Upson. 'It really irritates me when a notice says "wet paint" and it isn't wet. It gets my goat.'

'I bet you're the sort of person', said Sir Gordon, 'who when he passes a notice at the side of the road that says "flood", and the flood has all dried up, you ring the Highways Department angrily.'

'I do,' said Fred Upson. 'That gets my goat too.'

'Do you write to the papers about the misuse of the apostrophe?'

'When I have time. Wrong apostrophes *really* get my goat.'

'I wouldn't want to be one of your herd of goats,' said Sir Gordon.

Fred Upson looked mystified.

'I'd be being got the whole time. It would be most exhausting.'

'You think me a pedant,' said Fred Upson, 'but you forget how much time a man has on his hands when his job's a sinecure.'

Sir Gordon had heard the word 'sinecure' once before but had thought it to be some kind of remedy for nasal problems. Clearly it wasn't. He spoke carefully, not wanting to reveal his ignorance. 'Are you saying that you don't have to work very hard?' he asked. 'You should thank me for that.'

'Thank you?' erupted Fred Upson, angrily waving a sticker that said, *'SFN Holdings – Glass – Fragile – This Side Up'*. 'Thank you? Don't you realize that's what I hate about my fucking job?'

Everything about Fred Upson suddenly irritated Sir Gordon almost beyond tolerance. He felt gloriously released from the need to be nice to him any longer.

'Well, you may not have to do your fucking job much longer, F.U.,' he said. 'When the police come, we'll all deny that we were here, and there'll be no proof whatsoever, but there'll be your whacking great fingerprint on that banister.'

Fred Upson went pale.

What the letters SFN actually stood for

The last Friday of January might have gone down in the annals of Sir Gordon Coppinger's life as Black Friday, if the adjective hadn't been needed to describe the following Monday.

He was extremely tired. He'd been back to Dudley to help remove all trace of SFN Holdings from Big Mac's warehouse. That had not been such a difficult job, but he hadn't imposed on Keith Gostelow, Dan Perkins, or Adam Eaglestone a second time, so with less manpower it had still been a long Thursday night. He'd slept in the car on the way down, but even with Kirkstall's superb smooth driving it wasn't the same as a bed. He was running on empty.

He was also running on the joy of relief, though. He'd pretended to be cool about the big warehouse con, but deep down this new Gordon Coppinger (quite often now he omitted the 'Sir' in his thoughts about himself) hadn't felt confident enough to believe that his outrageously simple and cheeky scam could actually work when tested.

But it had. The tax people had peered round a bit but at no stage had they asked for any labels to be removed just in case there was a different label underneath. He had been

268

proved right in his belief that the idea of anything as preposterous as every label being changed in a whole large warehouse in the middle of the night would just not cross their minds.

So the telephone call was a complete surprise, a total shock.

A senior police officer known to Sir Gordon – what carousing they had enjoyed together in Dubrovnik, what laughs they had shared over Bellini after Bellini in Harry's Bar in Venice – telephoned with news of Fred Upson's arrest.

It seemed that HM Customs & Revenue had not been as naive as Sir Gordon had thought. They had simply gone back to the warehouse the next day and discovered that all the SFN Holdings signs had been removed. They hadn't needed to explore at all.

'The local police are well aware, Gordon – I hope I can omit the "Sir" but I like to regard us as friends?'

'Of course, Nigel. That night in Dubrovnik, eh? Fantastic.'

It was hard to say this with a sinking heart.

'One of the best nights of my life.'

'Ah, memories.'

'Quite. As I say, Gordon, the local police are well aware of – shall we say – the constructive working relationships that exist between you and some of us?'

'Absolutely.'

'However, clearly a fraud on this scale, the existence of a totally non-existent warehouse, if that isn't a contradiction in terms, in your own backyard as it were, cannot be swept under the carpet. The local officers have arrested Mr Upson and the owner of the warehouse, a Mr Archibald Stirling Inverness Macdonald.'

'Ah.'

There was a long, disturbing silence. Sir Gordon felt obliged to continue.

'I knew nothing about this,' he said hastily, hating himself for every single word, but what else could he say if his world was not to collapse and everyone who depended on him with

269

it. 'I am deeply and totally shocked. I've been horribly let down.'

In his fury at being forced to tell yet another whopping lie at a time when he craved, craved, craved the truth, Sir Gordon swivelled his chair so violently that the phone was jolted off the desk. He leant forward, caught it with an agility worthy of his goalkeeper Carl Willis – no, better than that – and placed it back on the desk.

'Are you still there?'

'Yes. Yes. I'm just terribly shaken.'

'I can imagine,' said the chief superintendent smoothly, 'and I'm glad and relieved to hear that you knew nothing of this. It corroborates what Mr Upson said.'

Sir Gordon had to hide his astonishment.

'Oh good.'

'Mr Macdonald claims that there was a financial arrangement between him and Mr Upson under which SFN could use the warehouse if and when needed. He didn't know what for.'

'What an extraordinary arrangement.'

'Exactly. It sounds pretty implausible to me.'

Sir Gordon gulped. Each lie seemed to hurt him physically. His throat was acid.

'I'm disappointed in Fred,' he said. 'I thought he was a good man.'

'Well, there you go, Gordon. He seemed quite proud of himself. Called himself "one of those rogue operators you read about". Rather pleased with his image. Bit unhinged, perhaps. The chaps in Dudley, where he's pretty well known, are astonished. They'd got him down as a follower rather than a leader every time.'

'Well, me too, Nigel. That's why I'm so shaken, but you'll know from your job how little we can ever know about another human being.'

'That is so true, Gordon. That is so true. Anyway, I'm delighted to hear that you aren't involved, though of course

270

I don't think we'll be able to keep you out of the court proceedings or the publicity.'

'No, of course not.'

Oh God. The publicity.

'So back to Mr Macdonald. You knew nothing of his involvement?'

Gulp.

'I'm afraid not. He and I go back a long way. We were at school together. He's the nearest thing to a lifelong friend I've got.' Oh, those last three sentences, what joy it was to be able to speak the truth. Now his heart sank as he approached further lies. 'He might have agreed to give Fred a free hand in the mistaken belief he was being loyal to me. That's all I can suggest. He's a good man.'

'Thank you. He has to be arrested, but Superintendent Molloy, who is the officer in charge, has no problem in releasing him on bail in the sum of twenty thousand pounds. Would you be prepared to stand bail for him?'

'Of course. No problem.'

'Excellent. Gordon, I really am anxious to be as accommodating over this business as I can, and I think I have persuaded the Super that if you give us a guarantee, with your reputation, we may be prepared to release Mr Upson on bail also.'

'I give you my absolute guarantee, Nigel. Fred may have done wrong – clearly has done wrong – but he's not a man to run away or shirk his responsibilities.'

Sir Gordon hadn't the faintest idea whether this was true; he was amazed that Fred hadn't passed the buck and he felt now that he really didn't know the man at all, but he didn't gulp this time as he told these lies. Lying begins to get easier quite quickly once you've set out on that road. In fact, you can very easily start to convince yourself that you're telling the truth.

'Good. Excellent. The main thing, of course, is your belief that he wouldn't run away – well, I suppose we can confiscate his passport, yes, I think that would have to be a condition – or that he wouldn't . . . um . . . harm himself.'

'Oh, I don't think Fred's that sort of person.'

'Good. Good. The money is a secondary consideration, but it is a serious offence on a pretty grand scale really, and I don't think we could set bail at less than three hundred thousand pounds.'

Icy horror gripped Sir Gordon. That was a very large sum. He felt a surge of panic. His head was swimming.

'Are you still there, Gordon?'

'Yes. Yes. Sorry. I was thinking. A decision like this needs thought. Yes, three hundred thousand is fine.'

'Excellent. He'll appear in court tomorrow morning. One night in the cells won't do him any harm. In the morning he'll plead guilty – apart from anything else we've got a whacking great set of fingerprints on a banister – and we'll release him on bail. Thanks, Gordon.'

'Thanks.' Sir Gordon still felt weak, still felt shaken, but he forced himself to end the talk on a polite, calm note. 'Your wife all right?'

He had failed to dredge her name from the database of his mind.

'She's fine. Going to visit her friends in Canada from August the seventh to the twenty-sixth.'

'Let me make a note of those dates. Maybe I can offer you a trip on the yacht.'

'Oh, that wasn't why I was mentioning it.'

'I know that, Nigel. But I can hear those Bellinis calling to me.'

'Terrific. That is a tremendous thought, I have to admit. Well, good to speak to you, Gordon, glad to hear from your own mouth that you were nothing to do with this. Never thought you were, of course.'

A ridiculous weakness stole over Sir Gordon. After he had put the phone down, he found that he barely had the strength to stand up. His legs wouldn't support him. He had to clutch the desk for support. He felt faint. He felt that he was going to pass out. He sat down hurriedly, held his head in his hands. He heard a faint squeak behind him. But was it behind him or was his head squeaking? Did your head squeak when you had a heart attack?

There was another, louder squeak and he realized that this one was definitely from outside his body, from behind him. He looked round with a mixture of alarm and relief.

The window cleaners waved at him and made miming gestures. They weren't skilful, there was no reason why they should be – ability to mime wouldn't be part of their job description – but Sir Gordon could tell that they were asking, 'Are you all right?'

Oh God. He couldn't bear their concern. He found it hard to tolerate that they had witnessed his weakness.

He smiled, forced himself to stand, gave them a thumbs-up, mimed, 'Is it cold out there?' They mimed, 'It's fucking perishing,' he gave an exaggeratedly friendly grimace as of one equal to another in this ghastly cold world, they gave him a thumbs-up, and he sat down again.

All this had cost him, but he had managed it. He had come through. He hadn't passed out.

Now he had to pretend to be busy until they had gone. He moved papers around, picked papers up, pretended to read papers, oh Lord, the window was large and oh heavens, the men were thorough, the nation was full of lazy workers and he'd been saddled with the most thorough window cleaners in the universe, but at last they had gone, and he was left blessedly alone with his panic.

Because this was what it was. A panic attack. Not a heart attack. At one moment it had been a panic attack caused by his fear that it was a heart attack. But now it was a panic attack pure and simple, and strangely that was worse, in a way, because more abstract.

273

He was panicking because he had been asked to stand bail altogether in the sum of £320,000. He wasn't panicking because it was a large sum. To him it was peanuts. He was panicking because for a moment it had seemed to him like a large sum, because, when he heard it, he had wondered if he could afford it. Of course he could afford it, but he had never, since he was in his early twenties, needed to panic about a sum of money. In that moment he had felt the vastness of his empire, the fragility of his empire, the possibility, never before contemplated, of the destruction of his empire. He had felt that he was losing control. There is no worse feeling for a control freak. And it was only a few weeks since he had agreed to pay £20 million for a small Turner without blinking an eyelid.

He knew that he didn't have much time. He must save Gordon Investments. He phoned Hugo and yet again couldn't get him. The selfish bastard had gone abroad. He arranged transfers of money from a few of his more profitable concerns, but he was only buying time, and that was bad business; it was always terrible business to throw good money at bad, he knew that, but reason had gone from him now, judgement had flown, and, which was even worse, he bypassed his chief accountant.

Dudleygate didn't break across the news channels until after the markets had closed, but then it was everywhere. There it was, on the radio, on television, on the Internet, on Google, on Yahoo, on Twitter, on YouTube, on Facebook: the warehouse that didn't exist for the holding company that held nothing. The arrest of Fred Upson.

He sent for Gavin Welland, his Head of PR. He arrived out of breath and looking more than a little stressed, but on this occasion there could be no suspicion that he was putting this on for effect. The media were besieging him, as they were besieging Helen Grimaldi asking to speak to Sir Gordon.

Now that it was public news, Sir Gordon felt calm again. It was as if the worst had already happened. Calmly and swiftly he and Gavin knocked out a statement together. It wasn't easy. They both realized that they were between a Northern Rock and a hard place. He couldn't admit any kind of involvement whatsoever, but to claim total innocence meant leaving him open to charges of incompetence and carelessness, with the left hand not knowing what the right hand was doing. It was his only option, however.

At seventeen minutes past six on that Friday evening Sir Gordon issued a statement: 'I am horrified by what has happened at SFN Holdings. I blame myself for trusting a long-standing employee too much. I have a huge range of profitable, well-run businesses in many walks of life and in my heavy schedule I took my eye off the ball in this particular instance. I must point out that there is no cause for panic. SFN Holdings is a very small player in my global world. It is a completely self-contained operation with absolutely no knock-on effect on my other businesses. I would also like to reassure any employees of SFN Holdings who can show that they too were unaware of this crime that I will stand by them. I have been too loyal, but I still believe in the value of loyalty.'

He spent the evening talking to journalists and giving interviews to the TV networks. He arrived home shortly after midnight, utterly exhausted but feeling far happier than he had earlier.

Christina was fast asleep, her breathing gentle and calm. She had been out to dinner as the guest of a leading player in the roses game. She might not even have heard what had happened.

Sir Gordon crept carefully into bed beside her. He wasn't at all sure how, or indeed if, he would sleep. It could be a long night.

He realized how lucky he had been in one respect. Nobody, but nobody, had asked what the letters SFN actually stood for.

He rather liked bees

He woke with a sense of excitement, almost a childish excitement, and he couldn't understand why. Then he realized. It was Sunday.

Now he was wide awake and astonished. He had rarely, in his adult life, woken with a feeling of excitement. Satisfaction, yes. Anticipation, often. Pride, regularly. Gratification, frequently. But excitement, pure and simple, no. And on a Sunday, never. The weekend had been a space that had to be filled, before he could get down again to his uninterrupted pursuit of money and the things it bought. How good it had been, yesterday, not to step into the Rolls, not to be driven up the Kingston By-Pass, not to enter the Coppinger Tower.

The morning had been marred by the need to tell yet more lies. He had assured Christina that he had known nothing about Fred Upson's crime, that SFN was of no importance, that the scandal would pass. But then she had gone out until the evening. Oh, bliss. She was having lunch with the wife of the owner of the local garden centre. They would lunch on salad and mineral water, it was too dreadful to contemplate, but then he didn't need to contemplate it.

He had lunched alone, blessedly alone, on rare cold beef

and Burgundy. And then he had gone into the television room and watched the match. Climthorpe United away to Doncaster, recorded by the BBC so that they could show the goals (if any) and piped through to him under a long-standing arrangement.

It's not easy to cope with stress, but one way of dealing with it is to find something else to be stressed about. That goes a long way towards explaining the amazing hold that football has upon a huge section of the public. Sir Gordon had rarely needed to escape from stress quite so urgently as he had yesterday. What better way to forget his troubles than to suffer ninety minutes of utter agony watching Climthorpe United, with five extra minutes of even greater agony added on? And to see your side win 1–0 away, not entirely deservedly, and with very little contribution from Raduslav Bogoff, and being under almost unbearable pressure for the last quarter of an hour as Doncaster strove for an equalizer, what masochistic euphoria. And part of the joy of it, and he had been dimly aware of this yesterday, was that he was just one of the team's supporters, no different from the mass of the team's followers for the duration of the match. How weird that he should obtain pleasure from not being different, not being special, not being superior, when he had worked his balls off for forty-one years just to become superior.

It would have been churlish not to celebrate victory in fine wine – a Gevrey-Chambertin was just the job – and to nod off in front of the east fire, what could be nicer? Christina was home blessedly late, and although she had been shopping in Godalming, she had only bought two pairs of shoes, so that was a bit of a result too. She had fancied a glass of champagne, so there had been no obstacle to his continuing to drink, and Farringdon had served a very good meal, and that had taken them almost to bedtime, and he hadn't thought about SFN Holdings or Gordon Investments or Germophile once all evening.

And now it was Sunday. They were planning a family Sunday. A traditional lunch here with Joanna and Kev and Emma, then while they went to visit Luke in prison, Joanna and Kev would go for a walk. (Going for a walk! Good God! Sir Gordon knew that other families had walks, and despite the sad surroundings he'd actually liked the walking element of his visit to the National Memorial Arboretum with Joanna, but even the thought of it, a Sunday-afternoon walk, in his own family, he couldn't believe that the prospect didn't depress him.) After the prison visit they would deposit Emma and Kev in a pub – what would they talk about? – and visit Clarrie in his home.

A family Sunday. No Luke, of course, and he was amazed to find how sad that made him feel. No Jack either (little did he know) and no Hugo (still abroad, absolutely infuriating, got five houses and he's in none of them, how spoilt is that? Apparently he's expected back today, oh God, let him have his plan of salvation).

But still, incomplete though it might be, a family Sunday. He'd never really experienced the concept of 'A Day of Rest'. Rest was not something that had ever attracted Sir Gordon. His batteries had never seemed to need recharging.

But things were different now. Sometimes, he realized, he had used his work as an escape from his personal life, from, yes, his family. Now he was ready to use his family as an escape from work. He was becoming more like most men, and he didn't mind. He no longer craved power. He no longer yearned for excitement. Waking up was enough of a challenge for him now. He looked forward to a quiet family Sunday.

On the other hand, he found himself wishing that it would not be quite so quiet. To his utter amazement, he realized how much he would like a grandchild. Of course, if Luke and Emma had a child, it wouldn't really truly be his grandchild, but he would enjoy it just as much as if it was. And what about Joanna and Kev? On the face of it, not promising. Nice lad, Kev, just can't picture him actually oozing sperm, can't see him slipping on a French letter even though he is a postman. And Joanna, great how she's blossoming, but just how far can she blossom? Might surprise him, though.

He ought to be getting up now, but it was lovely, despite all the problems that needed resolving, to lie in bed and muse. Did he realize, instinctively, that he would have no time to lie in bed, no time to think or to muse, in the days ahead?

At last he did drag himself out of bed.

When he went in to breakfast, Farringdon's face was grave.

'The police have telephoned, sir. I'm afraid they wish you to identify a body.'

Just for a moment Sir Gordon felt a shock of dread.

'Where?'

'Gravesend.'

Somehow, at the mention of Gravesend, he knew straight away that it was Jack. It was only human to feel relief that it wasn't . . . well, someone he really cared about, Joanna or Luke or Alice Penfold – how did she squeeze into the list? It was a shock, half pleasant, half worrying, to realize that there were people he cared about.

So he spent the morning of his family Sunday being driven to Gravesend and back along the M25 by Kirkstall, a man who seemed to have no family life. Like Jack. Having a family doesn't guarantee one a family life.

The sheet that covered the corpse in the mortuary was pulled back with great solemnity, just like on the television. Sir Gordon looked at the bloated face and the undernourished body, ravaged by water and time and the beginning of decomposition. It was not a pretty sight, but then again it had been almost thirty years since Jack had been a pretty sight. And although it wasn't a pretty sight he didn't want the moment to end. He had seen so little of his brother for so many years; he realized that he was starved of his brother, he wanted to just stand there and look at him and think about him and speak silently to him and tell him how he was more sorry than he could say for the way things had turned out. He dreaded the moment when the sheet would be pulled back over and his brother would be lost to him for ever. He thought of the games they had played, the games they hadn't had time to play, the moments they could have spent together and hadn't. He was overwhelmed by sadness and yet he didn't want to lose that sadness. But he had to speak. They were waiting for him to speak.

'Yes, that's my brother Jack,' he said softly.

The mortuary official was just about to pull the sheet back over Jack, and release Sir Gordon from his pain, but he said, 'Might I look at him for just a moment more?'

'Of course, sir.' The official's voice was coated in sympathy. 'Of course, sir.'

And further thoughts of what was and what might have been, of what was said and what might have been said, sent Sir Gordon Coppinger floating adrift and helpless, just like his brother Jack.

And then he had been looking for too long and could feel nothing more.

'Thank you,' he said.

The sheet was drawn over Jack's swollen body. Sir Gordon could feel a pricking in his eyes.

'If you can bear it, sir, Inspector Rice would like to have a word with you.'

'Of course.'

'Thank you. Much appreciated.'

'No problem whatsoever.'

How polite people can be, in the presence of death.

Sir Gordon was led from the icy mortuary into the fug of a small interview room.

Inspector Rice stood up and was five inches taller than he looked as if he would be, reminding Sir Gordon of that young

280

public-school lad he had sent to Porter's Potteries Pies only a few weeks ago, though that seemed to belong in a different life. He wondered, briefly, how the lad was getting on. He was to find out all too soon.

'This is very kind of you, Sir Gordon.'

'Not at all.'

'I'm sorry we had to send for you.'

'No, no. You had to.'

'We tried your brother Hugo as well, but apparently he's out of the country, back tonight. We needed to get it done, to be honest.'

'It sounds odd, but I'd have hated to have missed it.'

'Good. Good. I'm glad. Incidentally, I was speaking to the Chief Constable about you a few days ago.'

Yawn, yawn.

'Really? That's interesting. How amazing is that?'

'Yes. Quite a coincidence. Small world, eh?'

'Very small.'

Very small, yet plenty of room for clichés.

'He said he had a wonderful holiday on your yacht.'

Oh God. Not now. Please.

'Ah. Yes. He seemed to enjoy himself.'

'He most certainly did.'

Get on with it. These words are cheap.

'How can I help you, officer?'

'You knew your brother, sir, and I—'

'I have to stop you there, officer. No, I didn't. None of us did. The separation has been long.'

'Yes, of course. Of course. Very sad, sir.'

'Yes.'

'Very sad.'

You've said that.

'Very sad indeed. However, he was your brother, and – well – let's put it this way. We aren't looking for anybody else.'

'It was suicide, in other words.'

'We have no reason not to believe it was suicide. However, we pride ourselves on our thoroughness.'

Certainly do. Perhaps he should put Inspector Rice in his Alphabet of Boons to Celibacy in place of isthmuses. One thought of him could put a man off his oats for a decade. Oh no. Sir Gordon resented that irrelevant thought, and resented Inspector Rice for causing him to think it. This dislike of the man was irrational. It wasn't his fault that Jack had died.

'So I must ask you, sir, did you ever see any sign of suicidal tendencies?'

'No.'

'I see. None?'

'None.'

'Do you have any reason to suspect that it isn't suicide, Sir Gordon?'

'No. I'm certain it was suicide.'

'You have a reason for that, sir?'

'Yes. The life cycle of the wasp.'

In his sadness and anger Sir Gordon enjoyed a brief, vicious pleasure at the expression of utter bewilderment on Inspector Rice's face.

'The life cycle of the wasp, sir?'

'Yes. My brother Jack hated me and my brother Hugo for almost all his life. I mean, he really hated us.'

'I see, sir.'

It's amazing how many people say 'I see' when they don't.

'Not long ago, very recently, amazingly, he was interviewed in depth in a Sunday newspaper.'

'I see, sir.'

'He expressed his hatred of us in the article in no uncertain terms.'

'I see, sir.'

If you say 'sir' once more I'll scream. How much respect can a man stand?

'Thirty years of bile were poured into that article.' His voice was on the verge of cracking. Oh God, he didn't want to cry in the presence of Inspector Rice. He was saying what sounded like bitter words, and they were true, but as he said them he felt overcome by wasted love. 'Thirty years of hate. He had nothing more to say, and, if he said it, he had no one of that importance to say it to. He had nothing left to live for, after that article. His job was done.'

'I see, sir.'

'He stung us, knowing that afterwards he would die. Just like the wasp.'

On the way home, Sir Gordon realized that he didn't actually know whether it was the wasp or the bee that died after it had stung. He hoped it was the wasp. He rather liked bees.

A thing that they had never done before

A family Sunday. A normal family Sunday. Something he had never had. What a day to try to have it. What a start. Identify your brother's body, and then sit down to lunch.

They sat at the round rosewood (what else?) table in the great dining room and had the full works – roast pork, crackling, apple sauce, roast potatoes, roast parsnips, sprouts, broccoli, and carrots. Sir Gordon was being the Head of the Family to such an extent that it almost seemed as if he was playing at it. 'More apple sauce, Kev?' 'Please.' 'Good man.'

They drank to absent friends and the toast had a power that it rarely achieved. Jack. Luke. Hugo.

'Do you know,' said Sir Gordon, 'the other thing I regret, apart from our absent friends?'

'No,' said Christina. 'Of course we don't. So tell us. You're dying to.'

Sir Gordon raised an eyebrow very gently at this suspicion of sarcasm.

'I regret that we don't cook our own meals. I think the lives of those who have servants are as diminished as the lives of the servants themselves, if not more so.'

'I'll drink to that,' said Emma, 'but then I'll drink to anything.'

284

Sir Gordon poured her a generous slurp of the Margaux.

'Is it true you're painting a rubbish dump at the moment?' asked Kev.

'I'm painting the tip,' said Emma.

'Not the tip of the iceberg?' said Joanna.

'No, the tip of the tip. Not the whole tip, of course.'

'Of course not,' said Sir Gordon. 'Too ambitious altogether.'

It was the turn of Emma's eyebrows – and she had very dark, shaggy eyebrows on that solid, square face – to be raised, not quite so gently, at this more obvious sarcasm.

'I'm painting the bit where people dump their cardboard,' said Emma.

Kev tried to keep a straight face, and couldn't. He began to giggle. Joanna caught the giggle. They both went deep red.

Three times Kev tried to say 'Why cardboard?' and his voice dissolved three times into helpless giggles.

'I'm sorry,' he said at last. 'I really didn't mean to be rude. Seriously, why cardboard?'

'It's the challenge,' said Emma, looking at him so fiercely that he just didn't dare to giggle again, though he was very near to it. 'I mean, cardboard just has to be the most boring thing in the tip, but if I can find something magic there, wow.'

'Why should we look at a picture of cardboard?' asked Sir Gordon, endeavouring to keep any trace of sarcasm out of his voice.

'Well,' replied Emma without hesitation, 'it can have interesting shapes – angular, square, oblong – differently arranged, perhaps making amazing patterns, perhaps at random with no pattern, and yet forming a pattern despite that. Or you could see it as a narrative painting. You're the boss when you look at a picture.'

'A narrative painting?' asked Christina, sounding more as if she felt it was time she said something than because she was truly interested.

'These were once packages that held interesting things, exciting things, presents for children perhaps, eagerly, impatiently opened. Now the contents are being used, played with, eaten, and the cardboard has been discarded. You could see this as a very sad picture. Also I'm capturing a moment that will never be repeated. In a moment these boxes will be crushed. I like to capture moments. Like your Turner, Sir Gordon.'

'He isn't my Turner,' said Sir Gordon, 'and please don't feel the need to call me "Sir". I know how it must rile you. You're family, Emma.'

Emma looked astonished.

'Am I?'

'Well, almost.'

Christina looked astonished too. And not quite as pleased as Emma. It struck Sir Gordon as odd that the sexual jealousy still smouldered. If there was jealousy, could there not once again be love?

'I don't always like your pictures, Emma, but I love your explanations,' said Sir Gordon.

Kev blushed, and Sir Gordon had recognized that he did this when he was about to make some controversial comment.

'I don't want to be rude about your pictures, Emma,' he said, 'and I'd like to apologize for our synchronized giggling.'

'Me too,' said Joanna.

'Delivering the post isn't the worst job in the world,' said Kev, 'but it isn't the best either. On my day off I want to look at beautiful things, not cardboard and rabbit droppings.'

'But I want to show you the beauty in them,' said Emma. 'Give me a chance. Give cardboard a chance.'

'OK,' said Kev. 'Fair enough. Maybe Jo and I could come to your studio some time. How about next Saturday?'

'Deal done,' said Emma.

'No, I'd really like to see your stuff in creation,' said Kev. 'I'm not dismissing it.'

Sir Gordon and Christina had exchanged a barely perceptible glance of disapproval at the word 'Jo', but Kev had noticed.

'Do you dislike "Jo"?' he asked.

'We do to be honest,' said Christina. 'We love "Joanna".'

'Joanna?' asked Kev, meaning, 'How do you feel about it?'

'I'm more comfortable with Jo,' said Joanna. 'I don't think I'm quite up to being a Joanna.'

'Well, in that case I'm always going to call you Joanna,' said Kev.

Joanna looked at him in astonishment, and he blushed again.

'I think you're well up to being a Joanna,' he said. 'I think you make a wonderful Joanna.'

Now Joanna blushed too.

'If Jo's second best then it's Joanna from now on,' said Kev.

It struck Sir Gordon that Joanna and Kev were now indulging in synchronized blushing. Wisely, and unusually, he said nothing about this.

'I suppose if we're all going to see Luke, there won't be time for a walk,' said Joanna, as Farringdon served seconds. Why couldn't they serve them themselves?

'We can't all go,' said Christina. 'You could stay here and have a walk.'

'Lovely,' said Joanna.

Sir Gordon tried hard not to look at Joanna and Kev as if they were creatures from outer space, but really, to be excited by a walk, he just didn't get it. Hard though he tried to conceal it, Kev sensed what he was thinking.

'You don't like walking, sir?' he asked.

'Please, no "sir",' said Sir Gordon. 'No, I think it's unbelievably boring. But luckily Christina and Emma and I will be spared.'

They had apple crumble for afters.

It was quite a long drive to the prison, and Sir Gordon had suggested to Kirkstall that one of the family could drive them, but Kirkstall had looked so disappointed that he had changed his mind.

'You really want to drive, Kirkstall?' he had said.

'Yes, sir. I don't like Sunday afternoons,' Kirkstall had explained.

Once again, they were allowed the privilege of a private room. This recognition of what power he still had to pull strings only served to remind Sir Gordon of all the threats to this power that he was facing, though of course as yet he had no idea just how extensive those threats were going to be in the coming days.

They had decided in the car that Sir Gordon and Lady Coppinger would see Luke first, and then it would be Emma's turn to see him on her own.

It was the same drab characterless room and a feeble winter sun was slipping behind the high, spiked wall outside. Luke looked pale and drawn, though no worse than on his previous visit; Sir Gordon could see that Christina was a little shocked.

'So, still no bail,' said Sir Gordon. 'I thought you were being assessed by – who was it?'

Luke smiled. It was a strangely calm smile. Sir Gordon saw more of an adult in Luke's face as he smiled than he had ever seen in him before.

'A police psychiatrist, if that isn't an oxymoron.'

'That is ridiculous,' said Sir Gordon. 'And was he? I bet he was.'

'Was what?'

'An oxymoron, whatever that is, but it doesn't sound very bright.'

'No, Dad, it's a figure of speech. Never mind. And it was a she.'

'Ah.'

Christina gave Sir Gordon a look.

'She analysed the slashes I made to the pictures and found them to be sinister, with a random quality and a depth that suggests that I cannot be trusted not to harm myself, or you, or Emma, or all four of us, or anyone I happen not to like.'

'That is ridiculous.'

'Murderers get released and kill again. Child abusers get released and abuse again,' said Christina with a venom that made Sir Gordon realize just how little he had bothered to find out what was going on in her brain during recent years.

'It is disgraceful,' he said. 'All you've done is attack your own pictures and do a bit of minor damage to a gallery or two. It is outrageous. Don't worry, though. I'll have a word on the way out. I'll begin to pull strings.'

'Dad, I don't want you to pull strings.'

'What?'

'I . . . I've had time to think. And I'm really sorry for what I did, and I want to pay for it so that I can start off painting again with a clean sheet.'

Not with an unmade bed, then, thought Sir Gordon, but for the second time that day he resisted an unwise remark.

'Sorry, Luke, but that's nonsense,' he said. 'You've punished yourself enough. The whole thing was an exercise in punishing yourself.'

'There's another reason,' said Luke. 'I won't get a long sentence, I may not even get a prison sentence – though I probably will, they just love sending people to prison in this country. It's not nice in prison but it's not unbearable and I think the experience will deepen my work if I've got anything about me as an artist, which I think I have even if you don't.'

'I don't say that,' protested Sir Gordon. 'I don't know enough about art to say that.'

'Also, Dad, and this is important, it really is. I need to feel angry. I need to feel unjustly treated. That's such a trigger for me. That's what's missing in my work. Anger, that wonderful emotion, that emotion that's the only true emotion we can feel towards this world. Please, Dad, don't pull any strings. Promise?'

'Right. Right. I won't. I promise.'

Sir Gordon patted Luke on the shoulder. He actually felt proud of him. He wanted to say that he was pleased to hear Luke calling him "Dad", but he didn't, since Luke hadn't called Christina "Mum" once. For the third time that day he resisted an unwise remark. Was this is a record?

'Are you absolutely sure about this, darling?' asked Christina.

Sir Gordon couldn't remember when Christina had last called Luke "darling", but it came out very naturally as if she used the word all the time.

And then Luke said the word at last.

'I'm absolutely sure, Mum.'

Now Sir Gordon could see his way into telling what must be told – and it seemed that there was something that must be told every time he saw Luke.

'It's great to hear you calling us Mum and Dad, Luke, but . . . I'm afraid I have some bad news about . . .' He couldn't bring himself to use the words "your real dad". '. . . Jack.'

He told Luke the story of Jack's presumed suicide and his identification of the body that morning.

Luke looked agonized.

'I can't feel anything,' he said. 'I can't feel a thing.'

'Well, of course you can't,' said Christina. 'You never really knew him.'

Sir Gordon realized that he and Christina were hardly the people Luke needed to be talking to about his real father.

'You don't need to talk to us about this,' he said. 'You need to talk to Emma. We'll send her through.'

Christina kissed and hugged Luke and so did Sir Gordon.

'We're very sensitive all of a sudden, aren't we?' said Christina after they had left the room.

'It seems so, yes,' said Sir Gordon equably.

They were given the Governor's office to wait in while Luke talked to Emma, and again this evidence of his privileged position in society made Sir Gordon conscious of just how fragile that position now was. He was glad that he had promised not to pull strings. He might have found that he no longer had many strings to pull. They were given a newspaper to read. Sir Gordon managed to avoid the news pages entirely, but read about Climthorpe's away win at Doncaster twice. When he had done that, he just sat and waited.

'You aren't impatient,' said Christina.

'No.'

'But you're always impatient.'

'He's with his girlfriend. He's happy. In a moment he'll be very, very lonely. Why should I wish for that moment?'

At last Emma arrived. Her eyes were wet and her face was defiant. No words were spoken.

Back at Rose Cottage, Joanna and Kev were sprawled in armchairs, exhausted. They still had slightly damp hair. They had taken their boots off. They looked happy.

'You look happy,' said Sir Gordon.

He made it sound like a double entendre.

'And tired.'

He made it sound like a double double entendre.

'Well, we had a really nice long walk,' said Kev.

'We only got back a few minutes ago,' said Joanna.

The sad thing is, I believe you, thought Sir Gordon, but for the fourth time that day . . .

'It's really pretty round here,' said Kev.

'Yes, you'd have hated it, Emma,' said Joanna, and she blushed at her boldness.

'Oh, I don't hate beauty,' said Emma. 'I love it. Venice is the most beautiful place I've ever seen, but what's the point of painting it? It's already beautiful.'

It was Kev's turn to blush.

'There was one thing you'd have loved, though,' he said.

Joanna looked at him in alarm.

'A used condom on a cowpat,' said Kev.

Emma shook her head.

'Tempting,' she said, 'but no good. Staged. Somebody must have put it there.'

'Would that make any difference?'

'Of course. In putting it there they have created the work of art. There'd be nothing left for me to do. Great, though. I wish I'd seen it. Some people have all the luck.'

They all laughed.

But visiting your father who has Alzheimer's is no laughing matter as the final act in your attempt to have a normal family Sunday which has already seen you identify your dead brother and go to prison to visit your dead brother's son who for most of his life thought he was your son.

Sir Gordon apologized to Kirkstall for making him drive again.

'That's all right,' said Kirkstall. 'I hate Sunday evenings.'

They dropped Emma and Kev off at the Dog and Duck in Old Borthwick. His father would only be confused if there were too many people. That morning Sir Gordon had wondered what on earth the two of them would find to talk about. Now he imagined them having a passionate discussion about art. If only he could stay, except that his presence would distort the conversation completely. And of course he had to visit his father, even though there was no point; he wouldn't remember the visit in the morning.

His father was sitting in the communal lounge, which was extremely hot and smelt of urine and carrots. The room was absolutely stuffed with chairs and settees. There were cheap bookcases filled with books that looked as old and worn as the inmates. *Countryfile* was on the television. Some of the inmates were watching how to make a hedge with willow. Others were asleep. One woman farted magisterially. One man smiled. Nobody else took any notice.

Clarrie was deep in conversation with a very old woman with a skeletal face, hunched shoulders, and sparse, straggly hair. He seemed annoyed to be interrupted.

'Who the hell are you?' he said.

'I'm your son, Dad. I'm Gordon.'

'Are you sure?'

'Absolutely sure, Dad. And this is my wife Christina. And this is Joanna, your granddaughter.'

'Oh yes. Hello.'

Suddenly Clarrie was all good manners and charm, shaking hands with Christina and Joanna and saying, 'Very pleased to meet you. And I must introduce my girlfriend . . . um . . .'

He waved his frail old hand in the direction of the old woman.

'Hello . . . yes . . . I'm . . . um . . .' said the old woman in a very posh voice. 'So very pleased to meet you. I'll leave you alone with your family, Clarence.'

She walked off incredibly slowly, steering her way between the outstretched legs of the inmates.

'She forgot her own name,' said Clarrie. 'She did, silly cow. She forgot her own name. Do sit down.'

They managed to find spare seats and arranged them around Clarrie, although it was a tight squeeze.

'So, what exactly can I do for you?' asked Clarrie.

'Oh, nothing, Dad. Nothing,' said Sir Gordon.

'Really? Be pleased to help.'

'No, we've come to see you, Dad. To visit you. That's all.'

'Ah. Well, thank you. That's so kind. I'll see if they can find Margaret.' He called out. 'Hello! Nurse!'

Nobody came.

'Always short-staffed on a Tuesday,' said Clarrie. 'Don't know why.'

'Margaret's gone to Scarborough with the WI,' said Christina.

'Ah. That explains it. How's Hugo? That bastard hasn't visited me for ages.'

'He's been out of the country, Dad.'

'Best place for him. Can't stand the feller. Will they let him back in, do you think? I think it's probably a good thing if we don't try to find Margaret. She might be upset if she saw me with Audrey. Audrey! That's the name. Good company. Comes from good stock. Family live near Woodstock. Good stock in Woodstock, funny that. Jack came yesterday. He's a good boy.'

'He is. He is,' said Sir Gordon.

Sometimes they hardly got a word out of Clarrie, but today he was overflowing with chat, which made things a lot easier.

'One awkward question,' said Clarrie, lowering his voice. 'My memory's not too good these days, to be honest, and I know when you came in you told me this young lady's name, but I've forgotten it.'

'It's Joanna,' said Joanna.

'Now this is what puzzled me, do you see?' said Clarrie. 'Because you see I thought I remembered Joanna. And she was, to be honest, a bit of a mouse of a thing, and you're a lot prettier, you know.'

'Thank you, Grampa,' said Joanna, and she hardly blushed at all.

Sir Gordon and Christina both looked at Joanna and noticed for the first time that she *was* prettier. It had stolen upon her bit by bit. They smiled at her, they couldn't help it, and she smiled back, and when he saw all three of them smiling Clarrie smiled too.

'Thank you so much for coming,' he said. 'It's been very kind of you, but please don't think you have to stay. There are things I rather want to talk about with . . . um . . . you met her, I think.'

'Audrey.'

'Audrey. That's it. Audrey and I are what I believe is these days called an item. Have to be careful with Margaret of course, but there we are. She's a cracker and I can't resist her. That's all there is to it.'

They said their goodbyes. Kirkstall drove them to the Dog and Duck in Old Borthwick, where they had a quick drink with Emma and Kev, and then Kirkstall drove them all to Rose Cottage. Kev and Joanna got into Kev's rattly old car, Emma got into her rattly old car, and Sir Gordon and Christina stood at the steps of their vast cottage, their oxymoron, and waved goodbye until the two cars had disappeared, and that was a thing that they had never done before.

'I can't afford to get rid
of him'

He had expected Monday to be difficult, but he had hoped that the morning would provide a brief respite from his problems. At eleven o'clock he was due at the Coppinger Collection off Old Brompton Road, for the hanging of Turner's *Storm Approaching the Solway Firth*. His patriotic smile was ready.

Farringdon changed all that, the moment he entered the dining room. His face, usually so grave, was different. It was beyond grave. It was taut with dread.

'The newspapers, sir,' he said, in a sepulchral voice. Occasionally, since their conversation in the hospital, Sir Gordon had noticed just a hint of Brian peeping out, putting a bit of life, a slight twinkle, into those glassy eyes. Today the eyes were glassier than ever.

'Do I want to read them, Farringdon?'

'You most certainly do not, sir.'

'Should I read them?'

'You most certainly should, sir. Though reading is not required. We are in the realm of photography.'

Every paper published the same photograph of him. It showed him stark naked in the company of '*the svelte Slav*

Svetoslava', wife of his sadly inadequate centre forward, Raduslav Bogoff. Svetoslava Bogoff was also stark naked.

This scandal ticked every bad box. It showed up his widely publicized promise to Christina that he wouldn't stray again. It revealed that his claim to be dealing with his sex addiction was hollow. It proved that the rumours about why he kept Raduslav Bogoff in his team were true, thus losing him all remaining sympathy in the huge world of football. And, above all, it showed just how hypocritical his claim to be a patriot had been. All his guff about the beauty of British girls had proved to be just that . . . guff.

Only one thing could be said in Sir Gordon's defence. It wasn't true. It wasn't remotely true in any respect. It was a digital fabrication.

And of course this scandal, the only one that wasn't true, was the one that was most likely to destroy him. He needed to act, and quickly.

'There's not a word of truth in it, Farringdon,' he said.

'I should have been astonished had you told me otherwise, sir.'

'Yes, yes, thank you, but there's no time for all that. Abandon breakfast. Tell Kirkstall to be ready with the car immediately.'

Sir Gordon didn't yet realize that this morning, at a stroke, his life had become a subject of fascination for the millions of men who follow football, who use the great game as a crutch to get through this vale of tears. In pubs and clubs, on trains and buses, the mystery of why Climthorpe United continued to play Raduslav Bogoff, that famous misser of open goals, would be discussed today. Already, the first texted jokes about Bogoff and Sir Gordon's sex life were flying through the air.

Sir Gordon didn't know this, since he knew nothing about the lives of the masses. But he began to learn when he saw that there was already a crowd of paparazzi and reporters at the gates. Sex with a footballer's naked wife was far more newsworthy, in twenty-first-century Britain, than a tax scam involving a non-existent warehouse.

There was no way Kirkstall could drive on to the road without hitting photographers and reporters. Sir Gordon wound down his window. Cameras flashed and almost blinded him. Kirkstall had to look away.

There were cries of, 'Was she a good fuck?', 'Was it an open goal?', 'Did you miss like Raduslav?', 'What's the Bulgarian for "I'm coming?"', 'Is Christina on the transfer list?'

He shouted, 'It's not true', 'It's a pack of lies', 'I've been stitched up', 'Let me through.'

One woman cried out, 'Is it really not true?' He recognized her from his Guy Fawkes party. 'It's as true as it is that you're a nun,' he yelled. There was laughter. He had struck a chord. The young lady clearly had a reputation. As the laughter died down, he called out, 'Look. Play fair. I've always played fair with you. If I give you a photo and a quote, let me through. I must get to London.'

The crowd pulled back. He leant out of the window and posed with a very serious face. He said, 'I have only met this woman once and I have never had sex with her.'

Someone asked, 'Do you think she's attractive?' and he replied, 'I wouldn't touch her with a bargepole.'

They took their photos. Then they let him go. They had got what they wanted.

He phoned Gavin Welland, who agreed to mount a press conference.

'I have to go to the Coppinger Collection to pose with the Turner at eleven,' he said. 'Can we squeeze it in before that?'

'Better not. Need to give people time to arrive. Need a good crowd. Twelve-thirty. Still in time for the one o'clock news.'

'Where do you suggest having it, Gavin?'

'The foyer of the Stick of Celery, the symbol of your status, Sir Gordon.'

'Splendid, Gavin.'

'Remind the world how big your foyer is.'

'Tremendous, Gavin.'

'And, by implication, how big you are.'

'Terrific, Gavin.'

He rang Vernon Thickness on his mobile.

'Have you seen the papers, Vernon?'

'I have. Quite a goer from the look of her.'

'Shut up, Vernon. There are nine Premiership managers out of a job at this very moment. Vernon, this is a stitch-up. There's not a word of truth in it.'

'Of course not.'

'Vernon! I said, "This is a stitch-up. There's not a word of truth in it."'

'I said, "Of course not."'

'In the disbelieving tones of a dirty old man who wondered how much I enjoyed fucking her. Vernon, I repeat for one last time, "This is a stitch-up. There's not a word of truth in it." What I meant by those words was, "This is a stitch-up. There's not a word of truth in it." That is why I chose the particular words, "This is a stitch-up. There's not a word of truth in it," in the forlorn hope that you would believe that it's a stitch-up and there's not a word of truth in it. Now has that message got into your thick head?'

'Yes, boss. Sorry.'

'I hope you are. Now I want you to talk to the lads, and I want you to give them a message from me. Do you have any idea what that message might be?'

'"This is a stitch-up. It's a load of fucking bollocks."'

'Excellent. You've even improved it.' Sir Gordon changed his voice into a different gear, quieter, more earnest. 'Have you spoken to Raduslav?'

'Not yet.'

'Vernon, you know him better than me. Should you ring him or should I?'

'Oh dear. Difficult. I think you have to really, to be honest. It's difficult to talk about it second hand, know what I mean?'

'I agree, unfortunately, but I didn't want to step on your shoes. Right. Thanks, Vernon.'

Vernon Thickness gave him the Bogoff landline number and the mobile number. Both were engaged. This wasn't surprising.

The traffic was heavy and slow, this day of all days. As they crawled along the Kingston By-Pass he made notes about what he would say to the press. Every now and then he broke off to try the phones again, without luck. All his notes felt stilted, and in the end he crumpled them up viciously and decided to rely on his ability to think on his feet. Yet another mistake.

At last he got through, on the landline. Svetoslava answered. She sounded, not surprisingly, tense.

'I am so sorry about this,' he said.

'There are some wicked people in your country, Sir Gordon.'

'Yes. Does Raduslav believe you?'

'He wants to, but it is difficult for him to accept that all this is in every newspaper and it is not true. He is not used to this.'

'No.'

She spoke good English. She sounded nice. And . . . oh God . . . he had told the gathered press that he wouldn't touch her with a bargepole.

'Can I speak to him?'

'Just a moment. I'll see. He is upset.'

He waited for what seemed like a very long time. Then at last he heard Raduslav's voice, which was as heavy as his first touch tended to be.

'Hello, Sir Gordon.'

'Hello, Raduslav. I'm very sorry about this. I promise you, from the bottom of my heart, that there is not a word of truth in this. I have only met Svel . . . Svelanova . . .'

'Svetoslava.'

'Svetoslava . . . once. With you. This is made up. Fiction. I hope you believe me.'

'It is difficult. Why this? What for? People not liking me? Because I miss goals?'

'It's nothing to do with you. People want to destroy me, because I'm rich and successful. Please believe me.'

'Yes, I am sure . . . I think . . . Svetoslava is honest woman.'

'Good. Are you going in to train today?'

'I don't know. I am . . . what you say? . . . this way and that way.'

'Undecided.'

'Yes.'

'Go. Go, Raduslav and get it over with.'

'Yes, sir.'

When he put the phone down he felt very tired. He switched the phone off. He couldn't take any more. They were crawling towards Clapham. It was almost gridlock. He could do with forty winks but he was too stressed to sleep.

'I think we may need to go straight to the collection, Kirkstall,' he said.

'I think so, sir.'

He realized how rarely he spoke to Kirkstall. The man was so good, so reliable, always so calm. He really ought to take an interest. Why not now? Anything was better than worrying.

'Sorry to put you through that at the gate, Kirkstall.'

'It's all in the job, sir.'

'I never really speak to you, Kirkstall, I'm afraid. But my moments in the car are oases in my busy life.'

'I understand, sir, and I'm not the talkative type, never have been. I've got nothing to say that would interest anybody.'

301

'That in itself is interesting, Kirkstall. Would that millions of others were as perceptive about themselves.'

'That's right, sir.'

Kirkstall wove in and out of the traffic with rare skill, but, even so, they were proceeding only by fits and starts.

'But I should have asked you about your life, taken a bit of interest over the years.'

'I wouldn't bother if I were you, sir. You've seen my life. Driving's my life.'

They didn't speak again until they had crossed the Thames.

'There's worse lives,' said Kirkstall.

After that, neither of them spoke until they reached the Coppinger Collection.

The little ceremony in the main gallery of the Coppinger Collection at eleven o'clock that morning should have been one of the great moments in Sir Gordon's life. Instead, it felt like a nightmare. All the while, as he smiled his repertoire of smiles, proud but modest, simply patriotic, deeply appreciative, all the while as he listened to speeches in praise of his generosity, and tributes to the genius of Turner, all the while he was thinking about the press conference that he would soon have to face, and of the innocent wronged dignified Bulgarian lady whom, he had told the press, he wouldn't touch with a bargepole.

People are always surprised by how small the *Mona Lisa* is, and everyone here today was surprised by how small *Storm Approaching the Solway Firth* was. It didn't look impressive. It didn't look good value for the £20 million that he was by now almost certain that he couldn't afford.

The picture might have been small, but some of the dignitaries present at the ceremony were giants. Even Peregrine Thoresby, the Curator, who was over six foot, was dwarfed by his boyfriend David Emsley, the former Giant of Rosslyn Park, the beloved Big Dave of English rugby, and Sir Gordon found himself standing between Big Dave and the Earl of

Flaxborough, who was holding himself defiantly erect on this day of defeat. Sir Gordon felt very conscious of his lack of height. He was placing great store on the photographs of this event, which he hoped might help to revive his reputation, together with his denial of any affair with Svetoslava, in tomorrow's newspapers. Now he felt humiliatingly small, far smaller than he really was. It wouldn't have surprised him if one of the headlines had been *'Midget Tycoon saves Midget Picture for Nation'*.

But the worst feature of the whole event was that nobody spoke to him about the photographs at all. You might think it was a sad comment on their generosity of spirit that they found nothing supportive to say, or you might think it showed a welcome lack of malice and prejudice that nobody ventured a word of criticism, but to Sir Gordon the silence was deafening, and to him it was the silence of the closing of the ranks, it was a politeness so devastating as to feel extremely rude. He felt dreadful. He felt that, if he farted, the words 'Secondary Modern in Dudley' would come sliding out of his arse.

And oh, how he smiled, smiled as he listened to the speeches, smiled as he watched the picture being unveiled by the Marchioness of Tewkesbury (six foot two, where did they get them from, was it a conspiracy?), smiled as he said his own few words.

They had told him that they didn't want a speech, just a few words, and he had believed them. How naive was that? Now everyone was making speeches, government ministers were unrolling clichés by the yard and at least two people said that everything that needed to be said had already been said, and then proceeded to say it all over again. It was going to be tight to get to his press conference. Oh God. Missing from his own press conference! The end.

'Turner is so very British,' he said, 'and so very brilliant, and this is the sort of thing I always hoped to be able to

303

achieve when I started out on my career, to put something back for my country. This is a very proud day for me and thank you all so much for coming here to share it with me. The picture is not large, but then neither am I, and I think it appropriate that my speech should be short also. Thank you.'

Kirkstall, that calm, sedate, smooth driver, performed like Lewis Hamilton to get them to the Coppinger Tower on time. Bus drivers phoned their wives to ask them to get fresh supplies of tranquillizers. Taxi drivers made appointments with psychiatrists. A cyclist decided to emigrate. But they got there.

The moment they arrived, Sir Gordon felt better. Whatever had happened in the past, he was utterly innocent on this occasion. He drew confidence from this innocence. He found comfort in his familiar surroundings. He extracted gravitas from the walls of the Stick of Celery. He garnered joy from the knowledge that Alice Penfold was sitting there, behind her reception desk, watching him proudly.

Gavin's team had laid out chairs in rows. There were bottles of water on tap. No fewer than four of the newspapers represented had editors who had sampled the delights of his yacht. Nothing could go wrong.

Nothing did go wrong, until right at the end.

He spoke movingly about his failings, the sex addiction that he had worked so hard to conquer, the binding promises that he had made. He admitted that he no longer deserved the trust of the British people. He would have to win back that trust. He announced that he would fight to clear his name, and he would spare no expense in tracking down those who had committed this ghastly crime against the truth.

'In the past I have lied, and I have admitted it,' he said. 'Today I am lied against. I will not rest until you all believe me.'

There were questions, shrewdly managed and marshalled by the authoritative, easy-mannered, competent Gavin Welland.

The fourth question proved to be the fatal one.

'If you do not have a sexual interest in his wife, what has led you to persist with playing Raduslav Bogoff when everyone who has watched him feels he's not good enough?'

Concentrating only on the issue of the photograph, Sir Gordon was blind to other dangers.

'I paid twenty-five million for him, and now I can't sell him for peanuts,' he said. 'I can't afford to get rid of him.'

'Decision time'

Sir Gordon's remark about his centre forward caused only a modest stir in the foyer of the Coppinger Tower, where sex was the main interest of the press, but it brought an earthquake to Sir Gordon's heart. What would Raduslav Bogoff think when he heard it? What would it do for team spirit? There was a vital relegation battle tomorrow evening against Portsmouth at the Coppinger. How could the man shine now? How could he even play? He must go and speak to him. He must. Oh God, he could just imagine the scene in what was no doubt the most ridiculously ostentatious mansion within ten miles of Climthorpe. 'Darling, I am devastate. Sir Gordon, he only keep me because he cannot sell. How can I now have . . . how do the English say . . . the esteem of the myself?' 'Self-esteem, Raddy. And how can I have any self-esteem? He told the world he wouldn't touch me with a bargepole.'

It didn't bear thinking about, except that it stopped him thinking about other things that didn't bear thinking about. As the lift took him up to the nineteenth floor he consulted his mobile phone. Well, it was better than meeting the faces of the other people in the lift. Yes, he, the owner of the tower, the provider of all their jobs, found it difficult today to look any of his employees in the eye.

The phone told him that he had forty-three texts and twenty-seven voice messages. He pretended to hope that it had gone berserk – he'd never liked the little bastard, horrible little temperamental bugger – but he knew that it hadn't. The world wanted to speak to him. He couldn't speak to all the world at once. He switched it off.

Courage, Gordon. Garibaldi. He tried to march through the open-plan office towards Helen Grimaldi as if he had 10,000 Redshirts marching behind him, but he had an awful feeling that he looked more like Mussolini than Garibaldi, and Mussolini never had a biscuit named after him. 'Helen, can I tempt you to a Mussolini?' He was going mad. His mind was cracking up.

'There you are!' said Helen, and he realized how often she had stated the obvious in their years together. 'I've been trying to get you everywhere. Everyone wants to speak to you.'

'Everyone?'

'Well, particularly Wally Frobisher. He's going frantic.'

'Oh dear. Oh God.'

'And the three musketeers from GI. They're in a panic.'

'Oh dear. Oh God.'

'And your brother.'

'Oh! Ah!'

There was hope.

The phone rang even as they spoke.

'Sir Gordon Coppinger's secretary. How can I help you? . . . Hello, Fred . . . I'll see if he's in.'

He wished she wouldn't say that. It was pointless. She was his secretary. She was both efficient and nosey. She would always know whether he was in. She might just as well have said, 'I'll see if he wants to speak to you, because he may not – you are not actually his favourite person or particularly important. Hang on'.

Did he want to speak to Fred Upson?

307

Not particularly.

Would he prefer to speak to Fred Upson than to his accountant or the men from GI?

Definitely.

He nodded.

'He's in. Hang on a moment. I'm putting you through.'

He walked into his office, and suddenly felt a whole lot calmer. This was his domain. This was a place where he couldn't be interrupted.

He picked up the phone.

'Hello, Fred.'

'I'm out on bail.'

'Good. Good. I'm glad.'

'Thank you so much for that.'

'Don't be silly. All I could do. I've got far more to thank you for. It was fantastic of you not to involve me.'

'All *I* could do.'

'Meaning?'

'No one in the world will employ me now. No one. Except you. If I involve you you'll go to prison too and what good would that do me? My only hope is your survival.'

'That was brilliant thinking, Fred. Fantastic.'

'I must say I was pretty pleased with myself.'

'Fred, there is one thing. If they ask you what your motive was, as I'd have thought they almost certainly will, what will you say?'

'My motive?'

'Well, your scam, if you like.'

'Are you doubting me?'

'No, Fred, not at all.'

'I don't have a motive. I don't have a scam. There's absolutely nothing in this for me. I haven't cheated you in any way.'

'So what are you going to say if they ask you why you did it?'

'Oh, I see.'

'Exactly. It's a tax scam and you would not be paying the tax, so, if you don't have a motive, they'll know you were doing it on orders from me, and that will defeat your purpose.'

'Yes, I see. I'll have to think of something.'

'You certainly will.'

'I don't know that I can. That's not my mindset. I'm an honest man.'

'Oh, come off it, Fred. You've managed twenty years of systematic tax evasion.'

'I didn't mean morally. I just meant . . . imagination-wise. I'm not sure I'm capable of thinking up anything illegal.'

'You'd better, for both our sakes.'

'I'll think about it . . . Um . . .'

As he waited for Fred Upson to overcome his hesitation, Sir Gordon caught sight of the framed photograph of his brother Hugo. That pinched, puffy face didn't look like the sort of face you would expect help from, but he had a feeling that enormous help was going to come from that direction. He must get Fred off the phone and ring Hugo.

'Yes, Fred?'

'Sorry. I was hesitating because I know you're very busy, with . . .' Fred Upson clearly couldn't think of any ending to his sentence that wouldn't be tactless, so he just stopped.

'What is it, Fred?'

Sir Gordon only just hid his rising impatience.

'Can we meet to . . . well, discuss all this and maybe . . . see what sort of job you might be able to offer me.'

'Yes, yes, good idea.'

'Would Friday morning be any good?'

'Friday?'

Sir Gordon had already switched his computer on and his list of engagements soon floated into view.

'Friday, ten-thirty? Give you time to avoid an overnight stay?'

'Oh, thank you. Thank you.'

'Least I could do.'

Sir Gordon banged the phone down before Fred Upson could mention his expenses. He picked it up again immediately, before his accountant or the GI Three could ring, but he did it too quickly and the line hadn't yet been reconnected. He put it down again, waited for as long a time as he dared, heart racing – this was dreadful, he was becoming a nervous wreck. He picked it up and got the tone. He dialled Hugo's number. Be in. Be in, you bastard.

Hugo was in.

'Coppinger.'

Sir Gordon realized for the first time that they both answered the phone with that single confident, almost arrogant word.

'Oh hello, Hugo. It's me.'

'Ah! I've been trying to get you.'

'My phone's red hot.'

'Not surprising.'

'No. Hugo?'

The one good thing about all this, he reflected, was that it showed his heart to be in good nick. The hammerings it was surviving. Now his whole chest was tight, he could hardly breathe.

'Any news?' he croaked.

'I came back this morning with the bones of an agreement.'

Relief surged through Sir Gordon as if he had taken a huge slurp of scalding chocolate.

'Oh, Hugo. Thank you.'

'Wait.'

Now he was gulping again. If his body survived this call, he wouldn't need a BUPA check-up for five years.

'Then the news about this footballer's wife broke.'

'But it's all made up, Hugo. All of it.'

'I believe you. But will they? These are honest people, Gordon.'

They're bankers, but I'd better not say anything.

'The SFN business stretched things. People are reluctant to make a final commitment. You're going to have to hang on a bit longer.'

'Oh, Hugo.'

They talked then about Jack. Sir Gordon told him how moved he had been on identifying the body. Hugo said he was sorry he'd been away. In fact he said it four times, as if he hoped that repetition was a good substitute for emotion. When at last the call ended, Sir Gordon put the phone down slowly, let it rest for a moment, managed somehow to pluck up a reserve of strength, and dialled Adam Eaglestone.

Ten minutes later he met Keith Gostelow, Dan Perkins, and Adam Eaglestone in the anonymous surroundings of the David Lloyd George Conference Room, with Lloyd George staring out from behind him. Had he chosen this room because it reminded him of another flawed hero with a weakness for women? Or because the Welshness of the man, and the middle of his name, brought back a memory of Megan Lloyd-Phillips, the woman he most regretted not having fucked, by a short head from Alice Penfold, with Kim Novak putting in a spirited finish in the final furlong? Stop it, Gordon. Concentrate.

'So, what's the position and what do we think?' he asked.

'This . . . you know . . . this news today . . . um . . . although you've . . . you know . . . also today . . . I don't think your statement has . . . well . . . you know, really on balance. Sorry,' said Keith Gostelow, who had a loose plaster over a boil on the side of his neck. 'I think, you know, money isn't coming in . . . well, I mean it is, I suppose, but not enough to say, "Money's coming in," if you know what I mean, so we can ignore that, but I mean, the withdrawals . . . they're not . . . you know . . . I mean, they have slowed a bit since, you know, your press conference, but I mean, they are rising, in the sense of . . . you know . . . being above

311

what they were before they rose, even though, I mean, to be fair, they aren't rising as fast, but not rising as fast isn't really . . . I mean, is it? . . . it isn't . . . a decline. Is it? And it has come on top of lots of . . . in other unrelated fields . . . well, hasn't it? Let's face it, it has. So, no, sorry, I don't think we can . . . you know . . . much longer. If at all . . .'

'Thank you, Keith. Adam?'

'I agree broadly with Keith's analysis,' said Adam Eaglestone, who had a very small trail of tomato sauce down the front of his shirt. 'The bottom line at this moment in time is that at this moment in time your analysis, Sir Gordon, that what they're calling Dudleygate is not part of a meltdown in the Coppinger global picture, has not carried sentiment with it in terms of the average small and middle-sized investor retaining confidence in the stability of GI in terms of being unaffected by not only Dudleygate but other unfortunate incidents of a controversial character which, though completely confined to a sexual scenario and therefore irrelevant financially, are together creating a surge of unfavourable sentiment which has been slowed by your claims of innocence but which could push the reserves beyond the level not only of good financial practice but even to a situation in which there was ultimately, if not sooner, a totally insufficient pool of liquidity.'

'Thank you, Adam. Dan?'

'We have to close down the business, and we have to close it down now,' said Dan Perkins.

'Thank you,' said Sir Gordon. 'Thank you, gentlemen. Dan, in very few words, can we survive the afternoon?'

'Just,' said Dan Perkins.

'Thank you.'

'But I don't recommend it and I don't see the point,' said Dan Perkins.

'The point is that things will be happening in the newspapers tomorrow,' said Sir Gordon. 'Things which may turn

312

the tide of sentiment in my favour. I'm going to see Wally now, and tell him that I want to ride this out until say mid-morning tomorrow. Eleven o'clock tomorrow, let's meet here again. Thank you, gentlemen.'

Sir Gordon gathered up his papers and walked out of the room with a touch of his old authority. A few minutes later, he arrived at the Sir Walter Raleigh Room. Wally Frobisher was waiting for him.

'I've been trying to get hold of you all day,' Sir Gordon said.

'I've been busy.'

Wally repeated the advice of the GI Three. Sir Gordon repeated his insistence that they hold off until eleven o'clock the next morning. He expressed his faith in the effect on confidence that would be given them by the morning's newspapers. Wally expressed his doubt about the power of newspapers in today's world. Sir Gordon expressed his belief in the effect of the TV news, when he was seen smiling beside the Earl of Flaxborough and the Turner he had bought off him. Sir Gordon expounded on the trust he had in the common sense of the good old British public. Wally refrained from saying that he would think it very sensible of the British public if they believed that while the Turner painting *Storm Approaching the Solway Firth* was very nice, £20 million was a lot to pay for it and great good works could have been done for the needy in our society with that money. Sir Gordon emphasized how confident he was that there would be a flood of supportive Tweets, of messages on YouTube, of friendship on Facebook. Throughout the land people would be texting each other to support this great champion of the arts, of sport, of Britain.

Wally 'Proboscis' Frobisher, tough man though he was, found it difficult for quite a while to get a word in edgeways, and he certainly didn't have the courage to suggest to Sir Gordon that he had allowed himself to become deluded. He

313

also had the sense not to tell him at this late stage that for many years he had pointed out that Sir Gordon was over-stretching himself, that he had moved into too many areas, that he had been greedy, that it had been wrong to want a piece of everything, that there had always been a risk of a lack of liquidity when hard times struck, that he had not been wise – by which he meant that he had not listened to him, Wally Frobisher, which was a big mistake, because Wally was one of the shrewdest men who ever walked the earth.

'My brother Hugo has been trying to mount a rescue package for several weeks now,' Sir Gordon told him.

'What sort of package?'

'I don't really know. Something that would give us money to legitimize GI. Actually invest in the companies we claimed to be investing in. Retrospectively. I suppose.'

Wally stared at him, and didn't reply. Sir Gordon stared back. He had forgotten that he had never told Wally that GI wasn't legitimate.

'Are you telling me that GI is a Ponzi scheme?' asked Wally with every appearance of incredulity.

'You must know it is. You're so close to it, and you're clever.'

Wally gave a strange little smile that didn't reach his eyes.

'I may have suspected,' he said. 'I don't say I did, but with your reputation, and your volatility, which the public never sees, how could I say anything?'

'You didn't want to say anything. You like what I pay you too much.'

'Moving on from the past to the future, which *is* rather more important,' said Wally, 'I can't see anybody lending you money with that avowed aim, but I'm sure we could have got you enough money for some purpose or other and used it for that purpose or most of it for that purpose. Once you'd got it nobody would have done any very thorough checks on you, with your reputation.'

'Can you not get that money now?'

'Almost certainly not.'

'Will you try?'

'Why don't you try? You have more clout.'

'I don't know that I can bear to beg.'

'Good God, man, do you want to survive this or not?'

'Please, Wally, make some enquiries. Put out some feelers. Pave the way. Make it easier for me.'

Wally Frobisher shook his head at this unprecedented sign of weakness from his employer.

'Oh, Sir Gordon, Sir Gordon, why, oh why, did you go to your brother?' he asked.

'Because he is my brother, and because he knows more about banking than any of us.'

'I don't believe he'd take risks with the law. I don't believe he'd take risks at all. He's got very rich indeed without taking any risks at all. So he's got nowhere?'

'Apparently he has. Apparently he flew back into England last night with a rescue package. He's been negotiating all over the place.'

'So you have your rescue. Why didn't you tell me?'

'I don't have my rescue. Recent press stories seem to have rather put the kibosh on it. He's had to go back to them.'

'Oh, Gordon, Gordon, Gordon.' Wally turned to a picture of that other Walter, who was unlikely ever to have been called Wally. It showed Sir Walter Raleigh with Queen Elizabeth I. 'Oh, Sir Walter. Oh, Your Majesty. You wouldn't believe the naivety of this man. But they say every great man has a blind spot. What was your blind spot, Sir Walter?'

'Are you saying you don't believe in Hugo's integrity, Wally?'

'I am saying I don't believe in Hugo's integrity at all.'

Sir Gordon felt more tired than he had ever felt in his life. He was famed for his energy. He was admired for his stamina. He had boasted that he didn't need a lot of sleep. It was as if all his energy and stamina had been used up. It was as if he needed hundreds of hours of sleep to bring his average up to eight hours a night. His weariness was shocking to him.

Wally Frobisher's great nose was good at other things besides sniffing out fraud and detecting areas where profits could be made. He was sometimes able to catch the scent of other people's thoughts. And he detected Sir Gordon's weariness now, valiantly though the man himself was attempting to hide it. He had intended to tell Sir Gordon that even until last week there might have been a chance of getting the money they would have needed, but he didn't think Sir Gordon would be able to bear that news just now. There was no more that he could say. The man needed rest. He needed to go home. He needed his wife, if she was still close enough to him to behave as a wife.

'Till eleven o'clock tomorrow then,' he said. 'Decision time.'

A magic moment

She was sitting by the east fire, as he had known she would be. Her face was like the Berlin Wall.

'Sit down,' she commanded.

He didn't want to sit down. He wanted to tower over her. He wanted to pace up and down.

'Sit down,' she repeated.

He pulled a heavy armchair up to the fire, and sat down. He reached out his hand, and pressed a bell at the side of the fireplace. He could hear the bell ringing, far away, in the kitchens.

'What do you think you're doing?'

'Ringing for a drink.'

'You are not having a drink, Gordon. You face this without a drink.'

Farringdon entered.

'Yes, sir? Yes, madam?'

'I would like some of that marvellous Meursault, Farringdon.'

'Sir Gordon has told you what he would like, not what he will have, Farringdon,' said Christina. 'What he will have is nothing. I will have a glass of the Veuve Clicquot.'

Farringdon gave Sir Gordon an uncertain, worried look.

'That's right, Farringdon,' said Sir Gordon. 'Her Ladyship will have a glass of the Veuve Clicquot. I will have nothing.'

Farringdon made the long trek across the flat fields of Wilton extremely slowly, as if by doing so he could protect his master from the lashing he would shortly receive from his wife's tongue.

Only when the door to the kitchens had been firmly closed did Christina speak.

'What has been going on?' she demanded.

'Christina, I didn't do it. I've been stitched up.'

'Why should I believe you?'

'Oh God!'

It was a yell to make Dresden shepherdesses shake on mantelpieces. It was a cry dug out of frustration and carved out of despair. It was a cry of an intensity that astonished his wife. Immediately, she seemed no longer to be in complete control.

'There's no reason why you should believe me,' he said quietly, but still with intensity. 'That's what's so awful. I have lost the right to be trusted, and everybody knows it, and so I'm fair game. But I need you to believe me. I need it, Christina. I made you a solemn promise that I wouldn't stray again. If I broke that, we would have nothing left.'

Farringdon approached with Christina's champagne and all the speed of a tortoise that is sickening for something.

'Your Veuve Clicquot, madam.'

'Thank you, Farringdon.'

'And two Bath Olivers.'

'Thank you, Farringdon.'

Farringdon had never brought them Bath Olivers before. Sir Gordon realized that he was aware of the depth of their marital crisis and the only way he could think of to show his sympathy and support was to bring them two Bath Olivers – one each.

Farringdon ambled towards the kitchens. He seemed to move even more slowly than before. If he *had* been a tortoise he would have been hibernating before he reached the door.

Christina, watching him go, ate a Bath Oliver, took a sip of champagne, then ate the other Bath Oliver.

'*Have* we anything left?' she asked, when the door to the kitchens had been closed at last.

'Oh, I hope so, Christina. And I promise you utterly and totally that I have never been to bed with Svetoslava, that I have never seen her naked in the flesh, or wanted to see her naked in the flesh, and having seen her naked in the flesh in the newspapers I have even less desire to see her naked in the flesh.'

'I think perhaps I probably do almost believe you,' she said, with some surprise in her voice.

'Well, I suppose I have to be glad of the basic principle and ignore all the qualifications. Thank you,' he said.

'It's just that it has been difficult to believe you've turned over a new leaf after Mandy and Francesca and Sandy and Kerry and Ellie and Uncle Tom Cobley and all.'

Should he? Was there any point? But he found, to his surprise, that he wanted to. Anything to bring them closer together.

'I did live with a man once,' he said.

'Gordon!'

'No more lies. Before I met you, of course. I was young.'

'I can't believe this. You. Mr Heterosexual.'

'Dennis was really gay. I was just playing at it.'

'Dennis!'

'You may have known him, in Dudley. He was a very nice bloke actually. I've often wondered what happened to him. If he remembers when he sees me in the papers. If he's still alive. He was a quantity surveyor.'

Christina laughed.

'What's so funny?'

She became hysterical. She could hardly speak through her hysterics.

'What was his verdict after he'd surveyed your quantity?' she asked.

He had never seen her like this. He put it down to nerves. But it did irritate him. It trivialized his revelation.

At last her hysterics died down. Even on happy occasions there can be flat moments at the end of a burst of hysterics. After Christina's hysterics there was a long, indefinable silence, broken only by the spitting of a recalcitrant log. Then she rang the bell. Farringdon entered with the bottle of Veuve Clicquot. She waved him back towards the kitchens.

'Yes, please, another glass, but also Sir Gordon is ready for his Meursault,' she said.

Sir Gordon had the distinct impression that she was wanting to say something else, but she remained silent until the drinks arrived. They both stared mesmerically into the fire.

'Shall I get Coleman to put some more logs on the fire?' enquired Farringdon.

'No, Farringdon,' said Christina. 'We don't need Coleman. Sir Gordon can be log man. And you might leave the champagne and bring the bottle of Meursault. We would like to be alone.'

'I understand, madam,' said Farringdon gravely. It was more than Sir Gordon did.

He put two more logs on the fire and they waited for the bottle. Only when all this had been concluded and they were alone again did Christina proceed, and in a very low voice.

'What is the truth of our position, Gordon?' she asked. 'What is going on?'

The logs, piled on by Sir Gordon, blazed joyously. He had discovered a new talent. He had also discovered, after years of glumly watching while people did things for him, the pleasure to be had in doing things yourself.

'Is it all over?' she asked abruptly. 'Can we keep all this?'

He didn't answer immediately. He sipped his Meursault, a superb wine, yellow with age and richness, sweet and soft and buttery and indulgent and yet at the same moment by some miracle utterly dry and spare. Not many people who invested with GI could afford a wine like this. Fewer now. He sighed.

'We still have extensive assets,' he said. 'I still have all my factories, though they're not all doing as well as they were. I still have a vast property portfolio, much of it still healthy despite a few problems. No, we'll survive, though life won't be quite the same, I'm afraid. I may have to sell the yacht. You won't mind that. You never liked it.'

'Won't selling it be a sign that you're in trouble?'

'Not if I say it's a symbolic gesture to show that I am alongside the British people in their sacrifices in a recession.'

'Could you really tell a brazen lie like that? I mean, it's a bit different from lying to your wife about your love life.'

'I'm afraid I have wide-ranging practice at lying, Christina. I'm quite an expert.'

'I have to ask you, Gordon, is it true that you knew nothing about SFN Holdings?'

'No, of course it isn't. It was all my idea. I'm the one who needed a tax scam. I'm the one who pays the taxes. I don't feel guilty about that. I still pay enough tax in my opinion and I don't approve of half of what the government does with my money.'

It was such a relief to tell the truth and, really, it didn't sound at all bad when put like that.

He eyed the fire up, an expert log man already. He placed another log carefully. The fire responded. He couldn't help smiling proudly, even at this serious moment.

He poured himself a generous measure of the glorious Meursault.

He felt a great urge to confess the full situation, even to tell her that he might go to prison for a very long time. That shocked him to the core. He hadn't even told himself that yet. Suddenly to realize the possibility, here beside the east fire, a fire so hot that they had to move their chairs back due to his sudden discovery of his new skill with logs, that was truly disturbing. He tried to give a calm smile.

He couldn't yet tell her that GI was an enormous scam too. He was terrified that she would ask him about it. He didn't know how he would respond.

It was time to change the subject.

'The thing is, Christina . . .'

'Oh dear. I loathe that phrase. It never precedes anything nice.'

'The thing is – I'm trying to be truthful, Christina. I've grown absolutely fed up with lies.'

'Yes, I believe you have.'

This surprised him. He glanced at her. Her face was shining in the light from the flames. He thought that she had never looked prettier, and the thing was, the haughtiness had gone, the 'Her Ladyship' look had gone, this was a woman who just could, admittedly many years ago, have been voted Miss Lemon Drizzle.

'I've tried to be honest at last, and I find I'm telling more lies than ever.'

'I think that's the nature of honesty, Gordon, and meanwhile I wait patiently to find out what the thing about which you said the thing is, is.'

'The thing is . . . tomorrow is decision time. After tomorrow, I think we'll know our fate.'

'Oh dear.'

'It may be good. I'm not despairing. And whatever happens, we'll have all this. And we'll have each other.'

She didn't respond to this. He might have wished for a positive response, but on the other hand he knew that only a few weeks ago he would have been guaranteed a snort of derision, and of all the things he had experience of snorting, derision was the worst.

It was time to change the subject.

He gave a gentle cough. The message of his gentle cough

was, 'We have been discussing matters of great importance, but now we have to discuss something of even more importance. Us.'

He leant across and clinked his glass with hers. He wanted to say, 'I love you.' It was there, but it wouldn't come out.

'I still care a lot for you,' he said instead.

She noted the evasion with a small but not unpleasant smile.

'I see you now in the firelight and you look fantastic. I still don't think . . . anything will . . . well . . . happen tonight. I don't know why. I don't understand why.'

'Perhaps it's age,' she said.

'Oh, come off it, we're relatively young and virile for these days. You know that's not it. Unless you've gone off sex prematurely.'

'No.'

'Ah. Christina, I've never asked you, it hasn't seemed important, but now it is. Is there anybody . . . you know . . . in your life?'

'Not as such.'

'What do you mean – "not as such"?'

'Not exactly.'

'That's not much better.'

'I'm not having sex with anybody. OK, Gordon, I'll be honest too. I've had sex four times with someone else in the whole of our marriage. Just four times. The first time was nine years ago with a Finnish horticulturalist who specializes in climbing roses.'

'He climbed all over you.'

'Gordon!'

'Sorry. Sorry.'

'We met at a garden show in Melton Mowbray.'

'Melton Mowbray! I thought it would be somewhere like Montreux or Cannes.'

'I know.'

'And the other three?'

'Later the same night.'

'Good Lord. What a climber.'

'Gordon!'

'Sorry. So what about the "not as such, not exactly" man?'

'That's long-standing and occasional. Lunches. Dinners. Theatres. Opera. Company when you're busy. An occasional kiss. Nothing more. And we're very discreet.'

'Who is this man?'

'I'm pledged to secrecy, and it wouldn't interest you. He's nobody you know. That's all, Gordon.'

'So we still haven't a clue why we don't manage sex together any more.'

'Well, I suspect it was so very good for so many years that we're frightened that it just can't compete.'

'I never thought of it as a competitive sport.'

'Oh, I'm not talking of the sex, Gordon. That can be nice and gentle and get more gentle and fade into lovely warm companionship, I couldn't care less. I'm talking about trust. I'm not sure we could ever manage anything again without complete and perfect and justified trust. I think it would be a far bigger commitment than either of us has felt the slightest need to make for a very long time.'

'I think I'd hope that the gentle fading would take quite a long while to happen, but yes, I take your point.'

Now the fire did need a couple more logs and it was time to fill both their glasses again. As he did so, she leant over and kissed him, not exactly warmly, but still, a kiss is a kiss is a kiss, as Gertrude Stein might have said on one of her more affectionate days. He could feel his heart racing. He was approaching the important question. He was nervous. He was so glad to be nervous. It showed that he was alive. It showed that he cared.

'Do you feel that you could make that commitment?' he asked.

She took a sip of her champagne. She avoided his eyes, then gave him a swift look.

'I don't know,' she said.

They sat in silence for what seemed to both of them to be a very long time.

'Sorry,' she said.

'No, no,' he said. 'No, no. I like that answer. I was frightened you'd say no.'

Farringdon emerged from the kitchens and announced, as gravely as ever, 'Dinner is served.'

Amazingly, hungry though they were, they were not pleased to hear this. It felt, against all the odds, as if he had interrupted a magic moment.

He didn't think that problem would be any easier

Every morning now saw Sir Gordon propelled from sleep to reality as if fired from a cannon. Eleven o'clock, decision time, that fact hit him in the face like a snowball. It was a cold, crisp morning, too cold for snow, a perfect winter's day, but it might have gone down in the annals of Sir Gordon Coppinger's life as Black Tuesday, if the adjective hadn't been needed to describe the following Wednesday.

'You're very quiet this morning, Farringdon,' commented Sir Gordon as his butler brought the newspapers and his freshly squeezed grapefruit juice to the round rosewood (what else?) dining table.

'The whole world has words aplenty to say about you, sir,' said Farringdon. 'I thought I would spare you any further comment.'

'Thank you, Farringdon. You're a gem.'

'I have enjoyed every moment of our long relationship, sir, and it has been my fervent wish that I should perform my duties in such a way that it would not be entirely inconceivable that you would describe me as a gem, but to hear the realization of that hope from your lips is a joy almost beyond belief, sir.'

Sir Gordon longed to say, 'Stop taking the piss, Brian,' but he found that he just couldn't. They were locked into this stately verbal dance. He ventured a touch of humour, though.

'If you wish to lie down after that sentence, Farringdon, feel free. I can pour my own tea.'

'Sir is in waggish form this morning, despite the clouds that gather. Listen to me, sir. Determined to be silent, I find myself prattling on.'

'Life is rarely as we expect it to be, Farringdon.'

That adage proved true from the start. The newspapers were not at all as Sir Gordon had expected them to be. Yes, the story of the Turner was there. There was the picture of him with his fixed, frozen smile, surrounded by giants, looking ready to have his greatness diminished by the world. But it was not on the front pages, it was not given as much space as he had expected, none of the papers shouted about a great day for Britain. And yes, his assertion that the photo of himself with Svetoslava was a fake was there, but it was not given anything like the prominence of the original revelation. It read like a reluctant admission that his innocence was a possibility.

He reminded himself that the newspapers did not have their former influence. He persuaded himself that things would be more favourable on the networking sites, where the great British public would be expressing their love for him and their horror at the stitch-up. He almost convinced himself.

The Kingston By-Pass was clearer than he had ever known it. Kirkstall just whizzed along.

The sunlight was gleaming on the word '*Coppinger*' at the top of the Coppinger Tower. There was his name, shining out, ironically, in gold. It shouldn't be sunny today, and his name should no longer be in gold. Yes, it should. He wasn't giving up yet. Yesterday's weakness had been but a blip. He was a fighter again.

Outside the Coppinger Tower, there was, if not a forest, at least a sizeable copse of photographers and cameramen. He was news now whatever he did. He waved and smiled and said, 'No comment,' and hurried into the Stick of Celery.

Inside the huge foyer, everything was normal. Quite a few people were waiting for the lifts, the rubber plants all looked healthy, and so did Alice Penfold. There was nobody for her to deal with at the reception desk. He grabbed his chance.

'Hello, Alice, how are you?'

'I'm good. How are you, Sir Gordon?'

'Oh, I'm . . . I can't get used to saying "good" like you all do. I'm very well. In the pink, to use an even sillier expression. How's Tom? Is he good? Is he in the pink?'

'I don't know. He's away on a course.'

'Oh dear. All on your own?'

She held his glance for just a moment.

'Yes.'

He couldn't believe it. She was flirting with him. He felt hugely aroused. Junket in Orpington with a tattooed undertaker.

'So when's he back?'

'Not till Saturday morning.'

Her cheeks had gone pink. Quorn on a tour of Finnish garage forecourts with Morris dancers from Kettering.

'Sir Gordon?'

'Yes?'

'I'm sorry about . . .'

She stopped. She didn't know how to describe his catastrophe tactfully, bless her.

'Thank you. Thank you so much, Alice. Now you look after yourself. London's dangerous when a girl's on her own.'

'Oh, I will, Sir Gordon. I will.'

He forced himself away from her desk. He strode to the lift, trying to look several years younger than fifty-six.

The lift stopped five times before it reached the nineteenth floor. Nobody spoke to him. They avoided eye contact. They didn't know what to say. He was getting used to it, and today he had his defences ready.

He knew that there were 101 things that he should be doing, but he felt that all of them were dependent on the decision that would be reached at eleven o'clock.

He phoned through to Helen Grimaldi to tell her that he was planning his strategy for an important meeting and mustn't be disturbed except by Wally Frobisher and the GI Three.

He flicked through the Internet. He began to look up the latest share prices of those of his factories that were quoted. It wasn't good news, so he abandoned that. He had a brief look at Twitter. Nothing encouraging there. He took virtual reality tours of some of his more glamorous properties, but he knew in his heart that in reality most of them would not look so glamorous now. They had mostly been acquired in the late eighties and early nineties and they were showing their age. A huge need for redecoration and renovation and modernization was piling up. In an ideal world they should be broken up like old cruise ships and replaced by state-of-the-art new buildings.

Suddenly it seemed that in all his empire there was no comfort to be found anywhere. He forgot that he had asked Helen to stop calls, and felt that the whole world had abandoned him. It was as if he was lost in space, as if the walls of his great office were expanding away from him. It felt like the opposite of his claustrophobia and it was just as bad.

At twenty-five past ten he could bear it no longer. He phoned Wally Frobisher and arranged to meet him in the James Watt Conference Room, far away in the recesses of the seventeenth floor.

The James Watt Conference Room was the spitting image of all the neutral conference rooms dotted round the Coppinger Tower. It was dominated by a large reproduction of the portrait of Watt by H. Howard that hangs in the National

Portrait Gallery. Another reproduction of the same picture hangs in the boardroom of the Kwality Kettle Korporation.

Sir Gordon and Wally shook hands.

'I feel we should have a cup of tea,' said Sir Gordon.

'What?'

'Exactly.'

'What?'

'Watt.'

'What?'

'James Watt. He invented the kettle. We should use his invention, show him our respect. It may bring luck.'

'Good Lord. I didn't realize you were so superstitious.'

'Nor did I.'

'What?'

'We learn about ourselves in times of crisis.'

'Ah.'

They sent for two cups of tea.

It was strange, but neither of them felt that the meeting could really begin until they were settled with their cups of tea. This was a moment, in the middle of a huge crisis, for idle chat.

'Sir Gordon,' said Wally, 'I meant to apologize yesterday for . . . well, no, "apologize" is the wrong word, I was fully entitled. Let's say meant to express my regret that I was away on holiday in America while events were beginning to move so quickly.'

'Sod's law. Were you touring?'

'No, I was re-enacting the American Civil War. Terrific fun.'

'Who won?'

'It's not like that. There'd be no point in doing it if you changed the result. You have to work round to achieving the historical result. That's the fun.'

Sir Gordon had no knowledge of any questions he could safely ask on this subject. He had no idea who had fought in the American Civil War, let alone who had won. Luckily the tea came swiftly.

Sir Gordon astonished Wally by clinking mugs and saying, 'To Watt.'

'To Watt.'

Now Sir Gordon knew that there was no further way in which the discussion of the decision could be delayed.

'So,' he said, his heart thumping, 'have we news from GI this morning?'

'Not good,' said Wally. 'Not good. Almost irredeemably bad.'

'Almost?'

'Withdrawals have slowed since your protestation of innocence, which incidentally has been most inadequately publicized, but that was all we could expect in reality, nobody wishes to highlight the fact that he was duped. But investment is almost nil, Sir Gordon, so the good news is that we are losing a lot of money every minute, but a lot less every minute than we were losing yesterday.'

'Might that improvement not continue?'

'Marginally, perhaps.'

'Did you . . . um . . . speak to the bank, as we discussed?'

'I did.'

'And?'

'It's too late.'

'Can we not sell assets? The yacht. A factory. Properties.'

'First of all, not possibly within the timescale needed, no.'

'Can we not borrow against these expected assets?'

'I doubt it, quite honestly, but it would be fatal at this moment in time.'

'Why?'

It would increase even further the lack of confidence which is causing you to consider selling them.'

'But by that argument I'm trapped.'

'I think you are.'

'You should have seen this coming.'

'Sir Gordon, I have tried to warn you.'

'Not in so many words, surely?'

'No. You're a strong, powerful, stubborn man. We all have to send you coded messages.'

'But I'm not bright enough to understand coded messages. Please, Wally, answer me a question now. I've been on the Net this morning and I've found that the shares in my factories are falling. Why? Are people really buying fewer kettles, fewer cans of S'ssh!, fewer electric cars, fewer settees?'

'Possibly to a certain extent people are turning against your products, yes, but . . .'

'But my products aren't any worse than they were.'

'That isn't the point. The point is confidence. Very little on the Stock Exchange is about facts. Why do you think the word "sentiment" is used so often? The things that affect share prices most are emotions – hope, fear, panic. That's why the strong always win at the expense of the weak, the professionals at the expense of the amateurs, the rich at the expense of the poor. And that's why it is virtually impossible to change the system, since the people who would benefit from a change in the system are the people who have least influence. Incredibly, Sir Gordon, until recently you've been so brilliantly successful that you've never needed to know the first thing about economics.'

'So it seems.'

'And while we chatter, and James Watt stares down at us, you are losing a huge amount of money every minute.'

'So you advise . . .?'

'I honestly advise – and, Sir Gordon, I do know what a terrible moment this is for you – I advise that you close down GI forthwith.'

'How do I do that?

'You go to the thirteenth floor, you tell them that the game is up, you issue a statement, you record a phone statement, you apply an automated electronic response, no further money moves in any direction. They'll do all that, they'll be prepared, they'll be expecting this.'

'Are you coming with me?'

'Of course not.'

'What?'

'I think you're forgetting, Sir Gordon, that I know nothing about this. I am horrified to learn that GI is a huge fraud. I would not have believed it possible for you to get away with such a thing for so long. I blame myself for being naive and not showing due diligence. I am shocked, and saddened. I think you should go now. Every minute may be costing you millions.'

Sir Gordon took the lift down to the thirteenth floor. Now he looked at every person he saw and wondered if they had invested with GI, wondered if he had ruined them. He didn't know how he could bear it, but bear it he must, and therefore, bear it he did.

He entered the great open-plan office on the thirteenth floor. Here a great phalanx of pale men and pale women who barely saw daylight in winter were wrestling with phones and computers. They realized that this was a financial crisis. They were anxious, worried, some terrified, but it still hadn't occurred to them that the tedious enterprise on which they had wasted so much of their one stab at existence was a fiction and a fraud. Or, if it had occurred to them, they had buried their suspicions.

He walked calmly across this vast room, which he had never visited because he had never been able to face the enormity of his deception. He could face it now. Besides, there was no time for reflection. That is one good thing about an emergency. There is no longer any time for worry.

He told Keith Gostelow, Dan Perkins, and Adam Eaglestone that the game was up. They reacted like men who had been released from a nightmare but are already vaguely aware that they will soon be moving into that other nightmare, the rest of their lives.

At seven minutes past eleven that morning, Gordon Investments closed its doors. Well, not its doors, it didn't have doors, it didn't have offices outside which angry investors could queue and shout and throw stones. It closed its business utterly. It closed its telephone lines literally in the middle of many conversations. New callers received a message which stated simply, 'The GI office is closed.'

GI existed in the world of telephones and electronics, of communication without physical contact. It had once been described by a financial journalist as 'virtually virtual'. Now millions of investors were going to discover that it had actually been entirely virtual.

Sir Gordon, to do him credit – credit! He had no credit now – tracked down a loudhailer and addressed the staff of GI personally.

'Gordon Investments has failed,' he announced. His voice was strong, but it had a tremble in it. 'We are shutting down as of now. We are no more. You have no jobs. In simple terms, we cannot meet our commitments. This is a very, very sad day for me, but I know that it is also a very sad day for each and every one of you. I am hopeful that at a later stage – how much later I cannot say – we will be able to find the money needed, the immense amount of money needed, to pay each and every investor what we owe them. Should that happen, I will re-employ any employee who wishes it, albeit on a temporary basis. But none of this will happen overnight.

'In the meantime I have to tell you that I am giving you all as much commitment as I can still afford – four weeks' notice from next Monday. You will please continue to come in to clear up whatever still needs to be cleared up, and no doubt meet with liquidators etc. However, I am sure that your three managers, Keith Gostelow, Dan Perkins, and Adam Eaglestone – to whom I offer my sincerest thanks for their sterling work in this great enterprise – will be very flexible over your working arrangements, so that you can be free to go for interviews for other positions. And I have to say that I would like to think that my reputation, our reputation, is such that you should not experience too much difficulty in this regard.'

334

He knew that he was on the verge of tears, and he hated this, hated it for its sentimentality, its irrelevance, its insult to all their feelings, but hated it above all because he knew that, although his tears were genuine, very few people would believe them to be so.

'I wish you well, I thank you, goodbye,' he said very quickly, and then he marched off.

There was even a smattering of applause. He hated that above all. He hadn't even told them that it had all been a fraud. They would discover that very soon, and be ashamed of their applause.

At three minutes to twelve, after further consultation and anguished drafting with Gavin Welland, Sir Gordon issued another statement to the nation.

'This is a sad day. It is with enormous regret that I have to announce that Gordon Investments ceased trading at seven minutes past eleven this morning, due to adverse financial conditions which of course I hope to be of a temporary nature. It will not reopen for investment. All monies currently invested with us will be frozen at the sums current today, January the thirty-first, 2012, and will be paid to investors when circumstances permit. I fervently hope that this will be very soon. I must emphasize, in conclusion, that this sad news does not affect any other Coppinger operations in any way whatsoever.'

He shook hands with Keith Gostelow, Dan Perkins, and Adam Eaglestone. He thanked them again, his voice almost breaking, for everything they had done. He spared them the embarrassment of meeting his eye, although even as he did it he suspected that it was mainly his embarrassment that he was sparing himself from. He walked away. He could walk away from the great nightmare that was Gordon Investments, but now he had to deal with a problem much smaller in scale, the problem of one man.

That man was Raduslav Bogoff. And he didn't think that problem would be any easier.

Suddenly he was very sober

Kirkstall drove him to Climthorpe in companionable silence.

He had telephoned Vernon Thickness and been told that Raduslav had turned up for training, but was being even more surly than usual, and Vernon had been forced to suspend a seven-a-side practice game for fear the Slav's tackles would injure half his fellow players. Sir Gordon had suggested that he come down and talk to the boy after training. 'That would be a huge exception to our protocol,' Vernon had responded, 'and this is a six-pointer against fellow strugglers, so I'm not happy about it, but you're the money, so you're the boss and if you feel that's the way, you must do it. But I need him till one-thirty.' 'Fine,' Sir Gordon had said, 'I'll pop down to the training ground and watch a bit. You never know, it might inspire the lads.' Vernon's phone had been breaking up, so Sir Gordon hadn't been able to hear his reply clearly, but it had sounded strangely like 'Pigs might fly.'

Kirkstall turned right off the High Street into Wordsworth Crescent, then right again into Gerard Manley Hopkins Grove, straight on across a Park Lane that bore no resemblance to its famous counterpart, on to the end of sad, shabby Gasworks Road, past the absurdly named Badger's Grove Industrial Estate, and through the rusting gates that led to Climthorpe

United's unlovely training ground. The players were jogging over the spongy grass with a conspicuous lack of energy and enthusiasm, but they grew a little more alert when they saw their paymaster arrive. None of them had any idea about the collapse of GI. Mobiles were banned during training, despite grumbles. Nevertheless, unease was in the air – Bogoff's mood seemed to have transferred itself to half the squad – and Sir Gordon feared for tonight's result.

Vernon Thickness packed it all in at a quarter past one, and sent them on their way with the encouraging words, 'Right, you fucking tossers, if you play as badly as you've trained we've no chance tonight. Have a rest this afternoon and don't even try anything active, you haven't got the energy for one wank between the lot of you.'

'If I might add a word, Vernon,' called out Sir Gordon.

'Of course, Sir Gordon,' said Vernon Thickness with bad grace.

'Portsmouth aren't much cop and they have financial problems,' said Sir Gordon, 'so I think we can stuff them. I've put a lot of money into this club, lads, and I think you're good. I made a silly remark about Raduslav here, I put my hand up and admit it, but he's owed a bit of luck and I want you all to support him tonight, and support each other. Come on, lads, play out of your skins, for me. Thank you.'

The players began to move off towards their flashy cars. Sir Gordon approached Bogoff.

'May I have a word, Raduslav?' he said.

'What you got to say to me? I got nothing to say to you.'

'No, no, I understand, I understand your attitude, I'm not surprised you're not pleased.'

He hadn't realized before just how big the boy was. Either he was shrinking from all the stress or chance was placing him in the company of giants.

'Are you happy just standing here?'

'No. Horrid place. Dump. And it's cold. Cold wind.'

Thoughts along the lines of 'I didn't realize I'd paid

twenty-five million for a wimp' ran through Sir Gordon's veins, but all he said was, 'Would you rather go to a café or a pub?'

'No. These pubs I hate. Get it over, please.'

'Fine. I don't much want to stand here on this horrid afternoon either, Raduslav.'

It was not only cold but grey. There was wetness in the air, though none on the grass, as if there was a curtain of invisible drizzle hanging there. The training ground was surrounded by the backs of ramshackle industrial buildings. It truly was a dump.

'Raduslav, I repeat what I said earlier, that I have never had any kind of an affair with your wife.'

'I believe you. You tell the world that you not barge her with a boat pole.'

'Yes, what I meant by that, I mean, it was a way of saying that there was no way I would make advances to her because she was someone else's wife, so I used a figure of speech, perhaps slightly unfortunately chosen, to emphasize how inappropriate I would have felt it to be for me to make any approach to her with any tactile intent.'

'She speak good English, much gooder than me, she not liking this talk of the barge with the pole.'

'No, no, and I understand. Turning to . . . what I said on the television, which I . . . well, things are bad for me, I was under attack, I was in a panic, and I said an unwise thing.'

'Unwise, you say, but you don't say untrue.'

'No. No. Um . . . look, Raduslav, from the point of view of buying you as an investment, what I said is, if not fully true, very nearly so.'

'But I not an investment. I am blood and flesh.'

'Absolutely, absolutely you are blood and flesh and that is how we should look at you. That's my point. And please don't forget that it was me who thought you worth twenty-five million of my own money. More than I paid for the Turner.'

'I not knowing this Turner. Who does he play for?'

'No, Turner was . . . oh, never mind. Look, we've never really chatted, have we, you and I? You must come and visit me and my wife at our cottage, you and Svetoslava. There was such a crowd at the bonfire party, we couldn't talk. You'll get on well with Christina. Look, we can be friends. We've got off on the wrong foot, but—'

'For Mr Thickness, both foots are the wrong foots. Left foot is the wrong foot. Right foot is the wrong foot. Left foot, right foot, no good.'

'No, no, I'm not talking about your feet as feet. It was a turn of phrase.'

'I turn not very fast. I know this. I am big. I am bulk.'

'No, no, I didn't mean that sort of turn. When I said "turn of phrase" that too was a turn of phrase. Oh dear.'

'I'm a disappointing for you. I not scoring enough goals. I thinking always the crowd they shout, "Bog off, Bogoff," this is not nice to hear, but I thinking, "Sir Gordon has faith in me, he get me keeped in the team, because this Thickness, he has it in from me, but Sir Gordon, a great man, a clever man, he thinked I was good." Then on TV I see you and I thinking you are not thinking I am good.'

'I do. I do. Look, it's freezing. Let's wrap this up.'

'My coat, it is in the car.'

'Not that kind of wrap. That was another figure of . . . oh hell. Look, I still believe you can be a great player. I am glad I have bought you. I think you are wonderful. I think you will score goals tonight. Forget what Mr Thickness says. I'll deal with him later. I believe you will come good. I believe you will come good tonight. Play wonderfully tonight – for me. Now go, it's cold.'

'Thank you. You really believe? You honesty?'

'Absolutely.'

'Thank you. Thank you, Sir Gordon. I go home. I have steak. I like steak. I go to bed. I rest. I have fifty winks. You see, I speak some English phrase. And tonight, I score. Like I now believe you did not score with my wife. You see, I know another phrase. I am good now. I feel better now. Thank you.'

A BT repair man emerged from one of the surrounding buildings. As he walked towards his van he saw Sir Gordon talking to Bogoff, and he called out, 'About time you got a few goals, matey.'

'You see,' said Sir Gordon.

The bulky Bulgarian looked at Sir Gordon doubtfully.

'He thinks you should score more goals,' said Sir Gordon. 'He wouldn't think you should score more goals unless he thought you were good, would he?'

He walked Bogoff to his car, and shook his hand. He could see that Bogoff almost believed him.

He just didn't want to go back to Canary Wharf. It was a long way, and he would only have to come all the way back for the match that night. But the alternative was to spend the whole afternoon and early evening in Climthorpe on a grey, damp day. Which was worse?

Going back would be worse. That was where all the trouble was.

He longed for a drink. He craved alcohol with an intensity that he had never felt before. It was disturbing but it wasn't exactly surprising and so he decided not to worry about it and got Kirkstall to drop him at the Royal Oak, a large dark brick pub in Climthorpe High Street.

'I hope you don't mind waiting,' he said.

'I never mind waiting,' said Kirkstall. 'It makes a change.'

'Right. Good. Thanks. Well, fetch me when I ring, then,' said Sir Gordon.

The landlord was Irish, and on an impulse Sir Gordon ordered something he had never drunk before – a pint of Guinness. He had it with a whiskey chaser. Irish, of course. The instinct to please was as natural to him as breathing.

There were two flat-screen televisions in the pub, and they were both on but with the sound turned down. They were

340

both on Sky Sports News, but news flashes crept across the bottom of each screen and although they all seemed to be about sport there was obviously a risk of some other news being flashed up. He couldn't have borne that, not today. Luckily he managed to find just one dark corner in the cavernous pub from which neither TV was visible, and it was unoccupied. The few customers on this drab afternoon were all staring at one or other of the screens as if riveted by what they couldn't hear.

As he sipped the smooth, deep, dark, velvet beer, and rolled the occasional sip of malt round and round till the roof of his mouth burnt, Sir Gordon scrolled through his text messages and listened to his voice messages. There were lots of them, but most of them were requests from the media and he had nothing else to tell them. There was just one caller to whom he would respond. Hugo.

But could he respond? Wally Frobisher had said disconcerting things about Hugo, and they had struck home.

The thought that Hugo might have been insincere and might never have intended to help him had festered in his subconscious ever since yesterday. He had felt a distant awareness of it while he slept, and it had returned the moment he had made his decision, faced the thirteenth floor and delivered his speech on the demise of GI. He had been conscious of it, faintly humming like an insect in his bowels, while he talked to Raduslav Bogoff.

He needed to ring his brother, but first he needed to recharge his glasses.

'Good stuff?' asked the landlord.

'Good stuff.'

'That's my man.'

Back in his dark cave with its dark panelling and his dark drink, the afternoon hermit plucked up courage and dialled his brother. He had no idea how to react to the startling new possibility, but then he had no idea what Hugo was going to say.

'Hello, Hugo, it's me.'

'Hello, you.'

'You rang.'

'I did, yes. I've got bad news.'

'That's hardly novel, at the moment.'

'No. Bad times for you. I can't tell you how sorry I am about it all.'

A subtext flew into Sir Gordon's mind. I can't tell you because I'm not remotely sorry. Was that the true Hugo? God, this was going to be difficult. But what was the bad news? He was terrified.

'What kind of bad news?'

'Another bit of dirt dug up by a newspaper.'

Amazingly, Sir Gordon felt bathed in sunny relief. Nothing awful had happened to any of the people he cared about, to Joanna or Christina or Luke or even Kev or Emma. God, caring about people was a fraught business. Maybe, when he got more used to it, he would feel less raw, less unprotected.

'Oh?'

'*Daily Record*, tomorrow. It's about your Germophile project.'

'Oh?'

It was a while ago. It was hard to care.

'I raised a concern about it at that Indian restaurant.'

'You did, yes.'

What was Hugo playing at? How did he know about this?

'You promised me it was all above board.'

'I did, yes.'

'You got quite angry.'

'I did, yes.'

'They are alleging that it wasn't all above board.'

'Good God. Why, after all this time?'

'Easily explained, I'm afraid, Gordon. You've become an easy target. They now dare.'

Was that real sympathy in Hugo's tone, or was it pleasure coated in sympathy? God, this was going to be hard.

'You take a very cynical view of human nature, Hugo.'

'Well, I would say that you take a very rosy view, but then you've had things so easy all your life that you've never needed to face the unpleasant truth.'

Definite touch of waspishness there. Not looking good.

'So, what exactly are they saying in the *Daily Record* tomorrow?'

'They're saying that you knew you couldn't go ahead with it, that you didn't have the intellectual property rights, but you didn't let anybody know this. People continued to invest, you and your chums made a lot of money out of it and when you'd gorged yourselves you announced that you were pulling out and the small investors were left with worthless stock. Pretty classic case of pump and dump. So they say.'

'Strong stuff.'

'Well, I'm paraphrasing, probably. I mean, I haven't seen the article.'

Just for a moment, Sir Gordon had felt the hairs on the back of his neck rising as Hugo spoke. He had been paraphrasing, he said. Well, it had sounded very much as if a touch of the resentment attributed to the paper had been felt by Hugo. Now, in his new suspicious state, Sir Gordon felt that there had been a touch of genuine resentment, rather carelessly given away by Hugo. Was it possible that Hugo resented him, felt jealous of him, had an inferiority complex about him, in just the way that he felt about Hugo?

He needed to ask a question, and he needed to speak very carefully. He needed to keep any vestiges of suspicion or doubt out of his voice.

But Hugo spoke again while he was considering this.

'Where are you? You sound as if you're in an aircraft hangar.'

'It's disguised as an Irish pub in Climthorpe.'

'Good God. I think I'd rather be in an aircraft hangar.'

'I like it.'

Careful, Gordon. Keep this cool or you may let your doubts show.

343

Now. That question. Difficult not to sound as if he's suspicious. Got to ask, though.

'Hugo, how do you know about this article?'

'Simple. I've just lunched with the editor. He told me.'

'Ah.'

Perfectly credible.

'He's a friend.'

'Yes, I thought he was my friend too.'

'Gordon, this is business. This is his job. This is what he does. It's got nothing to do with friendship.'

Did he detect another slight subtext? How you've been wasting your time inviting people on to that boat of yours. On to which I was never invited, not once. Was there just a hint of that in the voice, or was he now really imagining things?

'Gordon, I'm really sorry about GI.'

Sincere?

'Thank you. And thanks for telling me, Hugo.'

'No problem. I thought, Forewarned is forearmed.'

'Thank you.'

'Gordon, tomorrow . . . after the funeral . . .'

Oh no. He'd forgotten all about Jack's funeral. That was all he needed, this week of all weeks.

'. . . let's lunch. Just the two of us.'

'Yes, fine.'

'On me.'

'Well, thanks.'

'We need each other at this time.'

Sir Gordon switched off and stared into space. How much of that had been genuine? He really didn't know. Was he really any good at all at sizing up what another human being was thinking? He hadn't the faintest idea.

He felt quite stupid.

Well, he hadn't done badly for someone quite stupid.

Till now.

It wasn't even that he liked Hugo, but he needed to feel

that there was something there, some sincerity, some . . . well, warmth was perhaps putting it too strongly . . . some fellow feeling between the two of them somewhere. With Jack gone. With Mum gone. With Dad in a different world.

Good Lord. Both his glasses were empty. He had no recollection of having drunk from them.

He thrust himself out of his slough of despair. He felt instead a rising anger. He would phone the editor of the *Daily Record*. His friend.

But first he needed to go to the bar.

'The same again, please.'

'Why change a winning format?'

'Exactly.'

'That's the ticket.'

He took his drinks back to his cave, and went to the toilet. The walls of the Gents were covered in newspaper pages recording the few exciting mentions that Climthorpe had ever received in the national press.

Climthorpe Boy Survived by Eating Python
Climthorpe Man Leaves Clothes on Beach
Arson Allegation over Climthorpe Landmark Destruction
Climthorpe Slam Six Past Sad Pompey

Good Lord. He hadn't known that.

Would they slam six past sad Pompey tonight? Oh God. He hoped so.

But first he had to phone Marcus Lewiston, editor of the *Daily Record*. Well, no, first he had to phone Kirkstall to say that he was about to phone Marcus Lewiston and he didn't yet know how long he would be.

'That's fine, sir. I have a very cosy little parking space here. You be as long as you like, Sir Gordon.'

Then he phoned Marcus Lewiston. To his surprise he was put through straight away on announcing his name. He was surprised that he was surprised. A fortnight ago he wouldn't have been surprised at all.

'Gordon, hello. Good to hear from you. How are you?'

Insincere bastard.

'Fine. Fine. How are you, Marcus?'

Well, so am I, because I just couldn't care less how he is.

'Great, Gordon. Never better. Where are you? You sound as if you're in an aircraft hangar.'

'I'm in an Irish pub in Climthorpe.'

'Good Lord. A far cry from Corsica, eh?'

'Oh God, Corsica. Marcus—?'

'I didn't think I could drink so much Ricard.'

'I didn't know there was so much Ricard. Marcus—?'

'It's odd, isn't it? It tastes wonderful over there. I can't drink the stuff in Bishop's Stortford.'

'I know. Well, no, I don't know about Bishop's Stortford, but I once ordered retsina in Godalming and it tasted horrible. Marcus? I've been talking to Hugo.'

'How is he?'

Oh God. How strange you don't remember when you've been lunching with him. Oh hell. Hugo was lying. Oh Lord, why am I so upset?

'Are you still there?'

'Yes. Sorry. I lost the signal. I believe you've got an article about Germophile in the paper tomorrow.'

'That's right. Just a little piece.'

'Making allegations, I gather.'

'That's putting it strongly, Gordon. Making . . . suggestions. Which, if they are correct, are justified as in the public interest.'

'Would it be fatuous to ask you to withdraw the article?'

'On what grounds, Gordon?'

'Our friendship. Your holidays on the *Lady Christina*. Don't they mean anything?'

'I remember them with pleasure. I must thank you for them, if you feel you haven't been thanked enough.'

'Don't they influence you at all?'

'Gordon, you'd hardly expect me to admit that I was ever influenced as a news man by anything as personal as a little holiday gift – which I would not insult you by calling a bribe because I can't believe you ever intended them as such – but let me give you a little piece of advice. I've met people on your boat, people with less integrity than myself, who are the sort of people who would happily indulge in a bit of quid pro quo, but don't expect too much from them. They aren't really interested in past holidays, only in the prospect of future holidays, and I think the view nowadays is that you are, frankly, to put it as mildly as I can, not going to be in a position to offer anybody any holidays on any boat for quite a long time to come.'

Sir Gordon had to take a consoling slurp of Guinness during this disturbing speech and was caught off guard when Marcus suddenly stopped. He choked in his haste.

'Are you all right?'

'Fine. I just choked on some Guinness.'

'Guinness in the afternoon. I envy you.'

Sir Gordon wasn't far from choking again on Marcus's words.

'OK, Marcus,' he said. 'I have to accept criticism and I have to admit that I haven't always been as good a boy as I should, but I've done some good things in my life—'

'—and we've gladly reported them.'

'Yes, well, this brings me to my point. This morning there were two stories about me, one about the purchase of the Turner and one reporting my statement that I was entirely innocent of any affair with Sve . . . Sev . . . Mrs Bogoff, which was printed in all the papers the day before. Neither article received much prominence, and I'm not singling you out, all the papers were the same and most were worse than you, but it was all a bit unfair and—'

'Gordon, you're rich, you've been hugely successful and you haven't been a good boy, and I can't believe you're complaining because we've been "a bit unfair". "Tycoon complains, treatment 'slightly unfair'." "Billionaire protests, behaviour 'a bit off'." Really, Gordon.'

'What I really meant was that I thought it was a fucking disgrace.'

'That's better. That's a bit more like the real Sir Gordon Coppinger. Gordon, three things. One, you can't expect any paper to give a denial as much prominence as the original story. Two, we printed that story in good faith. It came from a very reputable source.'

Hugo. Oh God. Hugo.

'Can you tell me who?'

'Of course I can't. We never reveal our sources. And three, we live by news, not olds. We've had so many stories of good things done by you, now it's bad things done by you that are news, so really the Turner and your protestation were stories we didn't want and only printed because we are in our way people of honour. The British people love to build a man up and knock him down, and we have to try to deliver that to them, within the confines of truth, of course. The Americans just like endless worship, and that is so boring. I'm afraid it's the price you have to pay for being rich and living in the greatest country on earth, and now I have to go, please forgive me, it's been a pleasure to talk to you, a real pleasure, I do envy you all that Guinness, and please give my very best to the more beautiful of the two Lady Christinas, your lovely wife. Goodbye, Gordon.'

Bastard. Smooth, smooth bastard.

Guinness. Smooth, smooth Guinness.

He walked slowly back to the bar. He felt weak with hunger, and slightly drunk, which surprised him as he had a pretty strong head. But of course he hadn't eaten since breakfast.

'Are you doing food?'

'From half past five, sir. We start early on match days.'

'Right. So the question is, what should I do in Climthorpe between now, which is . . .'

'Twenty-five to five, sir.'

'. . . and half past five, on a dark, cold, raw afternoon.'

'Well now, sir. They do say that the scones at the Valley tea shop are highly palatable, but they close at four-thirty.'

'That's teatime. A tea shop that closes at teatime?'

'This isn't London, sir, not by a long chalk. Now the other thing you could do . . .'

'Yes?'

'. . . is have a nice pint of Guinness – which is, after all, a form of liquid food, sir – and that would go down very nicely, in my opinion, with just a touch of help from the Jameson's.'

And so he did.

'Are you all right till six-thirty, Kirkstall?'

'As snug as a bug in a rug, sir.'

So he sat enjoying living like the Irish, so he did, and he had a pint of Guinness and a helping hand from the Jameson's, so he did, and he tried to forget his troubles and his resentments, so he did, but he failed, so he did.

Germophile. The memories went round and round in his head. The bitterness. The early hope. The genuine excitement. A product that could cure MRSA. What did people think he was? Of course he'd believed in it. He'd believed utterly in Jason Coldcall, its inventor. Why else would he have modernized that wretched factory in that decrepit industrial estate on the edge of Great Yarmouth? He recalled the debates over the name. People were divided into two camps, the Germophile camp and the Germophobe camp. Each name had some kind of logic for a product that fought germs and would make a fortune from fighting germs. Actually, Germophobe would have been better, but somewhere there had been an even better name, waiting to be discovered. What did it matter now? The truth was that he had not checked out Jason Coldcall enough. He had taken his word for it that he had

349

the intellectual property rights. He hadn't followed the details closely enough to discover that the product was suspected of having disastrous side effects. It was believed to cause cancer but in months, not weeks. He would never have got a licence to produce and sell it.

His disappointment had been huge and it had been real. He would not be the man to wipe MRSA from the land. He would not be the saviour of our hospitals. His dream had died and hospital patients would die too. Could anyone really blame him for not letting on for a while? Could anyone blame him for selling some of his shares at the top price and letting some of his colleagues sell some of their shares at the top price? The money had been a matter of almost no importance compared to the disappointment of the failure of the wonder drug.

Even this had been of less importance to him, however, than the fact that he had been conned. Jason Coldcall had conned him. He, Sir Gordon Coppinger, had been conned. He, Sir Gordon Coppinger, of Gordon Investments and SFN Holdings, had been conned. If that came out, if the story tomorrow suggested that, what a laugh the business world would have. And, even if it didn't come out tomorrow, if there was ever an inquiry, a court case, then that ridicule was just waiting to happen.

He ordered Irish stew, which he had never eaten, and which he washed down with two large glasses of very indifferent Rioja, but he simply had no more room for more Guinness, so he didn't.

The excitement rose in him as kick-off time approached, and Kirkstall drove him to the Coppinger Stadium. Germophile was forgotten – for the moment.

'I can get you in if you want, Kirkstall,' he said.

'To be truthful, sir, I find the excitement excessive,' said Kirkstall. 'I'll be very happy in the car park, and I'll be able to follow the game pretty closely from the noises of the crowd.'

An evening game at a big football ground. The floodlights shining enticingly, the drab streets around the ground only emphasizing their magic glow. All the people moving like Lowry figures, from all directions but all towards the ground, pulled by the magnetism. The night dark and cold, the air damp. Nothing to do in all the town to compare with the next hundred and ten minutes. Two halves of forty-five minutes, half time of fifteen minutes, five minutes of unbelievably tense added time, what a prospect.

GI closed down? Germophile investigated? Pff.

But to Sir Gordon's shock, when he stepped into the directors' box from the warmth and glamour of the luxurious boardroom, there was a storm of booing.

'Who are they booing?' he asked.

One man, braver than the rest, told him.

'You, Sir Gordon.'

All the drink that he had consumed – two large Scotches in the boardroom on top of everything he'd had at the Royal Oak – plus his exposure to the cold night air made him feel suddenly very drunk. That just added to the shock of the booing. He thought that this might be the worst moment of his life. The crowd, his crowd, booing him. Then he thought of how little money they might have and how they might have scrimped and saved to invest with him, their man, and he understood. But he disliked these thoughts so much that he tried to go back to his other scenario, in which they were fickle bastards. But he couldn't. He had become too honest, damn it.

At last the game began. Now he was safe. Now all he cared about was victory for his team, and goals for Bogoff. He hoped he was nicely rested after his fifty winks.

The game began slowly, both teams sizing each other up. For a few minutes the ball went nowhere near Raduslav. Then he touched it for the first time and a chorus of boos rang out, and a few half-hearted cries of 'Bog off, Bogoff.' Sir Gordon's heart went into overdrive. In his determination, the boy hit his pass too hard and it sailed past its intended recipient and was easily cleared by a Portsmouth defender.

Raduslav had one more chance but fluffed his shot. Now the whole of the Abattoir Stand burst into song in complete unison, the way football crowds mysteriously do – sometimes they seem to have a communal brain like a flock of starlings. They'd been working on their song, and it was a huge advance on 'Bog off, Bogoff', even though it wasn't likely to cause the Poet Laureate any sleepless nights.

Anger coursed through Sir Gordon's chilled veins as he heard *his* crowd, at *his* stadium, singing of *his* centre forward in *his* team:

'He's Bulgarian and he's bad,
To play him must be mad
He can't control the ball
What does he give us? Fuck all.'

After forty-two minutes of gradually imposing themselves on the game without creating many clear-cut opportunities, Climthorpe were given a rather soft penalty.

Raduslav was going to take the penalty himself. Oh God, this was risky.

The visiting fans jeered, but the home crowd were now silent, 17,319 hearts in 17,319 mouths.

Sir Gordon couldn't watch. He had to watch. He had been brave once. He watched.

Bogoff placed the ball, walked back away from the penalty spot, waited. The referee, Mr C.O. Cadwallader (Redcar), blew his whistle.

Bogoff ran towards the ball, kicked fiercely in the direction of the right-hand side of the net. The Portsmouth goalie groped in vain, the ball curved away from him, hit the post, and ran free. A chorus of jeers broke out, and again there came that chant.

A Portsmouth player hacked at the ball, and sent it far downfield. Nicky Tremlett, the Climthorpe defender, of whom a sporting journalist had once written, 'Tremlett is too large and strong to be called "as thick as two short planks"; he's as thick as three long planks', misjudged the bounce. The goalie, Carl Willis, his concentration broken by the penalty attempt, realized this too late, reacted too slowly, got to the ball but couldn't hold it. It squirmed away to the feet of a Portsmouth player and he toe-poked it into the net. Half time: 0–1. Exit to a chorus of boos and cries of 'Coppinger out.'

From boos to booze. Sir Gordon craved a large whisky, how he craved it. But no. He had a duty. Against all his normal practice, against what he saw as correct protocol, he was going to visit the dressing room, where he assumed that Vernon Thickness would now be delivering a half-time talk that would make Mark Antony sound like an assistant in the shirt department of John Lewis.

Sir Gordon entered the dressing room cautiously. The players were sitting on the benches that ran the length and breadth of the room, listening glumly to Vernon ranting.

'Vernon,' he said. 'I never tread on your feet, as you know, but may I say a few words?'

Vernon Thickness didn't look too pleased, but he said, 'Of course, Sir Gordon.'

'No "sir" please today, Vernon. I'm one of you. And I am gutted. I am ashamed.'

The players hung their heads.

'Oh, not of you,' said Sir Gordon. 'You weren't great but you were the better team. You can win this. No, I'm ashamed of those people out there. Our fans. *Our* fans. I've a good mind to sell up in disgust. You know what that would mean. The end of my money. The end of Climthorpe as a serious possible contender for the Premiership next year.' (When I've sold most of you, but he didn't add that.) 'What would stop

353

me from selling up? You. You have just forty-five minutes to persuade me to stay on.'

All the players stared at him in horror as the words sank in.

'Just one more thing,' said Sir Gordon. 'That was six inches away from being the most brilliant penalty. We all know how important six inches can be.'

The lads laughed, as Sir Gordon had meant them to. Good old Coppinger, the knight with the common touch.

'You're a very good player, Raduslav,' said Sir Gordon. 'You can do it.'

He went straight back to his seat. There might just have been time to nip into the boardroom for a quick whisky, but he was asking his players to be strong, so he must be strong himself.

Sometimes, in the fierce intensity of an evening match, it seemed as if there was no world beyond the floodlights, it seemed that the stadium was the only thing that existed. But this evening, in the cold late-evening breeze, this was a match that would have huge ramifications for the world outside. It was more than a match. It was a symbol of Sir Gordon's fate. It was a prophecy of his future. There was a chorus of boos again as he took his seat. The lads were playing for his reputation. This was far more than a football match.

The Climthorpe players began the second half as if their lives depended on it, perhaps because their lives depended on it. Surging forward, they left space at the back and soon found themselves 0–2 down.

Still they surged forward, and this time they got a genuine penalty for a clumsy tackle on a very determined Raduslav.

Oh no. This was too much. He was going to take this penalty too. The decision was greeted by a huge chorus of boos and whistles, which ceased suddenly as the home crowd realized that they had to give their own team a chance if they wanted to avoid being laughed at in their workplaces in the morning.

Even the Portsmouth supporters were silent now. The tension in the ground was almost edible.

Bogoff shot exactly as before, hard, low, towards the right-hand post. Again the ball curved away from the goalie. Again he groped for it in vain. Again it hit the post. But this time it struck the inside of the post, and went in. A great roar went up. Raduslav raced towards the Coppinger Stand in exultation, the other players piled themselves on top of him, two gay supporters in the seventeenth row looked at each other in sad shared envy, all was mayhem.

A second goal followed in the seventy-third minute, a neat trap, swivel, and shot from the new hero: 2–2.

It isn't easy to create a new chant in mid-match, but football crowds, derided for their lack of brains, occasionally manage something really witty. That did not happen on this particular night at the Coppinger. Indeed, there were those who claimed that 'He's Bulgarian and he's good, and he likes his Yorkshire pud' was the worst jingle ever heard on a British football ground. Sir Gordon actually rather liked it for its complete irrelevance, though he didn't admire the fickleness of the crowd who had created it.

On and on they went, attack after attack. The Portsmouth goalie made two great saves, the crossbar came to his rescue on another occasion. Climthorpe just had to win.

There were five minutes of added time. Bravely the Portsmouth players blocked shot after shot. But in the end, that evening, Raduslav Bogoff was just too good. He flicked the ball to Connolly, ran on, took the return pass, feinted, swerved, made room, hammered the ball. Back of the net: 3–2. Pandemonium, in which nobody heard the final whistle.

Boardroom. Warm. Bright. Buzzing. Smiles. Hugs. Whisky. Pretty woman. With the Portsmouth lot. Smiling at him. Long nose. Flat cheeks, lovely to nuzzle against. Portsmouth directors trying to smile bravely. Climthorpe directors replaying each of their goals at least twice. Beautiful breasts. Smiling at him. Soft, grey eyes. Smiling at him. No. No good. Promised Christina. More whisky. That second penalty, wonderful. Smiling at him. Redhead. Funny, can't remember ever having a redhead. No, you promised. You mustn't. Tattoos. Imagine that she's covered in tattoos. Couldn't remember what T was in his ABC, but it should be tattoos. '*Up Pompey*' all over her thighs, and '*Administration*' in a circle round her left breast. That's done it. Oh, the relief. And the disappointment. Bit more relief than disappointment. Not smiling at him. Knows he's lost interest. Praise of Bogoff. Worth every penny. More whisky. Oops. The ship moved, the wind's getting up. Wait a minute. Not a ship. Oh heck.

Kirkstall drove very smoothly indeed, letting the master sleep. Kirkstall had never seen him drunk like that.

He woke just as the Rolls turned off the M25. He had a horrid taste in his mouth, but he didn't mind, they had won: 3–2. Last minute. Wow.

Midnight came and went. Here, in black Surrey, Black Wednesday had officially begun. There was no reason why that should make any difference, but it did. Euphoria faded. Reality returned.

At the gates to Rose Cottage, three people stood waiting for him in the cold, black night. Hatred was the fuel that had kept them warm. They carried placards that stated '*Thief*', '*Crook*', '*Bastard*'. They had spittle at the ready. One of the globs of spittle slid slowly down the driver's window. That was so unfair. It wasn't Kirkstall they hated.

There were only three of them, but the depth of their hatred shocked Sir Gordon to the core. Suddenly he was very sober.

The Great Fire of Stoke

A man in his mid-fifties sits at a desk in an office in a factory on the outskirts of Stoke-on-Trent. It is half past two in the morning, and he is writing a letter. He is rather too smartly dressed for a factory, somewhat fussily dressed too. He has a cravat. You don't see many cravats in factories, or in Stoke-on-Trent, or anywhere much actually these days. The halcyon days of cravats are over. He is also wearing pink trousers. These too are not much seen in factories or in Stoke-on-Trent.

He is writing his letter with a gold fountain pen.

He finishes the letter, signs it with a flourish, reads it back. There is a gleam in his eye as he reads it. It is a gleam to chill the blood.

He puts the letter in an envelope, runs his tongue over the gummy part of the flap, closes the envelope carefully, and writes on it. He does not write a full address, only a name.

He puts the letter in the inside pocket of his jacket, which hangs as if not quite used to the process yet, as if new.

This is a fastidious man.

But there is nothing fastidious about what the man does next. He opens drawers in the desk in front of him, removes papers, strews them on the floor. Then he opens filing cabinets, and does the same. Soon there is quite a pile of papers on the wooden floor.

He opens a briefcase, a leather case, shabby, slightly battered, not

357

the sort of briefcase you would take to work in a bank, or a lawyer's. Or a factory on the outskirts of Stoke-on-Trent.

Out of this briefcase he takes a Thermos flask.

He goes to the door of the office and unlocks it, but does not leave.

He opens the Thermos flask and empties its entire contents on to the pile of papers. Its contents do not consist of coffee. Or tea.

He gets a box of matches from his pocket, strikes a match, drops it on to the paper and scurries to the door.

He opens the door, hurries through it, and shuts it. He does not lock it.

The pile of paper catches fire immediately, roars into flame. Within seconds it is quite a conflagration.

The man walks very slowly away from the office in the darkness. He does not turn any lights on. He can hear the fire crackling.

Before long the flames are bursting through the door of the office. The fire, fuelled by the petrol, has taken a firm hold.

The man walks away, slowly, feeling his way in the dark.

The fire is spreading outside the office in which it started. It is fierce. The man sees that it cannot be stopped now.

Now at last he switches a light on, revealing that he is in a vast room half the size of the factory building. It is criss-crossed with production lines. Above his head there is a tangle of railway lines, a complete model railway, with points, junctions, inclines and, tunnels. But this railway line is for pies, not trains. By day, pies with many different fillings slide along these rails, savoury trains recognized by sophisticated censors and sorted into their relevant pie sidings and loading bays. But nothing is moving now. There is silence except for the crackling of the fire.

Now he runs, hurtles towards a door, hurries down a flight of stairs, cries out his warning.

A burly man, slow of thought, slow of movement, awakens, hears the cries, stands, hurries, as much as he is capable of hurrying. He is wearing a boiler suit. He is in his early forties.

The fastidious man, who may not be as fastidious as he first appeared, points upstairs. The crackling of the fire is louder now, *the light from the flames is already visible, the fire is spreading fast.*

The burly man, though younger than the other, is slower, but he follows him up the stairs. At the top of the stairs the man in the pink trousers gets the letter from his pocket and hands it to the man in the boiler suit.

It's as if the man in the boiler suit has been hypnotized by the man with the pink trousers and the cravat.

The man with the pink trousers and the cravat runs full pelt back into the fire, which is already roaring through the factory. His hair is on fire, his clothes are burning, he is screaming. The other man watches, open-mouthed, transfixed, he should escape, but he cannot drag himself away, cannot, cannot, cannot.

The man with the cravat is no longer wearing pink trousers. He is wearing black trousers now. His screams reach a pitch and then die away. He is dead.

Just in time as the fire licks around his feet, the nightwatchman comes to his senses, runs away from the fire, down the stairs, and out, out into the cold, frosty night air. Breathlessly he dials 999, delivers his message, then is violently sick.

The factory is old and decrepit and contains a great deal of wood. By the time the fire engines arrive there is already no hope of saving anything.

Then the smells begin, amazing cooking smells, smells of steak, kidney, oyster, pork, apples, chicken, mushrooms, leeks, lamb, mint, game. Luscious for just a while are the smells that waft over the Five Towns in the light winds. As the meat begins to burn the smell grows briefly more luscious still, but then it becomes just the smell of burning, and that is how it stays long into the rest of the night. Indeed, it will stay as a faint memory of the disaster for much of the following day.

But people will talk that day, and for many days to come, of the wonderful smell that first awoke them that winter's night, how hungry they felt, how luscious it was. One man, from Burslem, has been a vegetarian for twenty-seven years, because he deplores the cruelty of abattoirs. That smell captures him so that he can no longer hold out against eating meat.

And soon it is like daylight around a wide area outside the factory, and the canals glow red with the reflection of the fire.

It is yet another blow for Sir Gordon Coppinger, and it is a tragedy for the man who was so desperate that he ran into the fire, but the people who witness it cannot think of it like that. They are human, and so they will say that they are glad that they hadn't been in Tenerife at the time, and as a result missed the Great Fire of Stoke.

'I'm so sorry'

He woke very abruptly from a deep slumber. His head ached and his mouth tasted as if he was chewing dust. Yet he felt happy. Why? Oh yes. Climthorpe had beaten Portsmouth 3–2.

More than that. Far more.

When he'd stepped into the house last night he had immediately seen a page of A4 lying on the parquet flooring of the hall. On it Christina had written, '3–2. Great!' Hardly a literary masterpiece, but the nicest letter he had ever received. She had never shown the slightest interest in his football before, even in the happy days. He had been able to forget all about placards and spittle, and creep into bed beside her feeling warm and . . . well, if she had been awake, if he hadn't drunk so much . . . well, who knows?

A floorboard creaked and his happiness evaporated. Someone was in the house. And he could hear voices, low urgent voices. There were people on the terrace, plotting, planning, whispering, creeping.

He eased himself carefully out of the bed in the dark. He was frightened. He was shocked. He couldn't believe the intensity of the hatred he had seen from those three people at the gates. And now, these people were in his house, and on his terrace. Hatred like he had seen could slit a man's throat.

He crept across the carpet, felt for the door handle, turned it gently, managed to leave the room without a sound from Christina.

He crept around the house, visiting every room, until he was satisfied that there was nobody there.

He opened one of the sitting-room windows, breathed in the chill night air, looked and listened. Then, cautiously, he opened the side door, and crept round the house. The lights came on immediately, and revealed nothing. The terrace was empty. There was silence, deep silence, suddenly broken by the loud barking of a fox.

He locked up, and crept back to bed. He was satisfied that there was nobody in the house or in the grounds, but his sleep for the rest of the night was disturbed, to say the least.

In the morning he seated himself as always at the round rosewood (what else?) dining table in the exact centre of the dining room, whose panelling was as Elizabethan as it could be in a house built in 1932. It was the first day of February, but he felt that there was a lot of winter still to come.

Farringdon emerged from the kitchens and slid gravely towards Sir Gordon like a train coming to rest at the buffers. He carried a glass of home-made apple juice and a pile of newspapers.

'Could you open the papers at the sports pages, please, Farringdon?' he asked. 'I want to read every report of the match I watched last night.'

'Yes, indeed, sir. A wonderful result. The kitchens are thrilled.'

'I suppose I ought to ask you if there's anything I should know in the news pages, though.'

'Three things, I regret to say, sir. None of them good.'

'Oh dear.'

'Sir Fred Goodwin has been stripped of his knighthood.'

Sir Gordon felt a surge of relief. He was expecting something far worse.

'You know, sir, the disgraced RBS man,' said Farringdon, misinterpreting Sir Gordon's silence.

'Yes, yes, I know. But why do you think I need to know this? Are you hinting by any chance that this should worry me, that I may expect similar treatment?'

'Good Lord, no, sir. That never crossed my mind. I just thought that the story of a fellow knight of the realm, also a financier, disgraced, might touch a nerve of sympathy.'

'Not in the slightest, Farringdon. He deserved it and I deserve it too, so if it happens, never mind, it was fun for a while.'

Sir Gordon smiled. It was a surprisingly peaceful smile.

'My knighthood no longer means anything to me, Farringdon.'

Just for a moment he felt really quite good.

'And the second piece of news?'

'There are . . . I was going to say "allegations" but perhaps a less strong word is in order, sir . . . let's say "hints". There are hints in the *Daily Record* of irregularities at Great Yarmouth in your project to produce a wonder cleansing agent that you hoped would wipe MRSA and several other scourges off the planet for ever.'

'I did, I did, Farringdon. Oh, the hopes I had.'

'I regret to say there are a couple of phrases of the kind these clever clogs in the media like to employ . . . *"Is this Sir Gordon's North Sea Bubble?"*, *"Will Germophilegate Join Dudleygate and Gordongate in the Pantheon of Coppinger Crimes?"'*

'Oh dear, bit contrived and bit strong. Bastards.'

'The gist of the piece is that when you found that you didn't own the patent you concealed this fact for many months and . . . um . . . feathered the nests of yourself and your cronies, sir.'

'As if I ever had cronies, Farringdon.'

'I have never seen any, I must admit, sir.'

'Why do you think they're coming out with this after all that time, Farringdon?'

Well, sir. It's a common British phenomenon, I'm afraid. Rats leaving a . . .'

Farringdon stopped hurriedly. For the first time in their association, Sir Gordon saw the man flustered. He even blushed slightly, and then he made things worse. 'Not that you are a sinking ship, sir.'

Sir let that go. He felt a bit sorry for the man.

'And the third piece of bad news?'

'Porter's Potteries Pies has burnt down, sir.' Even as he spoke Sir Gordon was aware that his response of 'What? What? Burnt down? Porter's Potteries Pies? Burnt down?' did not display the kind of calm that might be expected from the Garibaldis of this world. But surely he might be excused? His head had been reeling from bad news in the last few days.

'Oh, Farringdon, when's it to stop?'

'When Lady Luck turns, sir, one just has to wait till she turns again.'

Oh, if only you could talk, just for a few moments, like the Brian you are.

When he had finished his breakfast, he went to see Christina. This was quite against his normal custom, but things were not normal now.

She was still in bed. She was not a morning person. For many years he had been glad of this, had liked to slip out of the house without seeing her. This morning he wanted to see her, touch her, feel her.

She was still asleep. He felt for the end of the bulge in the bedclothes, stroked her feet, ran his hand up her body, bent down, kissed her on the lips very gently. She stirred and smiled, and he thought, Oh dear, is this the best thing that will happen all day? Her eyes closed again. He left her in peace and hurried out to the car.

There were now seven people at the gates, holding up placards and spitting at the Rolls-Royce. Two tents had been erected. These people looked so sad, so bedraggled, so cold, so dwarfed by the Surrey countryside that Sir Gordon actually felt sorry for them, until one of them threw a stone, which bounced off the side of Kirkstall's pride and joy.

Outside the Coppinger Tower there were more photographers and reporters than ever. There was also a crowd of angry protesters. Large numbers of policemen were present, holding back the crowds, and there were police vans everywhere. An elderly man in a dark suit was waving a walking stick at the building and shouting, 'Bastard.' Three policemen descended gently but firmly upon him.

Right in front of the building, beyond the police cordon, several people were erecting tents. There were five already.

Sir Gordon walked over to them.

'You're from Occupy, I suppose,' he said.

'We are,' said a very thin man with a straggly little beard. He looked to be in his early forties.

'Welcome,' said Sir Gordon. 'Not a bad day for it. Bit on the chilly side, but dry, that's the main thing. Not too uncomfortable for you, though it may get a bit cold tonight if this arctic weather in Europe starts to creep up the river.'

'Are you taking the piss?' asked the man, who was rather disconcerted.

'Not at all,' said Sir Gordon. 'But that does remind me. I can't let you into the building, I'm afraid, but the least we can do is tell you where the nearest lavatories are. Obviously I'm far too privileged ever to need to use a public toilet but someone in our building will know. And I'll get our Siobhan McEnery to organize some hot soup for you.'

'You *are* taking the piss,' said a top-heavy girl with a large head, huge breasts, and very thin legs.

'Well, just a bit perhaps,' said Sir Gordon. 'Not entirely.' He lowered his voice. 'Don't tell the police but I'm with you all the way. If you were me, and I was you, I hope I'd do what you're doing. Have a nice day, see you later, don't do anything I wouldn't do, it's a free country, and other meaningless statements.'

He strode into the building defiantly. He waved at Alice but didn't speak. He realized that he had only raised her hopes yesterday. He wouldn't make that mistake again.

The mail made no sense that morning. Emails danced meaninglessly before his eyes. There were hundreds of them, and only about one in thirty was an advertisement for ways to enlarge his penis. This, he felt, was just about the only problem that he hadn't got.

He could no longer comprehend his vast empire. He tried to look at the latest sales figures for his factories. He couldn't make sense of them. None of it mattered anyway. They were drops in the ocean. The vast debts of Gordon Investments would swallow them for breakfast, burp, and ask for more.

He raised himself sufficiently to go out and tell Helen Grimaldi that he wasn't going to answer his telephone that morning, and he didn't want to see anybody. She looked at him in alarm.

She looked at him in more alarm when he gave her a letter and said, 'There, Helen, that's a reference for you. A pretty glittering reference. In case you should need another job. You never know in this life, do you?'

Her hard square face softened. The sun was catching her soft little moustache and turning it golden.

'Sir Gordon,' she began. 'If . . . um . . .'

'Thank you,' he said. He felt a vague desire growing slowly, but it wasn't strong enough to be dangerous. 'I appreciate that offer, Helen. I . . . I know we never repeated . . . um . . . what happened, but I want you to know it was not because I didn't enjoy it.'

He was pleased that at least she didn't blush. He didn't mind Alice blushing – Alice could do no wrong – but he was horrified by the extent to which he seemed to make other women blush. He felt that he was now utterly useless, a spent force, an irrelevance, an obstacle, with just this one spark of talent – he could make women blush.

'It's just that it's too close to home,' he said.

'I know,' said Helen Grimaldi. 'You don't shit on your own doorstep.'

With these words he realized why it had never happened again, but he didn't tell her that. Her words, the fact that she could say them just like that at this moment in this context, slammed a door on all his feelings.

Back in his office, he wondered how on earth he would occupy himself till eleven o'clock, when Kirkstall would pick him up to take him to Jack's cremation in Gravesend. Since there was far more to do than any one man could possibly manage, there seemed no point in attempting to do any of it.

There was a peremptory knock on his door, the door opened as if it was a nuisance, and Gloria Whatmough, his Head of Charitable Giving, steamed in like a cruise ship.

'Good morning,' she announced, in a voice like a ship's captain barking instructions to a tug. 'Sorry to barge in. I hope this isn't a bad time.'

'Not at all,' he said. 'I don't have to leave for my brother's cremation till eleven.'

'Oh good,' she said. 'That's . . . Oh, I'm so sorry. That's . . . Oh dear.'

She collapsed into an easy chair at the other side of Sir Gordon's desk.

'Oh dear,' she repeated.

Sir Gordon realized now that she was nervous. Very nervous. Her hands were shaking. Her chins were wobbling. The blush ran down from her face on to her neck. She looked unhappy. She looked like a turkey that has just heard about Christmas for the first time.

'Um . . . what I have to say to you, Sir Gordon,' she said, 'won't . . . um . . . won't exactly . . . um . . . cheer you up at this . . . at this sad time.'

Sir Gordon didn't like the sound of this at all. He decided to try to help her out.

'Is it about the vicar support group idea?' he prompted.

'What?' She had obviously forgotten all about that. 'Oh. That. No. No, no. Oh no.'

'Or the literacy project?'

Although he had accepted that he would never now make love to Megan Lloyd-Phillips, it would be rather nice to see her again.

'No. I'm afraid that's rather had to go on the back burner. Um . . .' Gloria was now turning puce. 'We . . . um . . . the management committee, we had a meeting yesterday afternoon, and it was decided . . . not unanimously, I have to say, but by the required two-thirds majority, though only just, only just, that . . .'

She hesitated again, and seemed to go even . . . pucer. Was there such a word as 'pucer'? Sir Gordon didn't know, but he felt that, even if there wasn't, it would need to be created just to describe Gloria Whatmough's colour.

'Um . . . Sir Gordon, I think it can be no secret to you what I think of you as a . . . as a man . . .'

'Which I am.'

'Absolutely. No question. I'll say.'

She went even more puce than pucer, and still Sir Gordon had no inkling of what she was going to say.

'I'm afraid we have decided to take your name off all our charitable activities,' she said. 'I'm so sorry.'

'For Jack'

He couldn't face the people he might meet in the lift. He couldn't face his employees.

He went down the stairs, half walking and half running down nineteen flights of bare stone steps. He was an exile in his own kingdom. He was angry and upset. She was *his* Head of Charitable Giving. They were *his* management committee. This was *his* building. If a huge sign in gold letters saying *'Coppinger'* wasn't a hint of that, he didn't know what was.

And yet he understood why they had done it. That, of course, made it worse. Far worse. His name had become counter-productive. He didn't feel happy that he was counter-productive. Gloria, of course, had been at pains to say that she had not agreed with the recommendation. He'd been rather proud of his reply, proud that he had been able, even in the very moment of his humiliation, to say something as elegant as, 'Of course you didn't, Gloria. Chalices are rarely carried by the people who have poisoned them.'

In the car, smoothly driven by Kirkstall, he slowly ceased to seethe. A sense of desolation crept upon him.

Hugo arrived by taxi, and Christina was brought by their other driver, Meredith, a young man who lacked Kirkstall's conversational ability. Altogether there were thirty-eight people standing outside the crematorium – twenty-two photographers, thirteen journalists, and three mourners. Jack's widow had not been traced, Luke was still in prison, and Joanna had been refused the day off. Kirkstall and Meredith remained in their cars.

There was a deep chill in the crematorium. Sir Gordon, Christina and Hugo sat in the sixth row, as if expecting the front seats to fill up. The duty vicar had a bad cold. As his nasal, croaky words reverberated round the empty building, Sir Gordon found them desperately hollow. He knew that Christina also wasn't a believer, and he realized that he had no idea about any aspect of Hugo's inner life. The two of them needed to talk. He tried hard to think about Jack, but his thoughts wandered back to Hugo. Hugo had offered lunch. 'Just the two of us,' he had said. But how could they exclude Christina? The last thing he wanted at this time was a row with her. But he needed to talk to Hugo alone.

He looked at the coffin and thought about the swollen, decomposing body he had seen. He tried to think of Jack as a young man and was rewarded with a sorrow so sharp that he found himself trying to think about Hugo again. That caused him pain too. Suddenly from nowhere there came a vision of Alice, sweet Alice. And then he felt overcome by shame, shame at his thoughts, so that wasn't any good either.

The vicar's voice gave out almost entirely during the Lord's Prayer, revealing only too clearly that nobody else was joining in.

And then the coffin slid inexorably towards the flames, and it was over.

As they left the building, the cameras flashed, the journalists called out, it was a scene lacking in all dignity. Sir Gordon wanted to glower at the media throng, who were there only because they wanted to compare his life and Hugo's with that of Jack. But he didn't dare glower. He needed them. But he didn't dare smile either. What look could he possibly give, when all looks were unsuitable?

A young journalist, reputed to be one of the BBC's rising stars, asked him, 'How do you feel?' Maybe it wasn't as stupid a question as it seemed, because his reply, 'How do you think I fucking feel?', was widely quoted in the tabloid press.

As the brothers walked away towards Sir Gordon's car, Christina turned to them and said, 'Chaps?', making it into a question. Sir Gordon had never known her to use that word before. She even repeated it. 'Chaps?'

'Yes?' asked Sir Gordon.

'Would you mind . . . would you mind awfully . . . if I just went off?'

Relief flooded through Sir Gordon. He heard a voice saying, 'No, not if you have to. Why?' and he recognized it as his own voice.

'Well,' said Christina, 'I think you two brothers might like to be on your own together at this moment.'

Sir Gordon looked at his wife and felt, somewhat to his surprise, that she was being sincere on this emotional day. It made him feel almost at peace.

He didn't feel like that for long.

Meredith drove Christina off, and Kirkstall took the brothers towards central London. As they were on the South Bank, Hugo suggested a restaurant called the Old English Chop House, not far from Borough Market.

After a few moments of silence, Sir Gordon said, 'Well, that's that.'

Hugo wasn't quite so forthcoming. 'Yep,' he said.

Sir Gordon would have liked to have said more, but found that he couldn't. He had no idea whether Hugo would have liked to have said more.

The Old English Chop House wasn't actually an old English chop house. There weren't any old English chop houses any more. It was a new English chop house. It had tables and

371

chairs in dark wood with several alcoves, it had a wooden floor sprinkled with sawdust, it had a Welsh dresser with blue plates, but it all looked too shiny, too new. It was like a pretty girl in a bikini who has only got off the plane from Britain that morning. Give her fourteen days in the sun, and she would look wonderful.

They lunched off smoked eel with half a bottle of Chassagne-Montrachet, and lamb cutlets Reform with a bottle of the very best Margaux.

Afterwards, Sir Gordon realized that he couldn't remember any of the waiters, or even if they had been waitresses. Was this because he was cured of his obsession, his waiter hating, just as he seemed to be cured of his sex addiction? It struck him, wryly, that perhaps he was also cured of being a rich man and a financier.

He was not yet cured of being a gourmet. The food was unpretentious and good. The wines were superb.

Hugo began by telling him how hard he had worked to achieve the rescue plan which, having been achieved, had been so cruelly snatched from them by the SFN business, and by other revelations in the papers. How difficult the Swiss had been.

'Great sticklers, the Swiss.'

'Sticklers? For what?'

'Just for . . . stickling. It's in their blood. Well, in particular for propriety.'

Sticklers for propriety. It was a cliché. Besides . . .

'Propriety? When they have millions of secret accounts?'

'Ah. Sticklers for their interpretation of propriety.'

It was nonsense. Hugo started to say that some Korean bankers he knew had offered to contribute regularly. It was all cobblers. It was all ridiculously complicated. It was a made-up tale. There had been no rescue plan.

'I gather you went to lunch with Marcus Lewiston yesterday.'

'Yes,' said Hugo rather uncomfortably. 'He's a good chap.'

'Isn't he? Not.'

'What?'

'I thought he was my friend. He isn't.'

'Gordon, he was just doing his job.'

'The cry of the cowardly throughout the ages.'

'You're in a funny sort of mood today, Gordon.'

'It's a funny sort of day today, Hugo.'

'Nice eel.'

'Lovely eel.'

'I like eel.'

'I guessed you did when you ordered it.'

'You *are* in a funny mood.'

Careful, Gordon. Pull back unless you want a full-scale row.

Could he face a full-scale row with his brother?

Could he face a full-scale row with anyone at the moment?

'Gordon, I didn't offer to buy you lunch just for the wine, much as I knew you were having such a rough time that you probably needed it.'

Sir Gordon's heart sank.

'You want to ask me if there are any other scandals in my life, apart from Dudleygate and Gordongate and Germophilegate.'

'Gordon!'

'When I was seventeen I lodged in York in a little bedsit-type place on a picturesque street called Goodramgate. I left without paying the bill. There you are. Goodramgategate.'

'Gordon! I want to help you.'

Suddenly he knew for certain. His heart told him. His instinct told him.

'Help me, Hugo? In what way?'

It was Hugo who had forged the invitations to his Guy Fawkes party. Who else?

'I've had the police asking about you.'

I bet you have. The police have a strange habit of coming to ask about people when you've told them you've got things to tell them about those people. Of course. All the times we've been meeting you've been wheedling stuff out of me and feeding the press. How unbelievably naive I have been.

'I've not told them anything that could harm you in any way whatsoever.'

Oh no?

How could he have been so naive? Because Jack was dead, his mother was dead, his dad was senile, and at that stage he hadn't had good relationships at all with Christina or Joanna or Luke. Hugo had seemed to be all he had. It was amazing how much you could think in the blink of an eyelid when your mind was racing. Could Hugo see what he was thinking?

'Well, we're brothers,' said Hugo. 'We're all we've got, in a way. Especially now.'

Maybe Hugo *could* see what he'd been thinking.

'I was just thinking that.'

No harm in that admission.

He'd been beaten up after dining with Hugo and Hugo had refused a lift. Hugo had set it all up. Christ. Hugo wouldn't have worried if he'd been killed. Fuck Hugo.

'So, Hugo, how can you help?'

'I want to warn you about something, but I don't particularly want the authorities to know that I've warned you.'

'Why not?'

'Because I sometimes have to work with the authorities and I don't want to go down on record – or even be arrested – for having hindered them in the course of their duties. So I didn't want to phone you.'

Hugo had set up the digital photo with Svetoslava. Who else? Oh God.

'Why didn't you want to phone me?'

'Your secretary listens to your phone calls.'

'How do you know that?'

'Well, somebody does. I've heard clicks.'

Oh God.

'Not bad cutlets.'

'Not bad.'

'Gordon, the police intend to arrest you tomorrow.'

'Are you sure?'

'Absolutely.'

'How can you be sure?'

'I can't really answer that.'

'And why do you think I need to know that?'

'I just thought you might . . . well, I don't know, but . . . you might have plans. Last things you want to do, before . . . you know . . . I don't want to spell it out, but I'd have thought prison was inevitable. How's the wine?'

'The wine is sensational.'

'Good.'

Hugo lowered his voice. 'Or you might want to . . . I don't know . . .'

'Run away?'

'Well, it's possible.'

'Leave my clothes on a beach and start a new life?'

'Well, it's been done before.'

'Or . . . end it?'

'Well, that's been done before too. But no, I wasn't thinking of anything as dramatic as that. I was just thinking, you could . . . prepare yourself.'

'How? By praying?'

'Don't be silly. Do you think we could manage another bottle?'

'I think perhaps we could. For Jack.'

A plan was beginning to take shape

There must be hundreds, perhaps thousands, of people working in the Coppinger Tower who had invested with GI. He could hardly bear to enter the building. He felt that he had been cowardly in not having a confrontation with Hugo.

He walked across the foyer with eyes averted, not even looking at Alice. Alice!

He didn't get into the lift. He walked up nineteen flights of bare stone steps, not easy after his share of two and a half bottles of magnificent wine.

'You have a visitor,' said Helen Grimaldi.

The boy rose from his seat in the outer office, rose . . . and rose . . . and rose. Much too tall. He reminded Sir Gordon of another boy who had risen from his seat in the outer office, many moons ago, well, actually, amazingly few moons ago when you thought of all that had happened since. He almost thought it was the same boy, except, that boy had looked so innocent, so keen. This boy looked as if he had seen too many things, and wasn't keen on seeing much more.

'Hello, sir,' said the boy, holding out his hand. 'Martin Fortescue. You gave me a job at Porter's Potteries Pies.'

'Oh yes. Julian's boy.'

It was the same boy. What on earth had happened to him?

'Come through.'

'Thank you, sir.'

He led the boy through, and this time he let him sit in an easy chair. This time he looked as if he needed to sit in an easy chair.

'Have you come to tell me something about the fire?' he asked.

'Yes. Yes, Sir Gordon. I . . . um . . . I thought for a moment you hadn't recognized me.'

'No, no. No, no. Course I recognized you. So, bit of a catastrophe, eh, young Fortescue?'

'Awful, sir, and you see, it was all my fault. And that man's dead. I . . . I'm sorry. I can't . . . Nothing in my life has prepared me for this. It's all my fault, Sir Gordon. The fire. The death. All my fault.'

'Calm down, young man. Calm down. Nothing ever does prepare anyone for life. Now just tell me your story, very calmly.'

'I had to come and tell you. I feel so awful. I . . .'

'Yes, yes. We all make mistakes, Martin, just calm down, and tell me what happened.'

'Yes, of course. He seemed such a nice man. To think he's dead. Walked into the flames, from all accounts. It makes me shiver.'

'It's a horrid thought. And it seems the nightwatchman witnessed it. Think of him.'

'Henry's shattered, sir. We've had to send him for counselling.'

'Good. I'm glad you have. Look, suppose you tell me what happened, calmly, from the beginning.'

'This man called at . . . at the front office . . . yesterday. Yesterday. It was only yesterday. It can't be. Sorry. He wanted . . . he said he wanted to speak to a member of the senior management. Reception phoned Mr Trellis and he sent for me and told me he had to go to a hospital appointment, so I'd have to handle it. I went to see this chap, and he told me he was a novelist, he was writing a novel set in a . . . it sounds silly now, but at the time it seemed like a perfectly reasonable idea for a novel.'

'Set in a what?'

'A haunted pie factory.'

'Right.'

'And he wanted to know if it would be all right for him to come into the factory and stay all night and . . . well, soak up the atmosphere. I said, "There won't be much atmosphere, we close down at night. We used to work some nights but there's a recession." Sorry, I probably shouldn't have admitted that.'

'It hardly matters now.'

'No. No. And he said, "But that's just what I'm looking for. Darkness. Night. A man all alone."'

'So you just accepted his story?'

'Well, yes. I mean, he showed me a couple of books he'd written and some photocopies about him and it seemed he was a very well thought-of chap. Wonderful reviews. It all seemed very convincing.'

'Do you remember his name?'

'Yes. M.R. James.'

'Right. Well, obviously M.R. James must exist if you saw the books and articles. Just for interest let's look him up on the Net. Did you look him up on the Net?'

'To be honest, I didn't like to look as if I didn't trust him. It seemed rude.'

'You regret that now?'

'I regret that now.'

'Ah, here he is. Oh yes. Very famous. Very distinguished. Except of course it wasn't him.'

'No, but he was very persuasive, sir. You didn't meet him.'

'No, and I never will. It seems he died in 1936.'

'Oh dear.'

'Quite.'

'I'm very, very sorry, sir.'

'Don't be. I think he lived to a good old age.'

'I meant I was sorry for not checking properly, sir.'

'I knew what you meant. I was teasing you. Bad taste, awful taste, when this man was about to immolate himself. Sorry. Right. So you took everything he said at face value?'

'I'm afraid I did, sir. He was awfully convincing. He was a gentleman. He had perfect manners.'

'Of course. And your school motto was "Manners maketh man". I did tell you what a disastrous motto I thought that was. You obviously forgot.'

'I remember now, sir.'

'Don't forget it again. Every con man in the history of the world has perfect manners. Every serial killer in the world was a perfect gentleman to his neighbours. They are perfect because they are playing a part.'

'I think I've got a lot to learn, sir.'

'I think you've learnt a lot very quickly in the last twenty-four hours, Martin.'

'Yes, sir.'

'I'm sorry, Martin, I'm going to put you in a hard chair. I can't bear the way you're perching on that one.'

'I'll do it, sir.'

Martin Fortescue lifted the easy chair as if it was made of gossamer, took it to a far corner of the great office, picked up a hard chair, carried it over towards the desk, and sat down.

'That's more like it,' said Sir Gordon. 'Comfier now?'

Martin Fortescue tried to smile.

'Yes, sir. Comfier now. Sir, I feel terrible. I can only say again how sorry I am. The factory, gone after a hundred and thirty years. That man, dead.'

'All right, Martin, worry about the factory, but don't worry about the man. *He* burnt my factory down. *He* chose to walk into the fire he'd lit. Don't worry about him.'

379

'Oh. I forgot. He gave the nightwatchman a letter for you.'

'For me?'

'Yes. Henry gave it to me.'

Martin handed Sir Gordon the letter.

'Obviously, sir, I will hide nothing from anybody about my part in the matter.'

'That isn't obvious at all, and I'm very grateful. It reflects well on you. You're very brave.'

Martin blushed. Sir Gordon was beginning to realize that he was quite good at making both sexes blush.

Sir Gordon stared at the envelope, neat, elegant, expensive, if rather crumpled and sooty.

'Thank you, sir, but nothing you say can make me feel better about what I've done. If I can do anything to . . .'

'You can't. Oh, it isn't the end of the world, except for whoever this was.'

He had a feeling that he had seen that handwriting somewhere before.

'You made an error of judgement. The seriousness of the consequences is out of all proportion to your guilt. You cannot blame yourself for that.'

From a long time ago. A very long time ago. The writing a bit larger then, a bit more optimistic. Who? Who was it?

'Blame yourself for a silly mistake. Learn from it. Go home and wait and if I can find another job for you, if . . . well, there are lots of ifs as I expect you can imagine . . . but now I just have to see who this letter is from. It's hard. Blame yourself for being stupid enough to fall for a con. Don't blame yourself for the fire or this man's death. He's to blame for those. Off you go now.'

Martin Fortescue realized that he should have realized that he was being dismissed. He stood up hurriedly and anxiously and knocked the chair over. As it fell there was a loud crack.

'Oh shit. I'm sorry, sir.'

'Please. Please. Don't add the chair to the burden of your

guilt. It's an old chair and obviously it was weak. Off you go, and I promise I won't forget you, Martin.'

'Thank you very much, sir.'

The moment Martin had gone, Sir Gordon ripped open the envelope, destroying its elegance. He was hungry to see who this was from, hungry yet also afraid.

He looked at the address. It didn't mean anything.

He looked at the signature.

Oh God. Oh no.

The walls of the office were closing in, sliding towards him. Not for the first time, he wondered how a man could suffer from claustrophobia in an office so grandiose.

He was dreading reading this letter. He took it over to the wide picture window. He breathed in a draught of air, as if it came from the outside world, as if the window wasn't there. He looked across to the neat waters of what had once been the West India Dock, and, beyond the dock, to the line of warehouses that had been converted into restaurants and bars.

He forced himself to read the letter, there by the window, facing the window, facing the world.

Dear Gordon,

By the time you read this letter I will be dead, and you will have killed me as surely as if you had plunged a dagger into my heart. In fact, you have plunged a dagger into my heart.

Ours was a brief affair, and I never expected it to last. I knew you weren't really gay, I knew you were just trying something out, having a fling, experimenting, rebelling, showing your individuality, renouncing convention, however you want to put it. I knew you were using me, but that's what you do, isn't it? Use people.

Well, I suppose I've used you too. I'm a bit of a name dropper, always was. Sometimes I'd see you on the box and I'd say to my friends, "I've been up his bum." I sometimes felt a

bit guilty about it, felt I was revealing something you might
want kept secret. I couldn't care less now, of course.

So, you left me, you didn't just walk out, you did it quite
nicely, a little bit abruptly but to my face at least. But the
bottom line (unfortunate phrase!) was that you had no more
use for me.

I've never been bitter about it, but I suppose, looking
back, it isn't helping with the way I now feel about you.

Sir Gordon looked up from the letter, took a deep breath,
looked out, saw a group of people leaving one of the restaurants, and felt a deep yearning, a yearning for friends, a small
group of people sharing a simple meal, one drink too many,
lots of laughter, cries of 'Let's not leave it as long next time.'
Oh, the depth of that yearning.

He returned to the letter, reluctantly, fearfully.

In fact, I recalled some great moments we'd had, not just the
sex, great nights in the pubs in Dudley, wild rides on your
motorbike, that week on the canals, all the laughter, and, brief
though it was, I thought it had all been worth it. It was a long
time till I found anything as good, let alone better. But in the
end, I did find something better. Mick. What an ordinary name
for an extraordinary bloke.

The great thing about Mick was, he was never jealous, never
resented my past flings. So when I told him all about you, the
fun we'd had, he was very happy to agree with me to put all
our investments into GI. All of them, Gordon. And we took the
option of ploughing back fifty per cent of our returns. We
trusted you. I thought the sun shone out of your arse. Mick had
no knowledge of your lovely arse, but he trusted you too.

When my darling Mick died last year – cancer, not Aids, he
was always faithful to me – he left me all his money, and I left
it all, fool that I was, in GI. You say you hope to pay it back
and you may mean it, but you won't.

The money isn't the reason I'm killing myself. I'm killing myself because I can't live without Mick. The money is almost unimportant.

I say "almost" because you can't live without money and I do have refined tastes. Maybe if I could still afford nice meals, lovely wine, cruises, I could have cobbled together a way of living without Mick. I doubt it, though.

No, the money isn't the reason I'm killing myself. The money is the reason I'm setting fire to your factory. I so look forward to that. Only a few minutes now. My one regret is that I have to walk into the flames — God, I'm terrified of that — so I won't be able to see the whole great conflagration. I'd enjoy every minute of it.

I've admired you, albeit reluctantly, for more than thirty years. Now I hate you. I hate you, Gordon Coppinger.

Not long now. I hope it's quick.

Yours sincerely,

Your one-time friend,

Dennis

Sir Gordon folded the letter very carefully and put it back in his pocket. Even as he did so he thought it incomprehensible that he didn't crumple it up and throw it away.

He looked out of the window and wondered how many of the tiny people far below had also lost all their money with GI.

His head was swimming. He had tears in his eyes. He struggled back to his desk, as if his carpet was holding him back, as in a dream. He sank into his chair, and closed his eyes.

They came at him then. Dennis with a dagger as promised, hate in his burning eyes. Shopkeepers from Borthwick, people he'd known in Dudley, faces still as young as they'd been then; Kirkstall and Farringdon (he would never dare ask them if they had invested in GI); his scientists tying him up in seaweed; his kettle designers saying, 'You got us into hot water. Now it's your turn to be scalded'; his dentist saying, 'While I've got you in this chair, you bastard . . .'; all the people who worked in all the offices on all the floors of the Coppinger Tower; all the fans of Climthorpe United; and all the investors he'd never met from Land's End to John o'Groats. Hate in their burning eyes.

It wasn't nice. He cried, 'Go away. Go away,' and realized that he had actually shouted it out loud, here in his empty office; he'd have to be careful, he didn't want Helen Grimaldi to have him put away.

He looked up, and an elderly couple were sitting opposite him. Well, no, they weren't, because he wasn't there. His desk had gone, his office had gone, he had gone.

He was in the room with them and yet he wasn't there.

They were having their tea. A small slab of Cheddar, a hunk of bread, a cup of tea, no milk. They were shivering. They were cold. They had white hair and sweet faces. He had never seen them before.

They smiled at him, even though he wasn't there. That was good of them. They didn't mind that they had lost all their money in the crash of Gordon Investments. That was very good of them too.

Then the man was gone, the woman was still there, but her face was changing, she was growing younger before his eyes, she still had a moustache, but her skin was smoother, and now there was real concern in her eyes and suddenly she was Helen Grimaldi. And his desk was back. And, which was even more important, he was back.

'Are you all right?' she asked.

'Yes, yes, I'm . . . I'm fine.'

'Are you sure?'

'I'm fine, Helen. I'm fucking fine. Now fucking get out of here.'

She smiled.

'That's more like it,' she said.

She swayed her arse as she walked out.

So it was happening. He believed Hugo. It was coming.

He had always known that it would.

The thing was, though, that this afternoon was the first time that he had known that he had always known that it would.

All this despair was no use. It wouldn't help anybody.

A plan was beginning to take shape.

He was fibrillating wildly

Thursday isn't usually the day of the week that quickens the heart. February is rarely the month that stirs the blood. But Sir Gordon Coppinger hoped that Thursday 2 February 2012 would be very special indeed.

When Farringdon brought him his poached eggs and venison sausages he told him that he expected to be arrested shortly.

'I am most sorry to hear that, sir,' said Farringdon, 'and that sentiment will be shared by the whole household.'

'Thank you. I have some plans, Farringdon, that may delay my arrest. Things I need to do, set in order. Will you tell Her Ladyship that I will not be back tonight?'

'Certainly, sir.'

'Tell her that I will be doing nothing that I am ashamed of, and nothing that need cause her any distress.'

'Certainly, sir.'

'I wonder if it might be possible for you to tell her – I know this is asking rather a lot – that I love her?'

'I doubt it, sir. I never managed to tell Connie that in our eleven years together.'

'Connie. My word. Oh, Farringdon. My dear, dear Farringdon. I've never asked you a single thing about yourself, have I?'

'No, sir, and I've really appreciated your tact.'

It hadn't been tact, it had been self-centredness, but he didn't need to go into that.

'I'm sorry, Farringdon,' he said when his butler brought him his toast and honey. 'I shouldn't have asked you to say that to my wife. It was a momentary thought, a whim. Please feel free of any obligation.'

'Thank you, sir. I have to say that is a huge relief.'

Sir Gordon went through into Christina's bedroom, located her feet in the mound of bedclothes, pressed them gently, ran his hand ever so lightly up her spine, bent down and kissed her softly on the lips. He mouthed, in utter silence, the words he could not at this moment have spoken out loud, 'I love you.'

She stirred but did not wake.

By this time, there were about forty people waiting with insulting placards at the gates, but there was now a police presence and there was no violence.

As they drew near to Canary Wharf, Sir Gordon suggested that Kirkstall park round the corner.

'We don't want to risk any further damage to your beloved car, do we?'

'Thank you, sir. I really appreciate that,' said Kirkstall. 'I have to admit, sir. I really do love this car.'

Sir Gordon had never been able to understand how the man could so clearly be deeply devoted to a car he didn't own. Now, suddenly, he realized that he understood. The answer lay simply in philosophy. The car was no less beautiful because Kirkstall didn't own it. Ownership was therefore, it followed, unimportant. There flashed into his mind something from his schooldays, something one of the poets had said. Beauty is truth, truth beauty, everything else you learn at school is a load of old bollocks. Not in those words exactly, but that was the general gist.

It also struck him as they nosed slowly along – why were there so many cars, didn't people realize we were still in a recession? – that it was a bit late in the day for him to be having this revelation about ownership. He smiled wryly to himself.

He also was loving the car that morning. It was warm and sleek and smooth and almost silent. He dreaded stepping out of it and facing the crowds outside the Stick of Celery.

Kirkstall pulled up so smoothly that it was impossible to actually pinpoint the moment that the car stopped moving.

'I won't be going home this evening, Kirkstall,' he said.

'I can take you wherever you wish, sir,' said Kirkstall.

'I shan't be needing the car at all. You can have the rest of the day off.'

Kirkstall hid his disappointment bravely.

'Thank you, sir,' he said.

Sir Gordon stepped out of the car into air so cold it felt solid, and walked towards the Coppinger Tower. There was still a line of policemen holding back angry haters of his once-beloved self, but the crowd was a little smaller. In London he was already yesterday's news. The event was more of a ritual, familiarity was already blunting the sharp edge of the confrontation. The protesters were getting to know the names of the policemen, and vice versa, and they were all getting to know the names of the people from Occupy. 'Morning, bit parky for a protest.' 'You're telling me.' 'Sleep all right?' 'Not bad. Mustn't grumble.'

There were jeers as Sir Gordon strode towards his tower. Suddenly, momentarily, the hatred returned. One man shouted one word which echoed like a pistol shot off the tower blocks.

'Cunt.'

Sir Gordon stopped and looked at him and said, gravely and with dignity, 'Thank you so much for calling me after something that has given me so much pleasure.'

There were catcalls and jeers.

He strode into the foyer. This was the moment.

He was fibrillating wildly.

It has no future either

A middle-aged man with an unconvincing moustache sits alongside a very attractive young woman on a wooden bench in a wooden hut. He looks rather like a cross between Charlie Chaplin and Hitler, but he is unaware of this. The young woman is aware of it but is too tactful to tell him.

Large flaps in the front wall of the hut have been pulled back, affording a splendid view over a quiet corner of the Suffolk countryside.

The man and the woman are both peering at the scene with binoculars. The man is absolutely riveted. The young woman glances at him and is amused and pleased that he is so absolutely riveted.

There is some high wispy cloud, but now that January has passed there is the first faint hint of warmth in the sun. In the hide it is cool, however, and a salty little breeze is blowing in. The young woman shivers slightly but the man is unaware of the cold.

The couple have a clear view of only a small patch of the Suffolk countryside, but what an interesting patch it is, for this is the Minsmere Bird Reserve, belonging to the Royal Society for the Protection of Birds. It is situated on the wild Suffolk coast, where over the centuries houses and churches have been reclaimed off the cliffs by the merciless sea, and where the bells of drowned churches still toll at midnight. This place feels much further away from civilization than it has any right to feel.

389

The man is looking at a real birdwatcher's highlight, a rare pair of smew, small birds with sawbills and striking black-and-white plumage. He is unaware that this is a highlight until the young woman tells him that it is. He is just as excited by the sight of the much more common redshank with its slender red legs.

He has seen ducks – wigeon and teal and gadwall. The young woman has pointed out that there is a single whooper swan among a flock of smaller Bewick's.

He has been thrilled to see birds living up to their names – a marsh harrier, hunting and harrying low over the marsh; plump turnstones with their pretty tortoiseshell plumage turning stones at the water's edge in their endless search for food.

A couple of avocet, the RSPB's signature bird, fly in. They are large, elegant, and striking in black and white. They look as if they should be living in the 1920s and '30s. Their long, upturned beaks seem too delicate to trawl mud. The man thinks how relaxing it would be to be an avocet, never to need to ask, 'What shall we do today?', because today, like tomorrow, like yesterday, like every day, they will trawl mud.

A little owl sits on a telegraph post, almost camouflaged by it. The man empathizes with the little owl, for he has sometimes felt a bit little himself, but he doesn't think that the bird pines for greater size, or feels inferior in the presence of larger owls.

The most exciting moment for the young woman is when a male bearded tit peeps shyly out of the reeds. She has seen the relatively drab female before, but the male has a striking black moustache and looks smart enough to be going to a formal tit dinner in the reeds. The man does not recognize his kinship with the bearded tit. He has quite forgotten that he is sporting a moustache.

A barn owl glides on almost motionless wings low over the heath towards the marsh, a white shadow, a beautiful and dangerous spook. The man shivers for all unaware mice as he watches it. Thrilled though he is, he feels that it is taking unfair advantage by hunting during daylight.

Sometimes, as they watch and discuss and he questions and she explains, their faces are within an inch of each other. She longs to kiss him, but he seems oblivious.

He is oblivious. He is totally wrapped up in what he can see from the hide, this busy varied life of which he has not had the faintest inkling. He is happy. He is happy because he is existing utterly in the here and now, and in the here and now there is no past to haunt him.

But the sun is sinking fast. They cannot see the beginning of the sunset itself, but they can see reflections from it in the pools. The light is starting to fade. Birds are beginning to fly to their roosts. The afternoon is still short in these opening days of February, and soon the bird reserve will close.

That is the only trouble with the here and now. It has no future either.

And went to bed

A golden sunset spread over the wide East Anglian sky, deepening through mauve to cerise and scarlet. The chattering starlings flew back to their roost in vast numbers, and Gordon and Alice walked back up the gentle hill to her Ka. He was not *Sir* Gordon now. He had abandoned his knighthood for this one day.

Bats were circling the car park as Alice drove off, but she knew better now than to drive like a bat out of hell. The peace of the day was in her, and she drove steadily, gently, out of the magic, back to the reality of London. But they both knew that this was relative, that on another day it might have seemed as if they were travelling from the bleak and boring grey of the Suffolk coast back to the magical energy and artistry of London.

She had been astounded and deeply flattered, of course, when he had told her that she could take the day off, that he wanted her to take him out and show him a bit of her life. After arriving at the Coppinger Tower he had gone to his secret seduction suite on the twenty-second floor, changed into the Lycra cycling clothes he had bought the evening before, donned his absurd moustache, and walked out of the Coppinger Tower in disguise to pick up one of the bicycles

392

made available throughout London by the Mayor, Boris Johnson, using a key that Alice possessed. He had met her, on her bicycle, in Cabot Square in the well-manicured centre of Canary Wharf, and ridden with her through the streets of the East End to the little terraced house she shared with Tom in Hackney; she so much a part of her bike that she looked like a beautiful mythical creature, half human, half bicycle, he wobbling and terrified, and thinking suddenly of those reckless rides on his motorbike through the hills of Wales, Cindy clinging to him in a mixture of fear and desire. He wished he had that motorbike now.

As they rode out of Canary Wharf into the older, drabber, poorer world around it, several police cars had passed them going towards the Coppinger Tower.

'Coming to arrest me,' he had shouted. 'Go back now if you don't want to be an accomplice.'

Of course she hadn't gone back. Nothing as exciting as this had happened even in her dreams. To accompany this great man on the run from the police, this knocked birdwatching into a cocked hat.

But funnily enough it had been birdwatching that he had fancied, and so she had driven him down to Suffolk in the Ka through lovely East Anglian villages, to the Minsmere Bird Reserve.

Now, on the way home, he was teeming with questions on every aspect of bird life. How did birds sleep? Where did they sleep? If they slept all night in winter, how come they didn't wake up before it was light? If they slept right through in winter, how could they get by on so little sleep in summer? Did birds in the Arctic Circle stay awake for weeks in summer? What did the world look like to them? Did they see the same colours as us? Why was there so little difference in character between birds of the same species, when people were so varied? Why were all bitterns shy? Why were there never any vegetarian marsh harriers? He'd read that birds couldn't really think. Everything they did was instinctive. When they laid eggs and sat on them, they didn't know why, it was an instinct. Was that true?

She told him that she was certain it was rubbish. She had watched a couple of thrushes teaching their children how to fly. As blackbirds mature they learn not to build their nests too low. Tests had proved that cormorants could count. Birds were far more intelligent than people thought. Human beings were really very arrogant.

He sighed, remembering how arrogant he had been. Alice understood why he had sighed and ran her left hand gently up his right leg as she drove.

'I can't believe how arrogant I've been at times,' he said. 'You've read about SFN Holdings, of course.'

'Yes.'

'Do you know what SFN stood for?'

'No idea.'

'Stands For Nothing.'

'You mean the letters actually stood for "Stands For Nothing"?'

'Yes. Is that arrogant or is it arrogant?'

'It's fantastic. For all those years. Amazing.'

There was her delicate little left hand again, the fingers exploring the firmness of his right thigh.

'There's something I want to do this evening,' he said. 'It may surprise you.'

'It won't surprise me,' she said, and her fingers opened to try to encompass his thigh, though of course they couldn't.

'Do keep your eye on the road,' he said anxiously. 'And it will surprise you. I want to cook you a meal.'

'A meal?'

She kept her hand there but it was no longer applying any pressure.

'I've never cooked a meal for anybody in my whole life.'

'Well, you're right. I am surprised. Do you know what you're going to cook for me?'

'Something very ordinary, Alice.'

'Well, you can't try anything too extraordinary first time.'

'Exactly.'

'So come on, what am I getting?'

'It's a thing I had in a pub, and I really liked it, because at heart I'm a very simple man.'

'Oh, come on. Tell me.'

'Cottage pie.'

'Very nice.'

'You're disappointed.'

'I'm not. It'll be lovely.'

'With a slightly unusual topping they did. Potato, parsnip and horseradish.'

'Sounds good.'

'Well, I enjoyed it at that pub.'

'I'm hungry already.'

He didn't tell her that he had also been influenced in his choice by his memory of the shepherd's pie he had enjoyed so much at his last meal with Mandy, just round the corner but in what now seemed like a different life.

When they got back to London, they went shopping and he made another confession.

'I've never shopped for food before,' he said. 'Never ever.'

He asked her where the nearest supermarket was.

'We don't use supermarkets. We want there to be a choice of shops still available when our kids reach shopping age.'

'Of course.'

'If we have kids, of course.'

'Of course.'

'We'd better not shop in the shops I usually use.'

He didn't need to ask why. Tom might find out about him. They were silent for a moment. Tom. Kids. Reality hovered over their idyll.

But the moment Gordon started shopping, the joy returned. He took it all so seriously. Alice found it all so amusing.

'What's so funny?'

'The hard-headed business tycoon felt embarrassed that all he was ordering was ten ounces of minced beef. The great financier couldn't cope with kilograms.'

At the greengrocer's, Gordon bought potatoes, parsnips, carrots, and onions. He examined the green vegetables for quality and price, as if his life depended on it, and chose courgettes.

As they left the shop, Alice was trying not to laugh.

'What's so funny?'

'The billionaire shops with the eagle eye of a French provincial housewife.'

At the corner shop, he was so embarrassed at only buying horseradish off the friendly Pakistani shopkeeper that he asked Alice whether there was anything else she needed. He ended up giving her a present of four rolls of toilet paper and a bottle of Vanish. The shopkeeper found this as funny as Alice and asked if he wanted them gift-wrapped. Gordon paid for everything in cash. There was a risk that he might be tracked if he used a credit card.

Just as they were about to leave, he saw himself on the television. They were reporting that he had vanished. Absurdly, he tried to hide the bottle of Vanish, and he hurried Alice out of the shop. He had quite forgotten about his moustache.

To his relief, the television wasn't on in the off-licence. He bought a bottle of gin, a pack of six tonics, and two bottles of sound red Macon.

And so, on the evening of Thursday 2 February 2012, Gordon Coppinger donned an apron for the first time. It was Tom's apron and it was too small for him, which pleased him, even though he knew he looked ridiculous.

'I'll pour the drinks while you prep,' said Alice.

'Prep?'

'Prepare. Get ready. Chefs call it prepping.'

'How do you know all this?'

'We watch food programmes. We're huge foodies. Imagine it. Young people with a dining table!'

'I shouldn't be cooking for you. You're the wrong person to impress.'

And so, Alice poured gin and tonics, and Gordon began to prep, in that small pine kitchen in a terraced house in Hackney (not that far from Hair Hunters of; lucky he hadn't run into Mandy).

Every minute in this small kitchen was an adventure for this jaded man, with Alice watching him with amused affection and quiet excitement. He was no longer a man on the run. He was a chef.

'I'm chopping a big onion for the base and a carrot for sweetness,' he said.

'Sounds good to me.'

'Happy with garlic?'

'Yes, as we're both having it.'

She almost blushed.

He felt extremely clumsy as he chopped the onion. Some bits were tough to chop.

'There are tough bits on the outside of an onion even when you've discarded the skin. You should discard those bits too,' she said.

He dropped half the sliced onion while he was carrying it to the pan. He bent down, picked it all up, washed it under the tap, didn't know what to dry it on till she pointed out the roll of kitchen towel. Once so powerful, he thought wryly, now so clumsy.

He had no idea how to break a clove of garlic neatly off the bulb, and he found that when he scraped the carrots the dirt seemed to keep coming back. Actually, Alice had to help him quite a lot.

'It's not going to be my cottage pie at all,' he said.

'It is,' she protested. 'I'm just helping. You're doing it.'

'You're telling me what order to put things into the pan in.'

'You're putting them in the pan.'

He began to fry the onions, stirring them lovingly, watching with delight as they turned soft and buttery. Alice grew so excited by his enthusiasm that she came over and gave him an impulsive kiss.

'Now then,' he said, 'that's enough of that. Chef has to concentrate.'

He added the other vegetables in the order prescribed by Alice, then the mince when she thought that the time was ripe. He added salt and pepper without needing to be told. He asked her what dried herbs she had, and chose small quantities of thyme and marjoram.

The gentle argument rolled on below the surface throughout the whole thing. He did work some things out for himself. He realized that to mash potatoes and parsnips you needed to boil them first.

He had to be shown how to work the potato peeler. Her hands sat on his, gently, guiding him as he peeled the potatoes and, with more difficulty, the parsnips. She kissed him again proudly, as if he had done it all himself. He didn't know when he had been happier.

Some good smells were coming and a right old fug was developing in the little kitchen. On another occasion the smallness of the kitchen might have brought on his claustrophobia, but here with Alice it was a superb way of hermetically sealing him from the perils of existence. Quite a lot of people were searching for him. They would never find him here.

He asked her advice on how much horseradish to add, but he did the courgettes without any help, modelling them on the ones that the Rose Cottage kitchens produced and which he liked so much.

They both agreed that they had drunk enough gin, so they started on the red wine.

Tom phoned. Tom and Alice were of the generation that uses mobiles even at home, so impatient are most of them to be on the move. She went out to the lounge/diner to talk to him. Gordon examined the pie. It was browning nicely. He turned the oven down, put olive oil in a pan ready for the courgettes, and waited. It was going to be delicious. Alice was quite a long time, but she was living with the man and there'd be lots to discuss. He mustn't mind. Nothing must be allowed to spoil this evening.

At last she returned, just slightly worried at having been away so long. He gave her a huge smile of reassurance and saw her relax.

'Sorry about that,' she said. 'Couldn't hurry him off.'

'Of course not. How is he?'

'He's good. Going out on the piss. Not that he's a huge drinker. We're very dull.'

'You aren't.'

He was almost cross.

He asked her how he could heat the plates, with the oven so hot that they might break if he put them in it.

'Rinse them under hot water for quite a while and dry them quickly.'

He lit the candle, and soon the meal was on the table.

They ate in silence for a few moments.

'It's very nice,' she said. 'Lovely.'

'It's not got as much flavour as I expected.'

'You always think that when you've cooked something. I think for a first effort it's all amazing. And I love the courgettes with the lemon and black pepper. I've never had them that way.'

'Oh good.'

'Don't be disappointed, Gordon. You said you were doing something straightforward and that's what this is but it's very,

very tasty and the horseradish is a lovely touch and the courgettes are really cool.'

'Shall I warm them up?'

'No, I meant—'

'I know. I was joking.'

'I really am enjoying it, Gordon. Believe me.'

And at last he did.

'It's actually not at all bad, is it?' he said.

'It's gorgeous. Clever old you.'

It was cosy in the through lounge/diner, despite the rather stark, clean-lined modern style in which it had been furnished. The one rather old-fashioned standard lamp softened the whole room, as did the log-effect fire. This quite excited Gordon. He had never had a log-effect fire and it amused him that you could change the effect by remote control. He was like a child with it.

He asked her if she wanted a second helping. She said that she couldn't resist a small one. He tried to hide his pleasure, but couldn't, so he gave in to it.

She asked him, rather nervously, how he had made all his money.

'Don't tell me if you don't want to talk about it,' she said, 'but I'd really love to hear.'

'Why not,' he said. 'No, I don't mind. It's odd anyway. It'll feel as if I'm talking about someone else, someone I once knew.'

He refilled the wine glasses, and began.

'This Gordon Coppinger fellow, Alice, he made his money by thinking about nothing else but money from the day he left school, with no regrets, as soon as he was legally allowed to. He worked, he saved, he scrimped, he bought, he sold, he saved, he worked in offices, bars, restaurants, and when he'd saved enough he bought his first property. He rented it out, and when he could afford another one, he rented that out too. He got a rusty old van. He bought things and repaired them and sold them. He bought things off a tip someone he knew worked at, and he sold those things, and every time he had any money he bought other things with it. He had a bit of flair, I suppose, and he took risks but they were sensible risks and they came off. He started to buy shares, he was bold, I'll say that for him, and he was quick, he was shrewd, I suppose, he could smell money, and above all he was lucky. It was hard, hard work, Alice, but he did it, and it got to that point, in the world of money, where money starts to beget money and money comes to money and then it was easy, easy, easy. But Alice, he was greedy, he needed an old head to advise him, someone like me, and he did naughty things, illegal things, immoral things, and he has to pay the penalty now.'

There was silence when he had spoken, deep silence in the little lounge/diner with the steamed-up windows in Hackney. Alice's pretty little hand snaked across the table and took hold of his great hand and squeezed.

She offered him cheese, and he accepted, eating it with a knife and fork rather than biscuits as was his habit. She thought this a good idea, and tried it too, though she only took tiny slivers of cheese. They were on to the second bottle of wine now.

They couldn't resist watching the ten o'clock news. There he was, being hunted in vain. If you spot him, don't approach him, let us know.

'Why? Do they think I'm dangerous?' he exclaimed.

'Dangerous, you?' She smiled.

He stood up.

'I think it's time for bed,' he said.

She stood up so readily, so eagerly.

'I . . . um . . . Alice,' he began. 'I hope you don't mind if we . . . you probably weren't expecting this, or maybe you were, maybe I shouldn't presume . . . I hope you don't mind if we have . . . separate rooms.'

401

She looked at him in astonishment.

'I'll sleep in the guest room. I'll be fine there.'

'But . . .'

'Is it a disappointment? I'm sorry if it is.'

'But . . . Gordon . . . I . . . I thought . . .'

'I know you did.'

'I thought you . . . don't you . . .?'

She had too much pride and style to finish the sentence. He finished it for her.

'. . . find you attractive? Of course I do.'

'Is it the ring and the stud? Sometimes I do regret them.'

She sat down. He thought she was going to cry.

'I think you're beautiful. You're as beautiful as any woman I've ever seen. But you've given me something even more precious than your lovely body. You've given me my innocence back.'

She looked disappointed, and very, very young.

'I'm sorry,' he said, 'but if you look back on the day I think you'll find I've tried very hard not to give you the wrong idea.' He breathed out, expelling all his tension. 'I've had the most wonderful time. I've been . . . an unknown person . . . an ordinary man . . . a happy man . . . a privileged man.' He could feel that his voice was on the point of breaking. 'And I truly want to go to bed with you very much.'

'I can't believe we're having this conversation.'

'Believe me, Alice, I can't believe it either. Neither would anyone who knows me. I just want to do one good thing, Alice . . . just do one good thing in my life, before—'

He broke off.

'Before?'

'Before . . . whatever happens.'

'It may be a good thing for you. Is it for me?'

'Oh God. Am I being selfish to the last? I hope not, Alice. I hope it's good for you. I don't want to leave you with a guilty conscience.'

402

'I'm going to have a guilty conscience anyway. You shouldn't be here.'

'All right. I don't want to leave you with a *very* guilty conscience.'

He smiled, trying to make a little joke out of it. But Alice Penfold looked very solemn.

'I don't want you to be unfaithful to Tom,' he said. 'I want you both to be very happy and keep all your local shops open and bankrupt your supermarkets and see simply hundreds of avocets and curlews and have at least two happy and healthy children who grow up to have their own dining tables.'

He knew that she was now on the verge of tears.

He gave her a swift kiss on the cheek, and went to bed.

The message from his wife

He awoke with a sense of shock. He had no idea where he was.

He felt instinctively for a light switch, and saw, in complete bewilderment, a small, bleak, almost unfurnished room, with a picture of a flock of flamingos on the newly painted off-white wall opposite the bed.

It all came back in a glorious rush. Alice. The barn owl. Buying mince. Wearing an apron. Cooking. Eating in shared peace and joy.

He knew where he was, but again the question of who he was presented an altogether greater problem. The Gordon Coppinger of yesterday could surely not have robbed more than two million people of money that he had promised them? The Gordon Coppinger who had created a love nest in the worst possible taste in his tower block could surely not have behaved with such respect and good taste towards Alice last night?

He had told Alice that she had given him his innocence back. It was true. He had felt a kinship with himself at the age of – he worked it out – eight. It had been after that, somehow, that the itch had got into his soul, the itch to have rather than just to be, the urge to conquer, the need to acquire, the obsession with power, as he stepped on to the first rung of the ladder that would lead to Garibaldi. Garibaldi! Had he really thought he could go down in history as a leader? A shudder of self-disgust ran through him, but was it self-disgust? Had that self ever been himself? Had he played a part, for forty-eight years, that was not true to himself? Had all the damage that he had done been the work of an alter ego? Had that actually been a shudder of alter-ego-disgust?

It was perhaps lucky that he had very little time to ponder these considerations. Alice was at the door, ghostly as a barn owl, frail as a flamingo, slim as a snake, strong as an ox, telling him that if he was going to cycle in to Canary Wharf with her he would have to get up.

Of course he was going to cycle in to Canary Wharf with her. Reality beckoned. Yesterday had been a dream. No, it had not been a dream, it had been real, real, real, but it belonged to yesterday.

In her cold, cold bathroom he washed with a borrowed flannel. Tom's flannel. He shaved with an electric razor. Tom's electric razor. He got a tremendous shock as he saw himself in the mirror. He still had that moustache. All day yesterday, when he had been feeling so good about himself, he had actually looked absurd. Sitting in wonder beside Alice in the hide, buying mince, chatting to the Pakistani owner of the corner shop, all the time he had been wearing the moustache. As he chopped that magnificent onion – had there ever been such an onion? – and turned it golden in the pan, he had looked ridiculous in an apron far too small for him and with a little false moustache. They'd been alone, he could have taken it off, but neither of them had thought of it. As he'd been kissing her goodnight, so delicately on the cheek, feeling so good, believing that he was showing rare dignity, she had been kissing a man who looked like a cross between Charlie Chaplin and Hitler. Well, he had been forgetting that he was kissing a girl with a stud on her chin and a ring in her nose. They must have looked a ridiculous couple. Thank goodness there had been nobody there to see them.

In his sleepiness he almost began to shave the moustache off before he realized that wasn't what you did to false moustaches. Then he decided to leave it on in case he felt that he needed to enter the Coppinger Tower still in disguise.

He cleaned his teeth with Alice's toothpaste. No toothpaste ever tasted so good, so clean, so pure.

They breakfasted hurriedly on tea and high-fibre cereal.

Sir Gordon – he was facing reality today, so his knighthood was restored – had often felt embarrassed, in the morning, about things that had happened the night before. Feeling embarrassed about what had not happened the night before was a new experience for him. And he sensed that Alice was feeling embarrassed about the same thing. They were both shy with each other.

He had been so pleased that he had managed to resist taking her to bed without having recourse to his Alphabet of Boons to Celibacy. It's hard to say to a pretty young lady, 'I managed to avoid being tempted to have sex with you last night without having needed any recourse to thinking about Morris dancers or Orpington' (and even more tactless to say it to a young lady who is not pretty). He wanted to say something to assuage the disappointment she had so obviously felt, the extent of which had actually surprised him. But he thought that anything he might say would make the matter worse.

And then she spoke of it, and he was mightily relieved.

'I . . . um . . . I understand and appreciate what you did last night,' she said, 'or rather, what you didn't do. Thank you.'

'I just hope, Alice, that you and Tom will be wonderfully happy.'

'Thank you. Time we were going,' she added sadly.

'Yes,' he echoed glumly.

Goodness, it was cold. Achingly cold. The sun was just appearing over the horizon as they crunched over the frozen grass to collect their bikes from the shed.

He shivered as he clambered, a little stiffly, on to his bike. Alice didn't seem to notice the cold. She swung on to her sleek machine and was in an instant transformed from frail ghost to fit young athlete.

He wanted to rush to get into the warmth of the Coppinger Tower, but he also wanted to go so slowly that they would never reach it and his time with Alice would go on for ever. He also felt extremely nervous about the cycling, perhaps even more so than yesterday. More than once he almost fell off, and people hooted at him aggressively each time he wobbled.

The sun as it rose shone with no real power on the skyscrapers of Canary Wharf. Suddenly it turned the name *'J.P. Morgan'* to gold. Then it caught, at the top of their mighty tower, the single word – *'Barclays'*. The letters sparkled in the sun like diamonds. How those words, *'J.P. Morgan'*, *'Barclays'*, seemed to Sir Gordon to shine with strength, security and honesty. How bitterly he regretted his misdemeanours at that moment.

The sun had not yet reached *'Coppinger'*. He had an odd feeling that it never would. Nearer and nearer came the tower blocks. Nearer and nearer came the Stick of Celery. How strange it was to think, 'All that is mine,' and yet feel nothing.

The crowds outside the Coppinger Tower were smaller. The tents of Occupy had moved on. The man they were all protesting against had disappeared, was no longer there, so there had been no point in their staying. Strangely, though, he missed them, missed the attention. The entrance seemed forlorn without them. In fact, the whole place seemed forlorn.

He left his bicycle with Alice's. She would take it back to the Boris bikes rack later. They went into the building by the staff and deliveries entrance. There, in a dark corner, he gave Alice Penfold a brief kiss, said, 'Thank you,' in a husky voice, turned away rapidly, and walked to the service lifts.

He went up to the twenty-second floor. He unlocked the door to his secret seduction suite, and entered a world of playful luxury, scarlet and gold, rich in tassels and chandeliers and pastiche, redolent of past epochs and turns of centuries long gone, five stars in any *Good Brothel Guide*, and making the Café de Paris look like a provincial branch of T.K. Maxx. Here, in a four-poster bed in a tower block in Canary Wharf, he had pleasured, and been pleasured by, Jenny Boothroyd, Sandy Lane, Isla Swanley, Kerry Oldstead, Gill Goldthorpe, Ellie Streeter, and others from further back whose names no longer sprang to mind. He had not brought Mandy of Hair Hunters of Hackney here, she would have been overwhelmed. Nor had he brought Francesca Saltmarsh. She would have shrieked with such laughter at its absurdity that no sex would have been possible.

In truth he hadn't used it for a few months, and he knew now that he had been gradually moving towards a change in his lifestyle quite a long while before he had realized it, on that morning when he had woken up to find that he couldn't remember who he was. Now, on Friday 3 February 2012, with the air stale from disuse and stifling from wasted heating, the whole place looked vulgar and absurd and desperately sad. Here he had been king and prince and Don Juan and Garibaldi. Now he was a middle-aged man with a false moustache that made him look like a cross between Charlie Chaplin and Hitler, and he was changing out of Lycra after the last cycle ride he would ever have.

He looked into one of the gilt mirrors and was shocked to see how old he looked. All day yesterday he had felt just slightly older than Alice. He adjusted his tie, tried to make his clothes less crumpled, carefully packed his cycling gear into his bag, and set off for his office on the nineteenth floor.

He realized that he *still* hadn't taken off his moustache. He removed it slowly, carefully, not wanting to rip his skin, and stuffed it into a pocket.

He walked across the large open-plan office. Only about half the staff were at work that Friday morning. His world was leaking people as well as money. It was dying.

Her Grimaldiship looked as if she had seen a ghost.

'We didn't know if we'd ever see you again,' she said. 'We thought . . . we wondered . . .'

She began to cry. He couldn't believe it. He held open his arms, she stood up, came towards him, allowed herself to be hugged.

'Oh, Sir Gordon,' she wailed. 'Oh, it was awful, we had no idea where you were.'

He disengaged himself from her. She blew her nose.

'I was in top-secret talks, Helen, in a wooden shed in Suffolk and a safe house in East London.'

'I wondered if it might be something like that. Oh, Sir Gordon, it is good to see you. I mean, we go back a long way.'

People express their emotional feelings in different ways. Some people will say, 'I love you.' Others may say, 'Why, Miss Ryecroft, you're beautiful,' or, 'I don't half fancy you, Hayley.' Sometimes, especially in organizations, the best people can do is, 'We go back a long way,' but there can be a lot of emotion even in that phrase, and Sir Gordon was amazed to see just how much feeling Helen Grimaldi had for him.

'Fred Upson has an appointment this morning,' she reminded him.

'Oh yes. So he does.'

'Apparently you hinted that you might have some kind of job for him when . . . if you . . . I mean . . .'

Helen Grimaldi lapsed into confused silence. He wondered how she would have finished her sentence if she'd gone on.

'. . . when you finish your sentence', perhaps. The thought gave him a wry smile.

'He's . . . um . . . I expect you've always been too busy to notice, but I think he's a very lonely man.'

'Are you surprised?' he said.

'Sir Gordon! That isn't kind.'

'I'm sorry.'

She was blushing. He realized that she was fond of Fred Upson. She must be lonely too. He had a sudden aching wish that he could go back over his life and take more interest in people.

He was moved. He was. But he couldn't quite bring himself to say, of Helen Grimaldi and Fred Upson, 'I hope you'll both be very happy.' He bent down and kissed her on the cheek. He wished that he had just one good friend to whom he could email a description of the morning's happenings under the title of 'A Tale of Two Moustaches', but there was not one person in the world with whom he could communicate in that sort of way, and he entered his office feeling very, very alone, and rather ashamed of his thought.

The size of his office dwarfed him. His computer was on. There were 373 emails in his inbox. All over his desk there were piles of papers.

Helen entered behind him.

'Just to explain,' she said. 'All this stuff came yesterday. That's your mail. Those are external messages. That pile is internal messages. That one on its own is from your wife. Delivered by hand.'

'You saw her?'

'No. A messenger brought it up.'

She left him to it, and he felt very alone again. He couldn't face his post or his emails. He slit open the message from his wife.

'Meet me in the roof garden at 10:15. X'

His heart raced. Unsurprisingly, he didn't study the

handwriting carefully. That single kiss coursed through his veins, and with it came a surge of panic as he recalled how close he had been to going to bed with Alice last night, how strong he'd needed to be to resist an urge that he had never resisted before in his life.

He walked towards the lift, then thought that a malign fate might cause it to stick. He couldn't risk that.

He walked slowly up the stone steps to the top of the tower. He pressed the four security numbers with shaking fingers. He was like a shy boy on his first date.

The roof was bathed in sunshine, but the air was still cold and the garden was a sad place in winter, the rose bushes bare and stunted.

Christina was nowhere to be seen, but then punctuality was not her forte.

He found himself walking towards the low wall from which he had not long ago felt a sudden urge to jump. There was no such urge now. He looked out over the restaurant terraces of the West India Dock, deserted in the early morning. He looked at the tiny figures in their city suits making their way along the streets and paths, and suddenly ridiculous to him in their self-importance. He knew, in that moment, that he wasn't frightened of going to prison, life would still be worth living as long as he had regular visits from Christina. He might even start to read books and educate himself and find he was really able to head a literacy campaign. He might even be able to work with Megan Ll . . . no!!

It was absurd to feel again, now when she was going to be unobtainable, all the love that he had once felt for his wife, but he realized in that moment just how absurd love can be.

Two men emerged from the garden's tool shed very carefully and tiptoed towards him. They didn't need to be so careful. He was oblivious to anything except his thoughts.

Had he turned round, he might have recognized one of

411

them, the one with the thick neck, the one who had driven Kirkstall's car so jerkily after his dinner with Hugo.

But he didn't turn round.

'Grief makes you very hungry'

They do say – whoever *they* are – that when you fall from a high building, you lose consciousness long before you crash into the ground. Presumably this is an assumption derived from medical theory and research, unless someone once fell several storeys, landed miraculously on a large trampoline, made a succession of smaller and smaller bounces, finally came to rest, opened his or her eyes and said, 'It's interesting. I completely lost consciousness long before I fell on to this trampoline.'

So, on his fall from the roof garden of the Coppinger Tower on that fateful Friday morning, less than two hours after he had left his bicycle for Alice to take back, Sir Gordon might already have been falling into unconsciousness as he passed the picture windows of his secret seduction suite on the twenty-second floor, those windows out of which Jenny Boothroyd, Sandy Lane, Isla Swanley, and several other young ladies had been known to gaze in post-coital wonder at the lights blazing out expensively into the Canary Wharf night.

He would almost certainly have been unconscious as he passed his own office on the nineteenth floor, and, shortly afterwards, dropped past the gaze of a raw Fraud Squad rookie who looked up from his inspection of GI's books on the thirteenth floor and exclaimed, 'I think I just saw a body drop past that window, sir,' only to be told, 'Don't be ridiculous, Mulliner, and concentrate on your work, please.'

Past the almost deserted London office of Porter's Potteries Pies dropped Sir Gordon, past PR and HR and IT and Maintenance and the administrative offices of the Coppinger Collection and the Sir Gordon Coppinger Charitable Foundation and the London office of 'S'ssh! The Ultimate in Squeak Removal'.

Unaware that in a few seconds it was going to crash at speed on to a London pavement, his unconscious body sped past the now deserted Elgar Room and Wordsworth Room.

Fred Upson, out on a bail of £300,000, was walking towards the Coppinger Tower, with a red rose in his right hand and a list of his expenses in his breast pocket. He was blissfully unaware that the man with whom he hoped to discuss what plum post he might be offered in the Coppinger organization if, after all, things turned out not to be as bad as feared, was at that very moment falling at a rate of knots towards him.

Sir Gordon crashed on to the pavement just a couple of feet in front of Fred, giving him the shock of his life and an unconscious final F.U. on a cosmic scale.

Blood, sinew, saliva and other substances rained over Fred Upson, covered his trouser legs, slid inside his overcoat, spattered his face.

A police officer led him, shaking with shock, into the Coppinger Tower, where he took his foul clothes off, had a shower and put on some ill-fitting garments provided at short notice by Siobhan McEnery, that ace provider of things at short notice.

A porter took his ruined clothes and set off to drop them into the tower's state-of-the-art guaranteed-to-be-non-polluting incinerator. Suddenly Fred shouted, 'My wallet's in there.'

The jacket wasn't as soiled as the overcoat but the porter

still clearly found it extremely unpleasant to reach in and remove the wallet. It looked quite clean, but he held it as far away from himself as he could as he handed it to Fred Upson.

Fred presented himself at reception and told a very pale young lady, with a ring in her nose and a stud on her chin, that he had an appointment with Sir Gordon Coppinger. He realized that he wouldn't be able to see him as he knew that he had died, but he would like to see his secretary, Helen Grimaldi.

The pale young lady burst into tears as he talked about Sir Gordon's death. She could barely make herself understood on the phone to Helen.

'Nineteenth floor,' she gasped to Fred Upson, who of course knew that. Then she blew her nose.

Fred Upson walked through the open-plan office towards Helen Grimaldi. Some people were crying. He could see that Helen had been crying too.

'Oh, Helen,' he said. 'Oh, Helen.'

'I know.'

'I was walking along, Helen, thinking . . . nice thoughts. Suddenly, there he is, Helen, thunk, right in front of me, on the pavement, dead. Right in front of me. Blood everywhere. And worse than blood. Right in front of me. All over me.'

'Please, Fred. Don't go on. You're upsetting me. He was my boss. I liked him. I'm upset.'

'Oh, I know. It's awful. Sorry. Sorry. But it was the shock. Right in front of me, dead.'

'Please.'

'Sorry.'

'We'll not see his like again.'

'We won't.'

'He'll leave a gap.'

'He'll leave a huge hole. Helen?'

'Yes.'

415

'We . . . you and I . . . we go back a long way.'

'Years.'

'Years. Only once a month when I called for my monthly meeting with Sir Gordon. Oh Lord, I won't be having those meetings ever again.'

'We'll never see him ever again.'

'Only once a month, but things grow on you. Helen, I'm not one for big romantic gestures. We aren't in Dudley. But, as I was coming to see you this morning, I . . . I had a single red rose. Just for you.'

'Fred!'

'Ruined, of course, but . . . that's me and romantic gestures, eh? Also, Helen, I had a list of my expenses.'

He took the list out of his breast pocket.

'Will you shred it for me?'

'Shred it?'

'I don't think it fitting to claim expenses on a day like today.'

'Oh, Fred, that's . . . that's lovely of you, actually.'

'Will you read them first, though?'

Helen began to read Fred's list of expenses. It didn't take long: 'Third of February 2012, return train fare.'

'What do you notice?'

'It's a very short list.'

'Isn't it?'

'You haven't claimed for lunch.'

'Exactly. Why do you think that is?'

'I've no idea.'

'I have been much mocked over my expenses, but I have always been fair. Lunch today I did not regard as a claimable item. Why do you think that is?'

'I've no idea.'

'Because it's for pleasure, not business, and it's for two people.'

'Fred!'

416

'Hardly the day to, as it happens, but there you are, where do you start?'

'I know. You think, with a man like that gone, you'll never enjoy yourself again, never smile again.'

'He wouldn't want you never to smile again. He wasn't that sort of man.'

'He wasn't that sort of man at all.'

'And it's a known fact that grief makes you very hungry.'

No respecter of wealth

The last moments in the life of Sir Gordon Coppinger, who for so many years had lived for and by publicity, were seen only by Fred Upson and a Fraud Squad rookie whose surname was Mulliner. His brother Hugo was a man who lived in the shadows, held secret meetings well away from the public's gaze, and kept his money in accounts far from anyone's eyes, yet what we must assume to be the last moments in his life were recorded for posterity on CCTV.

Had he lived, and now that he had begun to realize at last just how much Hugo hated him, Sir Gordon might have been amused. Her Majesty the Queen had laid a sword on his shoulder, but the nearest Hugo came to her was being on CCTV during a security rehearsal for a helicopter flight under Tower Bridge, to be taken as part of a filmed stunt for the opening ceremony of the 2012 Olympics later that year.

What does the CCTV footage show? It shows Hugo walking too fast on to Tower Bridge. It shows him pacing up and down on that iconic monument. He is anxious, on edge. He expels air deeply. He looks at his watch twice. His tension has the security forces on edge. The picture quality is not good, but the watchers feel that they know him. Then one of them says 'It's that banker wanker. Hugo Coppinger.' It's

418

not surprising that they recognize him. His face has been in all the papers that morning. He has been forced, by public opinion, to give up his bonus.

Then a woman appears, also nervous. This woman they all recognize instantly. It is Lady Coppinger. Hugo's face lights up. He approaches her, holds out his arms to her, but the kiss she gives him on one cheek only is brief, embarrassed, lacking in warmth. The security forces are no longer on edge, but they watch on, gripped by the drama.

All we know of any relationship between Lady Coppinger and her husband's brother is that he telephoned on her birthday to ask if he could bring something for the Guy Fawkes party a few days later. It isn't much to go on.

Sir Gordon did ask her, one evening, by the east fire, if there was anyone in her life. She spoke of a long-standing relationship, casual and social. Lunch. Dinners. Theatres. Opera. An occasional kiss. Could this man have been Hugo? Well of course he *could*.

He looks, on the CCTV, as if his feelings are much deeper than this, but then Hugo Coppinger's feelings were held, as secure from inspection as his money, in the steely vaults of his heart. We'll never know. You never do know, with the Hugo Coppingers of this world.

What do we see then on the CCTV? Astonishment and shock, suddenly laid bare on Hugo's unprepared face. Hatred, hatred so deep it seems obscene to continue to watch. Who does he hate so much? Certainly not Christina. A moment later he is pleading with her, his weakness also so evident that we feel embarrassed to witness it. We can decide, with almost total certainty, that it is his brother Gordon whom he hates so much. In view of what happened, the police studied the footage, even called in an officer who specialized in lip reading. He detected the words, 'I still love . . .' A Pickfords' removal van passed by at this moment, obscuring the couple. The end of the sentence could have been 'you' or it could

419

have been 'him' or it could have been 'the deputy mayor of Dudley', but in the intensity of the conversation it surely had to be either 'you' or 'him' and in view of the consequences, and of the significance of that word 'still', it had to be 'him'.

When at last the van has moved off – traffic was heavy and slow that afternoon – Hugo is clearly shouting and Christina has turned away. She walks towards the southern end of the bridge, raises her arm in a casual, dismissive fare-well, but then suddenly stops, as if shocked by something Hugo has said, or by his tone perhaps. Sadly, Hugo's lips are not visible on camera at that moment.

Now everything is obscured by a red double-decker bus. London buses hunt in threes, and by the time the three buses have passed on their slow journey north, there is no sign of Hugo, no sign at all. A Japanese tourist is photographing three other Japanese tourists. The light is fading. Christina is standing on the pavement, frozen in shock.

Perhaps Hugo has just turned and hurried away, but that wouldn't explain the depth of Christina's shock. Has he fallen into the river? Impossible, by accident, on Tower Bridge. Has he jumped in? Has the river that claimed his brother Jack also claimed him? Are we being too fanciful now? And if he killed himself, why? Because he has been forced to give up his bonus? Surely not, he still has money enough. Because, now that he has engineered his brother's death and made it look like suicide, his life's mission is complete, like that of the wasp, or was it the bee? Was Hugo really so irrational? Or . . . surely more likely . . . did he have a lifelong passion, perhaps an obsession, over Christina, whom he felt his brother stole off him? Was he simply unable to bear the knowledge that he would never possess her, that his life's dream was just that, a dream?

A lot of questions. Only one thing that could possibly be described as an answer. Ten days later, Hugo's body was found on the marshes, beyond Gravesend, not twenty yards from the spot where Jack's had been discovered. The banker and the tramp, who had shared nothing all their lives, shared their final resting place. London's river, unlike the city through which it flows, is no respecter of wealth.

Scrambled eggs are
his favourite

Christina has decided to leave Rose Cottage and return to Dudley, where she is known to have consulted three estate agents with a view to purchasing a small shop and setting up a patisserie. She has changed her name back to Cindy.

Luke was sentenced to four months in prison. By the time his case came up he had served more than he would have got on parole, so he was released immediately. He has begun to try to find his real mother. He has not succeeded yet.

Emma is sticking by him. Her latest work, *Estate Agent with Catheter*, has sold for only £3,300, but a collector in Swanage has offered £360,000 for Luke's painting with '*F.U.*' scrawled on it, believing that it symbolizes the crisis in bourgeois society, so it seems that Luke's action in protest at the commercialization of art has had exactly the result he didn't want.

All Sir Gordon's commercial interests have been put into administration, including Climthorpe United, who have been docked ten points for going into administration and therefore relegated to Division One. Raduslav Bogoff has gone back to Bulgaria. Many of Sir Gordon's assets have been sold to raise money for the creditors, including the *Lady Christina* and three of his factories. The administrators are cautiously confident that the investors owed money by Gordon Investments will eventually be paid out in full at the value quoted on the day of its closure.

Fred Upson was sentenced to a year in prison. He appealed against the severity of his sentence, and it was increased to eighteen months. Helen Grimaldi has moved to his house in Dudley, and visits him in prison every week. She now regularly bleaches her moustache.

Mandy of Hair Hunters of Hackney has moved to Dubai.

Two pieces of happy news. Joanna married Kev last month. It was a quiet, humanist affair. Alice and Tom are getting married next June. I'm sure you'd be made welcome if you turned up. Alice hasn't told Tom about Gordon and almost certainly never will. They spotted a wryneck in their back garden in July. Some people have all the luck.

Farringdon has gone back to his East London roots and is calling himself Brian again. He is having an affair with a fortune teller from a circus. He will die in September 2043. She hasn't told him.

Kirkstall was given the Rolls-Royce by Christina. The administrators ruled that it was actually a part of the estate. He barricaded himself in it at a car park in Leatherhead, and after strong protests from the public, he was allowed to keep it. He is now refusing to pay a parking ticket of £2827.20 from Leatherhead Council. A psychiatrist has ruled that his grief at Sir Gordon's death has twisted his mind, but in the public's eyes he is something of a hero.

Francesca Saltmarsh has amazed everyone by getting engaged to a French polisher. He's very handsome, his name is Jean, and he lives in St Tropez. He's a French French polisher.

The only person who is completely unaffected by what on the surface seems to be the Fall and Fall of Gordon Coppinger, but just might seem to Christina and Alice and Joanna in particular to be the Fall and Rise, is Clarrie, Sir Gordon's father. He has no idea that all his three sons have died, two in the Thames and one outside a building beside the Thames. The staff at his care home tell him every day that one or other of his sons came the previous day, and he is very happy about their being such good, loving boys. He still calls them 'the boys'. Apparently this morning he's having scrambled eggs. Audrey prefers poached eggs, so he's feeling rather triumphant. Scrambled eggs are his favourite.